BUT WORLD ENOUGH AND TIME

But World Enough and Time

Anne Louise Bannon

Healcroft House, Publishers

Published by Healcroft House, Publishers
2591 N. Fair Oaks Ave., #408
Altadena, CA 9001
626-502-7416

First Printing, 2021

Dedication

To Stephanie Beverage and Susanna Apitz, who helped bring this story into being. I hope you like what I did with it.

Acknowledgments

This book began as my two girlfriends and I were having dinner one evening. Chatting about some other project I'd been working on, I told Stephanie Beverage and Susanna Apitz about an idea I'd been playing with since the three of us had been in high school together at least four or five years before.

Both of them encouraged me to write it and Stephanie even went so far as to do the basic historical research for me. Both made corrections and suggestions on the original version.

Sadly, I've lost touch with both of them, at least beyond the odd Facebook comment or two. But this story would not have happened without these two wonderfully strong, incredibly intelligent women. And I am grateful for their help and for the friendship we shared.

Contents

Chapter One

Desperation made people do some strange things. Roger York looked at the sleeping girl, then gently checked her pulse yet again. Endless days mapping DNA strings on the fastest machines in existence. Even more months carefully searching for the perfect hiding place as others developed the tools to keep prying eyes away. All for an experiment that could take an innocent life that had no reckoning of the risk she was taking. Worse yet, Roger had little hope that it would succeed.

Roger ran his hands through his soft brown hair, not short nor long, cut so he could go as many whens as possible. He looked around the room, double-checking everything, especially the power sources. They would be all right. But what effect would the *suspend an* have on Elizabeth? Nobody had tried it over a hundred years, and Roger was bringing the girl forward five hundred and fifty plus.

The only thing more dangerous would be to bring her forward through the time drop. He'd drop in and wake her up every fifty years as it was. She seemed a strong, intelligent woman, despite her ignorance. Hopefully, her mind would be strong enough.

As he picked up his hand unit, he checked everything once

more, then focused his mind on the coordinates for fifty years ahead. It was odd, but the timetron landed him within seconds of the coordinates he entered. It had never done that before. Must have been the power source so close. He brushed Elizabeth's lips with his own. Her eyes flickered open. She smiled at him. He was smiling back. At least that part of this fool's enterprise was working.

Each fifty-year jump felt better than before. Elizabeth showed no visible effects from her time asleep, nor did Roger's handheld unit show any. The special locks that prevented anyone from even thinking about entering the room were working perfectly. He left the 1990s almost bursting with joy.

Some years into the 21st century, a small ion retainer on the door fizzled and sputtered. The rest of the card flared up and died as quickly. A minute later, the door creaked open.

It wasn't that Dean Parker was unintelligent. He did have brains. Even his older sister, Robin, admitted that. Dean's problem was that he didn't use them.

Exasperated, Robin watched the rest of the tour move further and further ahead through the medieval castle. Dean was not with them. There was no question about it, the twenty-one-year-old party animal was what gave twenty-somethings a bad name.

"Hey, Robin!" Dean's voice hissed behind her.

Robin jumped. "Damn it, Dean, where have you been?"

"You're not going to believe this unless you see it." Dean pulled at her arm. "Come on."

"The tour is going that way. If we don't go now, we'll be lost in this ruin."

"Robin, this is important, very important. Please, for me?"

Robin looked at her younger brother. Sun-bleached blonde hair capped the tanned face with the handsome square jaw and white even teeth. How he'd found a t-shirt big enough to be oversized on his broad shoulders, Robin had no idea. Underneath the shirt was dark plaid Bermuda shorts, and under them, beat-up board shoes. His blue eyes shone down earnestly from his six feet, two inches of height.

Robin's heart melted. "All right, what's so important?"

Dean led her down the corridor the way they had come, and around a corner. Robin stopped him.

"Uh, Dean, doesn't the sign on the door you're opening say not to go in there?" she asked.

He shrugged. "Yeah, well, I didn't read it. Come on."

Before Robin could protest, Dean dragged her through an open door made of surprisingly fresh wood. Robin looked about the room, in wonder.

The room was filled with an unnatural brightness. Up against the middle of the far wall was a huge bed with thin gauze curtains hanging around it. On one side, the curtains had been pulled back. Next to the bed was a tall black metal cabinet with a vertical door to one side. On top of the cabinet sat a flat monitor, with a flat black plastic box with rounded corners and edges next to it. In front of the monitor was another flat, black box, about the size of a portable computer keyboard.

To the left of the bed was a wall bearing one of the tall

narrow windows with which all medieval castles were built. A young woman looked through it.

She could have been twenty. She could have been twelve. She was short, about five one, and pleasantly rounded. Her light blue dress was rough wool, with an extremely full skirt and matching bodice. The under blouse had very full sleeves and tied at the wrists. It had been pulled up to tie around the neck, but the ties were loose. Her reddish-brown hair was gathered into a bun at the back of her head, with the side parts left loose and curly.

She turned and saw Robin and Dean. "Oh! You've returned."

"Yeah," said Dean. "I brought my sister. This is Robin."

The girl looked at Robin skeptically. Robin's mouse brown hair was cut short, and she was wearing jeans with a fitted t-shirt over them. Not the most feminine of outfits.

The girl bobbed a curtsy. "Are you a sorcerer, too?"

She had a strong Southern accent as if she were from West Virginia.

"A sorcerer?" asked Robin when she found her voice.

"Indeed. You must be one," the girl replied. "This is a magic chamber. How else could you enter it? It travels to many magical places. At least, they seem magical. Especially the last one. I did see great silver birds in the sky, and strange colorful animals that move so fast!"

"But we're not sorcerers," said Robin. "Who are you, and what land are you from?"

"My name is Elizabeth Wynford." She curtsied again. "And I am from Kent, in England, a village called King's Church on Rother. My father has a small holding there."

"King what? Where the heck is that?" asked Dean.

"In Kent, which is south, on the other side of London from here," Robin told him. She checked her watch. It was two thirty-three. The next tour would start at three, but Robin wasn't sure she wanted to see the first part of the castle all over again. "What do you want me to do?"

Dean shrugged. "Help her."

Robin groaned.

"So, she's a candidate for a rubber room," Dean said. "Is it fair to leave her here all locked up?"

"Well, Dean, maybe she's supposed to be here."

"Come on, Robin. Didn't you hear the tour guide? Nobody's lived here for over five hundred years."

"What? You were listening?"

"It happens. We gotta help her."

Robin looked at Elizabeth. "Are you really locked up here?"

Elizabeth thought it over. "In truth, I've never tried the door. I was brought here by a magician named Roger. He puts me to sleep, then moves the chamber. He's very kind. He wakes me up and we talk. But he never lets me see the lands outside the chamber. In truth, I don't believe he ever will. This is the first time I am awake without him here. Did he send you?"

"Nah, we never heard of him," Dean said. He turned to Robin. "Well?"

"I suppose we can turn her over to the authorities," Robin sighed.

"But she's an American. Listen to that accent."

"The accent..." Robin paused as something tugged at the

back of her mind. Either the girl had done a lot of research or the unbelievable was somehow true. It couldn't be.

But at that moment, Robin saw the headphones on the bed. They looked like fine, plastic calipers with white pads, sort of like the ones used on heart monitors, on the ends. Robin picked them up. Tiny tubes ran together to the cabinet and plugged into the machine on the bottom. There were tiny air bubbles in the tubes near the white pads. Robin followed the tubes to the machine and opened the door. Inside were two bags made of a material Robin had never seen in all her history of engineering. The bags looked and acted like plastic but had the cool smoothness of glass. They contained liquids, one perfectly clear, the other a light green.

Robin looked at the monitor. Six panels filled the screen. Four appeared to be monitoring Elizabeth, including one that noted that the food source had been handled, but the seals were unbroken. The fifth noted the presence of two life forms without known aura prints. The sixth said "Home Base, ready."

Robin looked at the keyboard-sized box. As soon as she touched it, lights for the keys she expected glowed quietly. Without quite knowing why, she touched the sixth panel, then the keyboard where the number nine would be on the keyboards she knew. Three nines appeared after "Home Base." Robin touched one of the nines. It disappeared. Without thinking, she hit enter on the keyboard.

Blinding light surrounded her. Robin felt as if she were being sucked into herself. A long second later, she was standing in a darkened room. The light grew to where Robin could see clearly. The room looked like a refugee from the Star

Trek set. The walls were covered by white panels. On an adjacent wall were inset panels that were light blue doors, Robin thought. Next to one of the doors was a tall dark blue box-like structure that reminded Robin of an armoire. Up against the wall facing the other door was a dark blue table. Above that simple white shelves displayed numerous antiques, among them what looked like an iPod music player that had been taken apart and wired to an old-fashioned coffee grinder.

"A time machine!" Robin gasped. "What else could this thing be? Where the hell am I?"

She scanned the room. On the table was another flat monitor with a keyboard like that in the castle. The monitor was already on, but there were only two panels. One noted the presence of a humanoid life form without a known aura print. At the top of the second panel was: "XY17, HOME BASE, TIME: 14:46, DATE: 21990714."

"2199?" Robin mumbled. "Oh, my god!"

Almost two hundred years in the future, if the date was to be trusted, and given how Robin had arrived, there was no reason not to. This was either the strangest dream Robin had ever had or… It had the solid feel of waking, the vibrancy.

"Shit howdy," Robin grumbled. "How do I get back?"

Tentatively, she typed a couple letters on the keyboard. They appeared in the monitor's second panel next to a blinking cursor. She looked quickly for a backspace key but found none. She touched the two letters on the screen and literally rubbed them out. The cursor remained blinking.

"Cool."

She typed "Elizabeth" just to be typing something. Sure

enough, coordinates appeared on the screen, plus a map of England that blew up to show the neighborhood the castle was in. Robin checked her watch. The liquid crystal diodes had gone crazy and broken figures were swimming all over the face. But she had just checked the time before she'd been... transported. She entered the date she'd left and the time at two forty-eight. She touched the second panel and hit enter.

Another blinding light and she found herself back in the castle room, gasping.

"You are indeed the most powerful sorcerer!" Elizabeth gasped, backing away.

"Fuck!" said Dean.

"It worked!" Robin crowed. "Hot damn, it worked! Deanie, this is the most incredible thing I've ever seen in my life! It's beyond belief."

"Fuck," said Dean.

"Is that all you can say?"

"What the hell do you want?" Dean groaned. "One minute you're playing with that computer, and then you disappeared into thin air! Three minutes later, you're back. Hell, it was like 'Bewitched', or something."

"It's a time machine!" Robin yelled. "An honest to goodness time machine. H. G. Wells. Quantum Leap. This is it. The real article. Dean, I was in the future! Two hundred years from now!"

"That's impossible."

"You saw me disappear. What else could explain this set-up?"

"Well, it sure as hell isn't 'Candid Camera'. What are we gonna do?"

"This is a good question." Robin saw Elizabeth backed into a corner. "You okay?"

"You are so powerful. The spell you uttered..."

"It wasn't a spell. It was the machine." Robin grinned. "I'm no sorcerer. Honest. The machine just did it."

Elizabeth thought it over with all her might. "That is what Roger says. But I've never seen him disappear like that. Perhaps it is because I am asleep when he goes."

"Probably." Robin reached out to the frightened girl. "Look, I don't hurt people, and I'm certainly no sorcerer. Do you want us to wait here for Roger to show?"

Elizabeth looked out the window longingly. "You are at least as powerful as Roger is. And I do want to see the marvelous land outside. Will you take me?"

"Sure," said Dean.

"Wait," growled Robin. She pulled Dean aside. "Let's think this one through. She has no I.D. Look at how she's dressed. She's going to freak out there."

Dean chuckled. "Hello? She's already freaked, Robin. Maybe we should take her to the embassy in London and find out who her folks are."

"Dean, her folks have been dead for something like four hundred years."

"Huh?"

Robin turned to the girl. "Elizabeth, what year were you born?"

"The year of Our Lord, sixteen hundred and twenty-three."

"She's cracked," said Dean.

"Wrong, hockey-puck." Robin faced off with him. "She really is from the seventeenth century. Don't you get it? She's been sleeping? This Roger guy is from the way distant future and has put her on suspended animation to bring her forward for some reason." She turned back to Elizabeth. "Did Roger say why he brought you here?"

"Just that he needed me," she replied simply.

Robin snorted. "I'll bet."

Dean struggled. "Robin, this doesn't make sense. I mean, time travel's impossible, isn't it?"

"Now, it is. But there's no reason to believe it won't happen in the future. Hell, there are people in this day and age trying to work out ways to make it happen. And it must be they get it, because of all this."

"Yeah, right." The look on Dean's face grew even more pained. "It doesn't make sense. Elizabeth talks like she's from Georgia or something like that."

"No, I'm from Kent," Elizabeth protested.

"We know," Robin told her, then turned to Dean. "Her accent is what cements it. The theory is that the way people talked in Shakespeare's time and a little bit later is more like the Appalachian dialect from West Virginia. People there were very isolated for centuries and still use terms and rhythms very close to Shakespearean language. If Elizabeth were faking it, she'd be more likely to use a current English accent."

"Woh." The thought made its way through Dean's brain. "So now what do we do?"

"I don't know." Robin wandered about the room. She stopped by the cabinet, and not entirely sure why, picked up the flat box with the rounded edges.

"I'd like to see the land outside," said Elizabeth.

The lights suddenly dimmed and brightened.

"Shit, that's what happened right before you got back!" yelped Dean.

He grabbed Elizabeth's hand and ran from the room. Robin ran also, just barely remembering to shut the door behind her.

It took a moment for the man who appeared in the room to get his wind back. He whipped around. Already the monitor had tracked his aura print. It wouldn't matter once he had the girl. But the bed was empty. He brushed his reddish-brown hair out of his eyes.

All the suspend an equipment was there. But the girl was obviously gone. The lights dimmed and brightened. He turned.

"Hello, Roger," he said, trying to feign a smile.

Roger, still gasping from the drop, shook his head. "Donald, what are you doing here?"

"Just checking on the project." Donald put on his most innocent grin.

He was an average size man, somewhat shorter than Roger. Though both were predominately Caucasian, their features blended well in a host of cultures.

Donald watched Roger carefully. But Roger was far more interested in the girl's disappearance than why Donald was there.

"You shouldn't be here," Roger said, mildly. He glared at the monitor. "It wasn't my idea not to authorize you for the project and I don't want to talk about it anymore."

"I wasn't saying anything." Donald smirked. For all the

two men looked the same age, Donald was considerably younger.

Roger ignored him and checked the bed.

"I don't have her, if that's what you're wondering," Donald said.

"Damn!" Roger enlarged the fifth panel on the monitor. "Nothing. Absolutely nothing. Damn lock."

"No aura prints?" Donald moved behind the other man to where he could see the screen. "Oh, unknown. That will make them easy to find."

"Donald, leave," Roger growled as he went back to checking equipment.

"A thousand pardons, oh mighty one." Donald's bow was anything but sincere. "If it weren't for me, you wouldn't have had your girl in the first place."

Roger turned on him. "By getting her charged with witchcraft? That made it quite easy. And discreet, too."

"She never saw me."

Roger groaned and went back to checking equipment. "You're just lucky no one saw you start that fire in the gaol. I'll have enough to do to regain her trust because I know her shame."

"Well then, maybe I could—"

Roger's glare cut Donald short. He shrugged.

"Maybe I'll just look around a while."

Roger ignored him.

Donald walked casually out of the room, but once outside, he dashed down the corridor. Whoever had the girl couldn't have gotten far. But which way had they gone?

Back in the room, Roger sighed. Even though Donald

seemed to have accepted the Board's ruling on this experiment, Roger strongly suspected Donald was not feeling nearly as conciliatory as he pretended. It was no accident that the two of them had arrived so closely together.

Roger glanced at the door. More worrisome than Donald was that the keyboard and base unit had been used, and the hand unit was gone. Oh, and Elizabeth was gone. Roger glared at the base unit keyboard.

Thousands upon thousands of years of recorded history and in only seventy-five of them would it occur to a mundane that a keyboard, that primitive mess laid out to literally slow people down, not to mention a keyboard under glass, that this bleeding antique technology could control something. So naturally, that's when the ion lock failed.

And one of the two strangers who had gotten into the room had had enough savvy to figure the base unit out, which meant a mundane knew it for what it was, creating an anomaly on top of Elizabeth being outside the castle during the wrong when. Only another time traveler could actually use the hand unit. But the lost unit meant yet another anomaly and Roger shuddered to think what would be involved in cleaning up that mess on top of all the others. Sighing, he hit the key for home.

Chapter Two

"Oh, dear," sighed the matron as she looked Elizabeth up and down.

Robin held her breath as she and Dean stood in the doorway to the castle. She glanced over at Elizabeth, who looked more curious than frightened at that moment. Dean was putting on his best "bluff 'em out" look.

"The seventeenth-century group is meeting in York this weekend," the matron continued. "I do hope you haven't been terribly inconvenienced."

"No," said Robin with a quick grin. "As a matter of fact, we're just on our way there. Thought we'd drop in and see the castle first."

"Oh, good." The matron smiled in relief. "It really doesn't do to say so, but some of your colleagues are rather disorganized. I was quite afraid I was going to be bombarded with Cavaliers and their ladies." She smiled again at Elizabeth. "Lovely job, dear, but I do believe ties at the neck are not quite period."

Elizabeth looked puzzled, but before she could say anything, Robin gently took her arm and turned her toward the parking lot.

"Well, who knows," Robin told the matron as she pushed

Elizabeth past. "Not a lot of portrait evidence among the lower classes, you know."

"Huh?" asked Dean, following close behind.

Robin glanced behind them. "We've got an explanation for Elizabeth for the moment."

"Explanation?" Elizabeth asked.

"I don't get it," Dean said.

Robin stopped to catch her breath. "Historical re-enactors, Dean. You know, like the Renaissance Faire back home? There are clubs all over the place that dress up in historical costumes and make like they live in the past. They've got them for all different time periods. That woman just thought we were dressed up for a seventeenth-century group."

"This is my best dress," Elizabeth said. "But what did she mean about my ties?"

"Long story," Robin said, suddenly aware that she still held the small, flat box she'd picked up in the room.

"Oh, I got you," Dean said. "Like that group you were hanging around with when you were dating Steve."

"Steve is gay, Dean," Robin said through her teeth. The two had spent a lot of time in each other's company years before, together nursing their latest wounds in the dating wars. They'd become good friends and even business part-ners, thanks to their combined misery. Steve was finally in a solid, committed relationship. "Anyway, we've got other things to worry about." She glanced around. "I don't see any sign of this Roger character, but that doesn't mean he's not monitoring us. We'd better make tracks. We'll get Elizabeth back to the hotel and then figure out what we're going to do."

A car rolled past, and Elizabeth yelped. "That's the

strangest animal I've ever seen! It's huge! It looked so small from the window."

"Oh, great," sighed Robin.

Dean shrugged. "It's just a car, Elizabeth. Oh, wait. You wouldn't know what that is."

"It's a like a carriage," Robin explained, leading Elizabeth into the parking lot. "Only it has an engine. We give it fuel and it goes."

Elizabeth looked at a couple leaving one car and another small family getting into one. Near her, an engine roared to life. She started.

"It's noisy," she said, then gasped as the automobile slowly backed out of its parking spot. "There are people inside. But how does it go? There are no horses. It must be the most powerful kind of magic."

"Something like that," Robin grumbled, fumbling for the keys to the rental car.

The dark sedan, unfortunately, looked like all the other dark sedans in the lot. People were staring at Elizabeth, a few smiling as if they were in on the same joke. Robin couldn't help thinking if only those living history fans knew what an opportunity they were missing.

Dean found the car first and went straight to the right side. Robin pushed him away.

"Other side, Dean," she said, unlocking the door. "We're in England, remember?"

"Duh. Hey, Robin, I don't think Elizabeth is going to fit in that back seat."

Robin looked at Elizabeth's full dress and the tiny space in the back. "Dean, why don't you get in the back?"

Dean got in without complaining, for once. Elizabeth balked. Robin walked around to the passenger side.

"Elizabeth, it's okay, I promise," she said. She thought fast. "I know this seems really magical to you, but it's normal stuff for me and Dean. Unless you want us to take you back to the room."

Elizabeth took a deep breath. "No. I wish to see this magical land. I will see it."

Robin stuffed the girl and the dress into the sedan, then slid on the seat belt. She ran around to her side of the car and slid in behind the wheel, stopping only to gently place the black box she still carried on the dash.

As the car finally rolled into traffic, Elizabeth stiffened once again.

"It's so fast," she gasped.

"This is nothing," Dean chortled.

"Easy, Dean," Robin said, checking the speedometer. "About the fastest Elizabeth has ever traveled in her life was maybe fifteen miles an hour, assuming she got on a really fast horse."

"Roger took me on one before he put me in the room." Elizabeth's brow furrowed, but she said nothing more.

Robin sensed it was better to let the girl be and let her own thoughts drift far beyond the immediate situation.

It had been a rough year, spent with a man who had repeatedly shown her why he was not the man of her dreams as she had thought. Robin winced. She used to be better at getting out of bad relationships. But as her friend Steve had gently suggested to her, it was possible she was expecting too much from her men and not giving her relationships the chance to mature. So, she'd stuck it out with Rick, forgiving him again and again, until the night she caught him surfing for Internet porn and realized he was more interested in his laptop than in her.

In some ways, Rick was not unlike her father or her mother. Her dad, a top NASA scientist, had always been more comfortable withdrawn into himself while poring over code or formulas. Her mom was more outgoing, but it was a professional necessity. A surgeon with a specialty in cardiology, she had one of the largest and most respected practices in Orange County.

Although both her parents were devoted to their children, parenting and careers left little time for each other and neither really had the inclination to leave their respective worlds. They had drifted apart, divorcing when Robin was thirteen.

Robin wondered, not for the first time, if her parents' indifference to each other was why she never managed to stay interested enough to keep a relationship going for any length of time. With her thirtieth birthday coming up the next summer, it was a puzzle she wanted to solve soon.

"Hey, Robin," Dean said, suddenly leaning forward. "I got some classical on my iPhone."

He had jammed the unit into the new speaker dock he'd brought with him and had all but shoved it into Robin's ear.

"Not a good time, Dean," Robin growled, nodding at Elizabeth, who jumped at the music coming from the small speakers.

"Never mind." Dean slumped back in his seat.

Robin glanced in her rearview mirror back at Dean, who

had taken his iPhone off the speaker dock, hooked up the ear-buds, and was now lost in his music as he watched the countryside whiz by. Nothing much phased Dean. He spent his life sliding along, never really having to work hard at anything he tried, which may have been why he seemed so incredibly stupid at times.

On the other hand, he was about to start his first year of graduate school, having whipped through his undergrad work as a psych major. But then Dean had always been like that, acing his classes, but not retaining much unless it happened to interest him. And not much besides girls and good times did.

Robin didn't like to admit it, but she was jealous of her little brother, although she was no less accomplished. Female computer scientists were still considered an oddity, and every day, almost, was a struggle for respect among her colleagues and subordinates. With hundreds of high-tech startups out there, it was no big deal to be senior vice president of engineering, especially at age 29. That the company she'd founded after college was not only still around, but profitable, said a lot. She'd worked hard and she'd earned it.

And she'd been looking forward to a month in England, a trip she'd planned for herself and Rick. Except that that had fizzled, and her mother had pressured her into taking Dean instead. Stuck babysitting again. Robin glared briefly into the rearview mirror at Dean, then noticed Elizabeth.

She was very tense but determined to accept whatever came her way. Pretty gutsy, Robin thought.

"I'm wondering," Robin said aloud, finally. "Why are we running from Roger?"

"Oh, come on, Robin," snapped Dean, whipping off his earbuds. "He locked her up and put her to sleep. Who knows what else he did to her?"

"Roger was very kind to me," Elizabeth insisted.

Dean snorted.

"So why are we running from him?" Robin asked, looking at her.

Elizabeth thought. The odd thing, Robin noticed, was that Elizabeth was not struggling to understand something, but was instead calculating.

"He took me from my town," she said finally. "I cannot say I was unwilling. But perhaps he put a spell on me to make me go." Tears, real ones, filled her eyes. "I don't truly fear Roger, but I do believe he is a danger to me."

That much rang true, Robin decided. And she had to admit, Dean had a point about this locking up business. But why hadn't the girl been discovered sooner? Robin glanced at the black box. Perhaps it would have some answers.

They got to the little bed and breakfast inn just outside of Windsor in under an hour. As they parked the car down the narrow street, Robin could see Elizabeth clenching her teeth, bracing herself against more magic, probably.

Robin tried to think ahead a few minutes. What was coming and what would Elizabeth find magical? The inn was at least Georgian, but certainly no older than that. It wouldn't be dark for several hours yet, so there would be time to explain electricity. What about toilets and running water?

Robin took a deep breath and led Elizabeth and Dean into the inn. In their room, Robin made a point of doing the latch and putting a chair under the doorknob. Dean drew the curtains, putting the room in semi-darkness. The summer afternoon sun slipped through the cracks. Robin held off turning on the lights.

Elizabeth looked around in awe. She started when she saw her reflection in the mirror.

"Who could that be?" she gasped.

"That's you, Elizabeth," said Dean. "That's a mirror."

"Why, it is. But it's so clear!"

Robin gently set the black box from the castle on the night table. "Okay, gang. We've got to do some thinking here. We've kind of decided that Elizabeth is not going back to the room and Roger, right?"

"Yeah," Dean said forcefully.

"Elizabeth?" Robin asked.

"I do not want to go back there," she said firmly.

"Okay. So now what do we do?" Robin asked. "We have someone, who for all intents and purposes is a non-person, to bring up to speed on over four-hundred years of human advancement, and some yahoo from the future probably looking for us. Probably the smartest thing to do would be to send Elizabeth back to her own time, but how to do that..." Robin shrugged.

Elizabeth, for her part, was struggling with something again.

"Robin," she began, then paused. "What is the name of this land?"

"We are in England," Robin replied slowly. "Do you know the story of the princess who slept for a hundred years until she was awakened by a prince?"

Elizabeth nodded.

"Roger found a way to make you sleep for over four hundred years," Robin continued. "A lot has changed since then. That's why everything is so different and seems so magical to you. The human race has learned a lot in four hundred years. How to make carriages go without horses. How to make mirrors perfectly clear. How to talk to people through wires and through airwaves. All sorts of things, Elizabeth."

"Will you be able to take me back to my time?" Elizabeth asked in a small voice.

"I don't know yet," Robin said softly. "That box I brought with me. It could be a hand-held time machine, and if it is, I need to figure out how to use it, and I may not be able to. It's possible you may be stuck here."

Elizabeth, looking frightened, nodded slowly. "Then I must learn how to be in this land."

It was a long and difficult evening. Robin, against her better judgment, let Dean convince her to take Elizabeth shopping and then to dinner. But everything frightened the poor girl. She balked at passing through the automatic door at the clothing shop. She was mortified by the skimpy little shifts on display and insisted on wearing several layers of skirts and blouses at once. Dean told the clerks an outrageous story about Elizabeth's luggage being lost at a living history event while Robin tried to convince Elizabeth to give up her stays.

Things were a little better at dinner at the nearby pub. Elizabeth was shocked by the array of dishes but pleased by the grilled half chicken she was served. The television over the bar caught her eye, but she started crying when the bartender switched the channels, convinced that he had killed the elves she'd seen.

Because electric lights were already on in the shop and the pub, Elizabeth didn't really notice them, until they returned to the room and Dean thoughtlessly flipped them on. Elizabeth yelped, then panicked when Robin showed her how to work the switch and the lights went out.

The noise of the toilet flushing terrified her, and she did not want to use it until Robin insisted. Then there was the bath. Elizabeth resisted, so Robin undressed to help her along. It didn't help when Elizabeth was surprised that Robin really was a woman.

Dean insisted on standing guard that night while Robin and Elizabeth slept, just in case Roger came to get Elizabeth. Elizabeth went to bed obediently. Robin decided to stay up to look at the box.

The clock on the room's bureau was chiming two a.m. when Robin glanced over at Dean. He'd been sound asleep in an easy chair for at least an hour. From Elizabeth's bed came the soft sound of weeping. Robin went over to her.

"You okay?" she asked, gently sitting next to the crying girl.

"This place is so magical," she whispered. "I'm so frightened. I know you think it good."

Robin sighed. "Not all the time. And I understand how it would be really scary for you. Look, Elizabeth, I can't make any promises, but I'll do everything I can. I figured out how to turn this thing on, and it's responding to me. There's some sort of language processor in here, which is why we can still understand each other even though language has changed a lot in the past four hundred years."

Elizabeth sniffled and smiled weakly. "I don't want you to

think that I don't like it here. You and Dean have been more than kind."

"We do our best. Listen, why don't you get some sleep? We'll tackle the world tomorrow. Okay?"

Elizabeth nodded and rolled over.

Robin waited until she heard Elizabeth's even breathing, then turned the machine on.

The next morning, Dean woke up stiff as a board and to loud knocking on the room door. Stretching, he lumbered over.

"Who is it?" he called.

Elizabeth was sitting up in bed, looking worried.

"It's Robin," she hissed from the other side of the door. "Get that chair out from under the doorknob now!"

Dean pulled it away.

"Did you know she'd left?" Elizabeth asked.

"Uh-uh." Dean yawned as he opened the door.

"I didn't leave through the door," Robin said darkly as she slipped in and replaced the chair under the doorknob.

"What?" Dean shook the last of the sleep from his head.

Robin held up the box. "I got it to work. I sent myself back to 1920s New York, then here. Only I got here two days ago. I've been hanging out in Bath, so I didn't run into myself."

"You what?" Dean gasped.

"The time machine, Dean. I figured it out. It's actually pretty easy. Geez, these guys in the future have human inter-face down to a hey nonny."

Elizabeth cried out happily. "Does this mean I can go back to my place?"

"Yeah," said Robin. "It may take us a few days to get the

stuff together that Dean and I will need to go back with you, but we can get you back to King's Church on whatever it is."

"No." Elizabeth paled. "Please, let's not go there."

"Wait a minute," Dean said nervously. "You want me to go back, too?"

"Dean, it's the chance of a lifetime. Why wouldn't you want to go?"

"I like living!"

"It's not dangerous. And, Elizabeth, why don't you want to go home? Oh, wait. Roger, of course. He found you there once. I guess we'll have to find a way to re-establish you someplace else. We can do some research at the British Museum. But, speaking of Roger, we've got to get out of here. Now."

"He's here?" gasped Elizabeth.

"Somewhere around here," Robin said. "At least, I think so. I didn't see him, but the desk clerk said that he was asking about a girl in a seventeenth-century dress yesterday morning and if the clerk had noticed some lights flashing. Well, somebody named Donald did, and I'm assuming that's what Roger's calling himself now. Who else would be asking that kind of question? We're just lucky the desk clerk wasn't on yesterday afternoon when we came back with Elizabeth because she's really wigged-out about this guy. Anyway, we've got to get out of here before Roger or whatever he's calling himself comes back. And I don't want that clerk to see Elizabeth."

The three packed quickly. Dean took over checking out while Robin and Elizabeth slipped out behind him. They went first to London, where Robin insisted on checking into a hotel known for catering to business travelers.

"We stick out like sore thumbs," Dean protested, looking at all the people in business wear milling about the lobby.

"Come on, there're plenty of tourists here," Robin grumbled, although she had to admit to herself that she didn't see any. "Besides, they have the fast 'Net access I need. I've got major research to do."

Once in their room, Dean paced nervously as Elizabeth sat on the bed, again looking small and scared. Robin tried not to notice as she pulled her laptop from its bag and turned it on.

"It's like we're gonna have to stay in this room the whole time," Dean fumed. "That Roger guy is going to spot us in nothing flat around all these suits."

"I know," Robin finally conceded. "But, Dean, we can't just go back in time without knowing about where we're headed. We don't know any more about Elizabeth's world than she knows about ours. We've got to get the right clothes, learn new habits, figure out where to go. All that."

"Can you get that on the Internet?"

"A lot of it." Robin fumed as the computer booted up. Suddenly, compared to the time machine, it seemed ridiculously slow. She whisked her finger across the mouse pad and clicked. It was noisy, too, compared to the time machine. "We'll have to check in with the British Museum and a whole bunch of other stuff. I'm just hoping there's a re-enactor group around that can get us clothes that are reasonably close to the period."

"Maybe we ought to see if we can get Elizabeth a passport and stay here." Dean folded his arms belligerently.

Robin glanced back at the girl. "I don't think she's up to it, Dean."

"Well, maybe we ought to ask her." He turned. "Elizabeth, don't you really want to stay here with us?"

A pained frown creased Elizabeth's face.

"Dean, don't put pressure on her like that," Robin said, still focused on her computer. "Wait." Bolting out of her chair, she turned on the girl. "We should be asking you, Elizabeth. You were there. Geez, talk about a primary source."

"Huh?" Dean asked.

Elizabeth shrank back even further. Robin stopped and gently sat down next to her.

"Elizabeth, we just need your help so that Dean and I can fit in in your world," Robin said softly. "There's tons of stuff out there that's been written on life in historic England, but you were there. You know what's accurate and what isn't."

Elizabeth began to cry. "It's so hard. Dean wants me to stay here, and I would like to please him. But I do want to go home, Robin. And I don't know how to get there, and you're saying that I will know."

Dean settled down next to Elizabeth and held her while tossing a glare at Robin.

"And you came down on me for pressuring her," he growled triumphantly.

Robin sighed. "Elizabeth, I do know how to get you home. Or close enough to it if you don't want Roger to catch you again. I just want to know what it's like there. That way Dean and I can come and stay with you for a while. That is, if you'd like us to."

"I would." Elizabeth nodded eagerly. "It wouldn't be good

to let people know you're sorcerers, though. But we can say you're my cousins. That you've taken me in. We could say that a greedy baron has taken my father's holding and that you've taken me on your travels so that I might find a situation. Two brothers traveling with their cousin wouldn't be thought strange. We've had a baron take a few holdings in our town."

Dean started laughing. "Two brothers, huh?"

Robin glared at him. Elizabeth grimaced as she realized her mistake.

"I am very sorry," she said softly.

"Don't be," Robin sighed. "Compared to women in your time, I probably am pretty manly. I don't know. It would be safer, two guys and a girl traveling together instead of two girls and a guy. But I am a little lacking in the beard department." Robin stroked her chin. "Someone would be bound to notice."

"I've seen it before," said Elizabeth. "His voice was quite high, too. They said he had not his jewels."

"Elizabeth!" Dean gasped. "You're not supposed to know about that stuff."

"Get real, Dean," Robin retorted and got up. "You know, that's not a bad idea. I'm sure birth defects like missing scrotum were even more common then than they are now."

"Yeah, but people probably died from them sooner," Dean said, mildly disgusted. "Robin, you're out of your mind. We can't go back in time. We'd be spotted in a minute."

"Not if we do the research first," Robin said. "And we've got Elizabeth to help us. Of course, if you don't want to go...

I suppose I could leave you here by yourself, and if Roger shows up, you could handle it."

Dean swallowed, then made his decision. "Not that I couldn't take him. But I'll go with you."

"Oh, I'm so happy," Elizabeth said.

Robin could see that Dean still wasn't happy about the adventure, but she decided not to press the point. She, too, had her misgivings about fitting into seventeenth-century English society and felt guilty about manipulating Dean into the trip. But she needed his brawn. For all she knew, she was rushing into far greater danger than even a furious Roger might be. But a time machine. How could she let that go without exploring every when she had ever wanted to see?

Chapter Three

It took almost two weeks to get all the information and clothes that Robin wanted before she felt satisfied that she and Dean were ready to make the jump into the past.

The clothes had been the hardest part. Robin made contact with a historical re-enactor through an e-mail friend of hers. The re-enactor helped her find outfits through her group but was remarkably picky about authenticity. Oddly enough, Elizabeth wasn't, and in fact, pronounced several doublets and breeches as workable that the re-enactor turned her nose up at.

Dean, for his part, complained incessantly and tried again and again to interest Elizabeth in modern life. Again and again, Elizabeth reacted with fear or distaste. She refused to flush a toilet, although she liked toilet paper once she got the hang of it. Dean's favorite alternative rock and hip-hop groups made her shudder. She refused to wear any less than three layers of clothes and clung tenaciously to her stays. Daily showers were a struggle. Robin and Dean had to be very sure to keep her away from television sets because the "elves in the box" would start her screaming. And while getting her on the Underground was difficult enough, the only thing worse was driving the magic carriage.

Even eating was difficult. Elizabeth would not eat anything that came in a Styrofoam container because she hated the feel of the foam. That made ordering food in almost impossible. But getting her through the streets to restaurants was pretty much running the poor girl through a gantlet of terrors.

The worse part was that Robin insisted the three stay moving to make it harder for Roger to track them. Furthermore, Elizabeth begged not to be left alone in whatever hotel room they were in after the first day because the phone had rung and scared her.

Still, Dean persisted, but as the two weeks wore on, his protests became less strident.

Finally, Robin was satisfied. The night before the three were to leave, she had hers and Dean's luggage shipped to her office. All they had that night was what they could carry in the two homespun bags they would bring with them into the past.

The next morning, Dean made one last pro forma protest as he tested his saber.

"Are you sure about this, Robin?" he asked, swishing the sword through the air as he lunged forward.

"Put that damn thing down before you hurt one of us." Like her brother, Robin wore a shirt, breeches, doublet, boots, wide belt, and plain, dark cavalier hat.

"I'm not going to hurt anybody," Dean grumbled, sheathing his sword, nonetheless.

Robin tried not to groan. "Look, Dean, the only reason we're carrying weapons is that we'd get slaughtered without them. With any luck at all, we won't have to use them. Better yet, let's try not to." She looked over at Elizabeth and back at Dean. "Are you two ready?"

"I am," said Elizabeth, her eyes shining with joy.

"I s'pose," Dean grumbled as he picked up his bag.

Robin put the room key on the bureau, then, taking a deep breath, picked up the time machine and her bag. "Okay. We should all be touching."

She waited for Dean and Elizabeth put their hands on each of her shoulders, then focused her mind on the geographic coordinates and date in early spring 1642 that she wanted.

The bright white light was blinding, and the awful sucking sensation almost caused Robin to cry out. Just as she was certain she could bear it no longer, she found herself gasping in the middle of a muddy road surrounded on both sides by a grove of trees.

Dean and Elizabeth still had their hands on her shoulders and gasped as well.

"Why didn't you tell me about that sucking part?" Dean groaned as he fell away from his sister. He stumbled for a moment, then looked around. "Woh."

Robin nodded. The utter quiet was startling. Birds sang and a soft breeze rustled the trees. But completely absent was any sort of mechanized roar from airplanes, cars in the distance, anything.

"This is, like, weird, man," Dean said. "It's quiet."

"Your world is terribly noisy," Elizabeth said.

"You sure we're in the right place?" Dean asked.

Robin hid the time machine in her sack. "Well, we'll find out soon enough. Where's the sun?"

"Over there." Elizabeth pointed. "Are we far from King's Church on Rother?"

"Far enough," Robin replied. "We should be in Essex, about three miles from a village called Downleigh."

"Essex?" Elizabeth asked. "Why there?"

"It's got a similar economy to Kent and is far enough away we won't be running into anybody you know," Robin replied.

She decided not to add that with the English Civil War in their very near future, she had made a point of going where the fighting wouldn't be.

She looked around. "Let's see, it feels like late morning, so the machine got that part right. So, if the sun's over there, then that's east and the direction we want to go."

Elizabeth chuckled, both amused and puzzled by Robin's labored reasoning of something she knew almost instinctively.

The three set off. About fifteen minutes into the walk, Dean sighed.

"It's sure a long way," he grumbled another fifteen minutes later. "Are you sure you know where we are, Robin? We should have walked three miles by now."

"We've not even walked one," Elizabeth said.

"Huh?" Dean groaned.

"Dean, don't be such a wuss," Robin said. "It just takes longer because we're walking."

"I know that," Dean retorted.

"Yeah, and when was the last time you walked further than five parking spaces from anywhere? Geez, Dean, if the mall lot is half full, you insist on using the valet."

"Hey, I work out."

Elizabeth shrugged. "This is not a bad distance. It was five miles to the village from my father's holding and I walked there every other morning."

"Remember our magic carriages, Elizabeth?" Robin said. "We're used to getting a lot further a lot faster."

The glade had quickly given way to pasture and farmland. Paths led into the rolling fields, and the odd distant chimney could be seen behind the hills and hedges. Eventually, from the top of a rise, they first saw the village. It was little more than a scattering of half-timbered buildings strung along either side of the road. A gray stone church sat at the far end.

As they got closer, they noted a much larger house sitting at the edge of the village that had a sign with a faded picture of a bear and a stag hanging over the door.

"That's the inn," said Elizabeth.

She and Robin looked at each other and both took a deep breath.

Dean held Robin back. "Do we have any money?"

"No," Robin replied calmly.

"Then how are we going to pay for it?"

"We'll work. Now, do you remember our story?"

"Yeah, sure."

Elizabeth was already walking up to the door.

The inn was a two-storied house, white with dark timbers. The matching stable stood back from the road. Small chickens ran about everywhere, and behind the stable, a small cow grazed. Dean looked puzzled, and even Robin was taken aback at the animals' small size, even though she'd remembered that conventional breeding techniques were for the most part unheard of.

Abandoning the door, Elizabeth led the way around to the side of the house, where an older matron presided over a brick oven. The woman looked up as they approached.

"You'll be wanting rooms?" she asked in a tired voice.

"Please, mistress," said Robin. "We've run into some bad luck on the road. Bandits. We barely escaped with our lives and our weapons. But they got all our money. Might we exchange some work for a night's lodging?"

"Bandits, you say." The woman looked them over carefully. "Well, lazy brutes they must have been with you not having a scratch on you."

"We were fortunate," Robin said, silently cursing herself for forgetting that detail.

"Indeed. Where are you headed?"

"Where our fortunes take us," Robin answered. "My brother Dean and I have four older brothers. Our father has nothing for us. We have our cousin with us because a certain baron took her father's holding when he died, and she had no protection. We're looking for a good situation for her."

The matron lifted an eyebrow. "Indeed. Can you cook?"

"That I can and well, too," replied Elizabeth.

The matron turned on Robin and Dean. "And you young men. After adventure in the king's army?"

"Not really," Robin replied quickly. "Even if we were, we'd want to be sure our cousin was well placed and safe first."

The matron picked up her apron and wiped her hands. She was well-padded, but not fat, with wisps of gray and brown hair slipping from her veil and cap. Her teeth were mostly sound, what Robin could see of them, and her hands were rough and red.

"Well, fortune is with you," the matron said. "My man and my girl ran off last week, leaving me alone. I might as well take all three of you. There'll be wages to be had if you work well. I am Anne Ford."

"I am Elizabeth Wynford," she said curtseying. "And my cousins are Robin and Dean Parker."

"Dean?" Mistress Ford asked.

"Dick, actually," Robin said. "But we had a sister who could not say Dick and called him Dean, and the name stuck."

Mistress Ford laughed. "Good enough. You two go tend the stable. We've a merchant in town, and I want his horse fed and groomed promptly."

"Yes, Mistress," Robin said, suddenly reluctant.

Dean, however, headed for the stables in high spirits.

"Woh, that was easy," he said once they were there. "I figured we'd be walking for weeks before we found someplace to put Elizabeth."

"I know." Robin sighed. "I hope Mistress Ford isn't setting Elizabeth up to service the guests." She looked back at the house. Elizabeth had taken over at the oven and seemed happy enough.

"That's bogus. I guess we'll have to stick around for a while, huh?" A horse snorted and Dean grinned. "I'm being paged."

He went over to the dark brown animal and slapped its neck. "Boy, you sure are small, fella. Hey, Robin, you see any curry brushes around? Oh, wait, here it is."

Robin watched, slightly shocked. But Dean had always been good around animals and had taken horseback riding lessons when they were kids. Sighing, she looked around for a rake, found it and began raking out the foul straw and droppings.

Elizabeth appeared an hour or so later with bread and cheese for lunch.

"So, how is Mistress Ford?" Robin asked, trying to sound casual.

"Very kind," said Elizabeth happily.

"You don't think she's, uh, trying to set you up as..."

Elizabeth laughed loudly. "No! In fact, she gave me a very stern lecture indeed. If I so much as smile too kindly at a guest, she'll have me whipped. She runs a good inn and would not for the world risk the bad opinion of our neighbors. She's a godly woman, I assure you. But eat quickly. We've the ale to make and much else to be done."

"Ale?" asked Dean. "But I don't know how to make that."

"Mistress Ford says she'll teach us," Elizabeth replied. "She also told me to be wary of Master Ford and not give him any."

"Master Ford?" Robin asked.

Elizabeth nodded and rolled her eyes. "He's asleep next to the fireplace in the kitchen. Mistress Ford said nothing, but I could smell the drunkenness on him. Poor woman, saddled with a husband like that. It's no wonder they haven't any children. He probably hasn't gotten hard in years."

"Elizabeth!" Dean gasped.

Elizabeth shrugged. "It's probably a blessing for her that he can't."

"We'll have to keep an eye on him, I guess," Robin sighed.

"He'll get his share of ale," Elizabeth said with a snort. "They always do. But he'll not get any from me."

The ale making went well. It was not a complicated

process. First, they roasted barley grains and brewed them, adding hops, then put the cooled wort into a small keg, which still had caked on yeast on its staves. As Dean and Robin carefully brought the new keg down to the little cellar and fetched up the one that would be tapped that night, a king's messenger rode up and requested a room.

Dean stabled the horse while Elizabeth went after a chicken and wrung its neck. Robin got the rake and swept the rotting straw out of the common room.

Dean was sent down to the nearby river to check the traps there. Robin went to work setting up the trestles and boards to make tables in the common room. Her arms feeling like wet spaghetti, Robin spread fresh hay over the old. The musty room filled with the smell of hay. It was heavy work and Robin wondered how sore she'd be the next morning as she wandered into the kitchen.

Dean sauntered in with two dead rabbits.

"We only got two," he announced, holding them up. "They're kind of scrawny, too."

"Dean, you fool!" Elizabeth snatched the animals and hid them under her apron. She glanced upstairs. "Don't you realize there's a king's messenger here?"

"What did I do wrong?" Dean asked.

"Dean," Robin explained, "All game is owned by the King."

"So?"

Robin tried not to sigh. "It's illegal to hunt. Your catch is technically contraband."

"That's a dumb law." Dean shrugged.

"Nonetheless," said Elizabeth. "You don't want to let a king's officer see that you have broken it."

"It's like letting a police officer see your stash," Robin added.

Dean glared. "Hey, I'm not that stupid."

Elizabeth hid the rabbits under a pan. "I'll make a pie later. Robin, why don't you see if Mistress Ford needs anything else? I'll have Dean finish helping me here."

Robin nodded and left. Dean would not be able to be left alone for one minute. Although Robin had briefed him extensively before they had left, she had a bad feeling precious little had sunk in.

They finally got to eat supper just as the sun began its last descent to the horizon. There wasn't much and Dean complained relentlessly.

"Why don't we get any of that chicken?" he demanded, eyeing the small bird on the spit before the fire.

"It's for the king's messenger," sighed Elizabeth.

"He'll probably hog the whole thing for himself," Dean grumbled.

"That's his prerogative," Robin replied. "You've got food. Quit complaining."

"You call this food?" Dean held up a spoonful of watery broth with a limp bit of cabbage leaf dribbling off.

"You call McDonald's food."

"This isn't a meal. Watery soup, bread, and cheese."

"It's good soup!" Elizabeth protested. "Mistress Ford has been very generous. You've got more than enough to eat."

"Dean, what we're eating is a full three-course meal for most people in this time," Robin said.

"You're kidding." Dean looked at Elizabeth. "Is this what you ate all the time?"

"Usually less," Elizabeth replied. "Mistress Ford, fortunately, has a very prosperous inn. We'll see several villagers after the sun is down."

Dean opened his mouth to complain again, but not before Robin kicked him under the table. He scowled but remained silent. Robin went back to her own soup. It wasn't very substantial and even after they'd eaten, her belly gurgled with emptiness.

They had to eat quickly. The village men were already arriving, as they usually did, to pass the evening gossiping and drinking the strong, dark ale.

Mistress Ford watched Robin pull a draft from the keg and assigned her tapping duties. Dean was asked to keep order, and Elizabeth served. Mistress Ford kept a close watch on the money box and on her errant husband, who nonetheless got a solid snootful. Robin could see the small, wizened, toothless man drinking from others' tankards when they weren't looking.

It was a busier night than usual, as Robin later found out. The twenty-odd villagers that filled the common room had come to hear what news there might be from the king's messenger. The men seemed to have strong Royalist leanings, which Robin thought odd because her research had shown that Essex had been strongly Parliamentarian during the English Civil War. That was the other reason Robin had chosen it. Might as well get Elizabeth established someplace that supported what would be the winning side when the fighting got going.

Fortunately, it was still only the spring of 1642, and the fighting wouldn't start until that fall, although King Charles I would officially start the war in August. But that was still in the future, Robin had to remind herself, and for the time being among the villagers, the current political scene was only nominally of interest. The king's messenger didn't have much to say and retired early. But the rest of the villagers made an evening of it, with a small group gathered around the merchant, hungrier for local gossip than anything the merchant had to offer in terms of goods.

Dean sat next to the keg, watching everyone with a keen eye. Robin filled tankard after tankard as Elizabeth ran back and forth almost frantically. The men were putting it away heartily, which made Robin wonder. The strong ale had made hers and Dean's heads reel earlier that afternoon, but presumably, these men were used to the strong drink.

It was getting late when the merchant ambled over to Robin.

"Tapster, be a good man and re-fill my tankard," he said with an easy grin. "I gave the maid a shilling a while back and haven't drunk it up yet."

Elizabeth popped up behind him and shook her head. "Don't fill it until he's paid me the three pennies he already owes me."

The merchant laughed. "Girl, I was the one who gave you the shilling."

"I'm afraid not, sir."

This did not please the merchant. He looked at Robin and Dean in disbelief.

"The maid is confused," he said forcefully. "I know what I gave her."

"Elizabeth?" Robin asked.

"It was the king's messenger that gave me the shilling," Elizabeth replied. "I showed it to Mistress Ford."

She glanced at Dean and Robin a little nervously as if she didn't expect them to believe her.

"Hey, buddy, if Elizabeth says you didn't give her the shilling, I'll trust her sooner than I'd trust you," said Dean, who hadn't noticed Elizabeth's look.

"The word of a mere girl over my own?" bellowed the merchant. The room fell still as the men turned their attention to the three newcomers.

"Master Black, is there a problem?" Mistress Ford came up to the group, her arms folded across her ample chest.

"I gave your girl a shilling a while back and here she is denying it!" He was a short man with bull-like shoulders and chest, and he drew himself up to his full height.

"Ma'am, he owes three pennies yet," Elizabeth replied softly, her head bowed.

Mistress Ford looked over at Robin. "Well?"

"Elizabeth has a sharp eye and a good head about her," Robin replied uneasily. "If she says he owes three pennies, I'd believe it."

Mistress Ford smiled. "Nor would I believe your word so quickly, Master Black. You've bullied my girls before. Kindly pay up your three pennies or I'll have my man here escort you out."

The man dug into his filthy breeches and pulled out a small pouch, and laboriously fished out the three coins. Grumbling, he stalked away from the common room and went upstairs to his sleeping chamber.

Robin suddenly realized she'd been holding her breath and

let it out. There was the rumble of good-natured chuckling as the men turned back to their drinks and their conversations. Two got a little boisterous and pawed at Elizabeth. She evaded them with the weariness of long practice until Dean noticed what was going on and one by one tossed the men out to the bawdy cheers of the others. Robin made a mental note of the two men's appearances. She had a feeling they were regulars.

It was late when Dean and Robin fell into the makeshift beds Elizabeth had made up in the stable's hay loft. Elizabeth had a cot in the kitchen.

"Robin?" Dean asked quietly.

"Yeah?" Robin curled onto her side away from her brother.

"When are we going home?"

"When we're certain Elizabeth is firmly established here and has some sort of future."

"She's not coming back with us?"

"The whole reason we came was to leave her."

"Why?"

"Because she'll be happier here."

There was a short silence.

"We can't leave her," Dean said finally.

"Do you want to stay and grow old and die here?" Robin snapped.

"No!"

"Well, there you have it. Now, go to sleep. We have to get up at dawn."

Dean groaned.

"And no complaining, either."

Robin pulled the thin blanket around her shoulders. She had to admit, she wasn't all that keen on leaving Elizabeth herself. But staying. There was so much to learn that she hadn't thought about. How would she and Dean ever find a way to fit in?

Chapter Four

There was barely a flush in the eastern sky when Dean felt Robin prodding him awake the next morning. He grumbled, but it was quickly clear that his sister was in no mood to put up with his complaints. Not sure what was bugging her, he followed her out of the barn and on to their first task of the day, setting the rabbit traps along the nearby stream that flowed between the fields and a small glade of trees.

Robin kept muttering about the time, and sure enough, the King's messenger and Master Black were already awake and waiting by the time Dean and Robin got back. But it didn't take long to set up the table for their breakfast. In the meantime, Master Black took some bread and his horse and left quickly.

Robin and Dean joined Mistress Ford and Elizabeth in the kitchen to eat the porridge that Elizabeth had prepared. Then Dean was sent to bring out the King's messenger's horse, Elizabeth to tend to the now empty rooms, and Robin to take down the table in the common room. Mistress Ford went to milk the cow, which apparently refused to milk for anyone else.

Dean had the horse saddled and ready by the time the

messenger had eaten but got no thanks as the man mounted and rode off. Mistress Ford had also told Dean to clean the stables once the messenger was gone, and so Dean turned to his task.

The mess that was the stable overwhelmed him as he stood in the doorway. His stomach grumbled with hunger and he grumbled about how miserable it all was. He was still grumbling when Elizabeth came out to the stable, looking for an extra broom.

"Doesn't anybody, like, rest or something around here?" he said, tossing straws from the bench he was reclining on.

Elizabeth pursed her lips and avoided looking at him.

"And I'm really hungry here," Dean continued, oblivious. "If you want to keep me working, you got to feed me. I mean, I need fuel."

Finally, Elizabeth could bear no more.

"By the rood, you are the most spoilt, obnoxious, ridiculous person I've ever run across!" she snapped. She whirled around and fixed her blazing eyes on him. "You do nothing but complain. Poor Robin had to find all the information she wanted to be sure we could come here safely. You just complained that it was boring. You complained that you didn't want to come here. And now that we're here, you complain that the work is too hard and that there's not enough food. There is more than enough food. Mistress Ford is marvelous generous. As for work, you should be apprenticed to my old master. Even his journeyman was up before dawn. And the work, it was heavy, carrying huge pots of dye day in and day out, and look that you don't spill a drop, or the master would beat you. If you didn't move fast enough or mixed the dyes wrong, or whatever you did wrong, he'd beat you. Sometimes he beat his apprentices just because he felt like it. A delicate beast like you, you'd never be able to survive it. You can't even survive this! I should be ashamed of myself if I were you."

Dean slid backward on the bench as Elizabeth bore down on him.

"I can't believe that a great big man like you is such a weakling!" she continued relentlessly. "If I were you, I'd be on my knees every night praying to our Good Lord to relieve me of the grievous sin of sloth. I've never met anyone as lazy as you. You are just appalling!"

"Are you done?" Dean squeaked out.

Elizabeth glared at him. "Yes."

"Am I that bad?" Dean squeaked again.

"Yes."

"Oh." Dean swallowed. Even as his chest caved in on itself and his ears burned red, he realized that he was feeling ashamed of himself for perhaps the first time in his life. Even the chewing out he'd gotten in first grade for turning over his filled juice cup hadn't felt this bad.

Elizabeth still glared. Dean got up and grabbed a rake.

"I'm not really that lazy," he said, grasping for a defensive posture.

"Then show me," Elizabeth snarled. She picked up her broom, spun on her heal, and trounced out of the barn.

Behind her, she could hear a flurry of raking, but the satisfaction she should have felt was drowned in worry. She should never have spoken to Dean as she had. Once more, her quick tongue had gotten her into trouble. She glanced back at the barn. Dean, by rights, could have beaten her for her harsh speech. Instead, he was acting like one of her old master's apprentices caught misbehaving.

She frowned. Dean was so very odd. Robin, she could almost understand. But Dean didn't act much like the men Elizabeth had known. Elizabeth shrugged and returned to the house.

She decided not to say anything to Robin, who had just finished in the common room and was headed to the small garden. Robin seemed very unsure of herself, something that also puzzled Elizabeth.

It was no puzzle to Robin. She had spent most of the morning with her stomach knotted into a tight ball and there seemed to be no sign of it loosening. Making sure Dean didn't do anything stupid was bad enough. Robin was just as worried about fitting in and not doing something stupid and felt horribly out of place, herself.

It had taken far too long to set the traps that morning. She had managed most of the other work, and, fortunately, working in the kitchen garden seemed straightforward. It was late enough in the spring that most of the cabbages, beets, turnips, and carrots had grown enough that Robin was able to tell them apart from the weeds. But there were a couple rows that were newly seeded. Robin decided not to worry about them just yet.

Just as the sun reached the zenith, clouds started rolling in. The rain started as almost a mist just as Dean and Robin headed into the kitchen for lunch. By the time they had started working on the ale, the rain was a steady downpour.

The rain didn't stop a small group of village men from

showing up for their evening's tankard and chat. It was a quiet evening. Even Master Ford seemed to go to sleep much sooner than usual. The work had gone well. Mistress Ford was pleased enough to say so, and as she did, Robin felt herself relax for the first time.

The next day was much the same, but the day after that was Sunday.

Robin was mildly puzzled. It seemed as though the machine had dropped them three days later than she'd entered. She'd figured it might drop them earlier, but later? It didn't matter in the long run.

In England, in the Seventeenth Century, Sunday meant Church. The service was long and highly ritualized. Dean did not enjoy the church service. Neither did Robin. As she looked around her, she didn't think anyone else found it interesting. The pastor didn't seem to be very popular. Every so often, Robin heard someone whisper "idolator," "papist," or "Laudian." Dean was aware that something was wrong but couldn't understand what it was. Elizabeth explained that the pastor was too much like a Catholic for the strongly Protestant Englishmen.

Sunday did have one advantage, especially as far as Dean was concerned. It was a day of rest. After all the necessary work and church services were done, Mistress Ford let her three workers do as they liked. Which would have been many different things, but for the rain. The first two Sundays in Downleigh were spent relaxing in the kitchen next to the fire, listening to Mistress Ford recite the psalms while Master Ford snored in his corner.

But two and a half weeks after the three had arrived, sunshine took over. Three whole days had passed without even a mist, and that Sunday, after services and lunch, Robin announced that she was going to spend her day of rest enjoying the warm weather. Dean was about to say he wanted to catch some rays but caught himself in time and instead merely agreed that a walk was in order. Elizabeth quietly agreed also. Mistress Ford smiled but declined to join her workers.

As it turned out, Dean found a grassy slope facing the afternoon sun and decided to take a nap there. Robin and Elizabeth both rolled their eyes, but went on, following the stream for a bit before turning back.

"I can't believe I'm saying this," Robin said with a yawn, "but I think Dean's got the right idea."

"If we don't get too brown from the sun," Elizabeth replied. She stretched and wriggled her shoulders. "But the sun does feel good."

They headed up the slope to where Dean was stretched out on the grass. Robin froze as she saw the bright white wires coming from his ears.

"Dean, you jackass!" Robin snarled softly as she ran up.

"Huh?" Dean looked at her.

Robin yanked the earbuds from his head. In the still, the faint sounds of Green Day rippled out.

"Why, in heaven's name, did you bring you bring that damned iPhone!" she growled, glancing around, and praying she wouldn't be overheard. "Do you have any idea of the trouble we could get into if someone saw you with this?"

Dean shrugged. "What about that machine that got us here?"

"Do you see me pulling it out in the middle of the day?"

"Well, what about your towel?"

Robin blushed. Her reasons for bringing the small towel were even sillier than Dean bringing the iPhone. That Dean had found the towel was bad enough. Robin wasn't about to tell him why she had it. That didn't stop Dean from needling her about it whenever he got the chance.

"That I can explain," she said quickly. "But an iPhone is completely beyond the comprehension of anyone in this time period." Robin sighed as Dean shrugged and put the phone away in his sack. "Honestly, Dean, after all that witchcraft talk last night, you'd think you'd have more sense."

"Aw, come on, Robin. There's no such thing as witches."

"Of course, there are," said Elizabeth. "I know you two to be friendly sorcerers. But there are many who aren't."

"She's not the only one who thinks so either," added Robin.

"I heard Farmer Lynley say last night that his last keg of ale went sour the other day for no reason at all," Elizabeth said.

"With the weather turning warm, that's not surprising," said Robin.

"It hasn't been hot," said Dean. "Hasn't been more than seventy-five."

"That's hot for ale, lunkhead," Robin replied, still irritated with him. "That's why we have to be so careful."

"Mistress Teaseley's cow wouldn't give milk yesterday morning," Elizabeth continued. "They say that Mistress Barkett is nearing her time. If there is a witch in the village, the delivery may not go well."

"If there's a problem," said Robin. "It won't be because of a witch. But that won't stop people from thinking it. We'd better watch our steps for the next month or so."

She glared at Dean, who got up and stretched. The slope they were on overlooked fields on one side and the inn and the road on the other. Dean twisted his head to stretch his neck muscles and paused.

"Huh," he said.

"What?" asked Robin.

"That." Dean pointed to the far edge of the road from the village. "Somebody's kicking up a lot of dust."

There was, indeed, a good-sized cloud of dust rolling toward the inn. But through the cloud, Robin could make out about three riders, one of whom was carrying a red and gold banner on a pole.

"Soldiers," gasped Elizabeth.

"Is that something bad?" Dean asked.

Elizabeth frowned. "It could be. Perhaps they are looking to billet a troop, perhaps they are messengers. Hopefully, they aren't mercenaries. They are the worst." She started off down the hill. "We'd best warn Mistress Ford."

Dean and Robin followed behind.

"You think there's going to be any fighting?" Dean asked Robin softly.

Robin shrugged, her stomach going back to its tight position. "Who knows? There was nothing in any of the stuff I read to suggest it, but maybe there were smaller skirmishes here and there that didn't get recorded."

"So, what do we do if there is?" Dean tried desperately to sound casual.

"Try to stay out of it."

Dean nodded. "I can do that."

The riders galloped past the inn just as Dean and Robin approached the yard and Elizabeth and Mistress Ford were coming out of the kitchen. Mistress Ford sighed as the riders reigned in near the church.

"They'll be wanting billeting for sure," she grumbled. "Let's just pray they don't have a whole troop behind them."

Mistress Ford wandered up the road toward the church house, followed by Robin, Dean and Elizabeth and other gathering villagers. Robin noticed several boys running off toward the outlying houses. The news of the soldiers' arrival was grim enough to quell any lightness of spirit over a chance to run and be free on a day devoted to rest.

For some reason, the soldiers preferred the church house to the inn. Fortunately, they were alone, although word had it there were others like them looking for the Earl of Essex's militia. What they were doing riding about on the Sabbath was anybody's guess, but the general conclusion was that these were not the godliest of men and certainly worthy of deep suspicion.

Still, it being the Sabbath, it was deemed unseemly to do anything about it until the morrow. The next day, there was work to be done, and if the three riders had had any plans to move on, they certainly did not seem particularly inclined to do so. Masters Lightwick, Pelder, and Surrey spent much of their time in the village square eyeing the young girls of the village.

The inn was busy that night. Grumbling restless men filled the common room. Elizabeth served quickly, enlisting Robin's aid at the request of the alderman, a shrewd, older fellow named Greenfield. He was the richest man in the village by virtue of the fact that he owned his tiny farm. The rest were tenants on the land of the local baron.

As Robin served the last few tankards, Alderman Greenfield rose and shouted for quiet. The dull rumble slowly faded.

"Before we begin, I want all of you to be sure of your bill," the older man told the crowd. "I think it only fair not to cheat Mistress Ford since she has been kind enough to let us use her common room for our meeting."

"Where else could we meet?" said Master Whitby, a slightly stooped man with a pox-scarred chin. "We can't use the church with that papist there."

The crowd rumbled in agreement.

"Enough!" shouted the alderman. "We are not gathered here to complain about our pastor. Laudian or not, he is still a churchman of the Church of England. Besides, even if he would have let us use the church, we couldn't have because of why we're gathered here in the first place."

The men shifted on their benches and grumbled. A few cast wary eyes on Robin, Dean, and Elizabeth.

"The pastor says they were directed here to wait for others of the Earl's army," said William Smith, who called himself a tinker, although Robin noted that he was more of a general metal worker and certainly supported himself and his large family far better than tinkers traditionally did.

"Aye," sighed Master Greenfield. "And they are all younger sons of some quality, which is why they are staying at the church house. Our good inn is too far beneath their stature."

"And just how great is their quality?" sniffed another farmer whose name Robin couldn't remember. "We've had knights and a couple viscounts who have stayed at our inn before."

"More likely they just don't want to pay for their lodgings," said someone else.

"That may be," said Master Greenfield. "But the point is that they are likely to stay until whatever other comrades join them."

"Are we to let them live among us?" whined Master Southwood, another farmer. "Must we risk our children, our beasts, and our wives? They are not godly men and who knows what depravity they will visit upon us. Have you seen how they've looked upon the maidens of this town?"

"We'll risk nothing," Master Greenfield said. "But we must take adequate precautions. It's simple common sense. Keep anything of value locked up. Do not let your children or your wives go into the village unaccompanied. Keep your distance from them. Do not let your beasts run loose. Do not speak first to them. If one speaks to you, be civil, but no more. This isn't the first time we've had soldiers come among us."

Reluctant agreement rippled through the crowd.

"As for these soldiers," Master Greenfield continued, "I dare say if we don't give them any trouble, we'll have none from them."

"Alderman, what about the Parliament's militia?" called out Robert Loomis, one of the town's three weavers. "I've heard they've called men out across the shire."

The tension in the crowd thickened threefold.

"I've heard they're rooting out all the papists," said Charles

Loomis, Robert's brother and fellow weaver. "They've burned several homes already."

"Why are you worried?" asked the alderman. "We've no papists here."

"What about our pastor?" demanded Farmer Whitby.

"We can't be worried about him," returned Alderman Greenfield. "He is no papist, in any case."

"But what shall we do if we are called to arms?" called out Robert Loomis.

The crowd began shouting again. Clearly divided, the majority shouted against answering Parliament's summons. But it was a small majority, and the opposing minority was very vocal. Just as it seemed things were going to get completely out of hand, the alderman screamed for silence. He waited until the crowd quieted.

"Obviously, this is not a matter in which we are all in accord," he said. "I think it a disgrace upon our village that we should be prepared to take up arms against our neighbors, people we've lived with all our lives. If we are called to take up military service, each man shall have to answer to his own conscience. I recommend that we stop fussing over something that has not touched us yet and continue as good Christian neighbors should. Wench! Tapster! See to it that each man's tankard is full. I'll buy this round. After that, let each man drink as much as his purse and his head can handle!"

Loud cheering burst out. Robin and Elizabeth scrambled to act out the alderman's request. Once the drinking started, Robin and Elizabeth had little rest. The riot had been quelled before it started. The men talked and sang together despite the slight undercurrent of tension. There were no fights that night. Dean continued the spirit of good comradeship and gently escorted the drunks out instead of pitching them into the street.

It was late when he and Robin collapsed into the hayloft.

"I don't get it," said Dean, peeling off his doublet. "What's all this taking up arms and militia nonsense? And why is everyone so down on papists?"

"Papists are Catholics, Dean," Robin explained, with a yawn. "You remember that Henry the Eighth split from the Catholic Church, right?"

"Yeah."

"That caused a lot of turmoil in the country. Then Edward, Henry's son, came to the throne and turned England really Protestant. But there was even more turmoil when Mary, Henry's daughter, made the country go back to being Catholic. She killed a lot of Protestants during her reign, that's why she's called Bloody Mary."

"Wasn't she Mary, Queen of Scots?"

"That's another Mary. Anyway, when Elizabeth I became queen, she returned the country to Protestantism. She also instituted a lot of reforms in the church. But a lot of people felt she didn't go far enough. Being the good politician she was, she was able to keep a compromise during her years on the throne. Then James I came to the throne. He did the same things as Elizabeth, but not as well and those people who had been quiet under Elizabeth got mad again and caused trouble. Then Charles I ascended the throne. He got these people even more upset. They are the people that we know as Puritans. Right now, it's kind of derogatory nickname and not very prevalent, so I wouldn't call anybody that. Anyway, there are a lot of Puritans in Parliament right now, and they are insisting that the Parliament has a right to raise its own army, which they are doing. The people in this village who don't want to mobilize are the royalists, they support the king. The people who want to mobilize are in favor of the Parliament, and the best thing for us to do is to try and stay out of the whole bleeding mess."

"You think?" grumbled Dean. "Are you sure there's not going to be any fighting?"

Robin clenched her teeth. "I never said there wouldn't be any. I just said that according to what I read, there didn't seem to be any in this part of the country. Not every little thing that happened got written down. In fact, the vast majority of what goes on day to day, even in our own time never gets written down."

Robin punched her pillow into shape, while Dean flopped down onto the hay pile he used as his mattress. Robin paused, her head twisting as she suddenly strained to listen.

"What?" asked Dean.

Robin shushed him quickly. Then Dean heard it, too. The soft nickering of horses outside the stable and the rattle of the bits and reins. The two crept across the loft and down the ladder. Outside, they could hear the soft hiss of boots on dirt.

Robin led the way to the stable door and eased it open. Three men closed in on the kitchen door.

"Elizabeth," Dean whispered so softly even Robin couldn't be sure what he said.

Robin looked over the expanse of yard between the stable and the kitchen. The trouble was that even though it was only ten-odd yards across, there was absolutely no cover. A horse snorted from the other side of the stable. Robin motioned at Dean to follow her as she retreated inside and to the back.

There she found the hole in the wall that she'd been meaning to fix. Dean was confused but somehow knew that Robin had a plan. She softly pulled away the boards that had been covering the hole and scrambled through with Dean close behind.

The three horses that the soldiers had ridden into town on stamped quietly and snorted. Their reins had been left dangling in front of them, something Robin vaguely remembered reading was a trick cowboys in the Nineteenth Century had used to stop their horses if they fell off. It appeared that it was an even older trick than that.

She picked up the reins of the first horse, threw them around its neck, and swatted its hindquarters. Dean caught on and did the same with the second horse, and then swatted the flank of the third horse as Robin tossed its reins.

Robin winced at the loud neighing and thundering as the horses galloped back into the village. Dean nodded back at the hole, and the two slipped quickly through and back to the front of the stable. This time, Dean got to the stable door first, but after a quick peek, he threw the door open and charged into the yard.

One of the young gentlemen had already hurried around to where the horses had been left. The other two were occupied with dragging along a struggling Elizabeth. She was still in her nightdress and her hair flowed loose and wild but still didn't hide the gag covering her mouth.

Dean charged into the pair with a loud yell. Robin followed, with a quick glance to see whether their companion was coming back.

Surprise and his larger size were Dean's only advantages. The two let go of Elizabeth, who just fell back and watched. Dean concentrated on getting the one young man's shirt front in one fist and repeatedly punching him with the other.

Robin was a little more hesitant. All her self-defense training had been geared toward fending off someone attacking her. The second man was about to pounce on Dean when Robin ran full tilt into his side.

He staggered away as Robin bounced back. She gasped as he came at her, but years of seminars and practices and classes took over. She dodged at the last second and the man tripped. But the man who had been going after the horses got his arm around her throat. Robin slammed her knuckles into his upper arms. Yelping, he let go, but not before Robin whirled around and landed her elbow in his nose.

His companion, still on the ground, got a hold of Robin's one ankle. She turned and stomped on his wrist. Howling, he let go and Robin kicked him in the groin.

Dean hadn't fared as well. He'd gotten the shirt front, but the other man punched him first, and Dean staggered back. The two prowled around each other for a moment. Dean gasped, but he could feel the adrenaline kicking in. It had been a few years since he'd last gotten into a fight, but he was ready.

The man feinted. Dean backed off a little, taking the measure of his opponent. The man feinted again, but this time, Dean drove the attack with a powerful blow to the side of the man's head. Dean sent his next fist into the man's midsection.

As the man doubled over, Dean knocked him backward onto his seat.

The man scrambled up, but instead of going after Dean, he fled back into the village, with his companions staggering after him. Gasping, Dean looked back at Robin and then over at Elizabeth.

"You okay?" he asked them.

Elizabeth fumbled at the rag binding her mouth. Robin went over and helped her release it.

"I'm fine," Robin gasped as the rag fell from Elizabeth's mouth.

"I am well, also," sniffed Elizabeth. "But I was so afraid."

Mistress Ford appeared from the kitchen door. "What has happened here?"

Dean checked his teeth with his tongue and spat blood into the dirt.

Robin swallowed. "Those so-called younger sons of quality tried to kidnap Elizabeth."

"What?" Clutching a cloak around her nightgowned ample figure, Mistress Ford cast a worried look into the village.

"We heard the horses behind the stable," Dean explained. "When we came around front, they had gagged Elizabeth and were taking her with them."

Mistress Ford looked first at Elizabeth, then at Dean and Robin. "Do you know these men?"

Robin shook her head. "I've never seen them before."

"Nor I," said Elizabeth quickly. "I have no idea why they singled me out. I was asleep and woke when they pulled me from my bed."

"Did they say anything?" asked Robin.

Elizabeth shook her head. "No. They just put the gag on and as we left the kitchen, we heard the horses running off."

"But why?" Mistress Ford asked.

Robin shrugged. "They're new in town. Given their attitude toward the inn, maybe they assumed that Elizabeth wouldn't have much of a character to ruin. She's really plenty virtuous, but how would they know?"

"No, they wouldn't," sighed Mistress Ford. "I'll grant you, the three of you haven't been here that long, but I've seen no sign of ill behavior in her. Her face is as fair as they come." She looked gently at Elizabeth. "Are you all right? Did they hurt you?"

"No," said Elizabeth softly. "I was just frightened."

Mistress Ford looked up at Robin and Dean. "You boys sleep in the kitchen this night. I'll bring Elizabeth to bed with me."

"What about Master Ford?" Robin asked.

"He's asleep next to the cellar as it is." It was hard to tell whether Mistress Ford was more disgusted or bored with the state of her errant spouse. "Let him lie."

Robin returned to the loft to get the pillows and blankets. When she got to the kitchen, she was a little surprised to see that Dean had already made a bed for himself on the floor.

"You take Elizabeth's bed," he told her.

"Thanks." Robin debated asking him why he was being so nice, then took a deep breath. "You really laid into that guy. I didn't know you could fight like that."

Dean chuckled. "I used to belong to a fight club in high school." He stopped suddenly. "You won't tell Mom, will you? She'd kill me if she knew."

"Before tonight, I think I would have killed you, too."

Dean laughed. "You didn't do too bad with the street tactics."

"Lots of self-defense classes." Suddenly weary, Robin sank onto the bed. "The scary thing is it was almost fun."

"It can be." Dean shrugged. "But that gets old real fast. That's why I stopped."

"Oh. Well, goodnight."

"Goodnight."

Robin sank back into the silence, pondering the events of the evening. But before she could make sense of them, she was asleep.

Outside, Donald Long leaned against the stable and mulled over his next move. The young soldiers would have to be on their way before dawn, assuming they could still move, Donald thought sourly. As easy as they had been to manipulate, the townsfolk were already suspicious of them. If word of this evening's engagement spread, the three idiots might easily lead the townsfolk to him. Donald sighed. That wouldn't make getting the girl any easier. Not that it mattered. Since he had missed Elizabeth in London, it had to be here in Downleigh where he'd caught her. Travelling backward along the trio's timeline was confusing enough.

He'd have to find a way to get the townspeople on his side, but he wasn't sure he wanted to be that visible. Donald slipped quietly back to his hiding place in the cellar of the church. It was an ideal spot, long forgotten, but close enough to the center of the village that he could observe and hear just about everything that was going on. He decided to wait it out a few more days to perhaps pick up something he might be able to use.

Roger had always chided him for his impatience. Donald sniffed and smiled to himself. That self-important prick couldn't chide this time.

Chapter Five

The three young gentlemen soldiers were gone before the sun rose the next morning. Robin wasn't sure how it happened, but by noon, the entire village knew of the attack on Elizabeth the night before. Perhaps not as surprising was the way the number of attackers grew as the tale was told.

And with each telling Robin's and Dean's stock in the village grew. The villagers weren't ready to embrace the pair as their own. But they were more willing to accept them.

A little over a week after the attack, Robin accompanied Elizabeth to the church to deliver some cheese to the pastor. As they approached the square, where the village well was located, Robin heard the familiar hiss of children whispering behind her.

She whirled, hollering "Boo!"

Screaming, the children scattered, giggling as they pushed each other out of the way.

"You've gotten quite popular," Elizabeth teased.

"And how many men did I fight off?" Robin sighed. "Isn't the number up to twenty by now?"

Elizabeth laughed. The sound of another young woman's laughter echoed.

It belonged to Mistress Mary Smith, the tinker's daughter.

Standing next to the well, the pleasantly plump young woman was just dropping the last of a bit of laundry into her basket.

"Good day, Master Parker, Mistress Wynford," she said.

"Good day, Mistress Smith," Elizabeth replied. "How fares Mistress Blethen?"

Mistress Smith wrinkled her nose in disgust. A couple years older than Elizabeth, she worked as housekeeper for the village midwife. It was not unusual for the women of the village to have some help, and most of the older girls worked in other houses for several years from their late teens, waiting to marry until they were in their early twenties. As a widow, Mistress Blethen was quite poor, so working for her was considered something of an act of charity unless one hoped to eventually take over the widow's birthing trade.

"My mistress is well enough," Mistress Smith said. "However, she has decided that I'm not. She said I don't have the knack for birthing."

Mistress Smith sniffed with annoyance, then eyed Robin.

Robin didn't notice.

"Indeed," said Elizabeth, who had noticed the eyeing, but decided not to say anything. "I thought Mistress Barkett's laying in went rather well."

"No thanks to me, apparently."

"Mary Smith, will you be all day with those clothes?" called a rather stern voice.

Mistress Blethen, a tall, thin woman, moved stiffly as she emerged from the pastor's house. She carried a certain calm about her that could be very soothing when she was assisting at a birth or otherwise helping some ailing villager. Or the calm could be imposing, such as when dealing with a slow serving girl.

Mistress Smith rolled her eyes, smiled at Robin, then scuttled away, neatly dodging her employer. Mistress Blethen shook her head as the girl hurried down the street.

"Good day, Master Parker, Mistress Wynford," she said.

Robin and Elizabeth returned the old woman's greeting.

"Master Parker, I should like to speak with your mistress," Mistress Blethen said. "If she would be so good as to call on me within the next day or two."

"May I tell her what about?" Robin asked.

"Yes. She was interested in taking up midwifery, and both she and you, Mistress Wynford, are quite helpful." Mistress Blethen shifted uncomfortably, rubbing her lower back. "My rheumatism is getting worse."

"I'll tell her," said Robin. "You've just been to see the pastor?"

"Yes. He's doing better today."

"Oh, that's a blessing," said Elizabeth. "We've brought a cheese for him."

Mistress Blethen nodded. "Let us hope that will tempt him. Mistress Ford's cheeses are among the best in the village."

Robin held her peace. The pastor had developed a bad cough during the last rain, which had turned into a fever. Robin thought it was probably some kind of strep infection, but there was no way to explain that, not to mention any antibiotics to combat it. Still, he had gotten through the worst of the fever and word had it, was on the mend.

The pastor's housekeeper took the cheese gratefully. Elizabeth offered to visit the sick man, but he was sleeping, so the two returned to the inn. Robin made her way to the garden.

Elizabeth returned to the kitchen. Mistress Ford was skinning a rabbit.

"Oh, good," said the older woman. "I was hoping you'd come back quickly. We've had two guests arrive since you've been gone. That's the third today. We'll have to make extra bread for tonight."

Elizabeth went to work quickly.

"Mistress Blethen would like you to call on her," Elizabeth said, stirring the flour, yeast, and water together. "About taking on the midwiving."

"Yes, I thought she might," Mistress Ford replied. She smiled softly at Elizabeth. "You have quite the gift for it, too."

"Thank you, Mistress."

"Well, I think I shall take it on. With your cousins here, it will be easier to leave the inn. I just hope they don't get the itch to move on."

"So do I," said Elizabeth softly.

Robin and Dean had adapted well to her world, better than she had adapted to theirs, she reflected bitterly. She gave the dough she was kneading an extra vigorous push.

"As soon as the bread is set to rise, why don't you bring Dean and Robin some water?" said Mistress Ford, getting up herself and dropping the skinned and cleaned rabbit into the soup pot.

"Yes, mistress."

It didn't take long to finish with the dough, and Elizabeth soon had it on the kitchen windowsill, a clean cloth covering it.

Out in the garden, Robin drank deeply and thanked Elizabeth, who went on to the stable with the bucket of water and ladle.

Elizabeth stopped in the doorway.

"Dean?" she called.

"Over here." Dean appeared from one of the stalls. "What's up?"

"I brought some water."

"Thanks." He took the dipper and drank. "I can handle a break right now."

Dean reached above him to the beam above the doorway and lifted himself. Elizabeth leaned against the door jamb and laughed.

"Showing off again, Dean?" she teased.

"What for?" Dean grunted, raising and lowering himself at regular intervals. "There isn't anyone in the town bigger than me."

"I thought perchance you were a little jealous of good Master Thomas Barton."

"Of that sniveling twit? Hah!" Nonetheless, Dean stopped his lifting exercise and dropped heavily to the ground. "Just 'cause I don't want him manhandling you."

Elizabeth shrugged. "I can deal with his kind."

"Yeah, well, the best way to do it is to keep your distance. You gotta watch out for those type of guys. There's only one thing they're after, and it's not very nice."

"I know what he's after, Dean." Elizabeth rolled her eyes.

Dean almost flushed. "Let's not talk about that. You got some more water?"

Elizabeth handed him the ladle feeling perplexed. Dean

wasn't normally timid when it came to talking about the ways of men and women. Only around her did he avoid the subject.

"The stable looks so nice." Elizabeth offered at length. "Mistress Ford just told me how much she approved of our work."

Dean grinned and wandered back into the stable. Elizabeth followed.

"You trying to make up for yelling at me?" he teased.

Elizabeth thought. "Perhaps."

"I wouldn't worry about it. I deserved it." Dean picked up a little hooked tool and entered a stall. "This dummy here picked up a rock in his hoof," he explained indicating the horse. "I gotta get it out before he goes lame."

"I know."

Dean chuckled. "You know, Elizabeth, you got a lot of guts to chew me out like you did. I mean the way you think I'm some powerful sorcerer."

"But you are."

"I got no more magical powers than you got."

Elizabeth frowned. "But you work such powerful magic."

"Do I have any here? All I got is my iPhone, and you can work that. Believe me, if I had half the magic powers you think I got, I'd be using them."

"I guess. It just seems so difficult to understand."

"Things change, Elizabeth." Dean grunted as he worked the tool around the wedged-in rock. "People learn things. The dress you're wearing wasn't always in style, was it?"

"No. My stepmother told me about the ruffs the great lords and ladies used to wear around their necks."

"Do they wear ruffs now?"

"Not really."

"There you have it." The rock tumbled from the horse's foot. "And there we have this. Things are a lot more complicated in the twentieth century. But there are some things that never change, like people."

"Like Master Barton?" Elizabeth teased.

"Yeah, like him." Dean tried to sound cool, and just barely failed.

Elizabeth laughed.

"If you wanna play that way," Dean returned, equally merry. "There's a young lady in the village I've got my eye on, also. In fact, I'm thinking of paying her a visit next Sunday."

"Who?" asked Elizabeth, more disconcerted than she wished.

"I'm not telling." Dean grinned. He was enormously pleased he'd hit home.

"Hm!" Elizabeth snorted. "I don't think you do have your eye on somebody."

"Oh, yes, you do think so. You're not going to get her name out of me that way."

She turned on him. "That's not fair!"

"Oh, yeah, then why is fair for you to tease me that way, huh? I know damn well you can't stand Thomas Barton."

Elizabeth shrugged. She didn't know how to tell Dean she just wanted him and would do whatever she could to keep his interest in her.

"We don't have to be that petty, do we?" Dean asked.

"No. I don't want to," Elizabeth whispered.

It seemed as if Dean were about to move toward her, but he didn't.

"Yeah, well, I don't either," he said. "You know, you're about the only person I can really talk to, here or back home."

"Robin said you had many friends."

"Not many I can really talk to. Guys just don't talk that way, and all the girls I know, well, they're either too selfish to care, or they're too dumb, and all the smart ones, they put me down because I act so stupid sometimes."

"You just act stupid, Dean. You're not."

"Yeah, I know. Maybe I should live up to my potential more. I don't know."

Elizabeth shrugged. "At least this way you don't have to compete with Robin."

Dean laughed. "You know, that's why I can talk to you. I figure you got me pegged already, right? So why hold back?"

"I like talking to you, too." Elizabeth felt her face warm up.

"You do? Why?"

"Well." Elizabeth swallowed. "I can tell you what I think. You and Robin don't get mad when I say what I'm thinking. And you." She blushed even harder. "Well, Robin is truly kind, and I really like her, but she doesn't understand when I get afraid of your magic. She tries to, but she likes it so much, it makes her feel bad when I don't like it. You understand. And while Robin's funny in a quiet way, you tease me, and we have fun."

And Dean was a man and Robin wasn't, but Elizabeth couldn't quite bring herself to say it. She sighed.

"I shouldn't speak as if I don't like Robin as much as I like you. Because I do. It's just different."

Dean nodded. "Oh, I know. It's like I love my mom, but I wouldn't want to marry her. You like different people different ways. Like how you love your mom. Oh. Maybe I shouldn't talk about your family. You must miss them a lot."

Elizabeth shrugged. "In some ways. My mother died giving birth to me, and I've lost two brothers and a sister to death. People die very easily. One gets used to the idea, and one goes on. When I left with Roger, I knew I wouldn't see my family again. They are as good as dead to me, and I am dead to them."

"Sounds gruesome."

Elizabeth shrugged. Dean had no idea how gruesome it really had been, and Elizabeth didn't want him to know.

"I suppose it is gruesome," she said. "But then, we shall all die. I can't say I look forward to it. But it's a part of life. One must expect to see many people die in the course of a lifetime."

"I don't know." Dean sighed. "I've lived twenty-one years, and I've only been to one funeral, and only three people that I've known have died. Of course, people live longer in my time. We talked about that once in a class I had in college. In our culture, death is almost a taboo subject. In yours, it's just a natural part of life. That's weird."

"Well, we don't like dwelling on it." Elizabeth laughed merrily and playfully shoved him.

Dean reached around and sent a handful of straw flying into Elizabeth's face.

"Dean!" Elizabeth squealed. She threw a handful at Dean.

Dean grabbed another handful and chased after her with

it. He caught her near the door and stuffed the straw down her back while she pushed several straws down his front.

"Hey!" Dean yelped.

"Indeed, it is!" Elizabeth returned, trying to retrieve the straws from her back. "It itches, too."

Dean turned her around to tease her some more. But as he looked at her, he gently put his hand to her chin. Without quite thinking what he was doing, he kissed her mouth. She returned it, too. For an innocent girl, she had one hell of a kiss. Then again, Dean had known other virgins who led guys on without realizing what they were doing, just like Elizabeth.

As they pulled apart, Dean started.

"That was nice," Elizabeth whispered, and reached for more.

Dean pulled away. "Yeah, it was. Look, I— I better get back to work. Look at all this straw all over." He sighed.

Elizabeth sniffed and fought back her tears.

"Elizabeth," Dean groaned. "It was nice! Just a little too nice. Um. I don't wanta get carried away. That wouldn't be right. You're just too nice to do that to. You'd better get back to the kitchen."

"Dean!"

"Oh, all right." Dean bent and quickly kissed her mouth again. "But only a little, every now and then. You gotta be careful, kid. You'd better get going. I think I hear Mistress Ford calling."

Elizabeth sighed, grabbed the bucket, and stomped off. Dean was getting more puzzling by the minute. Why did he insist on treating her as if she were some fragile piece of pottery? Granted, women did have strong passions and desires, especially once woken in the marriage bed. Yet most men found that as an excuse to shun her or push her closer to temptation. Dean seemed to think she needed protecting, worse yet, from himself, as if his passions were at least as strong as hers. That was ridiculous. Everyone knew that men were in command of their desires.

Robin, working in the garden, hadn't seen Dean and Elizabeth's play. But she did see Elizabeth stomping off back into the inn and wondered about it. Robin didn't have long to ponder, however.

The rumble of a disturbance in the village softly floated into hearing, accompanied by the sound of running feet.

"Master Parker! Master Parker!" The boy was about 10 years old, and although Robin didn't know his name, she was reasonably sure his father was a regular at the inn. "It's the pastor, Master Parker. Mistress Blethen wants your mistress to come quickly."

"Of course." Robin propped her rake against the inn wall and hurried into the kitchen.

"Where's Mistress Ford?" she asked Elizabeth.

"In the common room, I believe." Elizabeth followed Robin into the common room.

Robin found Mistress Ford there and explained the errand.

"Yes, we'd better go immediately," Mistress Ford said. "Have Dean stay to keep care of the guests, but Elizabeth, you and Robin had better come with me."

Robin ran out to the stable to tell Dean what was going on. The boy danced impatiently in the yard.

Mistress Ford swept out of the inn. "Young Master Thomas, you say it's the pastor?"

"Yes, Mistress. He's gotten much worse. Mistress Blethen wouldn't say how bad, but she fears for him."

The party hurried into the village to the pastor's house. His wife sat in the common room weeping and surrounded by village women. Mistress Blethen stood at the top of a tiny stairway which led to the one-room upper story. Mistress Ford did not hesitate and went up the stairs. Mistress Blethen stepped aside to let them in the room, but it was clear it was too late.

The pastor lay in bed, his face contorted, but his eyes had been closed. Robin felt her stomach twist at being so close to death for the first time in her life. The others took the body in stride.

"Oh no," sighed Mistress Ford. "I came as fast as I could."

"There was nothing to be done," Mistress Blethen said. "He was having seizures. I thought it was fever at first, but he had almost none. It was probably a brain fit. He's had them before."

Robin looked around the room, anywhere but at the body. The glint of a something small and glassy on the floor near the door caught her eye. It was a glass vial without a stopper. But before she could investigate, Mistress Ford directed her to fetch Master Greenfield so that letters could be written to the bishop and a neighboring pastor so that the funeral could be held. By the time Robin returned, the small vial was gone, and the room filled with women preparing the body.

The villagers all turned out for the funeral the next day. The pastor may not have been well-loved, but he was respected and those who differed with him were decent enough not to say anything.

The bishop's reply came after the following Sunday. It had been an awkward day because the neighboring pastor had to first conduct services in his parish and then make the hour's ride to Downleigh and conduct services there, which made services late, indeed. Two days later, a messenger rode into the inn with a letter from the bishop.

Master Greenfield read the letter to the villagers in the church, who were quite thrilled to hear that Pastor James Middleton would be the new pastor, but that his arrival would be delayed by some weeks due to his need to discharge some final matters in London first. His credentials meant nothing to Robin, but the villagers seemed impressed, and the mood in the village lightened considerably.

Life once again settled into calm regularity. The weather grew somewhat warmer, although rain was a common event. It had felt strange and disorienting, at first, not to be aware of the hours and minutes and the date, especially for Robin. Then even she began to be less aware of the calendar and more in tune with the ebbing of spring into the early summer.

As the day of the new pastor's expected arrival grew closer, a soft ripple of anticipation began to fill the village. One night, a couple weeks before the new pastor's expected arrival, things got rowdier than usual, although it was all in good fun. But a couple tankards were cracked, and Master Smith took them home with him, promising them back in two days.

The two days stretched into a week before Mistress Ford asked Robin to go into the village to get them.

"He promised me I should have them today," Mistress Ford said.

"And how much did you agree to pay him?" Robin asked, going to the money box.

Mistress Ford chuckled. "Sixpence and not a hapenny more."

Robin was in high spirits as she approached the tinker's house. No one was in the yard, although the tinker's work-bench looked as though it had been recently occupied. Robin knocked on the door.

To her surprise, young Mistress Mary Smith came out.

"Oh, good day, Master Parker," she said smiling slyly.

"Is your father here? I've come for Mistress Ford's tankards." Robin began to feel uncomfortable, but she couldn't quite figure out why.

Then Mistress Smith shifted the top half of her body suggestively.

"I'll fetch him." She turned with a flounce and went into the house.

Robin swallowed. The stout tinker appeared quickly, tankards in hand.

"Good day, Master Parker," he asked heartily. "Any news for us?"

"Uh, no. I've come for Mistress Ford's tankards."

"Nothing else?" Master Smith seemed to be expecting something.

"No, sir."

Young Mistress Smith appeared again in the doorway with her coy, suggestive smile.

"You've met my daughter?" Master Smith asked, nodding at her.

"Yes, sir."

Master Smith moved in closer to Robin. "Mistress Ford gives a good account of your work."

"That's very kind of her." Robin squirmed. She had a bad feeling she knew where this was heading and was hoping against hope she was wrong.

"My daughter likes you," Master Smith said, giving the tankards a final quick polish. "That's important to me, you know. And she's at a good age for marrying."

"Is she?" Robin barely squeaked. "She'll make some young man very lucky."

"Yes, she will." Master Smith held up the tankards and inspected them. "Those are very nice mends if I say so, myself." He looked at Robin. "Why don't we just tell Mistress Ford that I took the sixpence, and you keep it for yourself?"

Robin shook her head. "I'll just take the tankards and here's your money. Thank you, sir."

Robin walked away if only to keep what little dignity she felt she had left. All the while, though, she felt Mistress Smith's eyes following her as she returned down the road to the inn. Robin made a point of not looking, but she was fairly certain that Mistress Smith was mostly watching her butt.

Robin found the kitchen empty when she returned, as was the common room. Feeling far too uncomfortable to question it, she put the tankards in the common room chest and went back to the garden to sulk.

Only as she got outside, she saw Mistress Ford coming into the yard from the creek.

"Is something wrong?" Robin asked.

Mistress Ford sighed. "My good master wandered off this afternoon. We've only just found him."

"Is he all right?"

"Of course." Mistress Ford rolled her eyes skyward. "Divine Providence has again seen to his care. I suppose I should be grateful."

Robin looked at her. "It must be very difficult for you."

Mistress Ford shook her head. "These days it's no worse than caring for an infant. I should have liked to have borne children, but not having them makes it much easier to care for him and the inn. Heaven knows, I've seen the worst of it from him. The beatings were much worse when we were younger, and he was occasionally sober. I'm alive today because he was drunk far more often than not. I like him better drunk. He's much easier to handle."

"I suppose," said Robin.

"Much easier. For example, if he lays claim to my obedience, he forgets that he has a minute later." Mistress Ford returned to the kitchen chuckling.

Robin gazed after her, suddenly realizing that Mistress Ford enjoyed a level of freedom and ownership that most women of her time did not.

A moment later, Dean came up from behind the yard, carrying the comatose body of Master Ford.

"Is he okay?" Robin asked.

"Yeah, just sleeping it off." Dean wrinkled his nose. "Man,

he stinks. We had homeless people in the detox unit that smelled better than he does."

"Huh? What detox unit?"

"The one I volunteered in a couple years back," Dean said. "Because I was applying to med school. You gotta show that you're, like, serious about being a doctor on the applications. So, you work for a doctor somehow or volunteer. I took enough of my buddies to the detox unit, I figured I might as well volunteer there."

"Oh." Robin wasn't sure if she admired Dean for volunteering or was appalled by his ultimately self-serving approach. "But you're not going to med school."

Dean laughed. "No, duh. Being a medical doctor was Mom's idea. But I found out last year I could still do the research I wanted to do on addictive diseases as a psychologist, which is what I wanted to do in the first place."

"You? A shrink?" Robin tried not to gape and failed.

"Yeah, specializing in drug and alcohol rehab. I've been planning on doing that since my friend Eddie OD'd." Dean grinned as he pushed past her toward the house. "And you thought I was slumming it with my psych major."

"Well, yeah. I apologize." Robin glanced toward the stream. "Where's Elizabeth?"

Dean looked around. "Out looking still. She should be coming back soon."

And, indeed, Elizabeth was. She clucked briefly over Master Ford, then returned to the kitchen and her work.

That night, Robin began to sense a certain uneasiness among the younger men at the inn. Or rather, she finally put her finger on the unease that she realized had been building for a week or so. A couple of the guys were giving her the evil eye and it suddenly struck Robin that she'd seen them trailing after young Mistress Smith after Sunday services.

Not surprisingly, after the two and their friends had drunk up enough courage, they approached Robin.

"Good evening, neighbors," Robin said to the five young men with far more cheer than she felt. "Another round?"

"Mistress Smith has her eye on you," said the oldest around the gaps in his teeth.

"And it shall do her no good, I assure you," said Robin mildly. "I have no interest in Mistress Mary Smith."

"And why not?" snarled a second young man. "Aren't our girls good enough for you?"

Robin swallowed. "They are the finest anywhere." She suddenly smiled. "But am I good enough for them? I think not. They deserve fine, strapping young men like you whom they've known all their lives. Woo to your heart's content, neighbors. In fact, I'll buy the next round and we'll drink to your success."

The young men seemed mollified for the moment, although Robin was hard pressed to say whether it was her words or the presence of Dean's more significant bulk that did the trick.

Either way, Robin hoped that Mistress Ford had missed the scene. But the older woman had not, not surprisingly since she'd heard the talk that Mistress Mary Smith had her eye on the tapster. As soon as the common room was empty, Mistress Ford tapped Robin on the shoulder.

"Masters Robert and James," Mistress Ford asked, not quite casually.

"It's fine," said Robin quickly.

"It's Mistress Mary Smith."

Robin blushed and swallowed. "She seems to want to marry me."

"Ah." Mistress Ford waited patiently. She didn't wait long.

"It's not like I want to marry her. Anything but. It's just Master Smith was pretty emphatic about the idea, and... And..." Robin swallowed again, trying to control her shaking.

"So, there is an offer." Mistress Ford pursed her lips.

"Can't you say you'll fire me if I get married?" Robin asked.

"That wouldn't do any good." Mistress Ford sighed. "I've a feeling Master Smith is planning on taking you in as an apprentice. Why don't you want to marry her? Is there someone else?"

"No. Yes!" Robin smiled hopefully. "I'm betrothed to her. I promised I'd come back when I'd made my fortune."

Robin watched Mistress Ford as the older woman smiled her shrewd smile and shook her head. "Not a good enough story, huh?"

"For some, perhaps, but not for Master Smith," Mistress Ford said. "He won't care about past promises. You haven't made any to him, have you?"

"Not even close. He didn't want to take the money for the tankards, said we should tell you it did cost sixpence, and I would keep it. I gave it to him and got out of there."

"I sympathize," Mistress Ford said. "Mistress Smith has always been a forward, willful thing. She'll be no better than an old scold. I warrant you. And lazy, too."

"They can't trap me into marrying her, can they?" Robin asked.

"No," said Mistress Ford. "At least, not easily. But don't give them the slightest opportunity. Avoid Mistress Smith at all costs. Beyond that, there really isn't much you can do until they force the issue. We'll take it as it comes. In any case, I have no intention of losing my tapster, or having that girl under my roof."

"Let's just hope he's not rich enough to build us a house," Robin grumbled.

The next evening, Farmer Whitby approached Robin.

"Hullo, tapster," he said with a smug smile on his face.

"Shall I fill your tankard?" Robin started. "Oh, it's full."

Master Whitby grinned, his teeth half rotted and his breath sour. "I hear you're to be married soon."

Robin smiled. "Strange. I haven't."

"Mistress Mary Smith, the tinker's daughter, she's quite pretty, isn't she?"

Robin shifted. Elizabeth came up just in time to hear the last remark and giggled. Robin glared at her. She'd told Elizabeth and Dean what had happened at the tinker's house that morning. Dean found the whole episode hysterical, but Elizabeth, at least, had sympathized. Robin glared at her.

"Yes, she is," Robin said to Whitby.

Whitby belched then sniggered. "A charming lass. I assume you have, uh, tried her charms, as they say?"

Dean snickered loudly as Robin gasped.

"I have not!" she snapped.

"My brother has no choice but to behave himself," Dean said, laughing.

"You're going to wait for the wedding?" Farmer Whitby pressed, highly amused.

"There will be no wedding," Robin insisted. "Where did you hear that I was marrying her?"

"From the bride, herself, and her father." The farmer moved in closer. "To be truthful, he doesn't fancy you much, but his daughter's heart is set, and what she wants, she gets."

"That's what she thinks," Dean snickered again and swaggered off before Robin could snap at him.

"They are both mistaken," Robin replied. "I have made no promises, and I have no intention of doing so. I don't even like the girl that much." .

Farmer Whitby just laughed and moved off. A few minutes later, Robin saw Mistress Ford talking to him. She wondered what they were saying. As they were closing down, Mistress Ford told her.

"It seems the good Farmer Whitby is doing his best to spread the Smith's rumor about," the matron said. "His kin have always been troublemakers. Anything to get a fight going, as long as they're not in it."

"Well, I have no intention of letting it get violent," said Robin.

"You may not have a choice," sighed Mistress Ford. "As if there isn't enough tension in this village as it is."

The next two days were thick and not only with political tension and anticipation. The weather turned very humid and cloudy. Afternoon showers were a way of life. But this was different. The rain did not come, and the weather was particularly warm, almost eighty degrees, Robin guestimated.

That night at the inn the men complained about the strange heaviness in the air. A storm was due, and it felt like a bad one. The next day, the rain still did not come. That night the tension was even worse. Dean broke up several small fights, ejecting the combatants into the street.

The common room emptied earlier than usual, much to Robin's relief. The humidity had left her feeling tired and worn, as it had everyone else.

"This may sound terribly lazy," Robin yawned. "But why don't we just leave the tables up tonight?"

Mistress Ford didn't get a chance to answer. Running footsteps on the road outside interrupted them and the door burst open.

"Mistress Ford!" a young boy gasped. "Please, come quickly, it's my mother's time."

"Mistress Martin?" Mistress Ford paused in wonder. "It's too soon. Well, never mind. I'll come. You've no older sisters to help. Is Mistress Blethen come?"

"Yes, mistress. I just sent her. She said to send for you and Mistress Wynford."

Mistress Ford sighed but gathered herself together and looked at Elizabeth.

"We must go," Mistress Ford said. She turned to the boy. "Robert, did you run here by yourself?"

"Yes," he replied. "Father thought it best to stay with Mother."

"He's probably panicking her," Mistress Ford muttered. She looked around and her eye fell on Robin. "Come with us. He'll need someone to wait with him. Hurry now. Mistress Martin births fast."

Dean ended up going, too. He and Robin never saw Mistress Martin. She was in the second room of the little two-room house, and curtains in the doorway closed it off. As soon as Mistress Ford entered the second room, Master Martin left.

Their three other small children besides Robert slept on the floor. Robert soon fell asleep also. Thunder rumbled in the distance. Elizabeth emerged suddenly.

"Dean," she said, seeing him first. "Take this bucket and get some water from the well."

Dean grabbed the bucket and hurried out.

Elizabeth went rummaging among the kitchen tools. "Ah, a good, sharp knife."

Taking the knife, she returned to the room. Thunder rumbled again, this time closer.

"It's not a good sign," said Master Martin.

Robin shrugged. She hoped it would rain soon. Dean returned with the water. He was about to enter the back room when Robin held him back. Instead, she called for Elizabeth. She emerged and took the bucket.

Lightning flashed and the thunder came close on its heels. Dean jumped. Thunderstorms were very infrequent in Southern California. Robin, who had lived on the East Coast for several years through college, was more accustomed to them.

Even more eerie than the weather were the moans that rose and fell in the other room. Robin knew what was going on, but the cries were still nerve-racking.

Robin watched Master Martin for his reaction. He'd been through it at least four times already. The minutes dragged by.

The storm's intensity increased with a lightning flash every two minutes, and the thunder came faster and faster.

The wind kicked in, but still no rain. An hour passed, then another. The good farmer sighed.

"It doesn't go well," he said.

The moans came thick and fast and turned into cries of pain. Dean was antsy. Between the moaning and the thunder, Robin marveled that the children did not wake up. Then she heard low anxious murmurs from the bedroom underneath the cries. In the next instant, a brilliant flash concurrent with thunder signaled a strike in the village.

The lightning continued, still close, and almost continuous. Still, the rain would not come. The thunder boomed, muffling Mistress Martin's cries. The children stirred but did not wake.

Outside, there were the sounds of people running and yelling. Dean went to the door and looked out.

"A house is on fire!" he exclaimed softly.

Both Robin and Master Martin started. In the second room, Mistress Martin let out one long last yell. There was a brief silence, then the sound of an infant's first cries. The rain fell, pouring down at full strength.

Dean ran to see if he could help at the house, which turned out to be Master Smith's. Five minutes later, Elizabeth appeared in the curtained doorway, drained, and bloodstained.

"It's a boy," she said breathing heavily. "A fine, strong boy."

She stepped back to admit Master Martin and Robin. Mistress Martin lay in the bed looking very weak and drawn. The tiny infant suckled at her breast.

The sudden downpour drowned the fire at the tinker's house. Little damage had been done, as the village discovered the next day. Mistress Ford and company wearily made their way home in the wet. At the inn, they discovered two leaks in the roof, unfortunately in guests' rooms. Already exhausted, Robin made a huge fire in the common room and she and Dean got further soaked bringing in straw from the stable for beds for the unlucky men.

Dawn was only an hour off when she and Dean finally toppled into a pile of straw of their own near the fire and fell asleep.

Chapter Six

It was late in the day in the middle of the week when one of the farm boys came running into the village with the news everyone had been waiting for – the new pastor was coming.

The villagers filled the town square within minutes, their faces turned expectantly toward the far edge of the village where the road led to London. Even the one guest at the inn had come along with Robin, Dean, Elizabeth, and Mistress Ford to take in the festivities.

Mistress Blethen joined the group from the inn, regal and complaining, as usual.

"It's good that Mistress St. John was able to go back to her family," said Mistress Ford about the former pastor's widow.

"But she left the house in such a state," replied Mistress Blethen. "I've been cleaning it all week. I'd just got done yester evening, and thanks be for that. When I came this morning, I found the new pastor's clerk rooting about."

Mistress Ford looked shocked. "A clerk?"

"It's extravagance, I say," Mistress Blethen replied. "But who are we to judge? I'm surprised that he hasn't come out to greet his reverence."

"I'll send Master Robin to fetch him," said Mistress Ford.

"Yes, ma'am," said Robin, who went straight to the pastor's house.

She found the clerk sitting by the kitchen fire, bent over something.

"Sir?" Robin asked.

The man jumped. He was a little taller than Robin, but not by much. His hair was a dark reddish-brown and his teeth remarkably white. There was something else about his features, something Robin couldn't quite put her finger on, as if his face could have been one of a thousand different faces.

"You're the new pastor's clerk?" Robin asked.

"Uh, yes."

"Then you should come outside. The new pastor is just now coming down the road and should be here any minute."

The man brushed off his hands. "Uh, yes. That probably would be a good idea. It's going to be interesting."

"How so?"

The man smiled and there was something indiscriminate about it. "I'm not sure he knows I'm here. He may not have gotten the letter, you see."

Robin shrugged. "We'll see, I guess. I'm Master Robin Parker."

She held out her hand to the clerk, who took it with a very odd look on his face, indeed.

"Uh, Master Robert Neddrick."

"Welcome to Downleigh. I guess we'd better get outside."

Master Neddrick seemed somewhat anxious to hide what he was doing, so Robin left the kitchen first, but waited to be sure the clerk would follow.

The crowd had just begun its welcoming cheer as Robin

and Master Neddrick came into the square. The hurrahs diminished slightly as the four men on horses came slowly up the road. Pastor James Middleton was the easiest to spot – he was the one severely dressed in black, a plump man with a haughty, sour look on his face. The three men riding with him, presumably as an escort to protect the minister out on roads filled with bandits, were wearing military dress, but without any of the King's colors or emblems. Nor did they wear the badge of the city of London. And one carried the flag of the Parliament.

Robin, at first, did not get the distinction. But the rest of the village did, and from there, Robin was able to piece together what was wrong.

Pastor Middleton, for his part, acknowledged the crowd but with the kind of disdain that suggested he tolerated their behavior but did not condone it. He got off his horse, then turned to the villagers.

"Greetings, my fellow sinners," he announced. "Today, I come before you humbly, as God's servant, to be your guide and counselor. Let us pray."

And he began a very long and very pious prayer, thanking God for seeing him safely to the village, and for the villagers, and for a great many things that had nothing to do with anything, as far as Robin could see. She was longing to see what would happen when he came face to face with Master Neddrick, but that young man waited in the doorway to the house until the pastor had greeted Master Greenfield and the other aldermen. As soon as the pastor made ready to go inside, Master Neddrick slipped to Master Middleton's side and whispered in his ear. The pastor nodded, and the two went inside, followed by the horsemen, who brought in Master Middleton's luggage.

And that was that. The villagers dispersed, almost in silence, but Robin could almost feel the buzz of comment from behind every house wall.

Like the rest of the village, Mistress Ford kept her comments to herself until they reached the inn, and the guest went upstairs.

"Hmph!" Mistress Ford snorted. "I won't say our last pastor was perfect, but this new fellow does not seem to be much of an improvement."

Robin shook her heard. "I'd have never believed it, but I honestly think that whoever decides these things actually found the one choice that's worse than what we had."

"If I may, I agree," said Elizabeth. "I've known his kind before. They are the sourest Christians that ever trod the earth."

"Anybody want to put up some money we'll be getting some hellfire and brimstone preaching this Sunday?" Robin asked.

"Or it will be wives, be subordinate to your husbands," Mistress Ford sighed, with a glance toward the common room where Master Ford snored peacefully away. "Well, we'd best be ready for this evening. The men will want to talk over the new pastor, and I'd be very surprised if, after Sunday, we'll be having anyone in for the evening."

That evening the inn was busy, with practically every man in the village there to talk over the new pastor. The consensus was that he was an improvement over the old Laudian, but how much depended on where one stood politically. The tension was almost suffocating, but the men were reluctant to leave. About the only thing they could agree on was that Pastor Middleton was not likely to approve of taking a pint or two at the local inn.

Later, up in their loft, Dean wondered aloud why everyone knew they were going to have to give up visiting the inn at night.

"I mean if everybody disagrees with the guy, why would they bother listening to him?"

Robin sighed. "Dean, have you ever noticed anybody to miss church around here?"

"No."

"They disagreed with the other pastor, right?"

"Yeah."

"But they still paid attention to his sermons and did what he said."

"Well, I guess so, but..." His voice trailed off.

"Dean, religion and government are very closely linked here. The pastor is a very influential man because of his position."

"And they think this new guy won't like drinking."

"Not exactly. Just social drinking, going to the local tavern for the evening. He's probably like... Well, remember Cousin Janet?"

"Oh, yeah."

"Remember when she got converted into that super conservative Christian group?"

"Boy, do I. They wouldn't let her dance even."

"That sounds like this guy."

Dean's eyes widened. "Oh, wow. Folks around here aren't going to like being told they shouldn't go visit the inn."

"Do they like it back home? Face it, Dean, people haven't changed all that much over the centuries. Like I said, we're in for some hellfire and brimstone Sunday."

Dean groaned as Robin rolled over to go to sleep.

As Robin predicted, the hellfire and brimstone overflowed from the pulpit. The entire service had undergone some radical changes. The altar was now the communion table and in the middle of the church instead of the front. Pastor Middleton wore no vestments. There was almost no ritual. If anything, the service consisted mostly of Middleton's incredibly long sermon.

It was not an easy sermon to listen to, nor could one sleep through it. Pastor Middleton had a very full, loud and grating voice. And he was the only thing that could have been worse than the previous pastor.

He preached from Revelations, showing how the signs were right for the return of Christ. He reminded Robin a little of a preacher she had heard down near Costa Mesa. It seemed both were certain the big event was due within their lifetimes. At least Robin knew Pastor Middleton was wrong.

Still, the man unsettled her and the other parishioners. Part of it was the way Middleton condemned the King. According to him, Charles I was one of the twelve heads of the Beast, if not the Anti-Christ himself. The unnerving thing about Middleton's attitude was that he had a good case for it. Only Robin's historical perspective kept her from squirming with the rest of the congregation, Dean included.

"You think maybe Pastor Middleton could be right about the king?" he asked in a concerned voice as they sat on the hill that afternoon.

"Dean, when we left the twenty-first century had Christ shown up yet?" Robin replied, irritated with the way her own fears were surfacing.

"No. I guess Middleton's wrong."

"My father never did hold with people who preached that the Judgment Day was upon us," said Elizabeth. "He said men have been saying that since Christ first left, and all of them have said the predictions in Revelations were coming true. Perhaps some are. All I know is that one should be as a good a Christian as possible, then Judgment Day can come at any time it wants and it makes no difference."

"I had a friend in high school who used to say that," Robin replied. "Or something like that. It certainly makes more sense than scaring people into behaving."

Dean just shrugged.

For the moment, it appeared that Pastor Middleton was not going to condemn the nightly gatherings at the inn, and so the men came out again the following evening.

But any friendliness was forced, at best. The men quickly broke down into cliques. Tension again made its presence felt. Dean prowled the walls. Robin filled the tankards with one eye on the patrons.

It started with an argument. Master Leaton and Master Dimsdale were certainly loud enough, but even though it concerned the conflict between the King and the Parliament, loud arguments were common and no cause for alarm. Then the two men jumped up and Leaton grabbed Dimsdale by the throat.

Dean happened to be on the other side of the room at the

time. He hurried over, but not before Dimsdale's friend came to his aid. Then Leaton's friend joined in.

The whole thing snowballed in seconds. Everyone was fighting. Dean and Robin frantically tried to push the combatants into the street before they tore the inn down. Then Elizabeth screamed. Weapons remained outside or Mistress Ford guarded them in the kitchen. Still someone had brought in a hunting knife. The knife's victim, Master Leaton, sagged to the ground clutching his arm as the crowd pulled back. The errant knife was on the floor and no one claimed it. Dean drew his sword.

"All right!" he bellowed. "I don't care what side you're on, get out before I use this!"

The common room emptied out within minutes. Elizabeth and Mistress Ford tended to the wounded man. It wasn't a serious cut as cuts went. But Robin fretted. The conditions weren't exactly sanitary, and no one knew that was even an issue. Worse yet, saying so could get her, Dean and Elizabeth into trouble.

"We'll need bandages," said Mistress Ford.

"I'll prepare them," Robin volunteered and hurried into the kitchen.

Elizabeth appeared a moment later.

"We need boiling water," Robin told her.

"Don't be silly," said Elizabeth. "We just need some cloth strips to wrap it with. Boiling water will only scald the man."

She picked up a cloth used for covering rising bread and returned to the common room. Robin shook her head, but there was nothing that could be done.

Across the road from the inn, Donald Long watched the

exodus from the inn. He'd heard the yelling and had debated going in but decided against it. It would be unseemly for the pastor's clerk to be seen in such a sinful place, and Donald didn't like being seen in the first place.

If only that Blethen bitch hadn't caught him in the pastor's house. He'd managed to stay hidden easily enough to help that other old fart to his eternal reward and to recover the bottle before anyone had noticed it, even with half the village there to see. Still, he was in an excellent position with the most powerful man in the village.

Donald faded quickly into the blackness as the door to the inn opened. He watched as Mistress Ford, Dean Parker, and the girl brought out an injured man. Donald sniffed. It was that hot-head Leaton, probably had gotten what he'd long deserved. On the other hand, Donald found himself musing, if there was some way he could blame the innkeeper's servants, maybe that would force the trio onto the road where there was less cover and easier access to Elizabeth.

And even if he couldn't get the village riled up over Leaton, there was his old favorite standby, the witchcraft charge. Not that it was easy getting people riled up about a young woman. Fortunately, Elizabeth was just a little too intelligent for her own good. It had been a stretch convincing her previous pastor that she had taught herself to read the Psalms by the power of the devil. Donald couldn't help savoring that little triumph once again.

But now Elizabeth was a stranger, and there were the Parkers to deal with as well. He watched as Robin Parker came outside and emptied a bucket. As clever as that woman was, she never seemed to notice when he was watching her.

He'd watched her arrive from the drop outside that B&B in Windsor. And she never saw him in London. But this time, he'd have to remember that she didn't know who he was, let alone that he was watching her. Donald grimaced. Travelling backward along her timetron's logged path did make the continuity a little confusing.

Robin returned inside. She and her brother were fitting in among the villagers rather well. Master Robin had even caught the eye of the town's prettiest maid.

Donald paused and smiled. Although others also considered Mistress Smith far too froward to be a worthy wife, "Master" Robin had far better reason to avoid marriage. But would simply exposing Robin for the woman she was get him Elizabeth? After all, more than one woman of the seventeenth century had taken refuge in the guise of a man. No, better to cast suspicion on all three, get Elizabeth alone long enough to get the job done, and save his ultimate revenge on Robin and Dean for the future.

The next day, Robin could almost smell the gloom as she walked through the village to the pastor's house with one of Mistress Ford's best cheeses for the clergyman.

Robin stopped first at Master Leaton's house to inquire after him. Sure enough, he had taken sick from his wound. Robin could see that his fever was quite high. His arm was swollen, and Robin didn't want to think about what it looked like underneath the bandages. She wished the family well, and sighing heavily, left the cottage.

Master Neddrick opened the door at the pastor's house and seemed strangely pleased to see Robin. He ushered her into the common room where the pastor was reading a pamphlet.

"Good morning, sir. Mistress Ford, from the inn..." Robin began.

"You are Master Robin Parker, are you not?" Pastor Middleton interrupted.

Robin shifted under the older man's odd scrutiny.

"Yes, sir," she said.

"Good sir, I'd like to talk to you."

"Yes, sir?" Robin noticed that the pastor was gazing at her chin. She fought the urge to hide it.

"I'm told you are not interested in wooing Mistress Mary Smith."

"No, sir. And I'm not the only one."

"But you're the only one without a beard." Middleton's eyebrow lifted.

Robin nodded. "I know, and I suspect you're wondering about that. There was an accident when I was a babe, and I lost my, uh, testes."

Middleton nodded and Robin hoped that he was not going to pants her.

"You are too big to be a woman," Middleton noted, looking up at her. "But not fully a man. You have been cursed, you know. But should you repent of your evil, you might be able to find favor again with God."

"Evil?"

"Serving ale to drunken fools. You are the tapster, are you not?"

"Yes, sir. But I don't serve drunks. We escort them out if they get too much."

Middleton shook his head. "It is an evil practice, drinking ale at an alehouse at night."

"We are an inn." Robin fought to contain her temper. "Surely you stayed in one on your way here. The highways are full of bandits. We are a necessary service."

"But to tempt your fellow villagers with the evils of too much ale in rude company, that is sinful." Middleton prowled around Robin.

"Then we won't anymore," Robin said. "Mistress Ford was saying this morning that it would be better to not serve after supper. The inn has been a meeting place for the village, especially since we couldn't use the church. But the men can meet elsewhere when needs be. Mistress Ford said that. She is a godly woman."

"Who rules her husband?" snarled the pastor.

"He's incapacitated. And she still takes good care of him."

"He is the prime example of what happens to a man who succumbs to the evil of strong drink, no doubt driven to it by his wife."

"It wasn't like that," Robin snapped.

Middleton stepped back. "Shall I have you flogged for insolence?"

"No, sir." Robin stepped back. "In any case, Mistress Ford sent you one of her best cheeses, here."

"Take it back. I'll not take the offering of a sinner."

Robin glared. "You don't even know her. I assure you, if someone is sick in this village, or ready for childbirth, she is the first one there after Mistress Blethen. If there is anyone who wants for anything here, they go to her and do not go away empty-handed. When beggars come, they stop at her door. They don't waste time going elsewhere because they will be turned away. How does that make Mistress Ford a sinner?"

"I know who is a sinner and who isn't," Middleton snapped, pulling himself up to his full height.

Robin dropped the basket with the cheese at his feet. "Then it should be easy to find Mistress Ford's tithe this Sunday and return it to her. And I assure you it will be in the collection basket. You can't miss it. It's the most generous one."

Middleton glared at her. "I suppose it is commendable that you show such loyalty to your mistress. But take care, Master Parker, that you do not end up following her into the gates of Hell."

Robin turned walked out of the house, not daring to say another word.

Back at the inn, she tried to avoid telling Mistress Ford what had happened, but Mistress Ford took one look at her and knew.

"So, what has gained me the pastor's ire?" Mistress Ford asked philosophically. "That I serve ale to the men of the village or that I rule my husband?"

"Both," grumbled Robin. "I'm sorry."

Mistress Ford shrugged. "I've friends enough in the village, and I shan't be serving after supper. It will take time, I suppose, but I'll prove myself the godly woman I am." She smiled at Elizabeth, Dean, and Robin. "I just hope you three won't look for a riper situation. I'm afraid I won't be able to be as generous with the wages."

"As long as I have food to eat and a roof over my head, I'm staying," said Elizabeth.

"And you boys?" Mistress Ford asked.

Dean looked at Robin, as did Mistress Ford and Elizabeth. Robin nodded reluctantly.

That was another problem. She and Dean couldn't promise to stay. They had to go home before they aged too much. It would be too awkward trying to explain completely the faded tans, wrinkles or gray hair that would be sure to occur if they waited around for Elizabeth to die of old age. Robin had no intention of remaining in the seventeenth century for the rest of her natural lifetime.

That afternoon, as the barley roasted for the ale, Robin stood just outside the kitchen in the yard, kicking at the small stones on the ground. Elizabeth appeared at her side.

"You are sad," the younger girl observed. "Your errand to the pastor?"

"No kidding," Robin grumbled. "I swear that son of a bitch is more conservative than some of the jerks in my time."

"How do you mean?"

"There are some very famous folks in my time who are very moralistic, just like Pastor Middleton." Robin let out a soft rueful laugh. "It's amazing how little people change. Yeah, I know there's a lot that has changed, and we do look at some things differently, but the basic human personalities sure as hell haven't changed one iota."

Elizabeth frowned.

"Robin, in your land," she asked slowly, "is there an England?"

"In the U.S., where Dean and I live, there's a New England. That's what we call what you call the Colonies."

"Is it the same land as the Colonies?"

"Yes." Robin looked puzzled.

"I'm trying to understand," Elizabeth explained. "You keep talking about centuries and time, and it seems strange that you should identify a place by a name that also means time."

Robin suddenly understood Elizabeth's confusion.

"Where's Dean?" Robin asked.

"Watching the barley."

"Maybe we'd better wait and go keep an eye on him."

Elizabeth laughed. "I wouldn't worry. Dean likes his ale too much to let the barley burn."

"You're right," Robin smiled. "Come on. Let's go to the stable. We won't be overheard there. We don't want anyone thinking we're witches."

Elizabeth shuddered, but Robin didn't notice.

In the stable, Robin sat down on a bundle of hay.

"Elizabeth," she said slowly. "Do you remember in the castle where we found you how you said you'd been sleeping?"

"Yes, and while I did, Roger moved the chamber."

"You also said you'd changed lands. But that wasn't quite right. You were still in the same land. Have you heard the story of the Sleeping Beauty? She was put to sleep for a hundred years?"

"Yes, I know it." Elizabeth nodded eagerly.

Robing took a deep breath. "That's what happened to you, only it wasn't magic, in the sense that it wasn't a spell. It was science. You see, a hundred years from now, a man named Ben Franklin is going to find out that lightning can be collected, that it's power can be transmitted, can be directed to a specific spot. A hundred years after that, a man named Thomas Edison will discover that this collected power, which is something called electricity, can be stored, and used to make light and to make wheels turn and a lot of other things. It's part of what I call technology, and you call magic."

"But how do you know these things will happen?"

"Because five hundred years from now, your Roger will find a way to make someone sleep for hundreds of years without dying or growing older. I know because that's what happened to you. You were sleeping for over four hundred years, Elizabeth. Do you understand that?"

She frowned. "I believe so. But why am I back in England as it was when I left?"

"Because Roger found a way to travel not only across land but across years and days. He found a way to travel backward and forward in time. He is from my future, as I am from your future."

"How long was I asleep?"

"Around four hundred years."

Elizabeth did the math. "That's impossible, and yet, it can't be, for I know it happened. This is so hard to understand."

"I know, Elizabeth." Robin put her hand on Elizabeth's shoulder. "Most of the knowledge that makes Dean's iPhone possible hasn't been discovered yet."

"But how can one change time?"

Robin shrugged. "I don't know. As I said, Roger is not from my time. He is from my future, which is even further ahead. In that time, they will know. It was an accident that Dean and I were able to find you and the time machine. All I know is how to work the thing."

Elizabeth nodded. "It's still not completely clear, but it's better. Come. Dean will need help with the mash." She stopped at the door to the stable. "And, Robin, please don't be too angry with the pastor. He means well, even if all he does is cause trouble. We do have to live with him."

"Yeah." Robin smiled. "That's the nice thing about you, Elizabeth. You're at least willing to try something new."

"It doesn't seem like it," she sighed.

"You did fine," Robin said. "You'd have never made it as far as you did in the twenty-first century if you were as narrow as old Middleton. You should be proud of yourself."

Elizabeth smiled. "You are so kind, Robin. I want so much to like your magic, or whatever you call it, because you do."

"I understand. I'm so used to it, I don't even think about it. I forget how frightening it must be to you."

Elizabeth nodded. Together, the two women left the stable.

Chapter Seven

That night, it rained, a steady, drenching rain. Fortunately, there was only one guest that evening, and he was able to go into the one room that didn't have a leak in the roof. Robin found pans for the other leaks.

But when the next day dawned clear and bright, Mistress Ford insisted that Robin and Dean finally repair the roof.

Robin had been putting off the job simply because she had no idea how to do it, and she didn't want to ask anyone. After all, everybody had roof leaks, so the odds were good that it was a common task.

Dean settled the matter with his usual ignorant grace. He asked Mistress Ford. She was amused but expected such a reaction from Dean. Robin smiled and listened.

The job took all the morning and lasted well into the afternoon. They had just finished repairing the last leak when they heard the shouting. From the rooftop Robin saw the men gathering near the church. They carried swords as well as clubs and other tools.

"What on earth?" Robin muttered and hurried down the ladder.

Mistress Ford and Elizabeth emerged from the kitchen with worried frowns.

"What's all the shouting about?" Mistress Ford asked.

"I don't know," Robin replied.

"I don't know if I wanna find out," said Dean, who had come down the ladder behind his sister. "Those guys look like they're gonna start busting something up."

Robin explained about the men.

"Dean, fetch your sword. You, too, Robin," said Mistress Ford. "We'll pray they don't come down here, but we'd best be prepared. Lock up the stable. Elizabeth, you and I had better get plenty of water ready from the well. There could be a fire."

The two guests at the inn were not happy about the approaching riot, but neither felt inclined to do any more traveling that day. They did ask Dean to see that their horses were saddled in the event a quick departure was necessary. Dean obliged.

Mistress Ford forbade Dean and Robin to get involved unless the inn was attacked, although they'd already assured her they had no intention of doing so.

Several of the women slowly made their way to the inn, along with the smallest children. It was almost as if they knew the men were going to stay on the far end of the village.

"Master Leaton died," said Mistress Loomis, although Robin had no idea which of the two Loomis brothers she was married to.

"Is anyone attending Mistress Leaton?" Mistress Ford asked.

"Mistress Blethen," replied Mistress Southwood. "And her daughters."

None of the women, however, were quite sure how the fighting began, just that it had.

The hours eased past slowly. The fighting remained on the far side of the village. Even with all the weapons, there were few injuries. The fight burned itself out late that night when Master Greenfield, at last, made himself heard over the noise.

Even with the night's unrest, Master Leaton's funeral was still held the next morning and most of the village attended, uneasily at peace with each other for the moment. Pastor Middleton had the decency not to bring up the political issues that had been at the center of the riot. Robin could see he didn't want another one.

That Sunday, Robin had to give Pastor Middleton credit for finding a topic for his sermon that would unite the villagers. The only problem was the topic he chose: witchcraft. Later that afternoon, Dean scoffed. But Robin was worried. The pastor's eyes had focused on her during some of the more accusatory parts.

Robin spent the next day completely on edge, just waiting for the townspeople to rise up and arrest her. Or even hang her straight out. But when nothing had happened by Tuesday afternoon, Robin began to relax.

Which was probably why Master Ford's bizarre behavior caught her so completely off guard. The man had never moved quickly. The times he had wandered off and gotten lost, he had gotten away because no one was watching him, not because he could move with any speed.

Robin was weeding in the garden when the howling began. It came from behind the stable, but by the time Robin was on her feet, Master Ford was tearing into the center of the village, his doublet and boots flying as he went.

"Dean!" Robin called as she chased after. "Bring a blanket!"

Dean had already seen the old drunk's shirt flying and ducked back into the stable, grabbed the first blanket he could get a hand on and hurried out after Robin.

They caught up with Master Ford near the town well. He'd lost his breeches and was just about to take off his drawers.

"Maggots!" Master Ford screamed, trying to tear the invisible bugs off him. "Maggots! Get them off me! Get them off me!"

Robin approached slowly. "Master Ford, it's okay. We'll get them off. Just hold still."

"No!" Master Ford's eyes widened in terror as he saw Robin. "Get away from me, demon. Get away!"

"There's no demon here, Master Ford," said Dean, with an oddly jovial lilt to his voice. He walked casually up to the terrified man. "Honest. It's just me and Robin."

"Maggots," Master Ford whimpered.

"Nah," said Dean. "We'll take care of it. Here, get this blanket on and we'll get you home. You'll be fine."

Master Ford let Dean wrap him in the blanket. Dean picked him up and cradled him as he and Robin walked back to the inn, with Robin picking up Master Ford's clothing as she went.

The street was empty, but Robin's skin prickled with the frightened stares of the villagers.

Dean bedded Master Ford down in one of the guest rooms.

"Shit, that was lousy timing for a case of the DT's," Robin grumbled as she brought in Master Ford's clothes.

"Those weren't the DT's." Dean frowned as he looked down at the now sleeping drunk.

"Then what the hell were they?"

Dean shrugged. "I don't know. But the DT's happen when you're in withdrawal, and I saw Master Ford drinking up from one of the cellar casks not an hour ago."

Robin dropped Master Ford's boots next to the bed. "Something weird is going on here."

"I'll say." Dean frowned again. "You know, I thought I heard someone talking to Master Ford behind the stable right before it happened."

"Hm." Robin turned and went out to the back side of the stable, with Dean ambling along behind.

Sure enough, it was clear that Master Ford had not been the only person back there.

"Look at these two sets of tracks." Robin pointed them out. "And there's been something of a struggle here. But where do the hallucinations come into it? Could somebody have doped him, you think?"

"How would I know?" grumbled Dean.

"It would have had to act awfully quickly. You know of anything that acts really quickly?"

"Why are you asking me?" Dean groaned. "I don't do that shit."

Robin rolled her eyes. "You volunteered at that rehab place, you said?"

"Oh." Dean thought, then shrugged. "I don't know, Robin.

I mean, IV works fast, but hallucinations? I don't know. I mean, they don't have LSD here, do they?"

"I doubt that." Robin went back around to the inn's yard. "But I seem to remember something about some kind of rye mold that caused hallucinations or some kind of craziness. But no one's growing rye around here. Besides, it would be affecting more people than just Master Ford." She shook her head. "It just doesn't make sense, unless someone's looking for a good excuse to get us in trouble."

It was Dean's turn to roll his eyes. "Oh, don't get started on that witchcraft thing again. Even Mistress Ford says the only people that get accused are poor old women with no one to take care of them."

Robin sighed. "You're probably right."

Still, an uneasy feeling grabbed hold of her gut and wouldn't let go.

Fortunately, the inn remained empty of guests. Mistress Ford shrugged and sent Dean and Robin to the stable just as it grew dark. Neither of the two were sleepy.

"So now what?" Dean asked, flopping back onto the hay.

"We twiddle our thumbs, I guess," replied Robin. "There's not much else we can do in the dark."

"You know, I don't think I'll ever take an electric light bulb for granted again."

Robin started. "What's that?"

Dean was about to tease her when the sound reached his ears.

"It's someone running," he said. "Sounds like he's headed this way."

"Uh, oh." Robin sat up. "You hear that rumbling? It sounds like that riot's about to break out again."

Dean swung himself down from the loft and looked out the hole in the stable's back wall toward the village.

"There's a whole bunch of torches gathered down by the church," he said.

"Terrific," grumbled Robin, swinging down to the ground herself. "More trouble."

Mistress Ford appeared at the other door with Elizabeth, their hair down and flying.

"Robin, Dean, hurry!" Mistress Ford hissed. "You three must flee."

"What's going on?" asked Dean.

"You've been accused of witchcraft!" Mistress Ford replied. "The men are gathering to arrest you."

"We're not witches!" Dean protested.

"That doesn't mean a damn thing!" snapped Robin. She turned on Mistress Ford. "Are you sure that's what's going on? How do you know?"

"Young Master Loomis," Mistress Ford said quickly. "He just came running." She stopped and sniffed. "There have been rumors, but most paid them no mind. Then Sabbath past, Pastor Middleton, and then today when my good husband called you demon. Master Loomis said most think it's nonsense, but the pastor is insisting."

Robin scurried up the ladder to the loft and gathered hers and Dean's belongings.

"Well, I'm not doing time," Dean grumbled.

"They'll hang you, idiot!" Robin growled, lowering the two sacks into Elizabeth's arms.

Dean swore loudly.

"I agree." Robin swung herself down from the loft. "But we'd better keep quiet. Mistress Ford, are you sure they won't accuse you?"

She shook her head. "They won't. Trust me. But you must hurry. You can take the road toward the coast to the fork, then take the road heading northeast. I've a cousin in a town called Charing Vale. It's on the coast. He runs the inn there, The White Bear. His name is Master John Miller. Tell him I sent you. He'll take you in and give you work. Here's bread and cheese and some other things for the journey, and your wages."

"Thanks," Robin's voice suddenly choked.

She reached out and held the matron and kissed her cheek. Dean quickly did the same. Elizabeth was held a minute longer. There was a soft rustle from the back side of the stable outside, and on top of that, the rumble of angry yelling.

"I hear the men!" Mistress Ford started and released Elizabeth. "Quickly!"

"Right," whispered Robin as she grabbed Elizabeth's hand.

They ran across the yard and ducked behind the trees on the other side of the garden. Robin had them all lay flat on their stomachs.

"They're too close, they'll see us leave," she whispered to the other two.

They heard Mistress Ford wailing in the yard.

"Such horrors I've seen!" she cried out as the men came up. "Most terrible wonders! They were witches. They heard you coming, and I saw them all mount their ravens, and they flew away before my very eyes!"

"Which way?" demanded Pastor Middleton.

"To the north, I think, but only for a moment," Mistress Ford sobbed. "To London! They flew that way! Perhaps they went to meet their master there."

"Perhaps they set down somewhere near here," called out a voice.

"We'll search the village," said Pastor Middleton. "Everyone to the inn's common room so we can decide who searches where and with whom."

The men trooped into the inn. Robin watched, vaguely aware that somebody was missing from the group. But there was no time to figure out whom. She waited a minute longer, then motioned to the others to get up.

"No running," she cautioned. "We'll concentrate on being quiet. Come on."

Robin led them toward the center of the village, although behind the houses.

Dean paused. "We're going the wrong way. We're supposed to go to the coast. This way's towards London."

"I know," Robin said. "We'll make tracks that way, then double back along the stream. Hopefully, that will put them off our trail. Now, be quiet."

They made good progress to the other end of the village, but as they left the last house behind for the road to London, they heard the pounding of a single man running. Robin pressed herself and Elizabeth into the shadow of a roadside tree. Carefully, she eased around to see who had run up.

"Damn," the newcomer muttered.

It was Master Neddrick, and Robin realized he had been the man missing from the group that had come to arrest her and the others. Dean shifted and a twig snapped. Master Neddrick's eyes fastened on the tree.

"You're lucky I need Elizabeth," he said, chuckling softly. "Otherwise, I would sound the alarm."

"You'll have to sound it, then," said Robin, slightly amazed at how confident she sounded. "What makes you think we'd give Elizabeth up?"

"This." He pulled something from his belt.

At that moment, the moon broke through the clouds and Robin rolled around the trunk of the tree. She made out the barrel of a pistol in Neddrick's hands.

"You got another one of those?" she asked.

Neddrick's breath caught, but then he chuckled. "You'll just have to guess."

There wasn't time for guessing. Dean crashed out from his hiding place and tackled Neddrick from the side. The two rolled and Neddrick banged at Dean's back with the pistol butt, but Dean had his arms almost pinned and Neddrick couldn't hit him hard. Dean got one hand on Neddrick's face, then he reared back, and rabbit punched Neddrick in the side of the head. Neddrick was just stunned enough. Dean kneed him in the breadbasket, then rabbit punched him again to make sure he was knocked out.

Robin and Elizabeth were already running toward London. They had gone almost a quarter mile when Dean finally caught up. Robin looked back toward the village. Small flecks of light – torches – bounced up and down in the distance. They seemed massed at the edge of the village and certainly weren't fanning out.

"Okay," Robin gasped. "Let's get off the road."

"Yeah," Dean gasped. "Elizabeth, you okay?"

"Yes," she whispered.

"Did you get the pistol?" Robin asked Dean.

"What pistol?"

"Damn. Neddrick had a pistol. We could have used it."

"I thought you didn't like guns," Dean said.

Robin shushed him in reply.

It was a long night. Robin led them across the stream, and they followed it back the way they had come to the inn's side of the village. It was slow going because Robin did not want to make any noise. Nor did she let them stop until they were several miles away. Even then, she watched while Dean and Elizabeth slept, until the first flush of dawn touched the eastern sky. Then she finally nodded off.

Elizabeth had been so tired when they finally stopped that she hadn't really noticed where they were. She awoke as the sun cleared the horizon and sleepily noted that the three had tucked themselves into the corner of someone's pasture, up against the hedgerow. Standing on tiptoe, she could just barely see over the wall of ivy-covered stones. There was another narrow field and then the road. Not far away, and well into the pasture, a stream rippled past. Elizabeth couldn't quite see it, but she heard it and guessed that it was beyond the small rise that shielded them from the rest of the pasture.

Dean awoke just in time to see Elizabeth walk softly off toward the stream. He yawned, then noted that Robin was still fast asleep. So, he followed Elizabeth.

He found her next to the stream, weeping.

"What's wrong?" he asked, plopping down next to her.

"What do you mean, 'What's wrong?' Isn't it obvious?" Elizabeth pursed her lips and tried to dry her eyes.

"Well, yeah." Dean shrugged. "It was pretty scary getting run out of town like that, but we're okay."

"We spent last night in a field. And even if we find Mistress Ford's cousin, there's no guarantee he'll be a decent, kind man. He could be horrible and cruel."

Dean put his arm around Elizabeth's shoulders. "Aw, we'll be okay. If this cousin is a jerk, then we move on. It's no big deal."

"But we were accused of witchcraft!" Elizabeth wailed softly.

"So? We're not witches."

"But, Dean—"

Dean shook his head. "So, what's the big deal about it?"

"It's witchcraft. Making pacts with the Devil."

"But we're not." Dean shifted around and gently took Elizabeth's chin. "Look, Elizabeth, it doesn't matter what they say about us. Well, except that they wanted to hang us for it. Which I think is pretty stupid. I mean, back in my time, we don't care about who you make deals with, and we're not going to hang you because of some stupid superstition. Heck, we don't hang people anymore, anyway."

Elizabeth looked surprised. "You behead even the common criminals?"

"No! We only kill murderers, and usually by giving them a poison that just puts them to sleep."

"What do you do with the witches, then?"

"What witches? There's no such thing as witches, at least, not like the evil spell magic kind. There are some people who call themselves witches, but that's just a pagan religion thing. Seriously, Elizabeth, people just don't care about that."

"This time, which is in the future." Elizabeth began thinking carefully.

"Yeah." Dean gave her a quick little squeeze. "So, you see, it's no big deal."

"It is here."

"Well, yeah, but we dodged that rap. We're okay."

Elizabeth nodded. She liked the feeling of Dean's arm around her shoulders, and she leaned her head against him.

"I feel better," she said softly.

"Cool." Dean grinned, then suddenly shifted. "Yeah, well, we'd better not get too cuddly."

"And why not?"

"Cause, well…" Dean grimaced and stood up. "I can't talk about it."

Elizabeth stood also but was not to be put off. "You said you could talk to me about anything."

Dean squirmed. "I know. It's just about how guys are and all."

"You mean what passes between man and wife," Elizabeth smirked.

"Well, yeah. And what do you know about all that stuff? I thought you weren't supposed to find out until the night before your wedding or something."

"What?" Elizabeth couldn't help laughing. "Where on this earth did you learn that? Of course, I know what happens in the conjugal bed. And I know about guys and all. I've had to fend off more than one, thank you."

"Well, you won't be fending me off." Dean folded his arms and stood resolutely. "I mean, you are a virgin, aren't you?"

Elizabeth gasped. "That's a fine thing to ask me! I am a maid, indeed. That you should even ask!"

Dean caught her as she stomped off.

"Look, Elizabeth, in my time, it's not unusual for a girl to have sex by your age. Sometimes, it's more unusual when they wait. I mean, it's no big deal. I don't care. It's just I figured if you knew the facts of life, then maybe you weren't, which was dumb, I know, but..."

Elizabeth melted under the gaze of his puppy-dog eyes. "I just don't understand, Dean. I mean, it's noble that you don't want to trespass upon my virtue, but to treat me as if I'm an infant in understanding, it's uncomfortable."

Dean sighed. "I guess I just don't know how guys in your time... You know, what they do when they like a girl if they want to date or something."

"Date?" Elizabeth frowned. "What is that?"

"Well, in my time, if a guy likes a girl, he asks her out to do stuff together, like eat dinner or go to a movie. Oh wait, you wouldn't know what that is. It's like going to a play. And if they get to like each other more and more, and fall in love, then they move in together and maybe get married and all that. And sometimes even the girl will ask the guy. And a lot of times, it doesn't work out, so you go out with someone else until you find just the right person. Anyway, that's how we do it and I was wondering how you do it."

"We don't." Elizabeth looked out over the stream. "If I was still with my father, then he'd be finding me a husband. There were a couple boys that I had my eye on, and my father was a kind man and would have considered them. But he would choose the man and I must needs obey his wishes."

"But what about falling in love?"

Elizabeth shook her head and chuckled. "What about it? That's all nice for fairy tales and other such nonsense, but a good wife learns to love the husband her father finds for her. Falling in love is rash and dangerous and not much good is likely to come of it." She paused. "Although the mistress I served before I left my village, she and her husband had fallen in love, and it was quite a happy union."

"Well, I'm not thinking about getting married yet," Dean said.

"I didn't think so." Elizabeth turned to him, her eyes warm and full in the early morning light. "Some young men do go and court their mistresses to try to win their hearts."

"I'd like to try this courtship thing," said Dean softly. "I don't want to make any promises, Elizabeth. I can't. I gotta go back to my time sooner or later, and we did come here to bring you back." He looked away and swallowed. "I just don't see how I'm going to want to leave you."

Elizabeth nodded sadly. "You can't stay here?"

"I don't know. I could, I guess. But there's lots of things about my time that knock socks off this one. Like not dying just 'cause you got your arm sliced open. We got drugs that stop that from happening. We got more food. You get to keep your teeth."

"That would be nice." Elizabeth softly touched Dean's arm. "I could try again. In your world. I mean, your time. There's much I don't understand, but Robin has been telling me a little about it and it doesn't seem so fearful when she explains it."

Dean grinned. "Nah. It's just confusing. I mean, when she goes on about her computer and stuff, it's like she's talking another language." He laid his hand on Elizabeth's cheek. "I still can't make any promises. About us, I mean. Heck, you could decide you don't want me."

"I very much doubt that."

Dean bent and they softly kissed.

"How about this," he said when they finally parted. "We'll hang out here in your time until we're sure about each other, and in the meantime, we'll keep this between ourselves. I don't want to go flipping Robin out until we have to."

Elizabeth looked back at the corner of the pasture where they'd slept. "Poor thing. She is very lonely."

Nonetheless, she kissed Dean again, with considerably more heat this time. Dean pulled back, gasping.

"Wo-oh!"

Elizabeth looked down in shame. "I am too forward."

"Yes and no." Dean looked away and back at her. "How long do you want to stay a maid?"

She laughed in response. "Until I am your wife and not a minute sooner. Good heavens, Dean, if I should get with child and you were to leave, it would be my undoing and that of the child's. I am amazed that the girls of your time don't fear for it."

"Well, they do sometimes. But we have ways of keeping pregnancy from happening."

"You do?" Elizabeth mulled that one over, and Dean could

see her mentally chalking up another point in favor of his time.

Chapter Eight

"Are you sure you've never seen Master Neddrick before?" Robin asked for the fifth time.

"No, nor can I imagine what he would want with me." Elizabeth was clearly tired of the question but bore Robin's pressing with patience. After all, Elizabeth was just as curious and confused by Master Neddrick's professed interest in her as Robin was.

The noon-day sun bore down on the travelers as they trudged along the road to the coast. They had spent the morning walking through the neighboring fields, but it soon became clear that no one in Downleigh had seen fit to search them out. Robin decided to give up worrying about Master Neddrick and focus on getting to Charing Vale.

Most of the land on either side of the road was either farm or pastureland. Robin remembered reading that most of England had been deforested since the Middle Ages or the Renaissance or something like that. Yet, here and there, small woods still stood amid the fields.

As the afternoon wore on, a brisk wind slid through the chinks in their clothes, and dark clouds piled up in the sky.

"Looks like we're in for some rain," Robin sighed.

"Think we could stay at an inn tonight?" Dean asked.

"I don't know. We don't have that much money, and we haven't seen a lot of villages." Robin glared at the sky. "We may not have a choice."

Evening approached and the three left the road for the cover of another small stand of trees with a clearing in the middle. Robin found sufficient wood just as Elizabeth finished laying out the blankets. Dean re-entered the clearing with a good fat rabbit and Elizabeth reached for the pot.

"You're back fast," she commented as she left for the nearby stream.

"Just a naturally good hunter, I guess." Dean grinned.

Elizabeth laughed and ran off into the trees.

"Got lucky, huh?" Robin smiled from where she was setting up the fire ring.

"Yep." Dean dropped the rabbit next to her.

Elizabeth screamed from beyond the trees. Dean started in that direction, but Robin held him back.

"Get the blankets!" she ordered as she grabbed the bags. "We can't afford to lose them."

Dean had them slung over his shoulder in an instant. He was about to dash off when Robin held him back.

"Silently!" she hissed. "We could walk into a trap if we're not careful, and that won't do her any good."

Dean followed Robin as she slunk down to the stream. From a screen of bushes they saw two men push Elizabeth down a path on the other side of the water. Robin nodded and silently she and Dean followed.

Ten minutes later they stood in a brake of trees and bushes around a large camp. Robin counted twelve men, most of whom were filling their tankards with ale from a medium-sized cask. The camp seemed to be permanent. There was a crude shack built on the other side. Primitive tents sheltered the area next to the shack. In the middle of the camp was a huge roaring bonfire. Elizabeth was tied with her hands behind her to a post next to the shack.

"Now aren't you glad we didn't go rushing down to that stream?" Robin whispered. "There may even have been a couple more waiting at our camp to take what we left behind."

Dean nodded sullenly. "But what are we going to do? We can't fight all those guys. I don't want to wait until they've gone to sleep. They might rape her before then."

"These guys are thieves, not rapists. There's a whole different psychology involved."

"Not when they're drinking. And look at how they're putting it away. I swear, Robin, I've seen perfectly decent normal guys turn into monsters when they're drunk. And these guys aren't even that good."

"You do have a point," Robin sighed. "But the two of us aren't going to be much good against twelve of them."

"If only there were more of us. Wait a minute." Dean grinned. "What if we made them believe there was more of us?"

"How, Dean?" Robin returned.

"We could yell, maybe. Or..." Dean dove for the bag he was carrying. "We could use my iPhone."

"Are you going to put the headphones on each every one of those guys?"

"No. I brought the speaker dock. Here." Dean pushed the unit into place between the two small speakers.

"Deanie, boy, I do believe you're onto something."

"Damn. I don't think I downloaded any concert stuff on here." Dean pressed through the menu.

"Never mind. Anything on there should scare the pants off those fellows."

"Just because you don't like it."

Robin rolled her eyes. "It has nothing to do with like. Elevator music would terrify these guys."

"Hell, it scares me."

Robin paused. "You've got a point."

Dean squinted as he quickly pressed the menu button. "Damn. I can't see the readout that well. I think I got some Motley Crue on here."

"It doesn't matter," Robin said through gritted teeth. "Just play something."

Dean shrugged and pressed the play button. The screeching tones of Van Halen filled the air. The men in the camp looked up thunderstruck.

"Panama?" Robin asked. "That's way old.

Dean shrugged. "It's a good tune."

Elizabeth started at the sound of the music, then laughed.

"I told you!" she yelled. "My brothers have come. They are very powerful sorcerers, and they will destroy you all!"

Robin and Dean stepped into the camp. The setting sun and the firelight threw strange shadows on their faces. Thunder rumbled over from the gathering clouds, underscoring the wailing iPhone. The men didn't wait. They threw down their weapons and ran full out. Robin and Dean let them. Within seconds the camp was clear.

Shaking her head, Robin walked over to Elizabeth and untied her. Dean went to the bushes and retrieved the iPhone.

"Nice build up you gave us," Robin said to Elizabeth. "I'm glad you kept your head."

"Hell, she's heard it before," said Dean. "She knows it can't hurt you."

"Just your eardrums," replied Robin.

Elizabeth shrugged. "I guess one can get used to anything."

Robin laughed. "Let's check this place out."

They found a huge buck being skinned in one of the tents. In the shack, under some recently overturned earth, was a small chest. Robin had a fair idea of what was inside. But the sound of thunder again made her decide to eat dinner first. They feasted on the buck, washing it down with plenty of ale from the cask.

In preparation for the foul weather ahead, Robin built a small fire in the shack next to the door and collected all the discarded weapons.

"Those men aren't going to want to stay out on a night like this," she explained. "So, we'd better keep a good watch. We may as well have the fire since one of us is going to be up watching. It'll be too cold otherwise."

"Fine," said Dean. "Can we open the chest now?"

"Why?" asked Robin. "It's too dark to see anything. Why don't I sleep first?"

"But the chest."

Robin glared. "We'll open it tomorrow morning."

Dean reluctantly agreed. Robin bedded down and went to sleep. Elizabeth waited up with Dean for a while until sleep overcame her. Around midnight, Dean decided that the patter of the rain on the roof was making him too drowsy, and he woke up Robin.

An hour later, as Robin poked the fire, she heard a twig snap outside the shack. Instantly, she was fully alert. She crawled over to Dean and shook him.

"Ermph?" he asked sleepily.

Robin put her finger to her lips. Dean blinked, then nodded. Another twig snapped, and whispering could be heard. Dean sat up and drew his sword. Robin drew hers also and removed a flaming branch from the fire.

The door flew open. Robin thrust the branch at the man in the doorway. He screamed and dodged. Others stampeded from the camp. But three were too wet and too worried about their loot to worry about sorcerers. Only one had a sword. The other two were armed with belt knives.

These two attacked first. Robin blunted the slashing blades with her sword and jabbed with her burning branch. The men backed off. Robin forced them out of the shack, glad that the rain had stopped.

Dean burst out after her. The swordsman took him. Dean parried the thrust with a gulp. It suddenly dawned on him that he was fighting with swords that could really cut. He charged forward, hoping his size would at least intimidate his opponent.

The swordsman was intimidated, but greed conquered his fears, and he met the charge with a parry and a vicious thrust. Dean barely dodged in time. He slashed at the swordsman. The swordsman dodged that, and thrusted. Dean parried. The swordsman thrusted again and again. Dean parried both thrusts, then thrusted himself. It was blocked. Dean felt his opponent's steel swish by his belly. He spun around and started in with a quick series of slashes and jabs. It was all the swordsman could do to parry them.

Meanwhile, the two men knife men danced just beyond the point of Robin's sword. One distracted her and the other tried to move in. In a split second, she slashed at the one and thrust the burning branch at the other. But the way her hand grew warmer told her that the branch was burning fast.

The men pushed her back further and further, moving in and dodging. Robin felt the cool of the forest against her back. She dared not step out of the camp, where possibly the others lay in wait. Leaves crunched underneath her feet and gave her an idea.

She was under one of the makeshift tents. One of the men lunged. She parried, then dropped her branch into the dead leaves. They burned hot and fast. Robin dodged around the flames. The men circled, utterly confused. As the flames died down, Robin cut the ropes holding the tent up. It fell and trapped the men.

Dean was still dancing around the swordsman. He had pushed Dean back in a strong counterattack but had yet to draw blood. Dean was finally backed up against a tree. The swordsman lunged. Dean dodged, and with a quick spin, pounced on the swordsman, and landed a good strong blow on the side of his head.

Out of nowhere, it seemed, the music of Van Halen filled the night. Dazed and frightened, the swordsman stumbled into the darkness. His two friends slashed their way out of the tent and ran off also. Gasping, Robin and Dean staggered back to the shack.

Elizabeth was sitting in the middle of the room holding the iPhone, still hooked onto its speakers.

"You do say it's magic anyone can work once they know how," she said.

Robin sat down heavily on the floor and laughed. Dean staggered over to Elizabeth, flopped down next to her, and hugged her.

"I would have worked it sooner, but I've never seen exactly how you worked the spell," Elizabeth sighed. "You're not angry with me, are you?"

"No!" Robin wiped the tears from her eyes. "Your timing was perfect. We had them down and you put on the finishing touch to get them good and scared and out of here."

"I'm proud of you, Elizabeth." Dean squeezed her again.

"Why don't you go back to sleep, Dean?" Robin yawned. "I'll finish my watch."

"Oh, all right." Dean crawled back to his corner and flopped down. "Goodnight, gang."

In the light of the early morning, the three of them searched the camp again. No more chests or other signs of loot were found. As she promised, Robin opened the chest as they breakfasted on leftover venison.

It was mostly good jewelry, among a small collection of copper, silver, and a few gold coins. Dean was all for taking the whole thing, but Robin said no.

"That jewelry could be identified," she explained. "And no one will believe that we found it."

"I guess not," sighed Dean. "But can we take the money?"

"We may as well," conceded Robin.

"Here, I've a purse," said Elizabeth, pulling a small bag from her bodice.

"We'll split it among us," said Robin. "That way if one of us gets robbed, we've still got something."

"At least we're rich," chortled Dean.

"We've barely a few pounds," said Elizabeth, and then she smiled. "But we are more comfortable."

"Do you think we could stay in inns from now on?" Dean asked hopefully.

Robin looked at Elizabeth, who nodded. Dean cheered.

"We'd better get hustling," Robin said picking up the two big bags. "People are a lot braver by daylight, and I don't feel like fighting those bandits again."

"Me neither!" Dean grabbed one of the bags from his sister and they were off.

Chapter Nine

The three had barely been on the road for an hour when they crested the hills that overlooked the village of Charing Vale.

"That was fast," said Dean.

Robin nodded. "I keep forgetting how close together everything in England is."

Charing Vale was a small village nestled in a little valley that opened onto the sea. The green hills rose sharply around the hamlet from the rocky beach. Two main roads went through Charing Vale, the one from inland, which ended there, and one that followed the coast. About half of town's inhabitants raised sheep on the surrounding hills. The other half of the populace made their livings as weavers, fishermen and other assorted tradesmen.

The town looked much the same as the other villages, with the houses in the main part of the village built narrow and close together. Their church was not the same gothic edifice other towns boasted. This was a square building with a small tower, built entirely of rough stone and with a shingled roof. Robin guessed correctly that the church had been built fairly recently, and by what would later be called a Puritan. What had become of the other village church, which had surely been there, Robin never found out.

It was market day and the people from all over the lonely coastland filled the center square of the village to buy and sell their wares. Robin smiled. Market day would mean that the inn was busy, and hopefully, the innkeeper would be interested in some extra help.

They found the inn near the center square of the village. It was built just like the other town buildings, except it was wider and stood apart from its neighbors. On the side closest to the center square was a flower garden that had once been neat and well kept, but now ran wild. Behind the house, the stable could be seen, with another neatly laid out garden, this time with vegetables, that had also been left to grow as it willed. Chickens scratched among the plants with a half-hearted air. The inn seemed deserted.

"That's strange," muttered Robin. She looked at the sign bearing the picture of a white bear. "The White Bear. This must be it."

"It doesn't seem to be doing so good," observed Dean.

Elizabeth shrugged. "They did say at the market it was the only inn in the vale."

"Then something fishy is going on," sighed Robin.

She pounded on the closed front door, braced for action. There was silence within. Robin pounded again.

"Anybody there?" she called.

A window opened above, and a thin, pinched-looking woman poked her head out.

"Be off with you!" she called. "Don't you know the inn is closed?"

"They didn't tell us that at the market," returned Robin. "We're looking for Master John Miller, the cousin of Mistress Anne Ford. She told us we could find him here, as the innkeeper."

The woman sighed. "Wait a moment. I'll come down."

She withdrew her head, and in a couple minutes, the door opened, and she admitted the three travelers into the gloomy best room.

"I am Mistress Mary Whiteford," the woman said. "Master Miller is my uncle. He has been ill since last spring. I'm the only relation he has living near him, so it has fallen on me to nurse him. I've a husband and children of my own to take care of. It's been all I could do to keep care of them and Uncle. That's why the inn is closed. You must have come from some distance not to have heard. It's been closed since the snow melted."

"We have come some way," Robin replied. "We're looking for work, and Mistress Ford suggested we come here to work for your uncle."

"That was kind of Cousin Anne, no doubt. But there's no work to be had. Uncle is better, but he is not well enough to open the inn again. It would be a mercy if he could. He hasn't much left to live on, and my husband is a poor man."

"We could open the inn and run it for him," volunteered Dean.

"Mary?" called an older voice. It quavered but had plenty of power left in it. "Mary? What visitors are there?"

"Two young men and a young woman." Mistress Whiteford crossed to the bottom of the stairway and called up. "Cousin Anne sent them to work for you."

"Work?" returned the voice with rising enthusiasm. "Do you mean re-open the inn? Send them up! Hurry! Send them up now!"

"Peace, Uncle!" Mistress Whiteford cried. "Don't excite yourself. You'll only make yourself sick again. I'll send them up if you promise to rest quietly."

"As you wish," sighed the voice.

With Mistress Whiteford's instructions not to excite the old man, Robin, Dean and Elizabeth filed into the bedroom occupied by Master John Miller. It was apparent that as a youth, he had been a formidable character. Age had ravaged his long frame, leaving it withered and gaunt. Still, out of the ancient face peered two bright eyes that darted everywhere and missed little.

"So, my good Cousin Anne sent you," he said. "What are your names?"

"I am Robert Parker, and this is my brother Richard Parker," said Robin. "But I am called Robin, and he, Dean. This is our cousin, Elizabeth Wynford."

"Can you work in an inn?" The old man watched them.

"Mistress Ford seemed pleased," Robin replied.

"Then why are you not still in her service?"

Robin smiled. "Let's just say it seemed expedient to leave in light of local politics."

The old man laughed. "Someone wanted you hanged, did they?"

"We were wrongly accused, sir," Robin said urgently.

"Oh, I believe you," chuckled Master Miller. "Cousin Anne wouldn't have sent you to me if she did not know you to be honest. Nor would you have known to ask for me if she hadn't told you to. But back to this matter of re-opening the inn." Master Miller coughed, then held his chest. "My heart, you know. I haven't been able to get out of bed since it first started, just as the snow melted last spring." He smiled weakly. "It seems such a strange thing, not to be able to get around, big healthy fellow, as I've always been. There's a lot to be done. The rooms must be swept and aired out, the gardens tended to. I expect the ale's gone bad. That should be the first thing to tend to, I imagine. Then we'll need fresh straw and oats in the stable, and flour and other staples to feed the guests. I can tell you who to go to, or Mary can. How do you brew the ale? In the way that Cousin Anne does? Very good. Then tend to that immediately. We'll open in two weeks."

"Two weeks?" asked Mistress Whiteford, entering the room with a bowl of soup. "How? All the supplies must be bought, and I don't suppose you've given a thought to how you're going to pay for it. You can barely afford to feed yourself, let alone three other people."

Master Miller looked so deflated that Robin felt compelled to speak.

"Good sir, if you will not take it amiss, we have a little money ourselves," she said. "We could purchase what's needed, and once the inn's running, you could pay us back out of the profits."

"Borrowing is not a good idea," snorted the old man. But need and interest in maintaining his chosen livelihood won out. "Well, I suppose I might. Not that I like this type of arrangement. But maybe it will push you three into working harder. The more money the inn makes, the sooner you will be repaid." He mulled over this new thought. "Yes. Yes. This could be quite satisfactory. Mary, go prepare the chambers. And you, young woman, Elizabeth, is it?"

"Yes, sir."

"How are you at nursing?"

"Well enough, sir. I spent some months nursing my grandmother before she died. She said I brought her a great deal of comfort."

Master Miller smiled with surprising warmth. "Yes, my child, I'm sure you did. And you'll help me back to health. Mary, when you're done with the chambers, go back to your children and stay there. I don't care to deprive them of their mother any longer."

"Yes, Uncle," Mistress Whiteford sighed, torn between her desire to be free of her patient, and her basic distrust of the newcomers.

Mistress Whiteford stayed long enough to make sure Elizabeth knew what she was doing, and to have her brains picked by Robin, who, once committed, was determined to make a success of the venture.

It was barely noon when Robin left the inn to purchase the barley and hops needed to get the ale brewed. Because of the time needed to ferment, that was the first step. She had to go some distance, however, to find the farmer Master Miller insisted she go to. Adding to the difficulty was the handcart she pulled after her. The farm was in the next valley over, and as Robin went down the steep slope, the cart banged against the backs of her legs.

The farm lay off the small road, surrounded by green pastureland dotted with sheep. Robin followed the small path about half a mile to the farmhouse.

"Is anyone here?" she called out, startling the chickens.

A middle-aged woman appeared from the house.

"Yes?" she asked, slowly. "And who are you?"

"I am called Robin Parker. Master John Miller sent me to purchase hops and barley from you. He insisted I go to no other."

"Well, it's a fine thing we have his recommendation. But isn't he too ill yet to reopen the inn?"

"Yes. My brother and I have come to work for him as a kindness to his cousin. We're doing the work until he is well enough."

"That's a mercy to him." The woman turned towards the fields. "James!"

James, or rather, Master Ashley, appeared within minutes. He was a stocky man, somewhat browned by the sun. Even though it was a cool day, perspiration stained his shirt. He, too, was a little suspicious of Robin until she explained. Robin wondered what was behind it but declined to ask. The couple was friendly enough, even hospitable, as they carried on their business.

The Ashleys had numerous children, ranging in age from infancy to fifteen. Robin counted at least seven. Mistress Ashley insisted on sharing their lunch with Robin. After they'd eaten, Master Ashley loaded the sacks of barley and hops onto the handcart. Then the oldest boy, a sturdy youth of thirteen, was instructed to help Robin up the hill with the cart.

With the boy's help, Robin made good time. As they reached the top, Robin turned to thank him.

"I don't dare go further," he said suddenly.

"Why?" Robin began, but to no avail, as the boy promptly turned away and ran off toward his farm.

Puzzled, Robin concentrated on maneuvering the handcart downhill. Near the bottom, a group of young men, they appeared to be in their late teens, joined her.

"You're new here." observed a dark-haired youth, his face scarred by acne or smallpox or both.

"Yes." Robin nodded. There was something not quite friendly about this group. "I am called Robin Parker."

"Ah. I am Samuel." The dark-haired one indicated his companions as he spoke. "This is Robert, Edward, Richard, Charles, and John."

"It's a pleasure to meet you, sirs." Robin nodded at them as they all walked.

"You haven't much beard," observed Edward happily, his own beard not being much to speak of.

"Uh, no," Robin replied.

"Yet you're so tall," said Samuel.

Robin shrugged. But before she could start her story, she was interrupted.

"What's in the sack?" asked John.

"Barley and hops," Robin answered.

"To sell?" asked John.

"No. I've just bought them. I'm bringing them to the inn."

"The inn?" cried Samuel in delight. The attitude of the boys changed immediately for the better. "It's reopening? Hurrah!"

"You'll have to wait a couple weeks. The ale's got to be brewed first." Robin smiled.

"God speed you on your way!" Samuel said. "Better still

we shall help. This vale has been too long without a decent tankard of ale."

Robin was glad enough of the help, although somewhat suspicious of the boys. But their motives were indeed centered on the ale. They arrived at the inn in record time, with the barley and hops in excellent shape. Robin thanked them and sent them off in high spirits. After taking a deep breath, she turned to the inn and the next step.

Of course, everything had to be discussed with Master Miller, but Robin didn't mind. There was something about the old man that caught her fancy. She sat up late in the evening with him, discussing the inn, at first, then other matters. The man was ignorant, but only because of the circumstances of his birth. Even at an age when many elderly people have no intention of learning anything, John Miller was eager for instruction and knowledge. Robin thought he would have made a fine scientist, had he the education available.

The next day was the Sabbath. The pastor of the village was a youngish man, approximately in his late twenties, with a mild demeanor and an educated speaking style.

Robin had taken one look at the communion table in the center of the church and guessed at his Puritan leanings. Between that and his black clothes and the way he launched into the service with almost no ceremony at all, Robin worried that she wouldn't get along with this fellow any better than she had Pastor Middleton, back in Downleigh.

But Pastor Layton appeared to be cut from different cloth. He did not speak down to his congregation, nor did his sermon go over their heads. He challenged without condemning. Although the other villagers looked suspiciously at Robin, Elizabeth, and Dean, Pastor Layton did not.

After the service, he held them in the doorway of the church. It was pouring down rain outside. He gazed at Robin strangely.

"Greetings," he said, shaking Robin and Dean's hands. "You are new in our village. Mistress Mary Whiteford told me of your arrival yesterday."

"That was kind of her," Robin replied.

"Well, your kindness in caring for her uncle is not to be overlooked." The pastor smiled. "I am Pastor William Layton. If you would be so kind as to tell Master Miller, I shall call on him this afternoon, as usual."

"We'll do that." Robin smiled awkwardly and shifted. Aside from the recent bad experience, the suspicion of the other villagers made her rather suspicious herself.

Back at the inn, they relaxed in the inn's best room next to a roaring fire.

"There's something strange about this place," grumbled Dean. "People don't like us already."

"They just don't trust us yet," replied Robin. "We're new here."

"That's not quite right," said Elizabeth. "True, they don't trust us, but it's not because we're strangers. There's something wrong in the village. People are afraid. There must be a band of highwaymen or other evil bandits in the county. Didn't you see that almost no young girls were at church? At least none that were not young children or mothers. Certainly, no comely ones."

"You mean the people are hiding their women?" Robin mused over this. "Hm. I wonder why."

"As I said, highwaymen," Elizabeth replied.

"Then why suspect us?" Robin returned. "We're obviously not highwaymen."

"True," Elizabeth conceded.

"Well, whatever the problem is," said Dean. "Maybe we'd better keep Elizabeth under wraps. I mean, if there's some sort of danger."

"You may have a point, Dean," Robin sighed and looked at Elizabeth.

She smiled. "I'll have enough to do here, don't worry. As a matter of fact, I do believe our master has woken."

Pastor Layton arrived carrying two books just as the bell in the church was tolling three o'clock. Elizabeth had Robin show him up to Master Miller's room, then prevailed on Dean to help her bring up food and drink for the guest and the invalid. As soon as he saw his visitor, Master Miller started struggling to a sitting position.

"Hold on, now," Robin scolded. "Let me help you."

"I don't want help," protested the old man.

"I know," Robin replied, adjusting the pillows. "But if you don't ease into more activity, you're only going to make yourself sick again. There, the pillows are fixed. Now, sit up slowly. I'll let you do it on your own this time."

Grumbling, Master Miller slowly pushed himself up. Robin slid her arms around his chest and pulled him back against the pillows.

Well, Pastor," Master Miller smiled. "What have we got today?"

"More of the same, I'm afraid," replied Pastor Layton. "It does take so long for things to get out here in the country. I did get one special item from my bishop. It's a pamphlet from one of John Donne's sermons. They were just published about two years ago. My bishop says they make excellent reading and are good for study. He'll send me the volumes as he can procure them. But I think I shall have to ask His Lordship for them. It costs far too much to send them, and I doubt my bishop will visit the vale any too soon. There's just too much going on, with the Parliament's militia and all."

"And your bishop is calling for it as strongly as My Lord, the Earl?" Master Miller grinned.

"Of course," replied the pastor.

"If he values his neck and his post, that is."

Pastor Layton laughed. "Perhaps. I know my bishop to be a most sincere man. But come, I know you are just jesting with me."

"I am?" Master Miller's eyes twinkled, so full of the challenge that Robin was hard-pressed to tell if the man had been joking with the pastor or not.

"Yes, you are. You are as staunch a supporter of the Parliament as ever lived in this valley. But I also know you will say anything to get a good debate going." The pastor smiled at Master Miller with genuine fondness. "Unfortunately, today I am somewhat out of temper for it. Young Master William Cowly was exceptionally vocal during his baptism. I have already read the sermon and will leave it for you to read at your leisure. Then next Sabbath we can argue it."

"That sounds good."

Master Miller nodded. "And what other books do you have for me?"

"Just the Donne poems and the Shakespeare."

"Shakespeare?" asked Dean, appearing in the doorway.

He carried five bowls, spoons, and some cloths. Elizabeth came in behind him, carrying a large black pot, and a tray loaded with bread, cheese, two pitchers, and a roasted chicken. Robin got up and shifted a small chest around to make a table with the tray.

"Will you dine with us, Pastor?" Elizabeth asked. "I'm afraid the cheese is still green. We only arrived Friday. I'm surprised the cow would milk. But she did, and I made the cheese yesterday. We've no ale, either, but the water is quite good."

"Considering the circumstances, you've laid before me quite a splendid feast, indeed." Pastor Layton smiled. "I shall be glad to share it with you. But first, let us thank Our Father in Heaven for His goodness in giving it to us."

Everyone bowed their heads as Pastor Layton made a good long prayer, giving thanks for a great many things besides the food. Robin's stomach gurgled as the "Amen" was said, and Dean most irreverently watched the chicken. But before he could eat, he had to run downstairs to fetch the tankards he had forgotten. Elizabeth busied herself serving the pastor, while Robin prepared Master Miller's bowl, taking care to give him small portions and only the leanest bits of the chicken.

"No cheese?" he complained, as he received his bowl.

Robin tucked a cloth under his chin. "No. You know why not."

"Why not?" asked Pastor Layton, as the old man snorted.

"Because cheese is full of the bad humours that hurt his heart," Robin replied.

"I've never heard that," replied the pastor.

"My father held it to be true," said Robin hesitantly. "He was most skilled in herbs and medicines."

"Your father?" Pastor Layton looked as though he was trying to make sense of something exceedingly difficult. "Perhaps you are related. Forgive me, Master Robin. You remind me of a lady I knew when I was a student in Oxford. She, too, was very skilled in the healing arts. Lady Eleanor of Hawkesland. Her husband was the Earl, Lord James Haverfield."

Robin shrugged. "Never heard of them."

"You are very like her in speech and manner. Even as I look at you, I see how your faces seem much the same."

"Well..." Robin paused. Her Ladyship could have been an ancestor, but it would hardly do to say so. "If Her Ladyship is a relative, she's a distant one. Anyway, Master John's heart is so weak, we have to be careful of what he eats."

The pastor mused over that bit of information, while Elizabeth rolled her eyes behind his back. Robin had insisted that she not give Master Miller any salt, instead directing Elizabeth to feed him garlic and onions. Elizabeth thought the whole idea silly. Salt was an important staple to her. How were they to preserve any meat without it? They'd need the meat for the coming winter.

Then there was the prohibition on cheese, which Robin said was naturally loaded with salt and bad fats. Master Miller was also forbidden to drink whole milk. Robin had Elizabeth skim the cream very carefully from the top, first. Elizabeth didn't think much of Robin's strange ideas but conceded because she couldn't argue against them.

Dean appeared with the tankards, and they all fell to the meal.

"Hey, books," Dean observed as he collected the pastor's bowl.

"Yes." Pastor Layton smiled. "The poetry of John Donne and the works of William Shakespeare."

"Shakespeare?" Dean asked delightedly. "Can I look?"

"Certainly." Pastor Layton handed him the book, which was quite large.

Dean opened the cover and whistled low under his breath. "Wow. A real First Folio."

"I wasn't aware there were any others." Pastor Layton looked puzzled.

"Oh." Dean caught Robin's warning glare. "Well, um. Maybe there aren't. Anyway, this is pretty bitchen."

"I'm glad you like it," replied the pastor. "Do you read much?"

"Only when I have to." Dean grinned. "Well, not really. I like Shakespeare." He turned a few pages. "Woh. This is hard to read."

"Is it?" Robin came over and took the book from him. The type was in that difficult old English style with all the s's looking like fs. The language was not translated. "That's interesting."

"What is?" asked Dean.

"Oh, nothing," Robin replied. "I'll tell you later. In the

meantime, the pastor's time is valuable, and we should let him spend it with Master Miller."

She returned the book to the pastor.

"You don't all have to leave," grumbled Master Miller.

"I'd best clear away these dishes," said Elizabeth.

Dean jumped up. "I'll help."

Master Miller and Pastor Layton both gave him an odd look as he filled the tray and picked it up. Elizabeth smiled indulgently.

In a few seconds, Elizabeth cleared the room of dishes and Dean. The afternoon whiled away peacefully. Robin listened as the two men discoursed, occasionally interjecting a comment here and there. The local baron, one Lord Roger Featherton had sponsored Pastor Layton's excellent education. The pastor was great friends with Master Miller, who had not had the same opportunity for an education. But instead of begrudging it of the pastor, Master Miller took advantage of it, receiving the pastor's instruction gladly.

Of course, despite being uneducated, Master Miller could frame an argument in the best academic style. Robin had to stop herself from laughing when Pastor Layton was forced to concede to Master Miller's better logic. Then she found herself drawn into an argument. She never noticed that Dean and Elizabeth did not return.

All too soon, it seemed, the village clock tower tolled the hour of five o'clock, and Pastor Layton stood and stretched.

"I must take my leave," he said. "My wife has surely made my supper and will be most distressed if I'm not there to eat it. Good Master Parker, you will have to continue joining our weekly discourses."

"Thank you, sir." Robin smiled.

"And bring Marlowe's 'Passionate Shepherd' next week," said Master Miller. "We'll see how Donne stacks up to it."

"How about Raleigh, also?" asked Robin. "If you have it. Since 'The Bait' is in reply to Marlowe, it's only fair to compare it to another reply."

"Raleigh was no poet," snorted Master Miller. "A Godless man."

"So was Marlowe," Robin shot back.

"I'll leave you two to continue the debate." Pastor Layton cut in, laughing.

Robin left to show him out. She finally noticed that Dean and Elizabeth had disappeared. But her mind was too full of Bait and Fleas and pleasant discourse to care where her brother was.

The next day, while Dean cleaned out the stables, Robin turned to the vegetable garden. Supplies were low, and while they still had quite a bit of money, it wouldn't last forever. Robin decided to see what she could salvage.

She harvested a good crop of cabbages, as well as carrots. She was pulling up onions when shadows fell across the garden. She looked up to see the six young men from two days before gathered around her.

"Hello," she said, sitting back on her haunches.

"Not brewing any ale today?" asked Samuel.

"This afternoon," Robin replied. "We figure the inn should be open in about two weeks."

"Should we tell him about..." started Richard, but the others shushed him.

"About what?" asked Robin. She stood.

"About, well," Samuel hedged, then shrugged. "There's another inn two vales to the north of here. They've been doing very well since Master Miller's illness. The owner won't like it that this inn has re-opened. But we don't mind."

"Don't like traveling that far, huh?" Robin grinned.

"That, and the innkeeper charges too much for bad ale," said John.

"Too bad for him, then," Robin returned. "My brother, cousin, and I brew very good ale, and a penny a tankard isn't too much, is it?"

The boys cheered. Elizabeth came outside from the kitchen.

"Robin, where's Dean?" she asked.

"In the stable," Robin replied.

Elizabeth left. The boys stared after her.

"Robert," hissed Edward. "Warn them."

Robert looked at Samuel, who nodded.

"They're not his spies," Samuel said, derisively stressing the "his." "She'd be with him, if they were, and they wouldn't be opening the inn."

"Who are we talking about?" Robin asked.

"Master Thomas Blount," replied Robert. "He's Lord Roger Featherton's steward, and a more crooked man never walked the earth. You'd better keep your cousin hidden. Any pretty creature he sees is soon taken away to be a lady in waiting for My Lady Featherton, or so he says. But most have returned beaten and carrying his bastards."

"Not exactly a nice person," Robin replied. "I suppose anyone new here is probably one of his spies."

"Many times," said Samuel. "We have to always be cautious. Worse still, there are those of our neighbors who will not refuse payment from him for information. The wise farmer in this vale only leaves his farm for market day, and then does not bring his best goods. Master Blount collects the taxes and is not afraid to collect more than his due if he thinks he can get it."

"Can't someone complain to Lord Roger?" Robin asked.

"How?" snorted Charles. "He's forever with the Earl, My Lord of Essex."

"Besides, we have," said Samuel. "Or one of the braver villagers did. Master Blount simply bought some false witnesses, and the other man was put in the stocks."

"His men wrecked my father's grain bin," John complained. "Then Master Blount demanded more money to ensure it wouldn't happen again."

Robin sighed.

"Protection money, pimping, his men control several gambling rackets," Robin told Dean and Elizabeth that evening at supper. "I swear this guy makes the Mafia sound like nice guys."

"The Mafia?" Elizabeth asked.

"A bunch of organized criminals, and they are really rotten fellows," Robin explained.

"So that's where all the girls are," said Dean.

"And Elizabeth should be too," Robin added. "If it isn't too late. Apparently, he's got spies all over."

"I'd like to see him try to take Elizabeth away," Dean threatened.

"Dean, here we can't afford to play any modern tricks," Robin warned.

"Well, there's other ways." Dean shrugged.

"We'll see," grumbled Robin.

Chapter Ten

Robin settled the tap in place in the bunghole and studied the cask in front of her. Her eyes met Dean's, Elizabeth's and Master Miller's, each in turn.

"This is it," she said. "If this isn't any good, we don't open tonight, and we're going to have a lot of angry villagers on our hands."

"So quit with the suspense!" Dean bounced impatiently. "Open the damn thing. Here, I'll do it."

"Master Miller should," said Elizabeth.

Robin looked over the old man. He was improving. He walked around a little as Robin let him, and Dean had taken to carrying him downstairs during the days so he could observe and talk with Elizabeth, or whoever was available.

"I don't know," said Robin. "You've been doing very well, but we don't want any overexertion to bring on another attack."

Master Miller snorted. "I'm not..." He sighed. "Perhaps I am that frail."

"I'm afraid so," said Robin. "But at least you're still alive, and not in any pain."

"I guess. Well, Master Robin, I delegate the responsibility

to you. But do be quick about it. We don't want the suspense straining my poor heart."

Robin smiled as she saw Master Miller wink at Dean. She took the tankard from Elizabeth and opened the tap. The dark brown liquid poured from the spigot and foamed in the tankard. After shutting the tap, Robin turned and handed the tankard to Master Miller.

"You get the first taste," she said. "But one sip only!"

The others groaned. Robin remained firm. Master Miller sighed and lifted the tankard to his lips. He took his time evaluating the mouthful.

"Well?" asked Dean.

Master Miller swallowed. "We open tonight with the best ale in the shire!"

"Hot damn!" yelped Dean. He grabbed a tankard.

Robin and Elizabeth both let out little cheers. Robin stopped long enough to prevent Master Miller from getting another taste of the ale.

"Oh, Robin," Elizabeth pleaded on his behalf.

"You guys just don't understand, do you?" Robin sighed.

"Please?" asked Elizabeth. Master Miller looked woebegone. "Just one more sip?"

Robin turned to the old man. "Do you promise, just one?"

"My solemn word, just one sip." Master Miller smiled.

Robin nodded. Master Miller put his lips to the rim and began drinking. And drinking. He did not stop until he had drained the tankard. Robin glared at him.

"You didn't say how long a sip." Master Miller righteously wiped his mouth on his sleeve.

"You old fox." Robin laughed. "You did that just as much to bug me as you did to get the ale."

Master Miller laughed also and refused to answer.

The opening that night was loud and merry. The market day prior, Robin had let it be known that it would occur. Her young friends spread the news most efficiently. They all were present, with their fathers, brothers, and other relatives. Edward, in particular, seemed to enjoy being there. Robin assumed it was his first time, and he was enjoying his new adult status.

One surprise was that Pastor Layton showed up. Upon his entrance, the room fell quiet. All eyes were upon him as he paid Elizabeth his penny and took a tankard of ale. He turned to face the room.

"There are those among my brothers who believe that drinking in a public place is a profane and licentious practice," he said slowly. "Perhaps it is. But I do not know that this is a good time to remind you of the evils of drunkenness. You'll know at least one tomorrow morning." There was quiet laughter. "St. Paul, in his letter to Timothy, strongly recommended that he take some wine for his stomach, so I guess one can infer that spirits are not to be condemned. I know good fellowship is to be commended, and I see plenty of that here. Also, by your patronage, an esteemed member of our parish is able to live off the fruits of his labor, as are his servants. And so, to your merrymaking, good sirs. Our Lord, Jesus Christ warns us against being glum believers. To the continued and improved health of our host, Master John Miller!"

With a happy roar, the crowd lifted their tankards then

drank. Master Miller, resting by the keg, wept openly. Robin sniffed back a couple tears, then went back to tapping. Dean sat by the money box, grinning, only leaving his post when someone pawed Elizabeth.

The next day, two horsemen stopped and asked for lodging. On market day, the following Friday, the inn's five guest rooms were full. There was continued speculation as to what Master Blount would do when he found out about the inn being open. But shortly after market day, word got about that Master Blount was being kept busy by His Lordship, which wasn't surprising, considering the political situation. In any case, the steward was safely in London attending his master.

Thanks to the news, the pall of tension in the vale lifted and Robin, Dean, and Elizabeth were quite pleased to find themselves welcomed by Master Miller's neighbors. As for the rest of the village, even the prettiest young women could sometimes be seen on the streets. The late spring days melted into the full warmth of summer weeks. There were periodic rumblings, for example in June, when the king, now exiled from London, asked for a military force from the local aristocracy. But most of the villagers seemed to feel that the dispute was among their betters and seldom worried themselves beyond the occasional wish that any fighting would happen elsewhere.

When the king raised his standard against the Parliament in August, that caught everybody's attention.

"Well, it'll be a war now," sighed Master Miller, the day the news arrived in the village. "It'll by the grace of God if it doesn't come here."

His health had improved considerably. Robin had him

working with her in the garden for exercise every day. But while he seemed hale and hearty, his full strength was long gone. He seldom complained, but Robin could tell he was not happy about the loss.

Still, the days and nights passed pleasantly. Dean noticed the slight change in the weather first.

"You know, it's getting colder in the mornings," he remarked at breakfast one day.

"Yeah, it has been," said Robin.

Elizabeth almost sniffed the air. "Autumn is coming."

"Come on, it's barely September," Dean said.

Robin sent him a warning glare, which he mercifully caught before Master Miller noticed anything odd about Dean's reaction. Robin took him aside later.

"Dean, I know it's just getting really hot at home this time of year, but most other places in the northern hemisphere, this is when the weather starts getting colder."

Dean tossed his head. "I knew that. I just spaced."

Robin rolled her eyes and walked off.

"I've been doing better!" he shouted after her.

He had been. It was almost as if he had finally melted into Seventeenth Century life.

The next day, however, the air was thick in the village, and it was not with the weather. The tension was back as word spread that Master Blount was back to oversee His Lordship's properties.

Business that night was slow. Thanks to the rumors in the market that morning, Robin had a strong feeling she knew who she would see at the inn that night, and he did not disappoint. It was about the middle of the evening when he entered the best room. He was portly, with a soiled shirt and open doublet. He had dark and greasy hair and he wore on his chin one of the fashionable pointed beards. He was accompanied by two large men, although neither were as big as Dean. Goons, Robin called them mentally.

The others made room for the three men willingly. Their stench was unbelievable. Their leader leered at Elizabeth.

"Ale for me and my friends," he ordered through gums half-filled with rotting teeth.

"One penny for each, first, sir," Elizabeth replied.

The man dug the coins out of his filthy purse and handed them to her.

"You've spirit, wench." He grinned at her. "More than the others."

"Thank you, sir." Elizabeth ran to get the tankards filled.

The men finished their ale quickly. As Elizabeth came to collect their tankards, the leader took her arm.

"I have need of a wench," he said. "I think you'll do quite nicely."

"Thank you, sir, but no." Elizabeth twisted free.

"I'm not asking," the man snarled.

He grabbed at her again, but she skittered back.

"She stays here." Dean appeared between the men and Elizabeth. He was calm and that, along with his size, made him very threatening.

The two men looked at their leader, their faces tentative, at best. Robin slid up next to Dean. The three men sized up the two, and the stares of the glowering crowd.

"Very well," said the leader.

He turned and left, his goons following.

"Well," said Robin trying to cover her intense relief. "I dare say we've just met the good Master Blount."

"Indeed, you have," said Master Shepwell, Samuel's father. "He's not happy about this place being open. His inn in the next vale has been almost empty all summer. The word has spread that you brew very good ale."

"We damn well better," said Dean.

"Master Blount is not a good man to have as an enemy," piped up one squeaky voice.

"We're not good enemies to have either," Robin replied brusquely and returned to the keg.

The next morning, Master Miller wanted to know what the commotion had been the night before.

"Master Thomas Blount wanted to take Elizabeth with him," Robin explained as she arranged the pillows on the bench in the kitchen. "None of us took too kindly to that."

"He didn't succeed, either." Master Miller smiled at Elizabeth, who was stirring porridge. Then he sighed. "He'll make trouble for us, that's for certain. We'll just have to weather the storm. There isn't much he can do. He's tried tangling with me before. He can't buy enough witnesses to do me in, or my inn, for that matter. The villagers will only be pushed so far. You've seen all the devices they have for getting around him. I've a few myself you haven't seen."

"I don't doubt it," said Robin. "Now you rest. If you're good, I'll let you take a walk in the town square today."

"Second childhood," grumbled the old man. "I'm not in the seventh age yet!"

"Not yet, you old Pantaloon," Robin teased. "But fast approaching it."

Master Miller snorted.

"What's all that about?" asked Dean.

"'As You Like It,'" Robin replied. "The 'All the world's a stage...' speech. Pastor Layton read it to us last Sunday. Remember?"

"That's right," said Dean. "Each man's acts being seven ages. What was the rest of that?"

"Come, my son, and heed my instruction," said Master Miller.

Robin laughed. Dean had built quite a rapport with Master Miller, as had they all in their own way. Dean's friendly ignorance gave Master Miller much room to show off his knowledge. Elizabeth tended to him like a dutiful daughter and often took his side against Robin's dietary rules. Robin stood up to the old man and challenged him, as he challenged her.

Of course, the debates were never quite as intense as they were Sunday afternoons when Pastor Layton stopped by. Robin sometimes worried that the intensity would strain Master Miller's heart. But he seemed invigorated by it all and not any the worse for it.

The Sunday following Master Blount's visit, there wasn't a debate. When Pastor Layton arrived, Master Miller sent Robin out of the room, saying he had business to do with the pastor that wasn't for young ears. Robin shrugged. Pastor Layton couldn't have been all that much older than she. But then she reflected Master Miller probably thought of her as being young because of her lack of a beard.

Robin wandered around downstairs of the inn, looking for Dean and Elizabeth. She couldn't find them but had to admit to herself, she hadn't looked that hard. She found herself wandering down the path that led to the ocean, which was only a couple hundred yards away.

It was a nice peaceful day. It had rained that morning. The sky filled again with clouds and mist. The trees along the path were just starting to fade, and here and there a leaf was turning red. They had been back in time for almost six months. Seventeenth Century life seemed to be the way she had always known life to be. The distant future of her birth seemed almost to be a dream.

Robin strolled along the beach, lost in her thoughts, wondering what Master Miller had looked like as a young man. She knew he had been married but had had no children. It seemed a pity he was so ill. He might have been a good lover.

Robin stopped, startled. Then she laughed. A sexual relationship with anyone in that time could have some serious consequences. Even without the emotional aspects, there were venereal diseases to consider, for which there were no cures at that time, or worse still, pregnancy. Robin wondered what the effects of time travel would be on an unborn child.

In the distance, she heard the church bell tolling five o'clock. She was surprised she had been away for so long and hurried back to the inn.

Robin's peace was shattered early the next day by the arrival of Master Blount. Dean had seen him coming down the road. He didn't wait for the steward to knock on the inn's door but hustled Elizabeth out to the stable with him. That left Robin to answer the knock and admit Master Blount. He insisted on talking to Master Miller, who met with him in the common room, along with Robin.

"As you may know," Master Blount wheezed. "I've come to the vale to collect the taxes."

"I'm not surprised," replied Master Miller coldly.

"I'll not take long with this, sir," Master Blount continued. "Your due is ten pounds."

"Ten pounds!" Master Miller almost jumped up in fury. Robin feared another attack. But Master Miller composed himself and seemed to be breathing normally. "Ten pounds. That is madness. I've barely made nine this year, what with my illness. And past years, I haven't paid over five."

"Nonetheless, that is your due." Master Blount pulled a paper from his grubby doublet. "It is decreed by His Lordship, Baron of this hundred, and sealed by his seal."

"Set in wax by your hand," grumbled Master Miller.

"Are you accusing me of improper conduct?" Master Blount pulled himself up in righteous indignation, but Robin could almost see the grin.

"I accuse no one. Ten pounds. Master Robin, pay the man."

"How?" Robin was astounded. She knew there wasn't much more than three pounds in the money box. She had pulled some to buy supplies on market day, then gave a complete accounting to Master Miller earlier that morning.

"I believe we have the money in the box. It just may take a little longer for me to pay you back."

"You owe us nothing, sir." Robin went and fetched the money, drawing the balance from her own precious reserves.

She took her time counting the pennies out, and the few shillings. There were a couple gold angels in the horde, but Robin wasn't about to let Master Blount have those. As soon as the steward had left, Robin checked Master Miller. He seemed all right, just angry.

"You'd better rest today," she said.

"I'll rest well enough when that whoreson is in his grave!" Master Miller yelled.

He slumped slightly on the bench, but it was clear he was just sulking and not in any pain. His breathing seemed normal, as well.

Robin sighed, then went out to the stable to tell Dean and Elizabeth that it was safe to go back into the house.

"Just watch him extra carefully," Robin told Elizabeth. "If he seems to be having any pain, or trouble breathing, call me."

But Master Miller seemed almost merry at lunch. Not that he had forgotten that morning's fleecing, but he had put it from his mind, as choler was not good for his heart. Robin rested a little easier. Later, she insisted he nap in the common room while they brewed the ale.

While they worked, Dean talked of all the ways he could get revenge on Master Blount. Most of them were childish pranks, at best, and reminded Robin of a B-rate teen flick she had seen. She kept checking on Master Miller all afternoon. He slept, his breathing deep and even.

They had just taken the wort off the fire to cool when they heard the thud in the best room. Dean and Robin tore into the room, with Elizabeth close behind. What Master Miller had been doing walking around, Robin had no time to wonder. He lay in a crumpled heap in the center of the floor.

There was no time for thought. Dean already had the old man lying on his back and tore open his shirt. Robin skidded to Dean's side, next to Master Miller's head. She glanced at Dean. He nodded. His hands were already in position over Master Miller's chest. Robin took a deep breath, forcing the man's head back, and clearing the mouth.

They worked for what seemed an eternity. Robin blew air into the aging lungs with all the force she could muster, while Dean tried to force the tired heart into beating again. Robin checked the pulse over and over again. Nothing. She blew some more. Her lungs ached. Perspiration dribbled down Dean's face. The form remained inert.

Robin checked the pulse one more time, then sat back shaking. Tears clouded her eyes, then spilled onto her face.

"Why are you stopping, damn it?" Dean yelled.

"It's no use, Dean," Robin sniffed.

"No, damn it! We've gotta keep trying. He's still there."

"It's too late." Robin softly touched his arm. "He's already growing cold."

Dean slowly sat back, forced to face what he did not want to. It wasn't real. It couldn't be. He jumped up and ran out.

"Dean!" Robin called after him.

"We must prepare him," Elizabeth said softly. "Come, help me set up the big table. We'll lay him out there. We'll use his linen sheet for the shroud. That would make him happy. Come. We'll prepare the body, then you must fetch the pastor. They'll have the mourning tonight, and we'll bury him tomorrow. It's a good thing the weather's so cold. He won't smell so fast. Come, Robin."

Elizabeth gently pulled Robin up. Her soft chatter was soothing, and the ensuing action eased the shock and the pain.

"But Dean..." Robin protested weakly.

"He needs to be alone," said Elizabeth. "I'll go find him in a bit."

"It'll be dark soon."

They set up the table.

"I'll take a lantern. Go fetch the sheet."

Robin obeyed. When she returned, Elizabeth had her spread the sheet on the table. Together they lifted the corpse, then wound the sheet neatly around it, knotting the ends.

"That's well done." Elizabeth smiled briefly. "Now go fetch Pastor Layton. I'll find Dean."

Robin stumbled out into the growing mist.

Mistress Layton opened the door and saw at once something was wrong.

"William!" she called, leading Robin into the house.

Pastor Layton was there in seconds.

"There is trouble," he observed.

Robin nodded. "Master Miller, he had another attack this afternoon. He's..." She couldn't say it.

Pastor Layton nodded. "Let's hope and pray God had mercy on his soul."

"Elizabeth said for you to come," Robin sniffed back the tears.

"Of course. Let me get my cloak."

"I'll have the boy send some supper over," said Mistress Layton.

"Thank you, my dear. I'm afraid I might be late."

"You stay as long as you are needed. I'll wait for you."

Robin turned to the door. Pastor Layton followed. The inn was empty except for the eerie presence of the corpse.

"Dean ran off," Robin said with much agitation.

"You loved the old man, didn't you?" asked the pastor.

"Yes, very much," Robin choked. "He was like my father."

"Then why don't you shed tears for him?"

"Because I'm a man." Or supposed to be one, Robin thought.

"Since when do men not weep for a good man?"

Robin turned. Within seconds the tears were released, and Robin crumpled onto a bench and sobbed. Years of loneliness and pain flowed out as Robin shed the tears that even as a woman, she had denied herself.

Elizabeth had hastily lit a lantern and hurried down the path to the beach. Dean had spoken often of his love of the ocean. He would be there, if anywhere.

She had buried her own grief in her concern for the others. There was time for mourning, and she would weep then. Someone had to stay level-headed to see that the funeral was properly arranged. Of course, there was her anger at that thief, Death, who had robbed her of yet another good friend. But others had robbed her, too, and would have given her over to Death. But no, there was no point in dwelling on that.

She found Dean on the beach, viciously tossing rocks into the waves, whose roar masked the sound of her steps. The fading light of the sun caught the tears on his cheeks.

"Oh, crud," he sniffed as she came up. "You would have to catch me blubbering."

"Blubbering? You're weeping for a good man. What shame is there in that?" Elizabeth held up the lantern so that he could see her.

"Where I come from... Well, I guess there isn't really. But guys just don't cry back home."

"And you do."

Dean wiped his cheek with the back of his hand. "Not around any of my friends."

"They don't seem very good friends to me."

"Yeah, well, they're all I got." He stopped and looked at her. "Except you."

"And Robin."

"She's my sister."

Elizabeth nodded. "She's worried about you."

"It figures." Dean tossed another rock into the waves. "Why am I getting on her case? It's not like we didn't try. Hell, she was right. He was getting cold right under my hands. I've never had anything happen to me like that in my life!"

"Never?"

"People don't die as easily back home, and when they do, it's in a hospital."

Elizabeth shivered, but Dean didn't quite notice.

"I never been so scared either," he continued. "And why Master Miller? Why not that bastard—"

Elizabeth put her hand on his arm. "Please, Dean. That's not for us to say. We must just accept it."

"Aren't you sad?"

"Very." Elizabeth suddenly sniffed, her own grief catching her unawares.

"Oh, Elizabeth." Dean gathered her into his arms.

Together they cried, holding each other, protecting each other from Death, the wind, and the mist closing in around them.

"I feel so empty," Dean whispered.

"I, too." Elizabeth looked up into his face, then reached up and found his lips with hers.

They held each other for a couple minutes longer, then Dean slowly steered Elizabeth up the beach to a small cave. She smiled when she saw it and led the way inside. Dean piled up some of the dried driftwood he'd put in the corner earlier that summer over the ashes of that previous Sunday's fire as Elizabeth lit a twig off the lantern. The fire caught quickly, the smoke sliding into the airy cavern above them.

The two just sat holding each other and watching the flames dance around the wood.

"I need this," Dean whispered after a while. "I don't feel so empty anymore. I don't think I ever did, at least not since you came along. Geez, that sounds corny."

"It sounds pretty." Elizabeth smiled and squeezed his hand.

"I swear, Elizabeth, sitting here like this with you, in some ways, there's nothing better. The world may be going to hell out there, but here I feel peaceful. I love you."

"I love you, Dean."

There was another long pause.

"We'd better get going," Dean said.

"Yes. Robin will wonder what happened to us."

"Yeah."

Reluctantly, they gathered themselves together and crawled out of their hiding place.

For Robin, there was no way to take refuge. But the young boys of the village gave her the most comfort. They showed up at the inn shortly after she stopped weeping, bearing lanterns and the supper sent by Mistress Layton. In the kitchen, she discovered the cooled wort.

"Oh no," she groaned. "This needs pitching."

"We'll help," volunteered Samuel. "Come on."

Pastor Layton smiled and suggested Robin find comfort in activity.

Dean and Elizabeth showed up an hour after sundown. At the same time, the villagers arrived to pay their respects. The visiting went on late, with many of them paying for the porter Robin offered freely.

"We'll not take the bread from your mouth," said Master Woolwich, one of the weavers. "That's already been done to-day."

Robin couldn't help but wonder at the way the news had spread about the exorbitant tax taken from the inn that morning. It was generally agreed that it had brought on Master Miller's final attack.

Robin yawned as the last guest left the inn. It wasn't particularly late, but Robin felt more than spent. Only Pastor Layton remained.

"You'd best get back to your wife," Robin told him.

"I've more important business, I'm afraid," he replied, then motioned at Dean and Elizabeth, as well. "Come with me."

They followed him to Master Miller's bedroom. Pastor Layton removed a panel from the headboard to reveal a hole in the wall. From it, he removed a metal box. He sat down on the bed, sighing before he opened the box.

"One sometimes wonders what signs a person may have had before death," the pastor said. "Last Sunday when he sent you out, Master Robin, he bade me make his will. Like many in this village, his fortunes were greater than anyone knew, to protect them from Master Blount's avarice. There are fifty guineas, give or take a shilling or two, in this box."

"So much?" Elizabeth gasped.

"A year's income for the inn," Robin said.

"He'd been saving it for a long time," Pastor Layton explained. "He didn't need much, being on his own, as he was. In any case, twenty guineas are to go to his niece, twenty to the church, and ten to you, plus the inn, the land it stands on, and all the livestock."

"To us?" Dean said in shock.

"He had a great regard for all three of you," replied Pastor Layton. "He said you were the most capable of running it. He didn't care to burden his niece with it. Here is the deed, made over to you."

"Terrific," grumbled Robin. "It's not that I'm not grateful. Oh, never mind. It's all for the better, I suppose."

"Guess we're kinda stuck, aren't we?" Dean chuckled.

"You said it." Robin noticed the Pastor's puzzled look. "My brother and I left our father to travel and seek out the world. We took our cousin with us because her father had died and had lost his land besides. We were hoping to establish her somewhere and continue with our travels. With the inn, she'll be in good shape."

"We don't have to leave her," said Dean.

"She can't run this place alone," Robin retorted. "We'll have to marry her off."

"Don't you think she should have some say in that?" Dean snarled.

"I'm sure she'll obey your wishes, as all virtuous women

do," said the pastor. "However, I wouldn't make any hasty decisions, nor would I let it be known too widely that you are searching for a husband for your cousin. Master Blount might find it too convenient. Marriage contracts are too easily made, and Master Blount can afford a lot of witnesses, for when he makes it and when he breaks it."

"I don't doubt it," grumbled Robin.

"Don't worry, Pastor," said Dean. "I'll see to it he keeps his hands off her."

Pastor Layton smiled. "If anyone can, it'll be you, and your brother's quick wits. Well, I must take my leave." He rose.

"I take it the funeral's tomorrow?" asked Robin.

"Indeed, yes, on the stroke of nine. We'll start the procession here. I don't favor such things, but the other townspeople seem to require it. I'll give the sermon in the churchyard."

"I'd best get chickens plucked," sighed Elizabeth.

"You rest," the pastor told her gently. "You've had a hard day. My wife is already seeing to tomorrow. You all should go straight to bed. You need sleep now more than anything. After tomorrow, you'll have an inn to keep running."

Robin showed the pastor out, then wearily took his advice. Dean was already snoring as she entered their room.

The next day Pastor Layton made a very short sermon, reminding the villagers that as Master Miller was, so would they be. But the brevity was largely due to the pouring rain. Robin didn't envy the gravediggers their wet job.

The funeral feast was put off until that evening. Mistress Layton and the other townswomen provided the food and drink. Elizabeth, having adjusted to having a kitchen all to herself, was perturbed to see it so crowded. But she acquiesced, allowing the townsfolk to pay their homage to a man they had long loved.

Robin was surprised that Master John Miller was so fondly remembered. His many good deeds were talked about for hours, and they were numerous. It was strange to see so many women in the best room. Usually, Elizabeth was the only obvious female there. But this night was a funeral, and there was some celebrating to do.

The crowd was far from somber. They'd done all their crying that day at the graveside. That evening was for happy remembrances and relief that they were not in Master Miller's place.

"Master Miller loved music and dancing," Samuel explained to Robin. "It's only fitting that we remember him that way."

Indeed, several people had brought pipes and drums. There was much singing. Robin, loosened by far too much ale, even joined in, as she could.

Despite the festivity, there were many curses leveled at Master Blount.

"I should like revenge," Robin confided to Samuel, very much in her cups. "I should like to get him back."

"Master Blount?"

"Who else?" Robin took a long pull on her latest tankard-full. "Murder's no good. It's too messy, and someone's bound to find out. Besides, if I kill him, his troubles are over. I'd rather make him live with something."

Samuel took a long pull and thought about it. "Maim him?"

"Too messy. We could get him in trouble with his boss."

"You'll need a lot of money to buy witnesses."

"I'll carve it in stone, Master Blount's a... That's it!" Robin knocked over Samuel's tankard as she slapped the table. "I'll get a gravestone for Master Miller, and I'll carve on it how Master Blount killed him."

Samuel gazed at the tankard, which, fortunately, had been emptied before it fell.

"My father does stonework," he offered, finally. "I'll send him to you first thing tomorrow."

"Okay. Do that." Robin hoisted her tankard to toast with Samuel then noticed his knocked over one. "Oops."

The two looked at each other and began to giggle.

Later, Robin staggered to bed, chuckling about her revenge on Master Blount. But she wasn't chuckling the next morning.

"Oh, shavings," she grumbled to Elizabeth, who had wakened her. "I need a Bloody Mary."

"A what?"

"Two ounces of vodka, tomato juice, a dash of Tabasco, three if you're hung." Robin winced as her stomach lurched. "You don't even know what any of that stuff is."

Elizabeth smiled. "You drank too much last night."

"You think?" Robin rolled over and pulled the blanket over her head.

"I've some hot porridge and some cabbage leaves downstairs for you."

"Cabbage leaves?"

"For your head." Elizabeth gently removed the blanket. "It's a good cure."

"About as good as anything besides aspirin, a Bloody Mary and time."

"Come along. The sun's been up two hours already."

Robin merely groaned and pulled the blanket back.

As if her headache weren't bad enough, Dean wasn't in the least hung and was in excellent spirits.

"I've only been hung once," he announced when Robin had finally staggered downstairs. "I was shooting tequila. Boy, I was sick then. That tequila crap is mean stuff."

Robin merely groaned as she bent over her porridge.

Elizabeth left to answer the knocking at the front door.

"No, no, come on in," she told the person who had knocked. "He's in the kitchen. This way."

With her was Master Shepwell. Robin glanced at him listlessly, then nibbled at a cabbage leaf.

"My son said you wished a gravestone to be made for Master Miller," said Master Shepwell.

"I did?" Robin grunted. Slowly memories from the night before slipped into place. "Uh, yeah. I guess I was feeling it pretty badly."

"Samuel isn't in much better shape," chuckled the farmer. "Do you still wish the stone?"

"Yeah, I guess I do," sighed Robin.

"It'd be nice," volunteered Dean. "What do we put on it?"

"I think a moral for Master Blount would be good," Elizabeth suggested.

"I agree," said Master Shepwell.

"But what?" mused Robin. "Wait, I think something's coming. Get me something to write with."

Elizabeth produced some charcoal and the back of a roasting tray, and the four of them went to work. One hour, and several revisions later, the inscription was set:

"Witness on this Stone before you stand

Read how Avarice killed an Honest Man

A greedy Taxman was the Bloke

And Master Miller's poor Heart was Broke

Forced to Pay more Twice he ow'd

The rest o' his Fortune on this Stone be Stow'd

John Miller

Died the 1st of October 1642

Aged 71 yrs

Cursed be he that moves this Stone or my Bones"

Master Shepwell copied the whole thing down with a quill pen and some ink on a piece of paper he had brought.

"There!" he sighed as he finished. He flourished the paper proudly. "I'm not the only stone cutter here, but I write the best, so I do the gravestones when they be needed."

"How much is all this going to cost?" Robin asked.

"It's not cheap, I'm afraid," Master Shepwell shook his head. "Maybe two pounds for the stone, three if you want a good one, then there's my labor to consider."

"Of course," Robin said quickly. "Five pounds for it all?"

The farmer looked startled. He hadn't planned on getting that much. Master Robin was known to drive a hard bargain.

"Yes, certainly," Master Shepwell stammered.

"You may have it in advance." Robin pulled a small bag from her belt. "Aside for some money which I withdrew for supplies, this is all the old man had to leave us, except for the inn and the property on which it stands, and the livestock. But we need those to live."

"Your love for him must have been great," said Master Shepwell.

Robin smiled. "It was. But I also don't want Master Blount to get any more of my late master's money than he already has."

"He may try," said Master Shepwell. "But I doubt he'll do it through the taxes for a while. My Lord Roger Featherton might find it a little strange that this inn was assessed twice in so short a time."

"We'll be ready," Dean said. "We've heard about his other tricks. It won't be easy to catch us napping."

"Easy, Dean," said Robin, still feeling the previous night's excess. "Why don't you show Master Shepwell out?"

The attack did not arrive that night. Robin doubted that Master Blount was waiting through any respect for the dead. Nor could she imagine Blount having the subtlety to wait and create a psychological advantage through tension. He probably just hadn't gotten around to it.

It was late the next night when the goons showed. The evening's business had been finished for a few hours, and the inn was quiet. Two of the guest rooms were filled, one with an official messenger of the Earl of Essex.

There were five men, large by local standards, one as tall as Robin, but no larger. Elizabeth heard them first, from her bed in the kitchen. They crashed through the street door. Elizabeth silently hurried up the second stairs and woke up Dean and Robin. The two heard the noise and Robin nodded.

The men were in the kitchen, throwing whatever food

they could find about. Two tore open Elizabeth's bed and tossed straw and ripped sheet everywhere. Dean ran out the back door and around the inn and locked the one kitchen door that led outside. Robin waited, hiding on the other side of the door leading to the best room.

When the men discovered they could not force the locked kitchen door, they started through the other. The doorway was narrow, and only one man could pass at a time. Dean had joined Robin by then and the two were ready on either side of the doorway.

As the first man passed through, Dean whirled around and landed his right fist square in the man's face. The man fell backwards into his companions, who tumbled into the kitchen. Robin grabbed the one man's feet and quickly dragged him, unconscious, into the best room. Elizabeth had the rope ready and tied the fellow.

At the same time, Dean's fists hammered into the next unfortunate. This man sighed as his chin cracked under a right cross and went out. Dean pulled him into the best room, as Robin tripped his friend and knocked him unconscious with a blow to the back of his neck.

The next two came out with swords drawn. The first tripped on his fallen comrade. Robin kicked the sword away, then dodged as he grabbed for her feet. He was up in an instant and faced off against her. She was taller, but he had more weight, and he decided to use it. He flew at her and his hands landed on her throat. Robin brought her arms between his and broke his grasp. She pulled back as he caught her shoulders and knee-jerked her. It hurt like hell, but it did not have the incapacitating effect her opponent expected. Stung, and angry, Robin charged the surprised man, pounding his belly with her fists, then kicking him where he had hit her. He was incapacitated.

Dean had an equally difficult time. It didn't matter to the swordsman that Dean was unarmed. Dean dodged, avoiding the jabs and slices coming at him. He knew he had to get in close to get the man but getting around the three feet of really sharp sword was not going to be easy.

Trenchers and tankards were all over the floor. Dean kicked a tankard under the swordsman's feet. He stumbled just enough to give Dean a chance to bend and throw rotting straw into the man's face. Under that cover Dean rushed him. He tackled the man, then got a good grip on the hilt as they fell. The swordsman had a better grip and hung on as the two rolled on the floor. Dean rolled on top, straddled the man, and banged the sword hand on the floor. The man's grip held as he struggled beneath Dean. Dean squeezed and banged the man's sword hand on the floor again. The grip broke. Dean threw the sword away and landed a fist in the man's face. He sighed and went out.

Behind Dean, one of the first three came to and stood up. In his hand was a knife. A whip lashed out and caught his wrist.

"I wouldn't do that," said the smooth educated voice of the Earl's messenger.

Robin staggered up straight.

"I'm sorry, sir, if your rest has been disturbed," she said breathing heavily.

"It looks like yours has been more disturbed than mine."

The messenger smiled as he surveyed the scene. "The two of you did this?"

"Well, they wrecked the place first," Robin said.

The messenger laughed. "Good for you. Why don't we get these men bound before you send for the sheriff?"

"Actually, I think he'll be here tomorrow, sir," Elizabeth said.

"Oh? Hm." The messenger thought. "I have heard of things like this going on in this village. I wonder if Master Blount has anything to do with it. He owns the inn two vales over. It's a nasty place. The ale's bad, the food is worse, and the rooms here are nice and clean."

"I'm glad we've got your good recommendation," said Robin.

"I'm glad to give it. I think I shall tarry here a while tomorrow to see what falls out. The Earl's business is not urgent, and he'd like to know about a dishonest steward."

"You're welcome to it, sir," Robin replied. "I'll not charge you for the room tonight since your rest was disturbed."

"You keep your money. This has been well worth it." The messenger yawned. "Well, good night. I'm going back to bed."

After Robin, Dean, and Elizabeth finished tying up the five men, they returned to bed also, with Elizabeth taking one of the guest rooms.

The next morning, Master Blount showed up promptly, his two personal goons in tow.

"Master Robin," he wheezed. "I understand you had some trouble here last night. I hope you understand that I am charged with keeping the peace here."

"Oh, it's been kept," Robin replied, allowing the steward to enter. "In fact, it's a good thing you're here. These five men need to be conducted to the local gaol."

She didn't smile outwardly, but the look on Master Blount's face as he saw his henchmen bound and gagged on the best room floor was even more satisfactory than she'd anticipated.

Better yet, he was prevented from making any untoward accusations by the presence of the Earl's messenger. There was little the steward could do but accept the situation as the local authority, so he had the five men escorted out, after hiring a cart and horse to transport the prisoners to the next town's gaol. Before he left, the Earl's messenger suggested that he would take it very much amiss if any more mischief occurred at his favorite inn. Master Blount departed, defeated.

Chapter Eleven

Donald Long sighed. The ale had gone sour again, and his flea bites had begun itching as well. Inns such as the one he was in, two vales north of Charing Vale, were the worst parts of time travel. Still, it would be worth it when he got Elizabeth. Then he would save what had originally been his experiment and show Roger up for the fool that he was before the Intelligenisa Board. Once Donald had accomplished that, he could finally collect his assets, particularly the gold and other valuables he'd hidden in the stash the Board didn't know about and get the hell out.

It had not been an easy summer. Finding the Parkers had not been difficult. He'd merely followed the directions he'd heard Mistress Ford give the Parkers as they'd left Downleigh. But he'd been delayed going after them by a week, and by the time he'd reached Charing Vale, Elizabeth had been as closely mewed up as the rest of the women in the village.

Getting the confidence of Master Thomas Blount had been no small feat, either. Fortunately, the extended trip up north had proved extremely valuable. However, on their return, Blount was furious when he found that Master Miller's inn was not only running but doing even better than it had before. Now, the old man was dead, Blount's squad of toughs defeated, and the Parkers were even more firmly ensconced.

Donald was reasonably certain this would be where he would finally get his hands on Elizabeth. It seemed unlikely the three would find yet another place to hide before they turned up in London later that coming winter. Donald blinked. It was difficult to remember that what was in his past had not yet happened for the Parkers and the girl. He shifted and scratched himself. The only part that was worth all this trouble was knowing how it would all fall out.

Outside the room, the floor creaked near the end of the hall. Blount was coming. Donald quickly reviewed his strategy. The next meeting would have to be handled carefully. Blount seemed ready to concede his loss and Donald couldn't afford that.

Blount entered the room and sank into the other chair without being invited.

"Do you want to hear the latest outrage, Master Warfield?" the fat steward whined to Donald. "They set up a tombstone over the old man's grave, accusing me of killing him! It isn't my fault if he couldn't bear paying his taxes. I agree it was a lot of money, but it's my due considering what his inn has robbed from my business."

Donald nodded sympathetically. "Are you prepared to act, then?"

"Act?" Blount shifted. "Act? What is there to do, I pray you? They've defeated my best men unarmed. I can't assess them anymore. And they never let that girl go anywhere without at least one of them. She's a froward lass. I don't see why she's caught your interest."

"Never mind that for the moment." Donald got up and began pacing. "Blount, we must put our heads together and outwit them. We must evaluate their strengths and their weaknesses and exploit the weaknesses."

"What weaknesses? Master Robin is as quick-witted as they come, as is Mistress Elizabeth."

Donald cut him off. "But consider, she always looks to Robin for direction."

"True, so does his brother."

"Ah, yes, Master Dean." Donald realized he was stroking his chin and abruptly stopped. "He's not nearly as quick-witted as his brother."

"He's no fool either, and he's as strong as three oxen."

"He can be, but I find his dependence on Robin a little more than touching." Donald smiled. "I think I do see a weakness we may exploit. We'll have to get rid of Master Robin."

Blount snorted. "How? We can't take him by force, and I don't dare risk outright murder."

"For heaven's sakes, we'll be far more subtle than that. No. Too many people might think an accident of Robin's a little too convenient." Not that Donald cared what happened to Blount. But he did have to keep the filthy weasel's confidence up. "Wait. Did you not tell me that the Earl's army is being called together for training and that you would need some men from this area?"

"Why, yes, I did." Blount all but began jumping and down. "Yes! That would be perfect! I was instructed by My Lord Featherton to choose the best men in his barony. I can get rid of some other troublemakers, too, at the same time. I wonder that I didn't think of it myself. With both Robin and Dean gone, there'll be ready access to the girl..."

Donald turned on him. "Not both! You may only conscript one male from each household."

"But..." Blount looked like he was about to cry.

"Patience. Once Robin is gone, we can take care of the other two. It's only a matter of time before certain things happen, and we'll have an excellent case for witchcraft."

"Witchcraft?" Blount laughed. "She's just a young thing, and besides, they're friends of the pastor. He'll be sure to testify for them. No one will doubt his word that they're not making contracts with the Devil."

"The pastor is the least of our worries. We'll arrange things so that it won't matter what he believes. Get enough hysteria in the village going, and they'll be hung before the pastor can say boo. Trust me. With Robin gone, it won't be long before Dean makes a mistake, and we'll have them. It's only a matter of time."

Blount looked confused. "A mistake?"

"Never you mind. You just go and see to it that Robin is conscripted. I'll see to the rest."

Blount wheezed off. Donald sighed in relief and went to the window for some fresh air.

Two days later the weather turned very cold. Robin shivered as she followed Elizabeth to Master Woolwich's house, near the end of the town.

"He'd better have that order ready," Elizabeth grumbled, quite chilled herself. "This is the second morning in a row there's been frost, and it won't get any warmer until next spring."

"We'll survive," Robin sighed.

"Hm!" Elizabeth snorted. "Of course, we'll survive. It's just that Master Woolwich promised that cloth over a week ago. I don't like being cold when I don't have to be."

Robin shrugged. "I've heard Blount's been making trouble for him."

"That's everyone's excuse. Master Blount hasn't been seen in the village since we ran him off."

Robin shrugged. Lax tradesmen were something Elizabeth knew and dealt with well. If her temper was a bit short, it was only because she did not relish the task. Master Woolwich was well known for producing the finest weaving in the vale. He was also known for taking his time to do it.

Elizabeth would have been more forgiving but for the cold weather suddenly upon them. No one at the inn had a cloak, and only Robin had a pair of gloves. Elizabeth had knit them the Friday before from wool she had purchased that day. She was still working on Dean's.

Robin knocked on the weaver's door. Master Woolwich admitted them.

"Ah." He smiled. "You are here for the cloth you ordered."

"I do hope it's ready," said Elizabeth as she and Robin entered the weaver's house. "You promised it over a week ago."

The weaver grinned apologetically. "I'm afraid I did, didn't I? But no matter. It's ready." He opened a chest standing next to the wall. "See? One of my finer efforts, if I don't mind saying so."

Elizabeth didn't reply, but went over the fabric carefully, measuring it against the length of her outstretched arm to her nose. Bored, Robin gazed out the front window.

"Hm," she said suddenly.

"What?" asked Master Woolwich, joining her.

"Master Roth's little boy came running down the street from the church," Robin said. "I wonder what's going on. He seemed awfully anxious."

"Who knows?" Master Woolwich waved it off. "We'll know about it soon enough. Are you satisfied, Mistress Wynford?"

"More or less," she answered. "This piece isn't as long as I asked, but it will do. I just don't care to pay for more fabric that I'm getting."

"We agreed four guineas for the lot," said Master Woolwich.

"We agreed for fifteen yards. There's only fourteen here."

Master Woolwich opened his mouth to argue but then saw Robin watching him.

"Well, I suppose you have a point," he said, suddenly sheepish. "Four pounds even?"

"Four pounds then." Elizabeth finally smiled, but it was a little tight. "Robin?"

Robin swaggered over and counted out the change. Four pounds was a lot of money, but they needed the cloaks desperately.

That night, the inn was filled with grumbling men.

"What more could the fiend want?" said Master Shepwell. "He's already bled us dry."

"I smell a plot," Master Whiteford said. "He's been much too quiet since our innkeepers defeated his men."

"He isn't that subtle," said Master Woolwich.

"But why call out the entire village and surrounding

farms?" asked Master Allsworth. "The steward has some trouble planned for us. You mark my words."

Robin was forced to agree, and while she didn't say so, she was worried. Master Blount was not that subtle. But missing the next day's noon gathering was out of the question.

The villagers gathered in the town's square well before the church bell rang the noon hour. As it did, Master Blount rode slowly up on a decrepit old horse, accompanied by his two goons, as usual, and followed by a youngish teenager wearing the livery of Lord Featherton.

"Herald!" Blount barked. "Read the proclamation."

The teen undid his scroll and cleared his throat.

"Let it be known that by the order of His Lordship, Roger Featherton, Baron of this county, one adult man from each household, to be chosen by his most faithful steward, Master Thomas Blount, shall be required to join the army of the Earl of Essex, and shall depart this day for training. His lordship also invites any willing young men to also join with their comrades in the service of the Earl and Almighty God."

"Fuck!" Dean grumbled, as the crowd grumbled around him.

"For once, I agree," Robin muttered.

"The men to be conscripted from Charing Vale are as follows," the herald continued. "Edward Skippington. Samuel Shepwell, Robert Farthingate, Robin Parker..."

"Fuck!" Robin gulped.

The herald continued reading but she did not hear of any of the other names.

"How am I going to get out of this one?" she squeaked.

Dean shrugged. "Better you than me."

Robin pulled Dean aside and his head down to her mouth. "Brother, dearest, this is the army? As in big on communal living? And I have a slight problem with living communally with men?"

"You do? Oh. Right."

Robin resisted the temptation to thunk Dean in the head.

"Robin," said Elizabeth, putting her hand on Robin's arm. "Maybe we can buy our way out of this. It'll cost a great deal, I'm sure. Master Blount has no great love for us. But maybe we can."

Robin's eyes lit up. "Great. The first ray of hope."

The herald had finished with his list of names. "All those who have been called shall come forward to be registered. Upon which they shall be dismissed for two hours to put their affairs in order and gather their weapons."

"Here goes nothing," Robin grumbled as she pushed her way up to Master Blount and the scribe who was doing the actual paperwork.

A few young men ahead of her bought their way out for thirty pounds apiece. Robin's hopes rose still further.

"So, Master Parker," wheezed Master Blount.

"I'm sure you're aware of how difficult it would be for me to leave my inn," Robin said as nicely as she could.

"I expect it is," agreed Master Blount. "Still, one must do one's duty."

"Perhaps if I were to offer my services in the form of money," Robin said.

"One hundred pounds," Blount said quickly.

"What!" Robin shrieked before she could stop it.

"It will cost you one hundred pounds to avoid conscription," Blount said calmly. "It's as simple as that."

"But those other guys got out for thirty," Robin gasped.

"So? It will cost you one hundred."

"Obviously, I don't have that much." Robin held onto her temper with both hands.

"What a pity. It appears you shall be joining us, then."

"What if I were to pay it off bit by bit, say three or four pounds a week."

"Out of the question. Scribe, register him."

Robin was reeling as she returned to the inn. Amazingly enough, Dean remained cool.

"Look, all you have to do is wait a few days, then ditch them," he explained.

"And the first place they'll look for me is here," Robin retorted. "I'll be caught and probably hung."

"No, you won't. We'll go home. Hell, we could take off now."

Robin swallowed, tempted. "What about Elizabeth?"

"We'll take another stab at re-adjustment." Dean turned to Elizabeth. "Won't we?"

Elizabeth nodded reluctantly. "Yes. We will."

Robin looked at her and shook her head. "That's not going to work, Dean. It's hardly fair to Elizabeth."

"But, Robin—"

"No buts. I'll have to go with them for now and then ditch. If we all try to take off, they'll catch us. I'll wait 'til they're not expecting it. When I get back, we'll just have to leave the inn, that's all. We can go to London, or something. Anyplace away from Essex." Robin paced. "I don't know when I'll get a chance to take off, so you guys sit tight and act as if you're planning on staying. Dean, you be extra careful. Keep that big trap of yours shut as much as possible. You really can't afford to get into trouble now."

Dean glared at her. "Robin, I'm not that stupid."

Robin softened. "I know. You've got a darned good head on your shoulders. But I can't help it. I'm going to be worried sick, no matter what. You take care now, okay?"

"Sure." Dean hugged her. "Don't worry. We'll be fine."

"Yeah." Robin turned to Elizabeth and hugged her. "You keep an eye on him and keep him out of trouble."

Elizabeth smiled warmly. "I will."

Robin took a deep breath, then the cloth and gloves that Elizabeth gave her, and left the inn.

Chapter Twelve

As Robin came into the marketplace, she was directed to stand with the other young men already there. Almost all of them were her young friends from the village. As usual, Samuel took charge.

The only exception was Edward Skippington. He stood apart from the others and listened to some final instructions from his father. His brother, John, joined the group after speaking with Master Blount.

It did not escape Robin's eye that Master Blount had chosen his most outspoken opponents in the village. She could see that it hadn't escaped the townspeople's notice, either. They stood about the square, staring sullenly at the little group of recruits.

At least Master Blount did not accompany them when they finally left. They were led by a middle-aged man named Master Strike. His enthusiasm was wanting. He marched them to a camp surrounded by forest, eight miles out of town.

Four groups of other young men, each from a different village, made up the camp. Each group kept to itself, Robin noticed with relief. She hoped it would stay that way. If worse came to worse, and the boys from Charing Vale caught on to her, she figured she might have half a chance of explaining her situation. As it was, she tried to remain a little aloof from her comrades.

They bedded down, each village group huddling close to its own fire. Some older men came around and distributed bread and cheese. Robin, disgusted with Samuel's efforts, took over building the fire. As she looked around, she smugly noted theirs burnt brighter than any of the others.

Later, after she slipped away to make a private pit stop, the quiet chill of the night and the brightness of the stars called her, and she paused, drinking in the peace. Then the sound of someone retching nearby startled her.

Going against her better judgment, Robin stepped through the brush. The sick person was young Edward. Concern took over and Robin went to him.

"Here, let me help," she said, announcing herself.

Edward was too sick to notice. Robin slid one hand under Edward's belly and held his forehead with the other. It didn't last long.

"Thanks," Edward gasped.

"You need some water," Robin returned and grabbed for the horn at Edward's belt.

He drew back. "That's a powder horn."

"Oh. Sorry." Robin noticed the two pistols stuck in Edward's belt for the first time.

Edward suddenly giggled. "It figures. How come when you make water, you don't bank it up against a tree like the other boys?"

Robin gaped. "What?"

"You pee like a woman, Mistress Robin."

"I take exception to that." Robin got a fistful of Edward's shirt.

"Oh, who cares." Edward walked out of Robin's grasp. "I'm certainly the last person to tell anyone."

"But..."

Edward pushed through the small grove. "Come on. We've got to get back to camp. They'll think we've deserted if we don't get back soon, and that would be unpleasant."

Robin sighed and followed. Edward knowing her secret made her nervous, and even more irritated at being found out so quickly. Robin debated ways to talk her way around it. But ultimately, there was nothing to be done, except hope Edward would not take advantage of the situation for his own profit or pleasure.

The others were still awake when they arrived. They sat around the fire talking softly.

"Are you sure it's the same time every night?" Samuel asked John.

"Close enough," John replied. "As if it made any difference."

"That's all I need." Samuel was not happy. "Does your father know?"

"Of course. He and yours were already drawing up the contract."

"It looks like you're for it, Sam," chuckled Robert.

"A hell of a lot sooner than I wanted," sighed Samuel. "But this makes for a more immediate problem, you know." The boys all looked at Edward. "You were sick back there, weren't you?"

Edward shrugged.

"It was probably just food poisoning," volunteered Robin. "He seems alright now."

There was a collective sigh from the group.

"I always am," said Edward simply. "At least so far."

"You mean this has happened before?" asked Robin.

"Well, just for the past two weeks," Edward replied. "I don't know why I always throw up dinner. Mother said she was always sick in the mornings. But then, she says it's different with everyone."

"What's wrong with you?" Robin asked.

"Nothing's wrong." Edward laughed. "I'm with child."

Robin laughed also. "That's one hell of a draft dodge."

She stopped laughing as the others looked at her. She looked at Edward closely. The features that had only seemed effeminate were suddenly very much so.

"Perhaps we've said too much," said John quietly.

"Why shouldn't he know?" demanded Samuel. "He's one of us."

"Besides," Edward giggled. "I was right about him, or should I say her? I caught him red-handed."

Samuel burst into laughter as he and the others began to see the truth also. Robin poised herself for action and glared at Edward.

"I thought you said you weren't going to tell anyone," Robin snarled.

"What are you afraid of?" Samuel asked her. "We're not going to give you away. Don't you trust your own townsmen?"

"I— I don't know that I should," Robin replied.

"Well, if we're not going to give Edward away," Samuel

said. "We certainly won't give you away. It's damned inconvenient is all, another female to protect."

"I can take care of myself," Robin replied indignantly.

"Edward's the same way," sighed Charles.

"So, what is your reason?" Samuel asked. "Edward, here, is hiding from Master Blount."

"My brother and I were driven off my father's land," Robin explained. "A greedy baron took over, killing our father and our cousin's father as well. Since I'm so tall, we thought it would be safer if there were only one woman in the party. After that, things just fell out the way they did."

"They've fallen out rather poorly for you, at the moment," sighed Samuel. "And for Edward. So far, we've been able to stay together and keep the others from finding out. But what if they put us into separate companies? You'll never be able to get away with it among strangers."

"There's always the possibility of desertion," Robin suggested.

"But which one of you men can we spare?" Samuel pondered.

"For what?" asked Robin. "To escort us home? I hardly think it's necessary. May I remind you who runs the inn? It's not my brother."

"Robin is known for being exceptionally quick-witted," Robert put in.

"Perhaps she could share one of the pistols," John suggested. "I don't mind teaching them both."

"It would be a good idea, in any case," agreed Samuel. "But we've got to figure out a way to get them out of here."

"Why don't we wait a few days?" Robin said. "We're a little close to home at the moment. Besides, won't they know to look for us there?"

"Edward will return as a woman," Samuel replied. "That's all arranged anyway. I suppose you could do the same."

"I suppose," Robin sighed.

"I know," grumbled Edward. "Who wants to go back to being a woman? You don't get to do anything."

"You won't have any choice in a couple months," retorted Samuel. "I think it's about time anyway. I'm tired of making it with someone dressed like me."

"Not tired enough," sniggered Richard.

Samuel glared at him while Robin smiled to herself.

As Robin bedded down, she thought about the new alternative presented to her. Returning as a woman would leave open the option for remaining in Charing Vale. It sounded attractive, at least remaining in the village did. Robin shared Edward's chagrin at returning to the feminine state. Women at that time had no rights and were little more than chattel.

Then there was the problem of Elizabeth. Robin had a feeling she knew why Dean was so anxious for all three of them to return home. Even though she tried, Robin couldn't close her eyes to the obvious attraction between the two. She only hoped Dean was using his head and behaving responsibly.

It was still a complication Robin hadn't bargained on. Elizabeth was terrified of returning to the twentieth century. Dean was equally determined to do so. Of the two, Dean stood a much better chance of surviving the seventeenth century than Elizabeth did of surviving the twentieth. But if he stayed, how would Robin explain his disappearance to their parents? At least Elizabeth didn't have that factor to confront. On the other hand, how were Dean and Robin going to explain Elizabeth's sudden existence?

The possibility of breaking the two up flashed across Robin's mind. She dismissed the notion. Somehow, Robin just couldn't do it. Her own failures made her just that much more determined to make sure no one else's attempts fell apart.

But how to explain Elizabeth? Getting her identification wouldn't be all that hard – Robin even knew someone who could get Elizabeth a legitimate Social Security Card under the table. But Robin could see other problems, mostly with her mother.

Elizabeth's virtuous obedience would appear as a very tempting inferiority complex to Mom. Then there might be problems if Elizabeth said something just a little bit wrong and Mom questioned the girl's ability to distinguish fantasy from reality. Mom was big on objective reality.

It was unfortunate, Robin thought, that her mother only accepted the possible as a necessary evil. One had to have imagination, she conceded, otherwise one could never have new ideas or inventions. But one could get too wrapped up in dreams and that sort of thing bordered on instability.

As Robin drifted closer to sleep, she found herself wondering if that had been the problem between her parents all along. Her father had always been anything but practical. Reality for him included all the possibilities his fertile mind could create. Admittedly, his only interest in fantasy was where speculation went on from knowledge. Robin had always felt closer to her father than to her mother. Perhaps it was because they had that sort of thinking in common.

No nearer to solving her problem, Robin drifted off to sleep.

The next morning, they were awakened early. Roll call was taken first thing. Two boys from one of the neighboring villages were missing. A message was sent to Master Blount to have them apprehended and flogged. After a small breakfast of hard bread, the new recruits were on their way. They walked steadily until noon when they were given a two-hour break and permission to hunt game.

Robin heard several gun reports as they ate.

"We'd best hurry," grumbled John. "The others will get all the game, and we won't have meat tonight."

"You're going to teach us to shoot now?" Edward asked.

John sighed. "I suppose so. Edward, give Robin one of your pistols and a powder horn and shot bag." Edward did so. "Now, these are German guns. They were my grandfather's. How he got them, we'll never know. Now, Robin, note the spanner is attached to the powder horn. Never undo it, or you can't wind the gun and it won't work unless it's wound. The first thing you two must look over is the lock. This here is the wheel. The spanner goes through this hole here to wind it. You can feel it catch. Don't do it now! Never wind the wheel until the gun is loaded. You can blow your head off that way. Alright, make sure the doghead is always lying flat until you're ready to shoot. Now, this is the flashpan cover, you push that back with your thumb like so, and press this button to release it. Back to the doghead. This piece here in the clamp is called pyrites. Edward, give Robin half of yours. You must make sure there aren't any cracks in the pyrites, or that it isn't sticking out too far in the clamp. It should look just like that." John demonstrated on Robin's pistol. "Alright, you two tell me what parts are what."

After John was satisfied that the two women knew the parts of the pistols, he went on to explain the process of loading, tamping, winding, and shooting. The shooting, itself, involved a great deal of stalking to find the game, for even if one were lucky enough to get the gun to shoot, its accuracy could not be counted on for targets over twenty yards away. Worse still, the guns were old and finicky, in spite of the good care they'd received.

John first had the women shoot at targets on trees. Robin stood with her feet squarely planted, her arms outstretched, both hands on the pistol, ready to absorb the kick. Edward tried to imitate the casual attitude of her father and brother and got knocked on her seat. John helped her up.

"See how Robin stands?" he told her. "And use a little less powder this time."

They didn't have time to try for any game that day. The others anticipated that and had provided. There were two rabbits and a quail. These were presented to Robin and Edward that evening for them to clean.

"I'll get the water and build the fire," Robin volunteered, hoping Edward would have the animals cleaned before she finished.

As Robin stalled about her tasks, she watched Edward at hers. Robin knew her lack of knowledge of womanly duties could get her into almost as much trouble as letting the whole camp know she was a woman. Edward proved adept at feathering the quail. Robin still had to clean one of the rabbits. She was awkward at best.

"It's been a long time," she explained to Edward.

Edward just shrugged and showed Robin how it was done.

The next day at the lunch break, John took Edward and Robin stalking. The pistols were loaded and ready and had been since the day before. John had insisted that the women carry the pistols loaded, just in case.

The first few attempts failed. Either the fowl were too far away, or they scattered and broke for the air at the wrong moment, or (and Robin had to admit this was the most likely) the two women had lousy aim.

Then Edward caught the tail feathers of a grouse. Robin stalked up on another, aimed the pistol and pulled the trigger. Instead of the familiar quick whir, nothing happened. The grouse took flight. Robin turned the gun to look at it. The pistol went off. Robin yelped as the bird tumbled to the ground. John laughed. Robin looked at the dead bird.

"I'll be damned," she muttered. "I wonder what the odds were of that happening?"

"Who knows?" said John. He came over with the bird. "I shouldn't like to bet on it. But I think I know what caused it." He took the pistol and looked over the wheel. "It's fouled, alright. You've got to clean the wheel part out every so often. The pyrites crumble into it and jam it. Edward, here! You need to see this too."

That night Robin got her first lesson in cleaning fowl, and a lot of teasing from the boys on her first catch.

"And how many of you know how to shoot pistols?" Edward retorted.

"Let them tease," Robin said. "They'd just better remember that my brother isn't the only one capable of throwing drunks out of inns and that he had help the night Blount's men came to visit."

The boys roared with laughter. But Robin noted with no small amusement that they slowed their teasing down.

"It's strange," Samuel confessed as they sat around the fire that night. "That I should find such good friends in two women. Then again, both of you have the hearts and minds of men. I never thought I'd like that in a woman."

Robin smiled. "Most men don't. I think it takes an exceptionally perceptive man to realize that a woman is more interesting that way."

The others shrugged. The more Robin thought about it, the more she realized just how much women had achieved in her century, and how amazing it was that they had achieved it in so short a time. That men's attitudes had changed as much as they had was no small thing. That attitudes still had a long way to go didn't seem to mean as much. It would take patience. There were centuries to overcome, and Robin suddenly felt just how many.

They joined the rest of the Earl's army late Friday afternoon. In the larger group, the smaller village groups hung together that much closer. Little was done that afternoon beyond setting up a more permanent camp.

The next day the training started. After roll call, each village group was called away by one of three officers to see what each individual could do. The unoccupied groups stood around, waiting, hunting, and starting small skirmishes amongst themselves to relieve the boredom and the tension.

The evaluations took the better part of the day.

"There's a rumor they're going to split us into different companies Monday," Samuel said that evening as they sat around the fire.

"That's not surprising," Robin returned. "I'll bet I can tell who's going to get put where."

"What do you mean?" asked Charles.

"It's simple," said Robin. "First, they wrote down what weapons each of us had, then they watched us drill with them. Edward and I will probably go to a musket company, Samuel will end up in a cavalry unit since he knows horses, the rest of you will go to the pike units. They're going to keep us as split up as possible to avoid conflicting loyalties."

"I don't want to go to a pike company," grumbled Robert.

"A musket company is more dangerous," said Robin. "We only get one shot at a time, and loading those guns takes forever. Samuel's probably in the best position of any of us."

"The cavalry's no guarantee he won't get hurt," said Edward.

"True, but Samuel's going to be support, probably a stable boy, or something like that," replied Robin. "Because he hasn't got a horse, he won't end up on the lines."

"The problem is," said Samuel. "Is if we are split up, how are we going to keep Edward and Robin out of trouble?"

"Fear not," said Robin. "I've got everything under control."

"Are you sure?" asked Samuel.

Robin glared at him. "I am essentially the same person I was a week ago. You would have taken my word for it then, why can't you now?"

"Because, well..." Samuel sighed. He had to admit Robin

had a good point. But trusting women just wasn't in his cultural mode of thinking.

Robin shook her head. The next day there was roll call, then church service. At the end of the service, Robin slipped up next to Edward and pushed her along. The others were following them back to camp at a more leisurely pace.

"What?" asked Edward, bewildered.

"We're leaving," said Robin.

"Where?"

"Here. We're going home."

"On the Sabbath?"

"It's our best chance. No one will know we're gone until tomorrow morning. We'll have a half day's lead on them, at least. If we wait any longer, we'll get put into other companies, and I don't think I need to tell you the risks of that. Let's hurry. I want to be gone before the others get back."

"But we have to say goodbye."

"We can't. If they don't know we're leaving, then they can honestly say they didn't know we were going to."

Edward sighed, but followed Robin's lead. They already had their cloaks, gloves, and pistols with them, and Robin had her sword, so there was no need to stop at the camp. They walked quickly, but quietly through the brush and then into the open farmland. Robin made a point of following the road but staying off it. Grumbling, Edward followed.

That evening they stumbled on a camp of itinerant farm workers. The workers invited the two travelers to share their meager soup, which Robin and Edward accepted with thanks. They bedded down with the group. Robin got up before dawn and woke Edward.

"Come on," Robin whispered. "We're leaving."

"Why now?" Edward yawned.

"I want to get some distance between us and them before the army finds out we've been here. Besides, they might have figured out we're deserters, and that means we're a source of income for them. They won't let us get away that easily if that's the case."

Edward shrugged and hurried after.

The day was cold and overcast. Late that afternoon, it started to rain. Robin left the cover of the forest for the road as they approached a small town.

"We'll stay at the inn tonight," Robin told Edward.

"Isn't that dangerous?"

"Perhaps. But would two fugitives risk it? I think not. Besides, we wouldn't have the money to."

Edward's eyes grew wide. "You mean we do?"

"I won't say how much, but I generally have more means than it appears. If you look poor, people are less likely to attack you."

Edward nodded. She was nervous but imitated Robin's confident manner. At the inn, Robin paid for a single room for the two of them and a modest meal. Shortly after they ate, Edward retired to the inn yard to have her evening sick session. Robin waited for her in the best room, then decided the two would go to their room right away.

"No sense in pressing our luck," she told Edward as she shut the door.

"It would have been fun," sighed Edward. "That'll be the worst part of going back to being a woman. No more nights at the inn. At least you'll be able to tap still."

Robin shrugged. "I don't know what's going to happen when we get back."

"You don't want to go back to being a woman, either."

"Of course not. The very idea of relying on my brother for his protection fills me with revulsion."

Edward grinned. "Perhaps it was a good thing you had to disguise yourself. You're too smart to be a woman."

"Sh!" Robin stared at a part of the wall near the floor. "Damn!" she hissed. "There's a hole there. I wonder who's on the other side."

"You think he could have heard us?" Edward was frightened.

"He could have. We'd better not say any more about it or anything else we don't want people to know. We'll keep watch tonight."

Edward nodded. "I'll take the first lookout."

"Thanks. I'll turn in now. Goodnight."

They left early again the next day. It was a long morning and still wet from the day before. Both Robin and Edward stumbled several times through the slippery ruts in the road.

Close to noon, Robin decided they should do a little hunting to get their lunch.

"And how will we cook it?" Edward asked. "The wood is too wet to build a fire."

"I can get a fire going anytime I want," Robin replied, smugly.

"Excuse me." said a strange voice.

Robin and Edward stared into a toothless grin surrounded by a graying two-day-old beard. It was all connected to a bent

over man, with stringy shoulder-length hair and filthy dis-
arranged clothes.

"Can I help you?" asked Robin cautiously.

"Perhaps I can help you," replied the man. "You wanted
some meat?"

"Well, lunch," said Robin.

"Very good," he said. "It seems we are well met. Would
you care to share my lunch with me? Save yourself the trouble of building a fire."

"It's not necessary," Robin shifted.

There was something about the man that tripped all her
internal alarms. But because she couldn't put her finger on
anything specific, she decided against snubbing his offer. No
sense in pissing him off, especially when he might run into
soldiers looking for deserters in the near future.

"It's my pleasure." The man bowed prettily. "Come be my
guests. I am called Henry. I am a lonely peddler. I don't often
get companionship as I travel."

He gave them plenty of cheese and bread for lunch and
even some fair porter. Robin was amazed he carried the small
cask, as well as all his wares, on his back.

"You like my wares?" Henry asked as he packed up after
the meal. "I've some beautiful silk."

He showed them a part of the bright red cloth. Fabrics had
never interested Robin in the least. Edward had been playing
boy for so long, she didn't have much interest either, and resented anything that smacked of the life she was returning to.
Robin did wonder a little about how a poor peddler got his
hands on such an obviously rich fabric.

Nonetheless, she accepted the peddler's invitation to

travel with him. They made good time, but by the time darkness approached, they were still miles from any village.

They bedded down on the edge of the road under the hedge of a nearby field. Robin slept fitfully that night. She guessed it was close to one a.m. when she heard a strangled squeak from Edward's direction. She turned.

Henry had gagged Edward and was binding her hands. He looked at Robin and laughed.

"I wouldn't try anything," Henry said. He whipped out a knife and placed it against Edward's throat.

Robin stood slowly. "What do you want?"

"Anything I can get." One-handed, Henry finished tying Edward and tied the other end of the rope to a tree. "I do want you to step over here."

Robin did as he commanded. In an instant, Henry had the knife at her throat instead of Edward's. Robin stiffened as he grabbed her crotch and explored.

"I thought I heard you two right," he said, grinning. "You were overheard in the inn, you know. I wasn't quite sure I'd heard correctly when I first saw you. You are rather large for a woman." His free hand reached inside her shirt. "I am a very lonely man."

"Why didn't you just ask?" Robin returned.

Henry seemed startled but didn't remove the knife.

"I mean it," Robin continued. "It's been very lonely for me too, for obvious reasons." Her hands crept up along his chest. "I could be very good to you if you'll put down the knife."

Henry chuckled. "I'm not going to fall for that."

Robin licked her lips with the edge of her tongue. "Are you sure?"

The knife edged away. Robin's hand shot up and the knuckles of her two forefingers landed in his eyes. Henry cringed. Robin socked him in the stomach. Grabbing her pistol, she brought it down butt first into the back of his neck. The gun went off. Startled, Robin nearly dropped it as Henry fell unconscious at her feet.

A few seconds later, Edward's anxious grunting brought Robin back to earth. She hurried over and removed Edward's gag, then set to work on the ropes.

"Where did you learn to fight like that?" Edward asked the moment her mouth was free.

"My father. Didn't yours teach you how to defend yourself?"

"Of course, but not like that."

"I guess my father knew a few more dirty tricks than yours." Robin shrugged.

The rope fell from Edward's wrists.

"Now what?" she asked.

"We get old Henry tied up." Robin picked up the rope. "We'd better get it done fast. We don't want him waking up on us."

In a matter of minutes, the grungy peddler was hog-tied. Robin turned him over. There was a clinking sound, and near the man's waist, metal gleamed in the dying firelight.

"Gold." gasped Robin.

Edward looked also. "Angels. Why would he be carrying those?"

Robin picked up the purse that had fallen, taking care to scoop the coins into it first. After quickly checking to see that her own purse was still intact, she then dumped the little sack's contents into her hands.

"All gold angels, alright," she said. "I get the feeling Master Henry is not only a peddler."

"I thought it strange that he would be carrying silk," Edward said.

"So, did I. We should have been more careful. But seeing as though we're none the worse for it..."

Edward's eyes glowed. "And we're richer, too."

"True. Let's see what else this guy's got on him."

They rifled Henry's pockets. All Robin found was a piece of folded parchment with a wax seal on it.

"What's this?" she muttered, taking it over to the fire to read.

She stirred the coals, then fumbled over the strange writing. Despite the language decoder that enabled her to hear the language as her own, yet speak it as the people did, writing continued to look just as confusing as seventeenth-century writing always had. Edward peered over her shoulder.

"Can you read?" Robin asked.

"Yes, father taught me."

"What does it say?" Robin handed the paper to her.

Edward paused, reading the paper over, then took a deep breath.

"It says, 'The bearer of this writ is in the favor of His Lordship, the Earl of Essex, for the return of deserters to His Lordship's army, and is given the privilege to travel throughout His Lordship's domain without hindrance by the Army.'"

"Hot damn!" Robin grinned. "That's a free ticket to safety."

"What do you mean?"

"If we carry that thing, as long as no one recognizes us as deserters, the army can't accuse us of being deserters. They can't bother us, by His Lordship's orders."

Edward gaped. "But it wasn't written for us."

"You think it was written for him?" Robin jerked her head at the still comatose peddler. "It probably belonged to some special friend of the Earl's who kept getting stopped and harassed by the army. You know what everybody on the road is saying. Half of the army is deserting, and the other half is looking for them."

"It's not that bad."

"No. But you know what I mean."

"Yes." Edward thought it over. "Are you sure we'll be safe?"

Robin shrugged. "We should be. As long as we play it cool, and the people who catch us don't know us. I suggest we still try to avoid getting caught." Robin yawned. "I also suggest we get some sleep."

"I'll watch first."

"Okay. Wake me in a couple hours."

Robin got to test her theory earlier than she expected. The next morning, the two had been on the road an hour, when five men on horseback overtook them. They reined in, surrounding the two women.

"Behold," laughed the captain. "Two young men out wandering by themselves. Perhaps they are trying to escape service in His Lordship's army."

"Hardly, sir." Robin stood up straighter and with more confidence than she felt. She removed the parchment from her doublet. "If anything, we've seen to it that others have done their duty."

She held the parchment up for the men to see. At the captain's signal, one of the others dismounted and looked at the paper.

"It's the Earl's seal, alright," he said remounting. "They are not to be bothered."

"Pray forgive us then, sirs." The captain bowed his head, then signaled his men.

They rode off in the direction they had come. Robin took a deep breath and smiled.

"Okay, heart, you can start beating again," she muttered.

"You were right!" gasped Edward.

"Well, we'd better start being extra careful again. We're getting close to the vale, and that increases our chances of running into someone who knows us."

"Such as one Master Blount."

Robin nodded. "Or one of his friendly henchmen. Come on, let's hurry."

Chapter Thirteen

I n Charing Vale, on the day of the conscription, Dean and Elizabeth followed the rest of the villagers as they followed the recruits to the end of town. But as the crowd sullenly dispersed and the pair slowly made their way back to the inn, Dean firmly decided to make the best of the situation.

"Well," he said as they entered the inn's kitchen.

"This is terrible," Elizabeth said.

"Yeah." Dean took a deep breath. "But there isn't much we can do about it. Besides, Robin's smart. She'll find a way out of it."

"I don't doubt it," Elizabeth said. "But what about us in the meantime?"

"That." Dean grinned as he put his arm around her waist and pulled her close. "Here's the thing. I've been giving this a lot of thought, see?" He looked away, then looked at her again. "Okay, when we talked about us before we got here? And I told you how in my time we have a way to stop girls from getting pregnant?"

"Oh." Elizabeth pushed away. "You would think of that!"

"Elizabeth, I'm not saying we have to. It's just that, you know, when I said that most girls in my time are doing it before they get married, and you were, like, wondering why they weren't all afraid of getting pregnant, it looked like you were kind of interested when I said we had ways to stop that from happening." Dean caught her hand and looked down at her sheepishly. "And I had this idea, and I wasn't sure what I was going to do about it, 'cause of Robin being around, but now that she's not, I thought, why not make it work for us, you know?"

Elizabeth pulled her hand away and crossed her arms. "And how do you propose to do that? We don't have any of your magic here."

"But we got sausage casings." Dean grinned.

"What?"

"Sausage casings. I got the idea last week when you were making those sausages. So, I tried it out, and it worked." Dean held up his handiwork. "See? I wasn't sure when I'd talk to you about it, but the way things are working out… You know, we've got privacy and you wouldn't have to sleep in the kitchen anymore."

Elizabeth sat down on her bed. "I don't know what to say. Dean, I want to please you, and if you truly believe I will not quicken, I guess I can believe you."

"You bet you can believe me." Dean flopped down next to her. "We're too young to have kids. I'm not going to take that chance."

"What chance do you take? All you have to do is leave, and you leave to another time where no one can find you."

"Aw, come on, Elizabeth. That may be some guys, but that's not me. I'm not going to get you pregnant until we're ready, and even if I did, I'm not going to walk out on you and the baby. That's just not right."

Elizabeth looked at him curiously. "You wouldn't?"

"Elizabeth, that is totally the wrong thing to do. Give me credit for some morals."

"No, Dean." She put her hand on his arm. "Of course, you have good morals. But here, in this time, when a man presses a maid to give up her maidenhood and she quickens, he's not likely to marry her, especially when she has no father or brothers to see to it that he does. What reason would you have to marry me when it would be more than easy for you to leave me behind?"

"Like I love you?" Dean got up and started pacing. "I mean, I don't want to get married now. We're kind of young. Believe me, I don't want to rush things. But, Elizabeth, I'm not leaving you behind. We'll give Robin whatever time she needs to get used to the idea, but you're coming back with us. Or I'm staying here." He paused. "Look. I don't want you to feel pressured. If you're not ready, you're not ready. That's cool."

Elizabeth smiled coyly. "You're sure I won't get pregnant?"

Dean held up the casing he'd fixed. "It's pretty solid."

"Hmm."

The conversation was ended by the arrival of a traveler. A second arrived shortly after. Dean put them in the two rooms furthest from Master Miller's old room, where he and Robin had been sleeping since the old man's death.

As soon as it grew dark, a larger crowd than usual gathered in the best room. The men grumbled incessantly about the conscription, especially unhappy that they were unable to do anything about it. It hadn't escaped anyone's notice that the departed young men were mostly Master Blount's least favorite people.

Dean took over the tapping. While the men understood, some of them still complained that Dean didn't have his brother's light hand on the tap. Dean sighed, but he had to admit Robin had always had a special knack for drawing beer.

Finally, the guests were bedded down, and the last of the drinkers left. A weary Elizabeth soaked the dirty tankards in the kettle while Dean scraped down the tables. He was tired. But Elizabeth could see he wasn't too tired to have forgotten about the suggestion he'd made that afternoon. The only problem was she was still unsure about it.

Dean appeared at her side.

"You don't have to if you don't want to," he said softly. "But if you want to come up and spend the night with me, I'd like that. We don't have to do anything but sleep, either."

Elizabeth frowned. "As if we were married."

"I don't know. If it makes you feel better, sure. Think of it that way."

"But we're not."

Dean kissed her forehead. "Like I said, if it makes you feel better to think of it that way, go ahead."

"It doesn't," Elizabeth sighed. She looked at him fondly. "I'll not come up tonight."

"That's fine. I can wait."

And he slid off upstairs.

A virtuous woman obeyed to her menfolk, Elizabeth reflected the next morning as she made the bread. Her father was gone, and while Dean wasn't her husband, he certainly could be. Therefore, she should give him the obedience that was his due. There was no problem with that. Elizabeth was glad to do it. But being virtuous and obedient didn't mean she couldn't get her own way.

One had to know how to handle men. Her stepmother had been an expert, and Elizabeth, another like her. The key was in knowing the man's weakness. Denying the bedroom privilege rarely worked well, and Elizabeth had been in no position to deny her father that, as he naturally never took it. But Elizabeth had controlled her father well, and with a minimum of tears. Tears were only for emergencies. It was too easy for a man to realize he was being manipulated.

Dean was a whole other challenge. It seemed women were not terribly obedient in his world, and he expected her to be the same. Even stranger that he expected her to have relations with him without being married first. Or rather, that he considered having relations without being married to be completely normal and that the women of his time did so frequently. It had to be an exaggeration. Elizabeth knew better than to trust a man's word when he wanted to bed her.

But there was something different about Dean's attitude. It was almost as if what she wanted really mattered to him. Elizabeth thought that over. Without her father, it seemed that Dean and Robin would have the final say over whom she married, at least, Pastor Layton had said so. But she couldn't believe that Dean would let her marry anybody else, not when she wanted him. On the other hand, Dean did not want to get married, himself, but wasn't ready to rule out the possibility.

It wasn't unusual for the great lords and ladies to marry at young ages, but most people in her station waited until their mid-twenties. That was so they could earn enough money to establish their own households first. But Dean and Elizabeth already had the inn. Elizabeth thought she'd heard Dean say something about getting ready to go to some sort of school that would make him a doctor of something or other, which she supposed meant he had resources in his own world to support a wife.

Which meant that they might as well marry, or at least, arrange their betrothal. With a public promise to marry, it would be a lot harder for her to be disgraced if Dean's little sausage casing were less than it promised to be. Elizabeth smiled. She'd have to bring him to the idea carefully, but it was just as well. People got married and produced children, and that was the way life was.

Someone knocked at the door of the inn. Dean was in the stables. Elizabeth wiped her hands on her apron and went to answer the door.

A scraggly looking man with a half-grown beard stood there with two sacks. He opened one.

"I've fine grain to sell, Mistress," he said. "Fine barley it is."

Elizabeth pawed through the grain and shook her head. It was mealy, and she thought she saw insects.

"No thank you," she replied. "None today."

"It's good barley, Mistress."

Elizabeth started as she noticed the ugly fellow leering at her.

"No," she said firmly and shut the door.

She returned to her work shaking. It had been a most unpleasant encounter, not unlike her encounter with Master Blount. Suddenly she smiled. A plan formed.

About three hours later, she was stirring cheese in the big heavy kettle. Dean came into the kitchen, bringing with him, as always, the smell of horse's breath and fresh straw.

"Hello, my lovely little girl." He came over and kissed her.

"Hello," Elizabeth replied.

One nice thing about Robin being gone, Dean was a lot more affectionate.

"I'm afraid lunch will be a little late," Elizabeth continued. "I've got to finish this. But I should be able to let it set in a couple minutes."

"Sure." Dean took a chunk of the previous day's bread. "How was your morning?"

"Unsettling, I'm afraid." Elizabeth sighed, then removed her paddle from the kettle. As she spoke, she pulled the kettle off the fire and set it on the hearth to cool.

"What happened?" Dean rummaged and found a rind from a wheel of cheese that had already been cured and aged some.

"Just a peddler. Oh, that reminds me. I'll have to buy some more rennet on market day. I used the last of it for this."

"Oh. Can we afford it?"

"I believe so."

Dean slipped up behind her and nibbled the back of her neck. "So, what was so unsettling about this peddler?"

"Nothing, really." Elizabeth frowned at the cheese kettle. "I guess it was just the way he looked at me. It was not unlike the way Master Blount did."

"You should have called me."

"I didn't need to. I just shut the door and he left. At least, I hope he did."

Dean went to the kitchen door. "You want me to check around?"

Elizabeth shook her head. "I don't think the peddler is who we have to worry about."

Dean shifted. "And who do you think is?"

"Master Blount. He's not one to give up easily. I don't think it was any coincidence he sent Robin off to the army."

"Well, don't worry, Elizabeth. He won't get his hands on you."

"He might if we're not careful." Elizabeth set about tidying the kitchen. "He won't try to attack you, Dean. You're too strong. But he could by deceit. And you haven't been in this world long enough to know how he could."

Dean thought this over. "Well, you've been here most your life. How could he?"

"He could have a contract of marriage drawn up between me and whomever he wanted, and I would be forced to honor it. I have no father to protect me."

"Don't I count for something?"

Elizabeth plopped down forlornly onto a stool. "Not that way. I'm sure the only reason he hasn't before was because he was afraid of both Robin and you. But with Robin gone. Good heavens, Dean, he could be writing up a contract now."

"So how do we stop it?"

"Well, if there were already another contract made, and it were public..."

Dean folded his arms. "Elizabeth, why do I suddenly get the feeling you're trying to talk me into marrying you?"

"I was only suggesting a betrothal. It's just as binding, except it can be broken by the mutual consent of both parties."

"Hm!" Dean snorted and paced about the kitchen. "You know, I'd swear you were trying to manipulate me into marrying you. And you probably are. The only thing that worries me is that I remember Pastor Layton saying something about this contract thing before." He sighed. "You got me by the short hairs, you know. If I don't go along with this, that SOB, Blount, tries the same thing and carries you off. If I do, I've got you holding a promise to marry you over my head."

Elizabeth sighed. "So, you don't want to marry me."

Dean squirmed. "Aw, Elizabeth, honey. You know I love you. Isn't that enough?"

"For what?" The strange remark startled her.

"For us. To be together."

"What has love got to do with that?"

Dean was equally startled by her response. "But we're talking about us."

"We're talking about marriage." Elizabeth began setting the kitchen straight. "I mean it's very nice if you can be in love with your spouse, but that's not why people get married."

"That's the only reason why people get married in my time."

She suddenly pouted. "Then, if you love me, why don't you want to marry me?"

"It's not you, Elizabeth." Dean groaned. She'd gotten him again. "It's, well... Oh, hell. Just cause you're in love doesn't mean you have to get married. There are lots of people in my time who just live together."

Elizabeth gaped. "They live as man and wife and never get married?"

"Yeah."

"That's absurd," she snorted.

"Well, that's the way it goes. Look, we're getting nowhere fast on this thing. Why don't we talk to Pastor Layton and see what he can come up with?"

Elizabeth turned away and smiled to herself. "That's an excellent idea."

It suddenly dawned on Dean that the pastor would sympathize with Elizabeth.

"We're not getting married, in any case," he said finally. "I don't even know if it'd be legal anyway. Technically, I'm not even born yet."

"A public betrothal should do the trick." Elizabeth smiled to herself as she found a small cheese and wrapped it carefully in a cloth.

"Yeah, well, you'd better keep in mind that if we do get betrothed, it's only to keep Blount's hands off you. Is that clear? I'm not going to marry you until I'm damn good and ready."

"Yes, Dean." Elizabeth bowed her head. "I'll try not to say anything more about it, except..."

Dean folded his arms. "What now?"

"We'd best go this afternoon. Not that I'm trying to push you."

"That's exactly what you're doing, and don't think I don't know it. You're damn lucky old Blount is such a big threat. Well, we're not going to be here forever. You just keep that in mind and remember I don't like being manipulated."

They never did. Elizabeth watched as Dean paced about the kitchen. He was stuck, and they both knew it. Perhaps it was just as well, Elizabeth thought. In any case, she had removed a major threat and had just brought them closer to what he wanted, whether he realized it or not.

Mistress Layton smiled with delight at the small cheese Elizabeth brought.

"Of course, it needs to be aged a little longer," said Elizabeth. "I just made it last week."

"It's very gracious of you," said the pastor's wife. "My thanks. I'll go fetch my husband."

Dean paced about the best room, glancing at Elizabeth every so often and sighing. It wasn't her fault. Even without the Blount hassle, girls in her time got married, and there was something wrong when they didn't. The poor kid. He did love her and doing the domestic bit had been fun that morning. But, for heaven's sakes, he was only twenty-one!

"This is rather unusual," said Pastor Layton, sweeping in. "I hope there isn't any trouble."

"We're trying to prevent that," said Dean. He glanced at Elizabeth, who remained silent, as all virtuous women did. "Uh, well, we remembered something you said about Master Blount trying to get up a marriage contract or something on Elizabeth. And, well, we thought we might try beating him to it."

"I see." The pastor nodded. "In other words, you and Elizabeth wish to be married."

"Why don't we just set up the contract today?" Dean smiled nervously. "We can worry about the wedding later."

Pastor Layton smiled. "Why do you wish to wait for the wedding?"

"Uh, well, I've always liked spring weddings." Dean winced internally at the unbelievably lame excuse that had just escaped his mouth. "And Robin! It wouldn't be terribly fair to go and get married without Robin there. I mean our only family. Besides, we haven't got any parents to pay for the wedding for us, and I don't know how much these things cost, but they can't be cheap, and, well, that funeral did set us back a bit. We want to save some money. You know, get off on the right foot, get Elizabeth a nice dress. Things like that."

"Yes, I understand completely." Pastor Layton tried not to laugh. Dean was not the first young man he'd met who was reluctant to become a husband. As the pastor smiled at Elizabeth, he realized just how caught Dean was. The girl had maneuvered him into it, no doubt about that. But there was a genuine affection between the two that warmed Pastor Layton's heart.

"Perhaps it would be best to wait," he continued. "Does Master Robin know anything of this?"

"Not yet," Dean sighed. "We didn't want to rub it in, you know."

"Ah, he has similar feelings for Mistress Elizabeth?"

Elizabeth giggled, and Dean grinned and shook his head.

"Nah," he said. "No way. He's just kind of lonely. But it's a long story, and real complicated, and it involves a few family secrets. Not that he's that way, you know. He's straight."

"I never doubted it." Their reactions puzzled the pastor. A stray possibility crossed his mind. It was not all that unusual in that village, although why Master Robin should have done so didn't make sense. The memory of a lady skilled in healing troubled him. Master Robin was so much like her, and if Master Robin wasn't what he said... Pastor Layton dismissed the thought. "I do have to consider one other thing. You say you are cousins. Just how close is the relationship?"

"Not close at all," Dean said anxiously. "Third cousins, maybe. We're more like friends of the family. We just call ourselves cousins."

Pastor Layton suspected that was closer to the truth than anything Dean had said. The pastor had always had a strong feeling the three had some secrets to hide, but he had no proof, and they were model members of the parish.

"Well, I have no objections to make," Pastor Layton said. "In fact, I think it's a particularly good idea. Not that I believe that you two have been anything but pure and modest in your dealings with each other. But I cannot feel that the two of you living alone together in that inn is particularly wholesome. Obviously, it is mostly recent circumstances that have provided the temptation, and I am glad to see that you are doing the right and proper thing." He turned to a chest and pawed through it. "Here now, I've a couple sheets of parchment and some ink. We'll draw this up right now."

"Uh, can we date it about two days ago?" Dean asked. "Just to be sure we beat you know who."

Pastor Layton sighed. "That's not very ethical, but certainly practical in light of recent occurrences. All right. I will. Now, what possessions do you own outright?"

"Well, there's my clothes," Dean said after some thought. "And my sword. I guess I own the inn, but so do Robin and Elizabeth."

"Well, Elizabeth's part shall go to you upon the wedding. Have you no money?"

Dean shrugged. "Just the inn's."

The pastor nodded. "And you, Mistress Elizabeth, what can you offer for a dowry?"

"Just my share of the inn," Elizabeth replied, ashamed. "We hold all the money in common."

"I presume that has been working very well." Pastor Layton sighed. "But it does make things somewhat awkward in this case. Neither of you has parents?" They shook their heads. "Then I shall have to take both parts for the moment. Mistress Elizabeth has offered her share of the inn as her dowry. Master Dean, what will you offer her in return?"

Dean shrugged. "My share?"

"Upon your death, certainly, but what about your children?"

"We don't have any children."

"With God's grace, you will. What will give them when you die? They'll be Elizabeth's also."

Dean frowned. "I'm confused. What's all this when I die stuff? We're setting up a marriage contract, not a will."

"Master Dean, this is a business negotiation. Acting in place of Elizabeth's father, I must see to it that provisions are made for her support both now and in the future. In turn, acting for your father, I must ensure that her dowry compensates for those provisions. Do you understand?"

"Yeah." Dean understood the contract part. Why it was that way baffled him.

"All right. Now I would suggest that your part be the restoration of her dowry upon your death, should she survive you, and that both shares go to any children you have together, if you survive her, even if you remarry. I would also recommend that she receive an allowance."

"Why? She can take whatever money she needs."

"Then let us guarantee that in writing. Say ten pounds per annum. Does that sound fair?"

"I guess." Dean shifted. "You sure you're not taking me?"

"Well," Pastor Layton thought as he gazed at Elizabeth. "Mistress Elizabeth is a strong, healthy girl. She should bear several good sons. She's a hard worker and an excellent cook. I'd say you're getting a good deal."

"Okay, then," Dean conceded, although he felt deeply disturbed.

As much as he hated the idea of getting married, he resented the pastor dealing with it as if it were just another business deal. Dean fumed while Pastor Layton did the writing, then signed the paper with two townsmen who had stopped by to witness it. Back at the inn, Dean let out his anger.

"He treated you as if you were a piece of meat!" he told Elizabeth as they spread the barley on the roasting trays.

"So?" Elizabeth was slightly amused by Dean's reaction, even as it puzzled her.

"But you're not. You're a woman."

"And that's exactly how he treated me. And he got a very good settlement for me."

"I knew I was being taken to the cleaners."

"It was a fair settlement." Elizabeth paused and looked at him sadly. "You don't think I'm worth it?"

Dean groaned, caught again. "Of course, you are. It's the way he evaluated you as if all I wanted was your kids and your elbow grease."

"That's what a wife is for."

"Not where I come from! And I'll be damned if that's the kind of wife you're gonna be. There's a whole lot of other important things that he forgot, like companionship, and love. Anything but kids and how much work you can do for me. Geez, he even figured all I wanted was boys!"

"Well, girls are a liability. You must pay dowries for them, and they're not cheap. I just wish I had more to offer you. If I were with my father still, you could have had a hundred pounds, plus five sacks of wool every year for five years. I heard him offer that once for me, but he couldn't get enough from the man." She sighed as they shoved the barley trays into the oven.

"Elizabeth." Dean pulled her into his arms. "I don't want any money. I just want you."

"Oh, Dean, you say the sweetest things."

That night, after the townsmen had left and the guests were bedded down, Elizabeth stole through the darkness upstairs to Dean's bed.

For Elizabeth, the days passed quickly. She said no more about the contract to Dean. But word spread fast in a village eager for any festivity, let alone a wedding. Elizabeth wasn't sure she and Dean would be able to stay long enough to accommodate the village. Nonetheless, she had protection from Master Blount and an excuse to be intimate with Dean, so she happily accepted the congratulations.

She only worried about Robin. If someone found out the truth about her, it was likely Robin would be hung and probably raped. Not a pleasant thought. Robin's quick wits were the only reason Elizabeth didn't worry about it too much. It amused Elizabeth no end that Robin, although a woman, had the heart of a man, and certainly more intelligence than most.

Dean, for his part, refused to worry about his sister, at least initially. He knew the consequences could be dire if she got caught. But that was if she got caught. Dean figured the odds were against it. Robin was just too smart.

If anything, he was too busy compensating for her absence to worry. There really wasn't all that much extra work to do since the garden was finished for the fall. But Robin had a knack for repair work that Dean did not have. Something around the inn always needed fixing, Dean noted to his dismay.

He accepted the ribbing from the townsmen about his upcoming nuptials with congenial indifference. They didn't have to know the truth. Once Robin was back, they would leave. With any luck at all, Dean could convince Robin to let them go home. He'd like to see the townspeople try to find them after that. And in the meantime, he still had his nights with Elizabeth.

When Robin still hadn't shown up after a week, Dean did start to worry. Elizabeth worried because there hadn't been even the slightest sign of trouble from Master Blount, and she knew that couldn't last.

"He must be planning something." Elizabeth sighed as she removed the bread from the oven that morning. "He's not the type to forget his revenge."

The weather had chilled even more, with an icy wind whipping through the village, tearing the last of the autumn leaves from the trees.

"So let him plan," Dean replied. He was taking a break

from the stables and warmed his hands by the fire. "Robin's gonna be back any time now, and then we'll take off. We'll be gone before old fatso has a chance to strike."

"That's if Robin comes back."

Dean bit his lip and hoped that Elizabeth hadn't seen. "Okay, I admit it's possible she won't. But I know her. Hell, she got us this far. She's no dope. I've got a lot of confidence in her."

"But what are we going to do if she doesn't come back?" Elizabeth fretted with the edge of her apron.

"Stay here, I guess. There's no place else to go, and I can't work that machine of hers, even if I could find it."

"I think I know where it may be."

"That hidey-hole behind the bed, right?" Dean shook his head. "I already looked. It isn't there."

"It must be somewhere she could get it easily. It's funny, right after Master John's death, I saw her cutting a piece of board. It must have something to do with where she hid everything."

Dean shrugged. "Who knows? Like I said, it's no help if I find the thing anyway. I can't work it. So, we're stuck here."

"That's not so bad, is it?"

"I guess not. But it's going to be awful hard on my parents if they never see me again. That, and…" He sighed and looked at her.

They'd had this conversation several times already. Some days, when Dean would expound on the wonders of modern medicines that cured and stopped the plague, on longer lifespans, on being able to keep one's teeth all one's life and light-bulbs and running water, Elizabeth looked as though she liked the idea. Dean could tell this was not going to be one of those mornings.

He wasn't sure what bothered him more, the fact that Elizabeth was still apprehensive about his time or that she'd follow him there whether she wanted to go or not. He kicked the andiron in frustration.

"I'd better get back to work," he said, turning for the door.

"Dean, your cloak." Elizabeth looked around for the garment.

But as Dean opened the door, he stopped. "What was that?"

"Dean, you're forgetting your cloak and your gloves." Elizabeth looked over at the hook next to the door, where the cloak was supposed to be.

"Sh!" Dean listened. "It sounds like someone screaming."

"It's probably a seagull." Elizabeth finally found the cloak and gloves on the chair next to the fireplace.

"That's no seagull. Somebody's in trouble on the beach." Dean ran off.

"You forgot your cloak and your gloves!" Elizabeth grabbed the articles, plus her own and ran off after him.

As Dean hit the beach, he saw a woman on some of the rocks near a seaside path. She pointed out towards the water. Others hurried up from the village. Out on the water just beyond the breakers, a small dark figure bobbed. Dean saw the small arm sweep up.

"We'll get a boat!" someone called.

There was no time, not with the water as bitingly cold as the icy wind driving the surf to fury. With no time to debate it, Dean shed his boots and doublet as he ran for the water.

"Dean!" Elizabeth screamed, but her words didn't register.

Dean dove headlong into the crashing waves. The freezing water shocked and numbed him almost to paralysis. He broke the surface and got a good strong breath. Years of experience took over. His arms moved up and over his head and kicked his legs from the hip. Dean swam across the surf, not against it, diving when a breaker was about to crash down on him.

He was five feet away when the boy sank. Dean dove once more and caught him. The low tide left a wide expanse of beach and Dean in water too deep to stand in. He treaded water as he checked the tiny victim. The boy had stopped breathing. Dean quickly turned him over his arm, forced the water out of his lungs, then set the child floating on his back. Dean bent back the head and blew life-giving air into the child's lungs.

This time, it worked. A few minutes later, the boy coughed and spit up more water. Sighing with relief, Dean cradled the boy in his arms and began the swim into shore. He let the waves do much of the work, floating in on his back, with the child on his belly. He stood the moment it was possible to get anywhere that way, holding the child next to him, giving what warmth his chilled body had left.

The noise on the beach was incredible. The mother screamed for her child.

"Get some blankets, damn it!" Dean yelped.

Elizabeth was there in seconds, wrapping Dean's cloak around the two.

"Let's get them back to the inn," she called. "There's a fire there and soup."

Close to exhaustion and chilled to the bone, Dean sank into the chair next to the kitchen fireplace. Someone had already relieved him of the child, and his mother sat across the fireplace from Dean, holding her son and crooning softly.

"Everyone else, stay out!" Elizabeth demanded fiercely. "We don't have room, and I need to shut the door to keep the warmth in. Oh, no! Goodbye!"

"He'll be all right," Dean gasped to no one in particular. "He's a trooper."

"What strange spell is he uttering?" the boy's mother asked.

"It's no spell!" Elizabeth snapped. She handed a bowl of soup to her. "Have him drink this. It'll warm him. It's only soup."

The woman sniffed at it anyway. "Well, it smells like it."

Elizabeth ignored her as she made Dean drink from another bowl, then stripped him of the wet cloak and replaced it with a blanket. Dean was shaking so hard he found it difficult to maneuver the warm bowl to his mouth. After the first few sips, the shaking slowed. Elizabeth ran upstairs.

"Damn, I'm cold," Dean grumbled.

"What took you so long out there?" the woman asked.

"I was saving your kid's life, lady."

She trembled. "With magic?"

"Aw, come on," Dean groaned.

"Dean, hush," Elizabeth commanded as she re-entered the room. "Here, Mistress, wrap the child in this."

The woman took the blanket in wonderment. "It's from your own bed."

"Yes."

"I don't understand this." She slowly began weeping. "I have seen something fearful, yet I feel I must be grateful."

Someone knocked loudly on the kitchen door.

"Mary?" called a man's voice.

"My husband," said the woman.

Weary, Elizabeth opened the door and admitted the young farmer.

"Mary, how is he?" The farmer rushed to the woman's side. Elizabeth placed him as Master Fletcher.

"Chilled now, but he'll be all right," replied Mistress Fletcher.

"I've heard the worst rumors," continued the farmer.

"He saved our son. That's all we need concern ourselves with," his wife answered. "Mistress Wynford has been exceedingly kind, too, even when I was not very charitable. I can only pray she'll forgive me."

Elizabeth nodded.

Master Fletcher stood. "Thank you, both. I don't have words enough to express how I feel but thank you. We'll go now. He's warm enough. It'll be best if we get him back to his own hearth as soon as possible. Thank you again."

In a few minutes, the people were gone. Elizabeth shut the door, then crossed over to the bed, sank down onto it, and sobbed.

"What's the matter?" Dean asked.

"Why did you have to stay out there so long?"

Dean rolled his eyes. "He had stopped breathing. I had to get that going again before I could bring him in."

"Did you have to?" Elizabeth all but shrieked.

"Would you rather I let the kid die?"

"No! It's just no one has ever seen anyone float in one place like that and come out alive."

"In salt water it's easy." Dean pulled the blanket even closer around him.

"Not like that." Elizabeth choked and glared at him. "There are those who fear you used magic."

Dean coughed. "I was just treading water. It's the first thing they teach you in swimming class."

"Dean! Master Blount was there, and he was smiling!"

"Fuck!"

"I knew he was waiting for something, and now I know what," Elizabeth sobbed.

"Don't worry." Dean sighed. He was too tired and too cold to move from the fire. "Come here. It's gonna be all right. I don't know how, but it'll be okay. They can't bust you for saving somebody's life."

"But they can for witchcraft, and that's what Master Blount will say you used to save that boy." Reluctantly, Elizabeth came over to the fire and knelt at Dean's side.

"Well, there's not much I can do about it now. I sure as hell wasn't going to let him drown. If I know Blount, he may have rigged the whole episode. Probably bribed the broad to bring her kid out there, and then he knocked the brat in when she wasn't looking."

Elizabeth trembled as she put her head in his lap. "You'll never prove it."

"So what? As soon as Robin comes, we're taking off. Who cares?"

"What if she doesn't get here in time?"

"We'll cross that bridge when we come to it."

In another hour Dean and his clothes were dry, and he was warm enough to function. He still carried around that deep chill that nothing can warm. Elizabeth fed him another bowl of soup.

Dean had just finished when Master Blount arrived to arrest the two of them. The charge was witchcraft. Elizabeth remained resolute and calm until they shut the gaol door on them. Then she burst into almost hysterical sobs.

"We're gonna be all right!" Dean yelled, shaking her. "They can't convict us. We're innocent."

"They can too!" Elizabeth sobbed back. "It's a curse I must live with."

"Don't be silly."

"But it's true!" Elizabeth tried to hold her tears back but finally gave in. "You may as well know the worst. Everywhere I go, Dean, I am accused of witchcraft. That's why I didn't want to back to Kent. I am a convicted witch there. Oh, Dean, I was innocent then, too. It didn't matter. I thought I was doing something good, learning my psalms. But I somehow learned to read them on my own and they all said it was by the power of the Devil because I could read other things, too. And I told Mistress Langley that the sheriff had the pox, which anyone could tell by the way he scratched himself, only she said I had cursed him, and he got it. And someone else said that I crossed my eyes at their cow, and it stopped milking. I don't even remember seeing the silly cow! But that's why I went with Roger. He got me from the gaol the night before I was to be hanged. And then there was Downleigh and now this. Dean, I must be a witch or something horrible to have this happen. Oh, you must hate me."

"What?" Dean gaped, then pulled her into his arms. "Don't be ridiculous, Elizabeth. There's no such thing as witches. Okay, maybe there's this pagan religion thing, but that's not us."

"But it is me. It must be. And now you know my shame."

"Shame, my ass. You're not a witch and neither am I. We're just damned unlucky and manage to get on the bad sides of the wrong people. That's all this witchcraft nonsense is. It's just politics. It was the same way with the Salem witch hunts. There's a play about it called 'The Crucible.' We did it in high school. You get on someone's bad side, and they call you a witch, and bang, you're in jail."

"But Master Blount can buy a lot of witnesses, and after today..."

"Don't worry. We'll get out of this. I don't know how, but we will. I've got this thing about being hanged. I figure it's not too good for my health. Now, hold on. Someone's coming."

It was Pastor Layton. He sighed as he approached the gaol. It was a small single room building near the church. One of Blount's goons accompanied the pastor.

"I'll examine them alone," Pastor Layton instructed the man. "You may come fetch me when I call."

The goon silently opened the locked door, admitted the pastor, then locked the door and left.

"Well," said Pastor Layton. "I have been sent by Master Blount to examine you for witchcraft."

"We haven't done any," said Dean stubbornly.

"I'm somewhat inclined to agree. But there are some things." The pastor shook his head. "You and Master Robin are a strange threesome. It's nothing I can put my finger on, of course. And today's event. By what power did you rescue that child?"

"By God's power, what else?" Elizabeth blurted out.

"But I must find out," returned the pastor. "Was it truly a miracle or an act of the devil? He is known to appear as an angel of light."

"But don't you think," interrupted Dean, "that if it was something evil, there'd be something fishy about it somewhere?"

"Of course," Pastor Layton answered.

"Well, I'm all right. The kid's all right."

"I know," said the pastor sadly.

"That's the whole problem," Elizabeth said suddenly. "Pray forgive me for being so forward, but that's it. You can't find any evil stench about the act. I can see you can't. It was a good innocent act, aided by the grace of God. The stench about it is that of Master Blount."

"True," Pastor Layton conceded. "But Master Blount is a powerful man, and he does have the ear of my bishop. Rest assured, I would far rather lose my post than let innocent people go to the gallows. But if I lose my post, your doom is sealed. What we need is time. I think that I might be able to stall the trial. I don't know for how long. Master Blount would have you convicted and hung by tonight if he could. All we need is a little bit more time. Then..." He looked at the two. "It has reached my ears that two young men have left the army, a Master Edward Skippington, and a Master Robin Parker. No doubt Master Blount knows this also and is looking for them."

"Then they shall be captured," said Elizabeth nervously.

"I'm not sure." replied the pastor. "As you know, Master Robin has very quick wits. An odd one, all right. If it be the same oddity as Master Edward's, no one will even look for them. I must go."

Before another word could be said, Pastor Layton called for the goon and left.

"I guess we sit back and wait," sighed Dean when they were alone again.

"I almost wish Roger would come along just now."

"I'll give you better odds that Robin gets here first."

Elizabeth shrugged, and Dean set about trying to make the floor a little bit more comfortable. Then they both sat back and waited.

Chapter Fourteen

R obin and Edward arrived in the outskirts of Charing Vale late in the afternoon as the sun was just beginning to set. Robin had them hide until full darkness could cover their entry into the village. The day was bitter cold, and the night even colder. Edward was anxious, once the sun set, to hurry to her home. But Robin held her back.

"Too many people are abroad yet," she said. "Look at how many houses there are lit up by candles."

They waited three more hours. The night grew colder around them. Finally, Robin decided it was safe. Edward led them through the dark streets to her father's house. The door was unbolted. Edward admitted Robin and shut the door silently.

"Wait here," Edward whispered. "I'll go fetch my parents."

"Who's there?" a voice coming from the stairs hissed.

"Father?" Edward asked.

"Bess, is that you?" answered the voice.

"Yes, sir."

"Who's with you?"

"Master Robin, Father."

"She's home!" a woman's voice called out. "Put away that pike, Matthew!"

The light of a small candle appeared at the top of the stairs. It was carried by a large woman in a flowing gown, her hair loose and flying about her nightcap. She hurried down the stairs, followed by her husband, who was similarly dressed.

"Oh, Bess, at last," the woman crooned. She found another candle in the best room chest and lit it.

"Bess?" Robin asked Edward.

"It's my real name," Edward replied.

Her mother turned to Robin. "Oh, Master Robin, I want to thank you so much for bringing my child back. I'm sure you know why she couldn't stay."

"I do, Mistress."

"It's such a blessing it was you who brought her," Mistress Skippington continued. "And that you arrived now when you're needed so badly."

"What's wrong?" Robin's heart stopped.

"Today, your brother and cousin were arrested for witchcraft."

"What?" Robin let loose a short string of obscenities, then turned on Mistress Skippington. "What did that idiot brother of mine do now?"

"We know them to be innocent," Master Skippington said. "It's more of Master Blount's evil. He simply took advantage of a most unfortunate accident that resulted in some most peculiar actions by your brother."

"But what happened?" Robin demanded.

"Master Fletcher's youngest son somehow contrived to fall into the ocean this morning, near that part of the beach closest to the inn." Master Skippington took a deep breath. "Your brother realized that to fetch a boat to rescue him would take far too long, so he dove into the waves and swam after the boy. As if that wasn't peculiar enough, he remained in the water with the child for a full five minutes before returning to the beach."

Robin knew exactly what had happened. She hadn't been raised on a beach for nothing.

"They just floated in one place for five minutes," Mistress Skippington cried. "I've never seen anything like it."

"Surely you've seen people swim before," Robin said.

"Of course," replied Mistress Skippington. "But staying in one place like that?"

Robin groaned. "It's simple once you know how."

"But why?" Mistress Skippington pressed. "It was frightfully cold out there."

"He was probably tired and catching his breath before trying to swim in," Robin explained, although she doubted that was the real answer. The truth would only frighten the others more. She hoped Dean had kept his mouth shut about that.

"That makes sense." Master Skippington nodded. "The trouble is that while most of the townspeople believe they are innocent, they were frightened, and Master Blount surely has paid for enough witnesses to guarantee a hanging tomorrow."

"I don't doubt it." Robin sighed. "Well, that settles it, we're leaving town. We were planning on it anyway. I sure as hell wasn't going to stay in the army."

"And why not?" asked Master Skippington.

Edward giggled. Robin glared at her.

"Somebody has to take care of my dumb brother," Robin

said quickly. Edward giggled again. Robin turned on her. "You, come here for a second."

Edward obeyed. Robin pushed her over into a corner, then checked to see that her parents couldn't overhear.

"Don't you dare say anything about me," Robin said with quiet firmness. "If I'm leaving, I've got to stay in disguise. Besides, you know anyone else who can get those two out of wherever they are?"

"But they all know you're quick-witted," Edward said.

"They know I'm quick-witted as a man. Everything changes once they find out I'm a woman. Remember, Samuel wouldn't listen to me after he found out."

"And you're smarter than he is. All right, I won't say anything. You're one lucky woman, you know that. I envy you."

"Thanks." Robin paused, then took the small purse they'd taken from the peddler and opened it. "Here's your share of the booty." She glanced over her shoulders to make sure Edward's parents couldn't see. She removed half of the coins and pressed them into Edward's hand. "You earned it like a man, you keep it like one."

Edward sniffed and embraced Robin.

"All right," said Robin in her normal voice as she pulled away. "Do you know where Dean and Elizabeth are being held?"

"In the town gaol, next to the church," said Master Skippington.

"That should be fairly easy to break them out of." Robin thought. "Who's guarding them?"

"No one," Master Skippington said. "They're locked in.

There isn't a locksmith in the town, and the nearest one wouldn't dream of crossing Master Blount."

"I don't think we'll need a locksmith. I'd better go get some things from the inn first. I do want to thank you for your kindness. I'll be off now." Robin turned for the door.

"Wait!" said Master Skippington. "I'll go with you. I can help you carry what you need from the inn."

"If I can't carry it, I can't take it," said Robin.

"But your brother can. I'll take his place until you are able to liberate him."

Robin sighed. "Thank you, sir. Your help will be much appreciated."

Master Skippington disappeared, then came back a few minutes later, fully dressed. Robin slipped out of the house with him following. As she approached the inn, she saw a dim light glowing in one of the upstairs windows. Master Skippington gasped.

"Ghosts?" he asked.

"Hardly," Robin replied. "I've got a feeling someone thinks there's more money in there than we've let on." She pulled her pistol from her sash. "Come on. But be as silent as possible. We'll want to surprise him."

With Robin in the lead, the two stalked silently up to the inn. The street door was half open. Robin slid through without a sound, Master Skippington did likewise. Footsteps above approached the stairs. Robin scuttled underneath the stairs, with Master Skippington on her heels.

Though the intruder tried to move quietly, the stairs creaked softly as he came down. He turned into the best room and Robin recognized him: Master Neddrick. He carried a small candle with him, and he went straight to the chest and rifled through its contents. Robin turned to him and aimed.

"Evening, Master Neddrick," she said.

Stunned, the tall man whirled around.

"I assure you," Robin continued. "You are well within accurate range of this pistol. It's amazing what one picks up in the army, isn't it? Master Skippington, would you kindly tie and gag the gentleman? Isn't it a funny coincidence that you show up, Master Neddrick, just as another manufactured witchcraft charge was brought against my brother and cousin?"

"You know this man?" Master Skippington asked, tying Neddrick's wrists.

"We've run into him before," replied Robin. "I don't know what he's got against us, except that he wants my cousin for some purpose. Odd how he just happened to have the ear of someone else who wanted to hang us for witchcraft. I wouldn't be surprised if he weren't behind this charge and my conscription into the army. It makes sense. Get rid of the brains of the family, and then move in on the others. It had to be you, Master Neddrick. Master Blount just isn't that smart or that subtle."

"Indeed not," agreed Master Skippington.

Donald Long glared furiously at Robin, at a complete loss for words. It was impossible. If the information he'd gotten in London was correct – and there was no reason to doubt it – the Parkers and Elizabeth would be in London in a week or so. Perhaps he would catch them on the road. But no. They'd recognized him in London. There had to be some way to get to Elizabeth. The DNA hadn't lied. Or had it?

Skippington applied the gag with added viciousness. They seated Master Neddrick next to the wall so his feet could be bound. Robin went through his pockets and only found a nasty looking knife. A quiet groan startled her.

"What?" She turned.

In the corner, Pastor Layton lay crumpled in a heap and was slowly coming to.

"Oh, no!" Robin scurried over to him. "What happened to you?"

"Master Robin?" asked the pastor weakly.

"Yes, it's me." She gently turned him onto his back.

"Praise be to the Lord, you've returned. Have you heard?"

"Yes. That's why I'm here."

"It's why I came. I came after dark, so I shouldn't be found out. I wanted to fetch some blankets for them and some food. I came in, and that's the last thing I remember."

Robin waved the candle in front of his eyes. They weren't dilated.

"You've been hit on the head," she said. "You should be okay. But you should go straight home and stay in bed for several days, at least."

He struggled to a sitting position. "I can't do that."

"You could die if you don't." Robin glanced around. "Master Skippington, will you help the pastor home?"

"Wait!" Master Layton cried out. "Master Robin, don't you understand? If there is to be any chance of them escaping conviction, I must present myself at the trial tomorrow and give evidence."

"There's not going to be a trial," said Robin curtly. "We're leaving permanently. I didn't exactly get an honorable discharge."

"But the inn..."

Robin sighed as she looked around the best room. "Boy, is Samuel going to be mad. Wait. Pastor, will you see to it that the deed is signed over to Samuel Shepwell when he returns? It's here in this chest." Robin ran over and got the piece of paper, plus some others. "Here it is. And here are Master Miller's notes on how to brew the porter, and where to buy supplies."

Pastor Layton smiled and nodded. Master Skippington came over to take the pastor. Robin slipped away and upstairs. Besides blankets and food, there were a few things she wanted that she didn't want anyone else to see.

Neddrick had been through Master John's bedroom. The hidden hole behind the bed was opened, and empty. Robin stuck her hand in and smiled. The false back she'd put in was still intact. She removed it and the three bags the remaining hole contained. In the bags were almost twenty pounds in various pieces of change: earnings from the inn, leftovers from Master John's money, plus the loot from the thieves. There were also a small black time machine, a terry cloth towel, and an iPhone and its speaker dock. Robin hurried back downstairs. Master Skippington had been replaced by Master Shepwell.

"Master Skippington told me what happened here. We met as he was taking the pastor home," Master Shepwell said. "I was on my way to the gaol, to see if I could bring anything to make Master Dean and Mistress Elizabeth more comfortable. Master Skippington said I should come here."

"Oh. Thanks. I just want to get as much cheese and dried sausage as we have into these bags. And blankets, and a pot or two."

"Master Skippington has already seen to that. I'll help you carry them. What about your prisoner?"

"Leave him. There's no way to carry him and everything else."

"Yes, there is. You have a handcart."

"Yeah. Hey, I've got an idea." Robin chuckled. "Yeah. That's perfect. Bring him along."

Master Shepwell brought the handcart around and dumped Neddrick into it. The two hurried along the quiet streets to the gaol. Robin was surprised to see that Dean and Elizabeth were still awake.

"We've enough food," Dean hissed through the bars as he heard them approach.

"What food, you dope!" Robin hissed back.

"Robin!" Dean replied with delight. "Boy, am I glad to see you. See, Elizabeth, I told you."

"I'll bet you're glad," Robin returned. She looked at the lock and nodded. "You two get as far back from the door as you can."

"Why?" asked Dean.

"Just do it." Robin pulled her pistol from her sash once more.

With the barrel on top of the door lock, she squeezed the trigger. Nothing happened. Robin glared at the pistol, hit it with the heel of her hand and squeezed again. The heavy iron padlock danced against the bars of the door. Robin brought the butt of the pistol down onto the lock. It fell away easily. She swung the door open.

"Where did you get that gun?" Dean asked.

"Never mind," said Robin as she re-loaded. "Just get your butts out of there."

"Just a second, we got some stuff to collect."

Robin nodded at Master Shepwell. As soon as Dean and Elizabeth emerged, Master Shepwell entered the gaol and dumped Neddrick in. Elizabeth gasped as she saw him.

"He was behind this," she said.

"No kidding," said Robin.

"Tis a pity," said Master Shepwell, shutting the door. "I wish you didn't have to leave. We've been looking forward to the wedding."

"What wedding?" asked Robin.

"Master Dean and Mistress Elizabeth are betrothed," replied Master Shepwell. Dean squirmed. "Surely you knew about that."

"Oh, they are?" Robin glared at the pair. "No, I didn't know. I'd sure like to know more, too."

"It's a long story," said Dean quickly. "Let's get out of here. Half the town probably heard that gun go off."

"Half the town is helping us escape," Robin pointed out. "Nonetheless, you're right. Is everything loaded on the hand-cart?"

"Yeah," Dean shook his head. "Sheesh, we've got enough food to last us a year."

"Hopefully, we won't need it for that long." Robin turned. "Master Shepwell, please convey our sincerest thanks to everyone."

"I will, Master Parker, Master Dean, Mistress Wynford, farewell, and God go with you."

"And you too," said Elizabeth.

They hurried off, slipping through the streets to the south road. Once out of sight of the town, Robin headed them off the road and across the fields to the London road. They traveled a couple more hours, then bedded down for the night.

The next morning, Robin had them up early and off again. But this time they stayed on the road because of the handcart. Dean and Elizabeth were silent. Robin saw they were waiting.

"All right," she said about mid-morning. "What's the long story, Dean?"

"It's no big deal," he replied. "We just had a marriage contract drawn up so Blount couldn't do the same and get Elizabeth that way. Elizabeth knows we're not really betrothed. It was just to protect her. That's the only reason I went along with it."

"That, and you knew it would be pretty hard to enforce a three-hundred-year-old contract," Robin answered cynically. One look at Elizabeth told her there was a lot more involved, at least on the girl's part.

"Hey, I wasn't thinking aboutdidn't think of that," Dean said.

"I'm surprised," said Robin. "I'll bet this whole thing was Elizabeth's idea."

"And if it was?" Elizabeth said, defensively.

Robin sighed. "Elizabeth, surely you realize that Dean cannot stay in the Seventeenth Century. That's going to make it awfully hard for you to marry him."

Elizabeth shrugged.

"Hey, Robin, can we stop for lunch?" Dean asked.

"I guess."

They pulled off the road into a little thicket. Elizabeth laid out a blanket and set out bread and cheese while Dean took Robin aside.

"Robin, will you please go easy on Elizabeth?" he asked. "The past few days have been really rough on her."

"What do you mean?"

"You want to know the real reason she didn't want to go back to her family?"

"All right."

"She was convicted of witchcraft. Roger pulled her the night before she was supposed to be hanged. She's really upset 'cause she thinks she's under some sort of curse that she's going to get busted for witchcraft wherever she goes."

Robin shook her head. "That's ridiculous."

"Maybe, but she really believes it."

Robin sighed. "You really like her, don't you?"

"Well, yeah."

"Do you want to marry her?"

"Aw, come off it, Robin." Dean flushed.

Robin paused, suddenly sorry she'd asked. Dean wasn't denying it and even a blind person could see he was just as hooked as Elizabeth was.

"You think it's time to go home yet?" Dean asked.

"And what about Elizabeth?"

"Bring her with us. She'll get along in our time. And people won't be trying to hang bogus witchcraft charges on her."

Robin frowned. "Maybe."

She turned away. Clearly, Dean had had enough of their adventure. But there was still Elizabeth. Robin found it hard to dismiss the memory of how frightened the girl had been in the future. It would be cruel to bring Elizabeth forward again. Yet how to resolve hers and Dean's obvious affection for each other?

"Why don't we try getting lost in the big city first?" Robin said finally.

"Huh?"

"London." She turned back to the blanket where Elizabeth was waiting. "Hey, Elizabeth, how do you feel about settling down in London for a while?"

Elizabeth smiled happily. "Oh, that would be most interesting. I've always wanted to go to London."

"Well, there you have it," Robin said triumphantly.

She did not see Dean winking at Elizabeth as if to suggest that they two were just going along to indulge Robin. Which they were.

In the gaol in Charing Vale, Donald Long paced relentlessly. Guards were mounted as the prisoner made every attempt to escape. It wasn't until after the January Assizes were held and he was bound and taken to Scotland that he fell into a sullen stupor, mumbling over and over that he couldn't have failed. The DNA had matched his. He was the baby's father. It was unquestionable. He was the baby's father.

Chapter Fifteen

T he journey to London was relatively uneventful, even though bad weather delayed the three for a couple days. Exactly one week after their departure from Charing Vale, Robin, Dean, and Elizabeth found themselves facing the northern edge of the City of London. It was almost dark as they crossed the city limits.

"Well, here we are," said Robin without enthusiasm.

"It sure smells," Dean observed.

Elizabeth shrugged. The dense collection of houses, all of them tall and hanging over the street, left the threesome feeling rather overwhelmed. People crowded the streets, as well as the odd horseman or two. The shadows were deep, and the gathering dusk made them worse.

"I suppose we should try to find out where we are," said Robin.

"Don't you know?" asked Dean.

"Dean, the last time we were in London, it was a hell of a lot more modern, and most of the streets were actually marked, which is more than you can say for these streets."

"What do we do?"

"Find an inn, which we'd better do pretty quickly." Robin

looked around. "From what I remember, these streets at night aren't exactly safe."

"Can't be that bad," said Dean.

"They make a dive bar in a Navy town look like a tea shop."

Dean nodded. "Maybe we'd better find an inn."

Taking a deep breath, Robin pushed the handcart before them into a gloomy side-street. Several houses had signs above the doors, but they were all tradesmen's lodgings. As the dark settled, the street emptied of people and Robin was concerned.

"What's this one?" Dean asked, looking at easily the thirtieth sign they'd seen.

"He makes candles." Elizabeth sighed.

"That he does," sneered a rough voice. "You need any?"

"No, we're looking for an inn." Dean turned to face a group of five very dirty, nasty looking men.

At that moment, the moon broke through the clouds. Robin saw something flash in the dim light.

"Dean, look out!" she screamed.

Swearing, Dean leaped back, just in time. The five men pounced. Robin pushed the handcart into them, as Dean drew his sword. But the five men almost overwhelmed them. One of them tried to take Elizabeth, but she struggled, kicking, scratching, and biting for all she was worth. Robin kicked one man, then suddenly found herself facing off two others. Yelling, she charged them, sword out and thrusting.

The men turned tail, as suddenly as they had attacked. Breathing heavily, Robin looked around. Elizabeth picked herself up out of the muck and wiped her hands off on her dress. Dean leaned against the candle-maker's door, gasping, and holding his right side.

"Scared them, didn't we?" he remarked with strained cheerfulness.

"Dean, are you alright?" Robin went over to him.

"Just scratched, I think," he replied. "Sure hurts like hell."

His head wove for a moment, then, with a groan, he slumped forward into Robin's arms.

"Dean!" Elizabeth screamed.

Robin struggled to stay upright under her brother's considerable mass.

"Dean," she whispered frantically. "Dean, please, no joking, this isn't funny."

"Is he dead?" Elizabeth asked, equally horrified.

Robin glared at her. "Damn it, help me, will you?"

"Hullo, there!" called a voice at the end of the street. "Is there a problem?"

A man in his early forties ran up, accompanied by a boy in his early teens. Both were wrapped in long black flowing capes.

"It's my brother," Robin sniffed. "We were attacked. He's been hurt."

"He couldn't have found a better place for it," said the man. He picked up one of Dean's arms and slid under it. "This here is my house. Come, Matthew, you help the lady get the handcart in the house, then show her to the front bedroom."

"But sir..." the boy began nervously.

"It wouldn't be very Christian to leave the poor fellow here," the man replied. "Remember the parable of The Good Samaritan."

Together, the man and Robin struggled, dragging Dean's unconscious form upstairs, and put him on a bed. The man lit a large candle and brought it to the bedside. Robin pulled away Dean's shirt where he'd been holding his side and swore. The cut was only about three inches long, but it oozed blood generously. Robin guessed it was deep. At least it wasn't spurting. She tore away some of Dean's shirt and pressed it to the wound. Elizabeth entered.

"He's still with us," Robin told her.

"He'll need bandages," she said softly.

"Yeah, boil them first, in clean water."

"But why?"

"Just do it, damn it!" Robin snapped.

"Come, my child," said their host softly. He placed his hand around Elizabeth's shoulders and led her out of the room. "There's water and a fire in the kitchen. We'll do as the master asks. I am Master Chandler."

As soon as she was sure they were gone, Robin allowed herself to break down a little.

"Deanie, you fucking big dope," she sniffed, blinking back the tears. "Mom's gonna kill me when she finds out I let something happen to you. You dumb cluck."

Dean moaned.

"You're gonna be okay. I'm right here. I'm gonna take care of you, just like when we were kids, okay? Come on, Deanie, you big doofus, don't die on me, please?"

Someone approached. Robin dried her tears. Master Chandler walked into the room.

"Master Robin," he said in his soft gentle voice. "I am only moderately knowledgeable about the healing arts. Perhaps if I sent for a surgeon."

"He wouldn't be able to do any more than I can," Robin replied. She lifted the bandage. "Damn, he's still bleeding. He should probably have stitches."

"A surgeon could do that."

"No!" Robin's vehemence surprised her. She ducked her head, ashamed. "No, please don't. It'll cost too much, and I don't trust surgeons."

"Perhaps you are right."

"Master Chandler, you've been extremely kind. I'm sorry I've been so rude."

"It's perfectly understandable. You are forgiven, my child."

Elizabeth returned with a bowl full of dripping cloths.

"Here are the bandages," she said.

"Are they wrung out?" Robin asked.

"No."

"Why don't you do that, then? We'll need some of them to dry, but they must stay clean."

"I've a rack we can use," said Master Chandler, leaving the room.

Elizabeth listlessly took the bowl to the window and wrung out a cloth over the street.

"Here, give me that," Robin said. "Maybe the hot water will help cauterize the wound."

Elizabeth glared at Robin as she snatched a cloth from the bowl. Robin sniffed.

"Oh, Elizabeth, I'm sorry. I'm so worried about him. I know you are, too. But damn it, I'm responsible for him."

"I know." Elizabeth blinked back tears.

"Oh, shavings. Anything happens, and you're the first one we forget about. That's not fair. I'm sorry."

Elizabeth sadly shook her head. "Robin, I know you haven't been yelling at me."

"I— if you've got that cloth wrung out, I'm not that good at tying bandages. You think you could show me?"

Elizabeth nodded. "I'll need help, anyway. It has to go under him, and I don't think I can lift him."

Robin smiled and nodded. It was Elizabeth's idea to use three cloths for the bandage. One to soak up the blood, and whatever else the wound would give up, another cloth to hold that one in place, and the third, the part that went underneath Dean, to tie it all together.

"This way we won't have to lift him all the time," Elizabeth explained.

"You've certainly got a head on your shoulders," Robin agreed.

The lifting process proved to be difficult. Dean was very heavy, and Robin was afraid to disturb the wound. But she managed it. Elizabeth's hands slipped quickly under the gap left, smoothing as she went.

While they worked on the bandage, Master Chandler slipped in with the rack, and their luggage, minus the handcart. The rack was a round one. Its legs were covered with hardened wax, but the bars had been scraped clean. Robin helped Elizabeth spread out the remaining cloths on the rack as Master Chandler left the room.

"You see, Elizabeth," Robin explained as they worked. "It's not the loss of blood that's putting Dean in so much danger.

Well, it is still dangerous, but do you remember what I told you about germs?"

"Yes, a little. I didn't understand."

"Okay. You know how moss and lichens in the forests grow on trees. Eventually, they kill the tree. Well, germs are sort of like that, except they don't always kill you, and they're so small, you can't see them."

"Then how do you know they're there?"

"You've seen pieces of glass that make things look larger, haven't you?"

"Yes."

"Well, using special glasses like that, that are very strong, somebody found out, or will, about germs. Anyway, boiling things kills these germs. If they get into Dean, they could very easily kill him, even more easily than the loss of blood."

Elizabeth frowned as she struggled to understand. "And boiling the bandages will stop them?"

"Well, there are other things, but we don't have them. What I wouldn't do for a bottle of rubbing alcohol right now."

"Rub..." Elizabeth stumbled over the word. "I wonder. Dean has a strange flask in his bag, and there are strange words on it. I'm afraid I can't read very well, but it does seem like it could be..."

"Rubbing alcohol?" Robin dove for the bags. "Where did that overgrown idiot get the brains to pack that? Hell, I didn't even think of it." Elizabeth shrugged, as Robin pulled the clear plastic bottle from underneath the iPhone. "That's the stuff, all right. Shavings. We're going to have to untie those bandages. It's just as well. We've got to keep them changed, anyhow. Don't say anything about this, okay?"

"Of course not."

"You're right. You'd know better than any of us to keep your mouth shut. I'm sorry, Elizabeth."

"It's all right." Elizabeth still felt hurt at being shut out by Robin's concern, but she couldn't help smiling at Robin's awkward attempts to make up for it.

Robin untied the bandage. The first cloth, she discarded and replaced with one of the drying cloths. This last cloth, she poured the alcohol onto first. As Robin applied the cloth, Dean stirred and moaned.

"It's hurting him!" gasped Elizabeth.

"It does sting like hell." Robin watched her brother closely. "But it's a good kind of hurt. You watch. He'll be better for it." She tied the cloths closed over the wound and felt Dean's forehead. "Damn. He's feverish. We'd better get some water and a compress. If we can get him to wake up a little, we'll have to start pushing fluids, so he doesn't dehydrate. In the meantime, we'll let him rest. He needs that the most now."

"Perhaps we should bleed him."

Robin shook her head. "He's already lost too much blood."

"But that's what's done for a fever."

"And how effective is it? Not too, I'm sure." Robin realized she'd rolled her eyes and, embarrassed, shook her head again. "Okay, it probably works often enough to keep trying it, but it's not a good idea."

Elizabeth nodded sadly.

"Elizabeth, it's not your fault." Robin hurried over to her and took her hands. "Your people just don't know these things. It's going to be another two and a half centuries before medical science really begins to get on its feet. It takes time, Elizabeth."

Elizabeth nodded again. "It seems so awkward. I like my life here. Things are so frightening in your world, and so complicated. Is that automatically better?"

"I don't know, Elizabeth," Robin sighed. "You're not the first to wonder that. Sometimes I do, too. Things have a direction here that my time just doesn't have. Sometimes I really wonder if running water and flush toilets are worth it." Dean stirred. Robin sat down next to him and took his hand. "I know medicine is. If we were at a hospital now, we wouldn't have to worry that much. The dumb lunkhead. I know I shouldn't call him that. He really is pretty smart. He just never had to use it. He was so cute as a kid. He won a beautiful baby contest when he was sixteen months. I was jealous for a week. Well, I was only nine. Then when he was three, he used to go out in the yard and pick flowers. And he always made sure he had a special bunch for everybody. He'd come waddling in, covered with dirt, and he'd say, 'A bunch for Mommy, a bunch for Daddy, a bunch for Robby.' He always called me Robby, 'cause he couldn't say Robin. He did that until he was almost four. Then he started it up again when he was six. That's when our folks got divorced. Mom went over and over it with him. But he was just too young to understand. It scared the hell out of him. I think that's why he's not as close as I am to our dad." Robin looked at Elizabeth. "You have no idea what I'm talking about, do you?"

"No." Elizabeth shrugged and smiled. "But it doesn't matter. I understand some. A child picking flowers is nothing mysterious. You were close to your brother as a child."

"In some ways. I was always taking care of him. I resented it sometimes. He was always tagging along after me, and all my girlfriends, what few I had, thought it was terrific because he was so cute. Then when he turned twelve, he rebelled. Suddenly, he didn't want to have a thing to do with girls, me included. Come to think of it, he didn't want to admit he had a family until he was seventeen. Of course, by then I was already out of college and on my own working, so it didn't bother me any."

"It seems strange to be so close to one's family," Elizabeth said. "My brothers barely knew me."

"How many kids did you have in your family?"

"Seven besides me. I had five brothers and two sisters. That's not counting the ones that were stillborn, and the three that died before they were five. The others were all alive when I left. I was the oldest. I had to run the house and raise the others when my stepmother died."

"And now you're gone. It's funny. We don't think of life being so tenuous in our time, and yet it is." Robin shrugged. "I'll go ahead and watch first tonight. I'll wake you when I'm tired."

"If you wish," Elizabeth replied.

Robin looked at her. She seemed so sad but willing to do whatever Robin asked. Robin felt guilty.

"I think I will go down and get some water for him first," she said suddenly and left.

While she was gone, Elizabeth picked up Dean's hand and held it to her cheek. It was so warm. But Robin knew what she was doing. Elizabeth kissed Dean's sleeping mouth. It did seem strange to be so close to someone. She kissed him one more time, then Robin returned.

It was a long night. Robin watched anxiously. She thought often of the time machine in the sack that she'd stashed under Dean's bed. Dean needed antibiotics. He needed clean sutures. But then Robin remembered the terrible crushing sensation as the machine worked. As dangerous as Dean's current condition was, Robin was afraid the trip ahead through time would kill him.

About four o'clock in the morning, Elizabeth insisted on taking a turn. Dean remained feverish throughout the next day and into the next night, but at least his belly remained flat and fairly soft. Robin took that as a sign that his colon hadn't gotten punctured by the sword. But there was still that fever. Robin fretted. Dean couldn't get any fluids into his system while he was unconscious. The few times he was awake, he was delirious.

"Come on, Deanie, just a little sip." Robin held the tankard to his lips. It was around midnight of the second night. "For me."

"Mom. I want Mommy," he mumbled and tossed his head.

"Mom's not here, Deanie. It's Robby. Please take a little drink."

"I want Kool-Aid."

"Pretend it's Kool-Aid. It's grape Kool-Aid. You love grape."

Dean took a sip, then another.

"That's a good boy. Try another."

Dean sipped again. "Where's Daddy?"

"He's working, Dean."

"Why is he going away? Mommy says he's not going to live with us anymore."

Robin blinked back her tears. Why, of all the rotten times in their lives, did he have to bring back that one?

"That doesn't mean we won't see him," she said, just as she had before. "We'll see him lots of times. Mommy and Daddy just think it would be better for all of us if they lived apart."

"I don't think so."

"I don't either, but they know better than we do, okay?" Robin hadn't been convinced then and was surprised to find that she still wasn't. She reminded herself that she hadn't been in her parents' position, and so had no right to judge.

"Robby, are you going away, too?"

"No, Deanie. I'm right here. I'm not going to leave you. You take another drink and go to sleep."

Robin did leave for a few minutes as soon as Dean was fast asleep again. She needed to use the chamber pot and refill the tankard. Dean seemed even warmer if that were possible. At least the bleeding had stopped, and the wound showed no signs of infection.

When she returned to the door of the room, she stopped. She heard whispering, but it wasn't in English. She looked inside. Master Chandler was kneeling by the bed. In the dim candlelight, he traced something on Dean's forehead. She watched him continue whispering for a few minutes longer. Finally, he made the sign of the cross on himself. It was then that Robin noticed the purple satin stole around the man's neck. She smiled as she realized what he'd been doing.

Master Chandler removed the stole, kissed it, then gathered the little book, crucifix, and tiny pot that he had been using. He turned, then froze as he saw Robin. She was surprised by his reaction, then she remembered.

"No, don't be frightened," she said. "Trust me. I won't turn you in. I'm not like the others."

"Are you one of us?" Master Chandler asked.

"No. I'm just better educated, and a hell of a lot more tolerant."

"Pray forgive me." Master Chandler nodded toward Dean. "The sacrament is not usually administered to those not of the Faith, but Saint James admonishes us to pour healing oil on the sick."

Robin smiled. "I don't mind. At this point, I'll take any help I can get."

"Your faith is like that of the Good Centurion." Master Chandler smiled. "I shall return to my chamber. God grant you a good night."

Robin slipped into her place next to the bed. "Master Chandler, thank you, for everything. I know how dangerous it is for you to take us in like this. In fact, I would keep your secret from Elizabeth. She isn't as tolerant as I am. And if Dean recovers, I'd keep it from him as well. He wouldn't turn you in, but he doesn't always watch what he says, and he might give you away accidentally."

"Thank you for warning me. These are dangerous times, and not only for those of my faith, I suspect, but for all England. Still, we are a church under persecution. I must be more cautious if I am to continue serving my people."

This last was muttered as Master Chandler left the room,

and it seemed as if he were warning himself more than anybody.

The next morning, Elizabeth entered the room somewhat irritated. Robin had failed to wake her yet again. But Elizabeth's heart melted when she saw Robin fast asleep at the foot of the bed.

The morning sunlight streamed in through the window and onto Dean. His color looked a lot better, and he seemed to be breathing more easily. Elizabeth picked up his hand and held it to her cheek. It was cool to the touch, though not with that awful coldness. Her hand stroked his cheek, then lay on his forehead. The fever had broken. Almost in tears, Elizabeth bent and kissed his lips. He returned it. She pulled away as his eyelids fluttered open.

"You didn't have to stop," he said weakly.

"Oh, Dean!" Elizabeth whispered. She sat on the floor next to him. "How do you feel?"

"I don't know. Weak, kinda tired. My side is sore. Geez, did I have one hell of a nightmare."

"You've been hurt badly. We feared for your life."

"Oh. Where's Robin?"

"What the hell's going on?" asked a sleepy voice from the foot of the bed. Robin shook the last of the sleep away, then bounced to her feet. "Dean?"

"Yeah. You okay?"

"Fine. You sound normal. Do you know where you are?"

"Uh, London, sixteen something or other."

Robin felt his forehead. "I'll be damned. The fever's broken."

Dean coughed weakly. "Have I been sick?"

"Yeah." Robin grabbed the tankard and turned away. She tried not to choke on her words. "You were delirious a couple times. I'd better get you some water. You're probably a little dehydrated."

She hurried out before her joy could betray her.

Chapter Sixteen

With Dean out of danger, Robin and Elizabeth were left with a little free time. Elizabeth found her place in Master Chandler's kitchen and set about putting it straight, grumbling all the while about the basically inept nature of men. Robin found herself in the shop, first watching Master Chandler at work, then helping where she could.

"Master Robin, do you have a trade?" Master Chandler finally asked.

"As a tapster," Robin replied. "My brother and I were running an inn before politics and a certain enemy forced us to leave the village."

"You won't find much of that work around here, I'm afraid," Master Chandler said thoughtfully. "All the families that own inns have more than enough help."

Robin sighed. "I'll take whatever work I can find, then. I don't intend to continue burdening you."

Master Chandler laughed. "You're no burden. I'm deeply in debt to Mistress Elizabeth for straightening out my kitchen. Many of my brothers seem to manage very well on their own. I don't." He sighed. "But enough of that. To continue, there really isn't any work available. You might be able to get a laborer's position, but those are very scarce."

"I'm not adverse to learning something new," Robin said.

"You're a little old to apprentice. It's been a long time since I've had one. I could do with the help, though. Hm. How do you feel about the candle trade?"

Robin smiled. "It's as good as any. Better than most, I suspect."

Master Chandler chuckled. "Who knows? I'll take you on, then, and your brother when he's well enough. I dare say a man of his bulk could be quite useful for lifting things." He breathed in deeply. "Just as long as Mistress Elizabeth stays. It's been so long since I've had the smell of fresh bread coming from my kitchen."

A week passed, then another. Dean remained bedridden, although it was mostly at Robin's insistence. He was not a patient invalid, but he remained cheerful. He ran Elizabeth ragged with his demands. Robin was ready to strangle him. Elizabeth intervened, eventually convincing Robin that she (Elizabeth) was quite happy to do the running, as indeed she was.

Robin worked hard. Master Chandler was very gentle and patient in his instruction but was also a demanding master. He expected nothing less than Robin's best, and she was often surprised to find she was capable of so much.

Elizabeth was equally fond of Master Chandler but in an exasperated way. Master Chandler was an extremely charitable man. Beggars were frequent visitors, and none went away empty handed. Elizabeth quickly learned to make extra bread, cheese, soup, and ale to accommodate the hungry. Master Chandler never gave away more food than Robin, Elizabeth, and Dean needed. But it was not unusual for him to skip a meal or two to make up for what he had given away.

It was this habit that exasperated Elizabeth the most. Master Chandler was already bone thin. His clothes were in tatters also. Yet the day after Elizabeth had mended his much-needed cloak, he came back without it. He had given it to a poor young man who had none. Master Chandler worked tirelessly all day. Then many evenings found him on the streets, visiting sick people and performing other good acts, or so Robin said. She went with him, to provide some defense against the many villains who came out after dark, as Master Chandler refused to carry a weapon.

One morning, toward the end of November, when the three had been with the candlemaker for almost three weeks, Elizabeth went upstairs to check on Dean. He was awake and waiting for her.

"At last!" he sighed. "Robin was just here, grumbling about what a baby I've been. Hell, she won't let me out of bed."

Elizabeth smiled. "You're getting out this afternoon. Robin wants to change the bedding."

"I know. My chamber pot's full, and will you make sure there's no one on the street before you dump it? I can't believe the way you throw everything out of the window. You're lucky there isn't a Health Department around to bust you."

Elizabeth just shrugged. It was the way one did things. But Dean never seemed to understand that.

"You seem bugged," Dean observed.

Elizabeth shook her head. "Not really. I'm tired perhaps. I didn't sleep last night."

"A nightmare?"

"No. I just didn't sleep." Elizabeth hurried out of the room with the empty chamber pot. In the small yard just outside of the kitchen, she rinsed out the pot, another of Robin's wishes. Wearier than before, she climbed back up the stairs to Dean's room.

"So, what exciting things are going on?" Dean asked the moment she entered.

"Nothing, really." Elizabeth busied herself tidying the room. "Master Chandler and Robin just got up. They were called away again last night. Robin said it was a sick neighbor."

"There's a lot of those around here."

"About average, I expect. Anyway, Master Chandler is teaching her to dip candles. It should take most of the day. He's so fussy."

Dean chuckled. "No kidding. I hear he's going to start in on me as soon as I'm up."

Elizabeth smiled. "It's a good trade. Master Chandler would be doing very well if he didn't give everything away." Taking a deep breath, she checked Dean's bandage. The wound had scabbed over and looked strangely clean.

"Does that bug you?" Dean asked suddenly.

"It shouldn't." Elizabeth paused, then went back to retying the bandage. "It's a great virtue to be charitable. I just fear for his health. He's so busy thinking of everyone else, he forgets to take care of himself. I don't know how he survived all those years alone."

Dean chuckled.

"How are you feeling?" Elizabeth asked.

"Terrific. I'm just real bored, and..." Dean snickered.

"What?"

"I just realized it's been one hell of a long time since we last made it."

"Oh." Elizabeth bit her lip. That was also what was bugging her. It had been a few weeks, and she was missing it worse than she'd thought possible. "I don't know if you're well enough yet. Robin said even the slightest strain could start you bleeding again, and I'm not going to ask her about it."

"I know." Dean sighed out loud this time. "It's mostly because of her that I kind of want to right now. You said she'll be busy all day. It's going to be easy for her to catch us any other time."

Elizabeth carefully sat down next to him. Dean's hand reached up and stroked her cheek.

"I don't want to be pushy," he said. "If you really don't want to, that's okay."

Elizabeth smiled ruefully. "I always want to, Dean." She bent and kissed his mouth. "That, I'm afraid, is my biggest problem at the moment."

Downstairs, Robin and Master Chandler bent to the tasks at hand, oblivious to the proceedings above them. They were so absorbed, they didn't notice that Elizabeth took over an hour to come back to the kitchen. Master Chandler scraped the seams off some molded candles, while Robin dipped wicks into the vat of wax.

It was slow, monotonous work. It had to be done very carefully, or the wax would not be even over the entire surface. Nonetheless, Robin found herself able to let her mind wander.

She was nervous about the night before. Some men of Cromwell's army had come across the pair as they hurried to the house of one of Master Chandler's flock so he could hear confessions. The soldiers were more than a little curious about what two honest citizens were doing on the streets at that time of night. Robin made up a long song and dance about how Master Chandler was her stepmother's brother, and how her stepmother was quite ill and had begged for Robin to fetch her beloved brother that she might see him one last time. The four roundheads seemed less than convinced, but they let the pair go on their way. Robin was reasonably sure they hadn't followed.

Still, Master Chandler's true profession was dangerous. It was true that Catholics were no longer being hanged or burned for their faith. But they remained convenient scapegoats for any and all trouble, and with the current turmoil, there were troubles aplenty.

There was no point in trying to tell Master Chandler to stop risking his neck. His entire life was centered on serving the tiny group of Catholics in the surrounding neighborhood. What Robin couldn't understand was why she was willing to take such a silly risk with him, and furthermore, endanger Dean and Elizabeth as well.

Of course, the time machine provided a nice escape route. But what if the three were separated? And could Robin leave Master Chandler to end his days in some filthy, wretched prison, however willingly he might endure it?

On the other hand, bringing Master Chandler forward in time would only complicate things far worse than they were already. After all, the original objective was to bring Elizabeth back and get her established on her own. Or was it? The more difficulty they had in establishing Elizabeth, the more Robin was forced to examine her own motives for taking the trip backward in time.

She was certain Elizabeth's welfare was at the bottom of it. The girl couldn't function in the twenty-first century, or could she? Whether or not she could was irrelevant. She belonged in her own time, and that was that. Still, there was that nagging fear that Robin was taking full advantage of the situation to satisfy her own curiosity.

Perhaps she was, but what was wrong with that? For one thing, Dean could have died as a result. Even with the rubbing alcohol, the smartest thing to do would have been to go back home, wait for the wound to heal, then try again. But how to explain the wound to their mother?

Even supposing they could explain the wound, and Elizabeth, there was always the possibility that whatever batteries there were that ran the machine would run down, and they couldn't return Elizabeth. The machine had to be driven by an unknown, at least in her time, type of power. The amount of power it took to transcend time had to be formidable. But what it was outstripped even Robin's ability to guess.

"Careful, Master Robin," Master Chandler's voice shattered Robin's thoughts. "You have to keep watching. I know it's boring, but in time you will have the skill enough to let your thoughts wander. In the meantime, concentrate on slowly, carefully and evenly."

"Yes, sir."

Master Chandler chuckled. "Be ever watching. Do not let

the day of the Lord catch you sleeping, or your master, either."

Robin smiled. Master Chandler was easily the happiest, sweetest, most giving man she had ever met. That night she woke with a start, realizing that she had been dreaming about him. Robin sighed, then laughed it off. It was ridiculous. She was a man, and Master Chandler had no interest in men that way, or in women either. His whole life was dedicated to the service of God, and His people. Robin rolled over in her bed and went back to sleep.

The next day, shortly after lunch, Robin was checking out Dean's cut, when she heard someone knocked at the front door. Elizabeth answered it. Less than a minute later her voice rose upstairs, shrill, and angry.

"That's absurd!" she cried. "We've no Papists here! We're all good members of the Church of England."

"Damn!" Robin hissed, her heart in her throat.

"Yeah, she has been awful touchy the past two days." Dean sighed.

"You idiot, they probably want to search the place."

"Uh, oh. Did you hide our stuff?"

"Damn, that too." Robin dove under the bed for the sacks. "Where's Master Chandler?"

"How would I know? You won't let me out of bed."

Robin ignored him and ran out of the room with the sacks. She bumped into Master Chandler in the hall.

"What's the noise?" he asked.

"Sh! They're searching for Papists. You'd better get your stuff together. I wonder if there's a place we can hide it upstairs."

Master Chandler chuckled. "Of course, my son. You've things to hide, too, eh? Well, come along. Elizabeth seems to be holding them at bay, but she can't much longer."

Robin followed the priest into his room, where he quickly gathered his stole, crucifixes, books and the small shrine dedicated to the Blessed Mother.

"The candle, too!" Robin grabbed it and hurried after him out of the room and upstairs. "The wax is too warm. They'll be sure to notice and wonder why you were burning a candle in the middle of the day."

"Good thinking." Master Chandler stopped at the head of the stairs and looked up. Above them was a board ceiling. Robin had never really noticed it. But it dawned on her that she had yet to see a ceiling that didn't have rooms on top of it. The top floors in all the buildings she'd seen all had just the roof between them and the sky. There was no access to this extra floor.

Master Chandler looked at her and chuckled. "There's no way to get up there, is there? Well, that's what I tell everyone when they ask. It used to be an apprentice's loft that got sealed up many years ago before I got here. Only I unsealed it for just this sort of emergency. That board, there, see it? It's loose. If you'll just give me a hand."

"Never mind. I can get it more easily myself." Robin pushed up the board easily. "Terrific. All they've got to do is touch that and we're undone. I'll just have to hold it down on top. You can hand everything up to me."

Robin did take the precaution of taking the sack with the iPhone and time machine with her as she hoisted herself into the loft. Master Chandler chuckled as he handed up the sack with the money.

"Hiding from the tax collector, are you?" he said. "I would, too, if I had any to hide."

"There's not that much there," Robin replied. "Well, maybe there is, but it won't last forever."

"Too true."

"Get downstairs, quickly! I can hear them!"

Robin set the board in place, then sat down on it. After about ten minutes, she heard the voices coming up the stairs to the third floor.

"All this bloody work," wheezed one voice loudly. "And for what? Nothing, I tell you. There's no Papist here."

"Master James, will you cease with your complaining?" said a second. "The sheriff said we were to check this house and we will. Those soldiers seemed damned certain those two on the street were priests, and this is where they said they came from."

"That wench downstairs is not hiding anybody. I've never seen anyone so insulted in my life."

"I wonder what's up there?"

"Nothing. My cousin lived in this house before the candle-maker came. It's an apprentice's loft. My cousin had it sealed off to keep out rats."

"It could have been unsealed."

Robin held her breath and leaned on the board where it should have been nailed down. The jabs were ineffectual. The two men were probably short and unable to put much pressure on the loose board.

"So much for that," grumbled the second voice.

"See? I told you. Nothing. What an utter waste of time."

"Come along."

The two went off, the first complaining. Robin waited until Master Chandler called to her.

"They're gone. It's safe to come down."

Robin cautiously lifted the board. Master Chandler smiled up at her.

"Whew!" she sighed as she slid down. "That's not a very safe hiding place. What would you do if someone came searching when you weren't here?"

Master Chandler thought it over. Robin got the feeling it was the first time he had ever considered the possibility.

He shrugged. "I don't know."

"Well, I do know a way to fix that," Robin said. "Mind if I do it this afternoon?"

"Are you that concerned for your fortune?" Master Chandler asked with an amused grin.

Robin grimaced. "Not really. I'm more concerned about your neck, and Dean and Elizabeth's also, and, if you don't mind, mine. If you get caught, we're in for it, too."

"Perhaps you are right." Master Chandler sighed. "Have at it, then."

Robin's device was ingenious. It involved poking one of the knots in the wood up and out of the board, releasing the spring on top holding the board down. The knot was jammed in very tightly and required the use of an innocent looking dowel to poke it out. Robin showed both Master Chandler and Elizabeth how to work the device in case of emergency, and where she was keeping the dowel in her room. Master Chandler had explained to Elizabeth he had helped Robin hide their cache of money but had not told her what he had hidden. Elizabeth suspected nothing and remained peeved and out of temper for the rest of the day.

Her temper did not improve over the next couple weeks, and when she awoke one morning before sunrise feeling nauseous yet again, she sighed. It was more a nuisance than anything else, but it was the third day in a row. Elizabeth dressed in the dark and went downstairs.

There, a candle burned in the kitchen, a sure sign that Master Chandler had been called away during the night. Elizabeth thought it very wasteful, but if anyone could afford to waste candles, Master Chandler could. She went to the buttery, hoping to find some of the crusts from the evening before still there.

They were. Elizabeth nibbled on one gratefully. She wondered at the instinct that told her to seek out food when it was her stomach that was upset.

At that moment, the back door swung open and Master Chandler and Robin scurried in on a blast of cold outside air.

"So where have you been now?" Elizabeth asked.

"Sick neighbor," replied Robin. "Whew! It's cold out there. What are you doing up so early? It's not even five yet."

"I couldn't sleep," Elizabeth said. "I'd better stoke up the fire. You two look frozen."

"Not really," said Master Chandler cheerfully. "I think I shall just hurry to bed. But thank you for your kindness."

He scurried away upstairs as Elizabeth shrugged. Robin yawned.

"I probably should, too," she grumbled and stretched. "Oh,

before I do, Elizabeth, you got any of those clean rags around? I've got a feeling one of those days is coming up."

"So soon? Oh no, it must be. It's the ides of December."

"That we are." Robin looked at her quizzically. "Is something wrong? You don't forget things like that."

"No, I don't. It must have been Dean's injury. I've been so busy worrying about him, I haven't thought of much else."

Robin laughed. "You worry too much about him. He's doing fine. He's been lifting stuff without signs of strain. The wound has healed over. He doesn't need to be spoiled."

"I wouldn't worry about that, Robin." A fierce glint flickered in Elizabeth's eyes. "One thing I do very well is manage men."

Robin rolled her eyes skyward. "Managing people is not the idea. At least not in my time. I'd hate to be a woman nowadays. I'm not kowtowing to some stupid jerk just because he's a male. If a guy thinks he's better or smarter than me, he'd better damn well prove it. Well, goodnight."

Robin yawned again as she swaggered upstairs. Elizabeth rolled her eyes skyward, then returned to her crust. She paused. Robin's "days" had always followed Elizabeth's within hours. Robin wasn't early, either.

Elizabeth swallowed her crust uneasily. She'd been feeling nauseous for three days, and only first thing in the morning. Then there was that strange instinct. Maybe she was just upset. She had been thrown off when Dean had first awakened her, and Robin had had the same problem when they first returned to England. It seemed plausible, but deep inside, Elizabeth knew the truth.

Chapter Seventeen

E lizabeth kept her morning nausea and her secret to herself. By Christmas Eve, there was no doubt in her mind what her problem was. The only trouble was how was she going to break the news to Robin and Dean? She didn't think either of them would be happy about it. Yet she feared Robin's reaction more than Dean's.

Dean, for his part, sensed that something was amiss, but thought it was probably the whole marriage thing again and decided to let Elizabeth tell him what was going on when she was ready.

Robin was simply too preoccupied to notice anything going on with anybody. She told herself she was concentrating on the candle trade and keeping Master Chandler safe out on the streets. But finally, on Christmas Eve, she had to face facts. She was falling fast and hard for Master Chandler.

They had slipped out just after the clock had struck eleven to a house in the neighborhood, where Master Chandler said the solemn Midnight Mass. Afterwards, they only stayed long enough to greet everyone there, and then were sent off home.

"What a night," Master Chandler sighed with deep satisfaction, as they stepped outside. He adjusted the cloak Dean had loaned him and chuckled, his breath making little clouds in the cold air. "It's beautiful tonight. I do believe the clouds are clearing. Look, you can see a couple stars, and wait, there's the moon. I can't wait until tomorrow. I do hope Mistress Elizabeth will be pleased."

"About what?" Robin asked.

Master Chandler smiled mysteriously. "I've arranged a little surprise for the three of you. You've all been working so hard."

Robin shrugged. "I guess. I don't mind. It can be pretty satisfying."

"Working hard and well usually is."

"It is." Robin shivered a little in the chill, then looked away. "Do you ever get lonely, like for a woman?"

Master Chandler chuckled. "As in desiring a woman's flesh, I take it. Is that what's been troubling you, my son?"

"More or less."

"You're young and healthy. It's no surprise. Even I occasionally feel the yearnings." His smile grew utterly beatific. "But then I think of Christ crucified, there's no more glorious thought."

Robin pressed on. "Don't you ever regret giving all that up?"

"A family, you mean?"

"And, you know, relations with a woman."

Master Chandler smiled and shook his head. "I've never regretted it. I've found such inexpressible joy in God's service."

Robin forced herself to smile. "I can see that."

Master Chandler paused and looked at her. "Are you thinking of taking up the religious life?"

"Hardly." Robin wanted to talk him out of it. "It's too dangerous."

"For the body, perhaps." Master Chandler trudged on. "But far better for the soul. I can think of no greater pleasure than to look upon God's face and offer Him boundless praises." Master Chandler's face all but glowed. "It's the old Pauline dilemma, I'm afraid. I want so to continue here, serving His people, and yet to be with Our Lord is such a far greater thing, I can't help but long for it." He chuckled. "But bound to earth I am. I'll make the best of it. Well, here we are already."

In the kitchen, Master Chandler stopped long enough to give Robin his blessing before they went upstairs.

Robin went to bed feeling vaguely annoyed, but less with Master Chandler than with herself. She remembered reading somewhere that women who continually fell for inaccessible men had some issue or other, and she couldn't remember what it was. But it certainly seemed to be her pattern.

The next day, after church - Master Chandler made a habit of showing up like any other neighbor at the regular Church of England services and always with his new household in tow - Robin wearily made her way upstairs to her room. Dean followed her.

"There's gonna be a lot of people coming over," he told her.

"Yeah, I know." Robin pulled off her boots. "I'm going to try to catch a few before they get here."

Dean watched her for a moment. "You seem kinda depressed."

Robin glared at her left boot. "I don't know."

"Elizabeth said you were."

"Did she say what about?" Robin snarled.

"Hell, how's she gonna know?" Dean's voice got more defensive than he intended.

Robin backed down. "I guess she wouldn't. I shouldn't have snapped."

Dean sat down next to her. "Is it Christmas?"

"What do you mean?"

Dean shrugged. "It just doesn't seem like Christmas. There's no tree, no presents, no carols, just an extra-long church service."

"Wait 'til this afternoon."

"Well, if it isn't Christmas, what are you bugged about?"

Robin sighed. "I don't know if you'd understand. You'll probably think it's silly."

"Try me."

Robin gazed out of the window. "I think I'm in love with Master Chandler."

"So?"

She glared at him. "Dean, for starters, I'm a man, or supposed to be one."

"So, tell him the truth. He'd probably understand."

"Like hell, he would." Robin got up and started pacing. "And even if he did, there's the whole time issue. I'm not staying here for the rest of my life and bringing him with me is not going to happen."

"You could work around that, maybe go back and forth a lot."

Robin rolled her eyes. "It's not that simple and even if it was... Dean, it just wouldn't work. He's too absorbed in his candles and his charity work to be absorbed in me. It's the same problem I always have. Inevitably, I fall for the guy whose first love is something else. "

"Or just plain not available." Dean sniggered. "Who was it when you were in college? That married physics professor?"

"Let's not go through the list." Robin stopped. "How did you know about that?"

"Mom told me. She was a little worried. I mean, it sounds like fear of intimacy issues to me. You know, 'cause of her and dad."

Robin's heart sank. "You know, that's the part that really sucks about you becoming a shrink."

"I suppose." Dean shrugged. "It could be worse. I could do the whole analysis thing."

Robin flopped back onto the bed. "It doesn't matter. Sometimes I wish I really were a man."

"Why?"

"Even in our liberated times, Dean, men are usually very threatened by women who are smarter than them."

Dean laughed. "It's not just the men. Why do you think I play so dumb all the time?"

Robin looked at him. "You may have a point. But guys can still get away with it more easily than women can."

"In some ways." Dean's voice suddenly turned sour. "I haven't had much luck."

"You, Don Juan?"

"Do you see me staying with anyone? Sure, I messed around with a lot of girls. But they're all dumb bunnies, and they made a lot of stupid demands. All they wanted is sex, and I need more than that."

"No kidding." Robin sighed. "Why can't people understand that?"

Dean shrugged. "I don't know. I wish I could tell you, Robby, but I figure, if it's beyond you, it's gonna be beyond me. Maybe you'll just get lucky someday."

"Maybe." But Robin wasn't holding out much hope.

"Hey, Robby, remember when Mom and Dad broke up, and you used to take care of me?"

Robin shivered. "Boy, do I."

"I used to think then that I had the greatest, best damned big sister a kid could ever have. I still do."

Robin sniffed and turned to her brother. "Deanie, you are easily the most incredible, frustrating, aggravating creature I have ever met. But I love you more than anybody on this earth!"

They met in the middle of the room. Dean's large arms almost smothered Robin as they hugged each other. Robin couldn't hold back her tears any longer, and Dean caught himself sniffing also. Downstairs came the sound of knocking and merry singing.

"Hey, Merry Christmas, Robby."

"Merry Christmas, Deanie." Robin pulled away and wiped her eyes. "We'd better get downstairs."

"Yeah. Say, Elizabeth told me they give presents out on Twelfth Day. You think we can get together some neat surprises for then?"

"I think we could. Why don't we talk about it later? They're calling us now."

Downstairs they found not only a small crowd of neighbors but a fully cooked feast of chicken, roasted vegetables, soup, bread, apples, tarts, and cakes waiting for them. Elizabeth was in shock.

"Where did all of this food come from?" Robin asked, aghast.

"W-well," Master Chandler stammered, flummoxed himself. "I had asked Mistress Saunders to provide a dinner for us, so Elizabeth wouldn't have to cook. That was my surprise."

Dean laughed. "Looks like they surprised you."

"Indeed." Master Chandler laughed, also. "Well, good neighbors, we can't eat all this ourselves. Will you please join us? Oh, dear. I hope there's enough porter."

"We made an extra keg last week." Elizabeth couldn't hide her smile as she shook her head yet again at Master Chandler. "Robin, could you help me?"

"Hey, I can get it." Dean cut in. "Come on, Robin."

They headed to the cool room while Elizabeth helped the neighbors set up the food and the hot spiced wine. The revelry lasted late into the night. It was close to dawn before the last of the guests departed.

People continued to visit for the following twelve days. Many of them were people Master Chandler had helped during the year, coming to return the charity they had received. The tributes flowed in. Most of them went right back out again with other needy people.

Despite all the visitors, Dean and Robin each got a chance to visit the local marketplace separately. Elizabeth had already run her errands, long after conferring with Robin as far as funding went. On each of the twelve days, Elizabeth served a piece of fruit or some other sweetmeat to everyone. She also smiled with yet another secret, this time a happy one.

The big day, of course, was Twelfth Day. Again, the neighbors were expected. But that morning was reserved for Master Chandler and his new household. Elizabeth produced a magnificent breakfast for the occasion. After they had eaten, all hurried away to their respective rooms to gather all the secrets they had been so carefully guarding. They returned to the best room minutes later, tense with happy anticipation.

Elizabeth displayed her gifts first.

"Robin said I could have some money, and I was able to get some linen and wool." She displayed the two shirts and the cloak. "Here, Dean, this one is for you, and this shirt is for you, Robin. And, Master Chandler, you may have your cloak on one condition."

"What is that, my daughter?" Master Chandler's eyes glowed.

"That you not give it away. Do you promise? You must have something to keep you warm, or you'll catch your death."

Master Chandler laughed. "I must promise then, I will not give it away." He took the cloak gladly. "Now, I must present my gifts. Master Robin, behold your first mold, and the tools to carve it with. I have the same for you, Master Dean."

"Thanks," replied Dean, although his smile was a little indifferent.

"Thank you, sir," Robin replied. She understood what the tools meant in terms of Master Chandler's regard for her abilities.

"And for Mistress Elizabeth, I have this." Master Chandler

flourished his prize. "I am afraid you will have to cook it your-self."

"A pheasant!" Elizabeth glowed. "Oh, how wonderful! I don't mind cooking it at all. It's been so long since I've had any, and I do love it. Thank you, sir."

"I guess it's my turn," Robin began awkwardly. "I really didn't know what to get, so I did my best. Here, Dean, I got you this Shakespeare book, the folio."

Dean burst into laughter. "You would. Thanks, Robin."

"And, Elizabeth, please don't get mad. I got a real good deal on it. I just hope it fits." Robin presented the dress. "It's just a work dress, but yours is getting a little worn."

"Indeed, it is." Elizabeth couldn't help laughing to herself. However masculine Robin might be at times, the woman in her had won out and found the one thing Elizabeth had been hoping for. "If it doesn't fit, I can fix it."

"Good." Robin flashed a sheepish grin. "And for you, Master Chandler, I got this. It was the best one I could find."

Master Chandler took the bottle of wine and looked at it.

"I shall relish this," he said when he, at last, found the words.

"Hey, it's my turn!" Dean burst in. "Look at this, Master Chandler. Isn't it cool? You can stick it in your boot and have an extra for when you're wandering around at night."

It was a knife, clearly meant to be a weapon as opposed to the belt knives worn by nearly everyone and used for eating. Master Chandler accepted it chuckling.

"I got one for you, too, Robin." Dean handed it to her.

"Thanks, Dean." Robin laughed, mostly because Dean had

blown it yet again. She put the knife in her boot just to placate him.

"And I got this for you, Elizabeth," Dean continued, blissfully ignorant. "Why don't you close your eyes?"

"As you wish." And Elizabeth did.

Dean slid the chain and pendant over her head. "Now, look."

Elizabeth opened her eyes and felt the chain with her hand. She looked down at the pendant in wonder. Suddenly, she jumped up and ran upstairs crying.

"What?" Dean was flabbergasted.

Robin sighed. "Dean, that cost a fortune, didn't it?"

"Only ten pounds."

Master Chandler laughed out loud. "An entire year's salary, young man? Still, I've seen other boys do even more foolish things. And I must say, Elizabeth does deserve it."

The dimmer switch in Dean's brain slowly slid on. "Maybe I'd better go talk to her."

"Maybe I'd better," said Robin.

"Nope." Dean held her back. "I did it. I'll talk to her."

"All right." The sudden display of responsibility surprised Robin, but she decided not to comment.

Dean found Elizabeth in her room. She sat on the bed crying.

"I guess I went a little overboard," Dean said.

"Oh, Dean, it's beautiful!" Elizabeth sniffed. "It's just far too rich for me."

"No, it isn't." Dean sat down next to her and cradled her in his arms. "Even Master Chandler said you deserved it."

"But..."

"No, buts. Remember that contract? You're supposed to get an allowance. So, I spent it for you."

"Ten pounds?" Elizabeth gaped. "Oh, Dean, so much! And that was for after we're married. And we're not, and..." She buried her face in his shoulder, sobbing.

Dean sighed. "Elizabeth, did you have to bring that up?"

"Pray forgive me, Dean, but I must now. It's more important than ever."

"Why? I mean..." It hit Dean. "You're not trying to tell me you're..."

Elizabeth sniffed and nodded. "I am. I'm certain now."

Dean groaned his favorite obscenity.

"I'm sorry, Dean." Elizabeth looked at him fearfully.

"But you can't be. I mean, we've been using that—" Dean swallowed. "We didn't that one time, did we?"

Elizabeth ducked her head. "I forgot. It's my fault."

"It is not. I'm just as responsible for remembering."

"How are we going to tell Robin?"

"Don't even." Dean got up and started pacing. "She'd have my butt in a sling so fast."

Elizabeth shook her head. "We can't hide it forever."

"You're not too far along, are you? We'll just have to go home. It's no sweat. We can get an abortion. Hell, I'll even pay for it."

"You mean kill it!" Elizabeth was horrified.

Dean continued pacing. "Elizabeth, will you get a hold of yourself? It's no big deal."

"It is so!"

"All right, maybe it is. But it's the only sensible choice. For crying out loud, we can't support a kid right now."

Elizabeth scrambled to her feet. "If you can buy me a necklace, we most certainly can."

"Yeah, here. But it's a whole different story back home, and that's where we're staying."

"Yes, Dean." Elizabeth bowed her head.

Dean sighed. "Damn it, Elizabeth. Don't go all subservient on me."

"That is my place."

Dean heaved an even greater huge sigh. "One of these days you'll learn. Look, it's going to be all right. I'll figure something out. Okay? Are you going to trust me?"

She sank back onto the bed, weeping once again. "I always have."

It took Dean a moment to realize what she was really afraid of. He plopped down next to her and bundled her into his arms.

"Look, I'm not going to abandon you," he told her softly. "Whatever happens, we're going to do this together. And I'm not going back home without you. Honest, Elizabeth. You're the best thing that ever happened to me and I love you and it's going to be all right. I don't know how yet, but it will. I promise."

Elizabeth sobbed even harder. "Thank you, Dean."

Dean held her tightly and rocked her, wondering what on earth he'd gotten himself into.

Chapter Eighteen

Dean made up his mind. He was not going to panic. Never mind that Elizabeth's news made it impossible to enjoy the afternoon and evening. He briefly debated telling Robin and getting her advice. Very briefly. Dean took one good look at her and completely lost his nerve. Nonetheless, he refused to panic.

The next morning, he thought the whole matter over carefully. The important thing was to get Elizabeth home before she got too much further along. If an abortion were even possible in the seventeenth century, it could quite easily kill her.

Dean crept upstairs. Robin had made merry a little too late the night before and was still sound asleep. Elizabeth had shown Dean how to work the loose board some weeks before. Dean retrieved the dowel and went to work.

He found the time machine easily enough. Just in case, he left the secret loft and scurried out of the house. By this time, he was familiar with the labyrinth. He slipped down two or three streets to a small courtyard. It was deserted, which wasn't surprising when one considered that it was just barely after dawn, and very cold.

Dean turned over the machine in his hands nervously. He

remembered Robin saying something about it being so user-friendly even he could use it. That was no help. He pressed the button on the side. The button glowed for a second. Dean wondered what to do next.

It was hopeless. Dean had a bad feeling that screwing up would only get him into worse trouble. He pressed the button again and hurried home.

Robin was still asleep when he got there. Elizabeth and Master Chandler were busy in the kitchen. Furtively, Dean hurried up the stairs and re-hid the machine.

It seemed the only thing left to do was to tell Robin the truth. But when she arrived downstairs, she was so surly and grouchy, Dean lost his nerve again. There was still a little time. Dean decided he would just have to wait for a good opportunity.

The next day was the Sabbath. The day after that, Master Chandler returned from one of his errands without his cloak and with a very guilty look on his face.

"Master Robin, you'll have to help me," he whispered very quietly to her in the best room. "Elizabeth is sure to be very angry with me."

"I don't doubt it." Robin chuckled. "You barely lasted three days."

"I didn't give it away. I loaned it," Master Chandler said earnestly. "The poor young man was freezing. He said something very curious about not checking the date before homing in. In any case, he promised to bring it back as soon as he got himself one."

Robin grimaced. "I've got a bad feeling that's the last we'll see of your cloak."

"Oh, no! He was very sincere. A good bright honest face."

"Famous last words." Robin took a deep breath. "Well, I'll explain to Elizabeth. You may want to lay low for a little while."

She left Master Chandler in the best room and went back to the kitchen, struggling for the right words.

Elizabeth was not very understanding.

"Why that...!" She groaned, too furious for words.

"Now, Elizabeth. He really did believe he'd get it back. He may just yet." Robin sighed.

"He's not that stupid." She whirled away out of the room.

Robin shook her head as she heard Elizabeth calling for Master Chandler in the best room. There was no answer. Master Chandler must have taken Robin's advice and gone out again.

Robin started as she heard Elizabeth pounding up the stairs. Master Chandler was rarely in his room during the day. Furthermore, Robin would have heard him answer Elizabeth's call if he had been. Robin bolted upstairs.

Elizabeth stood in the doorway of Master Chandler's room, gazing inside in shock.

"Elizabeth," Robin said softly.

"What are these things?" she whispered, pointing at the small shrine and its candles. She turned on Robin. "You knew, didn't you? I thought at first it might be. But then I thought, no. Robin wouldn't support that. How could you!"

"How could I not?" Robin said with quiet anger. "Damn it, he saved Dean's life!"

Elizabeth was shaking. "He's still a filthy papist!"

"Yes, he is. He's a priest, too."

Elizabeth whirled away. "How could you have allowed such a thing?"

Robin exploded. "And how can you say that after all we've been through? After all the times someone's wanted to hang us for no good reason besides hating us!"

"He's in league with the Devil!" Elizabeth ignored her and paced in the hallway.

"He sure as hell doesn't act like it! It seems strange to me that someone working for Satan is gonna go around giving the food out of his mouth to anyone who needs it. Or risking his life out on the streets night after night to care for the sick."

"Have you ever been to their services?"

"Yes. Have you?"

Elizabeth remained silent but had to stop pacing.

"Good lord, Elizabeth," Robin continued. "How can you hate them without even trying to understand what they're all about? That's why there are witch trials and all sorts of nonsense like that. That's why we keep getting accused of witchcraft. People are so busy hating what they don't understand, they refuse to take a chance on maybe finding something good. It's no wonder a little scratch can kill you around here."

"But all I've ever known was that it was evil." Elizabeth sniffed, suddenly very unsure.

"Elizabeth," Robin sighed. "You know people to the very core of their being. I ask you. Is Master Chandler evil?"

"This is so hard." Elizabeth sank down onto the floor and cried. "I know he isn't. But must I deny everything I was ever taught?"

"I'm not saying you have to become a Catholic. I'm just saying that it's a stupid reason to hate somebody. That's all it really boils down to. You disagree, so you hate each other and try to kill each other. It doesn't strike me as being terribly Christian."

"It isn't," Elizabeth agreed. "So why does it happen?"

"I don't know. Some of it's a lack of education. But that's not all of it. One of the worst bigots I ever knew had college degrees coming out his ears." Robin slumped down next to Elizabeth and put her arms around her. "They're still fighting it in my time. There are laws against discrimination, and people still hate."

Elizabeth sniffed. "Maybe Master Chandler has the right way of it. He risked his life to take us in, and I'm sure not all who receive his charity are papists. He treats everyone the same. Oh, Robin. How am I ever going to understand?"

"I don't understand a lot of things myself. But I think we're both a lot closer to understanding now than we ever were."

Elizabeth nodded and laid her head on Robin's shoulder.

The situation continued to perplex Elizabeth. She knew that Robin was right, as she was about many other things. But how could practically everyone else around them be so wrong? Perhaps it was not for Elizabeth to figure out.

The next day, Donald Long found himself carefully watching the candlemaker's house from across the street. In Bath, Robin had found him before he'd found her. Or would. And Elizabeth had clearly been pregnant there. The question was when did Donald get her that way? At least, if he wasn't successful in London, there was always whatever the next stop on the timetron showed - Downleigh, where the Parkers and Elizabeth had come from.

As another tall, thin man approached, Donald stiffened. Roger. Donald wondered how Roger had figured out the Parkers were at the candle-maker's. The timetron's log only showed a turn-on in the neighborhood.

Roger York smiled as he looked at the sign. This was where the man called Master Chandler had said. Roger patted the cloak on his arm. The candlemaker would be surprised to see it back. He had tried to seem trusting. But Roger doubted the man was ignorant of basic human nature.

He knocked and entered. A young man dipping candles looked up and smiled casually.

"May I help you?" the young man asked.

Roger smiled back as he looked at the young man a little more carefully. There was something a little bit odd about him. He was taller than most men of the time, about five nine, and slightly built. But that wasn't what made Roger pause.

"I understand this is Master Chandler's home," Roger said finally.

"Yes, it is," replied the young man. "What can I do for you?"

"I've come to return this cloak. Master Chandler loaned it to me yesterday."

The young man laughed as he came over. "I don't believe it, but great. I'll see that he gets it. Thank you for returning it."

"Please tell him how grateful I am." Roger handed over the cloak, surreptitiously gazing at the young man.

"Certainly."

There was an awkward pause.

"Well, good day, sir," Roger said, and headed out.

"Good day."

Outside on the street, Roger paused. That little oddity was coming. A moment or so more thought and he would have it. It did almost in a flash. The young man had had no beard. He wasn't merely clean-shaven. Roger was sure there wasn't any beard to shave.

A hormone imbalance could easily explain it, and that sort of thing wasn't unheard of. That would also explain why the young man's voice, although tenor in range, had an immature feel to it. Of course, another explanation might be that the young man wasn't a young man, which would make sense given what the surveillance disk in the castle had shown. And if what Roger had found among Donald's research was accurate, Roger had found Robin Parker and very probably her brother and Elizabeth and the missing timetron.

The sound of someone slipping on the icy cobbles destroyed Roger's chain of thought. Just on the edge of his peripheral vision, he saw a familiar form as it righted itself just in time to give Roger a glimpse of his face before he took off running. Donald, damn him. Roger hurried after.

"Well?" Robin asked Elizabeth as they looked out the upstairs window to the street below.

"He's running off," she replied. "I saw something in the shadows. I get the feeling he did, too, and that's what he's chasing."

"But he is..."

"Roger? Oh, yes. I recognized his voice. It's a good thing I did. I almost started to come down."

Robin frowned. "He was looking at me strangely. It can't be that he recognizes me. He's never seen me that I know of."

"Perhaps it's because you do look a little like a woman," Elizabeth said gently.

"No one else seems to think so." Robin was surprised by the bitterness in her voice, then stopped. "Wait. Maybe he did recognize me. There had to be some sort of surveillance in that castle room. Great. I wonder how much he knows about us."

Elizabeth shrugged. Dean burst into the house.

"Elizabeth! Robin!" he bellowed.

They ran down the stairs. Dean was breathing heavily, and his face was flushed with exertion.

"What is it?" Elizabeth cried.

"You guys aren't gonna believe who I almost ran into!" Dean gasped.

"Who?" asked Robin.

"That Master Neddrick dude."

"Are you sure?" Elizabeth squeaked.

"Oh, damn!" Robin snapped at the same time.

"I'm positive it was him," Dean answered.

"Did he see you?" Robin demanded.

"I couldn't help it, Robin." groaned Dean. "I didn't know he was there. But then I got this weird feeling that someone was following me. I turned around and there he was. That's what took me so long to get back. I hauled it out of there and ditched him."

"We'll have to flee again." Elizabeth wrung her hands.

"I hope not," Robin sighed.

"But, Robin," Elizabeth protested. "Roger was just here, and now Master Neddrick."

"Roger?" Dean squeaked. "Aw, crap, Robin. How the hell did he find us?"

"How the hell would I know?" Robin fidgeted as she wandered aimlessly around the best room. "All right. For the moment, we'll have to assume we put Roger off. And just because Neddrick's seen Dean doesn't mean he'll be able to find us. We're innkeepers. People just don't change trades like we have. Neddrick's probably not looking for candlemakers. We'd better sit tight for a while. If we take off running now, while they're both so close, they might spot us again. Not to mention the fact that it's the middle of winter. That's no time to be hitting the road."

"We could go home," Dean suggested.

"Not with Roger this close on our heels," Robin said, then sighed. "Look, we don't want to go rushing into anything. Give me a day or two to figure how to get home without leading Roger to us."

Both Dean and Elizabeth reluctantly agreed.

But Robin didn't even get until that evening. She was grateful that Master Chandler was off on some errand when the men arrived that afternoon. Dean and Elizabeth were in the kitchen. Robin worked in the best room.

They burst in, ten strong, without warning.

"We've come for the papists!" their leader announced.

"There are none here!" Robin yelped indignantly.

The men swarmed all over the place. Robin couldn't stop them.

"What the hell's going on here?" Dean demanded, bursting into the room.

"Bind the two of them!" the leader commanded.

Elizabeth slunk up the stairs. Three men pounced on Dean. He thrashed about, but the men knew their business and quickly had him face down on the floor and tied. Robin decided against struggling.

"And where do you think you're going?" A man caught Elizabeth on the stairs and roughly dragged her down. "You whoring wretch!" He cuffed her, then tied her.

A minute later, there were sounds of cheering upstairs.

"Look what we've found!" two other men called as they ran down the stairs carrying Master Chandler's vessels and crucifixes.

"They're mine!" Robin cried out. "The others have nothing to do with it. Please, let them alone."

The leader spat in her face. Robin flinched. The other men whooped with glee as they spilled the hosts onto the floor, then ground them into paste with their heels. Robin could hold it no longer. Her tears spilled down her cheeks, thinking of how sacred the small pieces of bread were to Master Chandler. He valued them above gold, even.

At the gaol the men took Robin away. Dean and Elizabeth were pushed into a cell filled with rotten straw. As the jailer stalked off, Dean wrinkled his nose at the stench. There were sounds of soft squeaking and scratching.

"Oh, no," Elizabeth sighed, terrified.

"Terrific. Rats," grumbled Dean. "It would sure be nice to have a cat around."

"Don't say that!" Elizabeth hissed.

Dean shrugged. "At least it's not witchcraft this time."

Elizabeth shuddered. Dean came over to her and wrapped his arms around her.

"Hey, we'll get out of this. We have all the times before," he told her.

"But there was always Robin before."

"She's gonna be okay. I know she is. She's probably escaped already."

"Dean..." Elizabeth's voice broke.

"No. We've gotta keep our spirits up. We'll get out of this. We will. We've just gotta believe that."

Dean's confidence faded completely late that night when they brought Robin to the cell. She was unconscious. Her eyes were puffy and bruising. Blood had dried underneath her nose and along the corner of her mouth. From her temples rose a sickening stench, and they were bright red with dark circles around the patches.

"What the hell did you do!" Dean flung himself at the bars of the door, and yelled, swearing, after the jailer. "Can't you face me? What did you do?"

"Dean!" Crying, Elizabeth pulled him back from the door. "Here, help me lay her out."

Dean choked. "She's dead?"

"No. Help me make her more comfortable. Come, Dean. Here's some straw that isn't so old. It'll make a good pillow."

Dean complied meekly. A few minutes later, they heard the clanking return of the jailer. Dean stiffened but resolved not to lose it again.

"It's good of you to come, your reverence," the jailer was saying. "But I don't see as how it's worth it. I've dealt with these papists before. They're as stubborn as they come. Worse than most."

"And all the more needful of Our Lord's mercy, my good sir," replied the man with him. He was wearing black, and his face was shadowed over by the wide brim of his hat. Elizabeth gasped. "Would you take a chance on losing these poor souls to the Devil just because you lack faith in God's power?"

"I 'spect not, your reverence. Well, here we are. Just yell loudly if you need me. I'll be at the end of the corridor."

"Thank you muchly, my good man."

The jailer unlocked the door, admitted the tall, thin newcomer, then locked the door behind him. The man waited, standing perfectly still until the jailer was well out of earshot. Then he shifted into action, bending over Robin's still form and reaching for her pulse behind her jaw.

"Weak but holding on well." He shook his head. "The beasts."

"Who the hell are you?" Dean demanded. Something was wrong with the newcomer's actions, but Dean was at a loss to say what.

The man turned and removed his hat.

"Roger," sighed Elizabeth.

"Oh, hell!" Dean approached menacingly. "You get away from her!"

Roger shook his head. "She needs treatment, and you are far too young to be qualified or capable of giving it to her."

"I got basic emergency care." But Dean stopped.

"I am a certified sub-medical, which trumps you several times over." Roger bent over Robin once again. This time he probed with his fingers, searching for broken bones. "I appreciate your distrust. However, there is not time for it. Will you help me remove her boots?"

"I'll help you...!" Dean advanced again.

"Dean!" Elizabeth yelped, stopping him. "Please. I know he's after us, but I don't think he'll hurt her. Please, Dean. We need his help."

Dean looked at Elizabeth, then sighed. "All right."

"Good." Roger shifted around. "You hold her leg stable while I remove the boot. There we are. Now, the next one." He nodded as Dean did as he was asked. "You've got quite the touch."

"It's in the family," Dean stammered. "My mom's a doctor. Back home."

Roger smiled over at Elizabeth, a little sheepishly, then turned back to examining Robin.

"I suppose I should have stayed in the castle," Elizabeth said softly. "I'm sorry, Roger."

Roger shrugged. "It doesn't matter now. Although you should refer to me as Reverend James for the time being." He looked over at Dean. "I've been talking to your neighbors. Let's see. If you're Dean, then this is Robin?"

"Yeah. She's my sister. Well, she's supposed to be my brother." Dean shuffled again. "Robin Parker. I'm Dean Parker."

"Yes. I understand that." Roger nodded as he finished his examination. He removed a small flask from somewhere inside his cloak. "Well, the good news is that she doesn't seem to have any broken bones or internal bleeding."

"What's that?" Dean asked, nodding at the flask.

"Phenyl-trichloroacenol. Something I seriously doubt you've heard of."

"That's not surprising," Dean shrugged.

Roger smiled. "It's a powerful restorative, excellent for quickly healing contusions and other minor cuts. If your sister is to do any time traveling tomorrow, she'll have to be in much better shape. Open wounds are very dangerous in the drop. Those burns on her temples worry me a little."

Dean nodded. "I wonder how those happened."

"Probably made with a poker. Quite common for this era. I suspect she probably fainted from the pain. I have a salve that will hopefully hold through the drop. But first this." He dropped some of the liquid from the flask onto his forefinger. Opening Robin's lips with his other hand, he slid the forefinger between her teeth. "There you go. Now, start swallowing." He massaged her neck. "It's also good for anesthetic purposes. Let's get some more down." He repeated the performance.

Robin stirred. Roger set the flask down and removed a tube from his cloak. He applied some of the contents to the burns.

"Oh, good." He smiled. "She's accepting it already. There's a good chance it won't even scar."

He replaced the tube in his cloak, then fed her some more liquid from the flask. Robin stirred again, this time waking.

"They didn't know. I promise you," she whispered, her eyes still closed. "The candlemaker had no idea."

"It's all right," Roger said. "I'm not an inquisitor. But do me a favor and drink some more of this."

Robin sipped, then took another good swallow. Roger

pushed for one more long drink. She took it. Her eyes fluttered open as he took her pulse.

"Who...? Oh. You're the young man who returned the cloak."

"Yes. Roger," said Elizabeth softly.

"What!" Robin yelped weakly. She feebly struggled.

"Hold on! Hold on!" Roger pinned her. "You're still too weak to try moving around. Rest now. Give the medicine a chance to work."

She moaned softly. "Everything feels so funny like my whole body's gone to sleep."

"That means it's working."

"What are you doing here?" she asked, laying back on the straw again.

Roger smiled. "I'm supposedly trying to convert you three to the true faith, and hopefully they'll just keep you jailed instead of hanging you."

"They'll never believe it," Robin groaned.

"Why shouldn't they?"

"Hey, I'll convert," Dean volunteered.

"It doesn't matter," Elizabeth said. "We're already converted. Roger is just going to tell them that he converted us because they think we're Catholics."

"Precisely." Roger nodded.

"They'll never believe it," Robin sighed.

"Why not?" asked Roger.

"Because I confessed." Robin sniffed. "It was the only way I could think of to save Master Chandler. They'd heard there was a priest in the neighborhood. I knew they'd go after him, so I told them I was the priest. Threw some Latin at them.

Dominus vobiscum and a few plant names. That convinced them. I just hope Master Chandler doesn't get the same idea to try and save us."

"He already did," Roger said. "Fortunately, I convinced him that I had a better plan that would allow him to escape and serve others. I've got some other members of his parish holding him down now just in case."

"Thank God," Robin whispered.

"It looks like my plan isn't going to work though." Roger sighed. "They'll hang you for sure now, and probably torture Dean to find out if he's a priest also."

"Your reverence?" the jailer called.

"I'm quite well, sir," Roger called back. "I'll call for you shortly." He stood and thought for a long moment. "There are other options."

"Why don't you just zap us out of here right now?" Dean suggested.

"Because I do not carry the timetron with me. Once I've made it through the drop, I hide it, so I can move about freely without detection by the locals. We'll have to make the break, as it were, tomorrow. I seriously doubt they'll carry out the execution right away, not with a civil disturbance on, but there's no point in chancing it. I'll have to try and find out their plans for you. That shouldn't be too hard. I'll be back tomorrow morning, in any case. Robin, you will be feeling a lot better in a couple hours. You'll still be weak for another eighteen hours, at minimum. But I would recommend appearing more like they would expect."

"Yeah," Robin whispered.

"I think I've got a plan coming." Roger smiled. "Yes. It's

there. I'll be spending my night refining it. You three rest up, and whatever happens, keep your heads. It's your only chance."

Roger called for the jailer, and a few moments later was gone.

Chapter Nineteen

The bells of nearby Saint Paul's Cathedral were the only clue Robin, Dean and Elizabeth had that dawn was upon them. Robin decided that she would go ahead and take a chance on hinting to their captors that she was in better shape than they thought by putting on her boots. It was more than likely the jailer had never noticed they'd been removed the night before. By wearing them, Robin was ready for action.

She got up and walked around the cell, stretching out. Then she laid back down in the position she'd been in. Her temples felt sore and had an almost clothlike feel to her touch. She could tell the area around her eyes was very swollen, yet it didn't hurt at all.

As Saint Paul's tolled eight o'clock, they heard the jailer come.

"It's more than they deserve, sir," he said to his companion. "But I admire you for trying."

Tall and cloaked in darkness as before, Roger nodded as the jailer opened the cell door. There was silence until the jailer left.

"Here, I've brought food." Roger opened the cloak and brought out cheese, bread, and some fruit.

"Oh, wonderful!" gasped Elizabeth, who had been trying to hide her nausea. She ate greedily.

Robin and Dean also made short work of the supplies.

"I brought your weapons, too." Roger tossed the two swords, the belt knife and the pistol to Dean and Robin. "I searched Master Chandler's house last night. I didn't find anything else." He looked at Robin. Her face remained blank. "Things aren't quite that grim. Fortunately, the inquisitor has other commitments today, so he won't be ready for you, Dean, until tomorrow sometime. I've been able to arrange for some help around dusk. I'll expect you to be ready. Basically, I'll get the jailer to open the cell again. We'll disarm him and go from there."

"Why can't we just do that now?" asked Robin.

"We wouldn't get past the front door," Roger said. "The help I've arranged will be creating a distraction and will help cover us as we leave."

"I say you oughta just get your little machine and zap us home," grumbled Dean.

"Dean, you dope!" groaned Robin. "There are a lot of things we've got to consider before we do that."

"Your sister's right," Roger said. "We'll take care of those later. I'd better leave. Robin, you continue resting. It's a little risky pushing you this soon."

"Well, the alternatives aren't exactly the greatest," Robin replied. "I'll be fine."

Roger smiled warmly. "Yes, I believe you will."

With that, he left.

About the middle of the afternoon, someone approached.

"It's Neddrick," Dean hissed to Robin, who was again laying down.

The tall man with the dark reddish-brown hair stood and leered at the door to the cell.

"Well," he sneered. "I can't tell you how satisfying I find this. Of course, Mistress Elizabeth, you're the one I really want. You know, if you just go ahead and give yourself over, I might find a way to get the three of you out of this mess."

"But I don't know what you want from me," Elizabeth said.

"I do," growled Dean. "You ugly, sick... You make me want to puke!"

"So be it." Neddrick nodded at Robin's prone form. "You're next, you know, unless I prevent it. I can. I'm good friends with the inquisitor. I'll have her, either way. You may as well spare yourself the pain."

Dean swallowed but did not answer.

"So be it." Neddrick turned and left.

As the time passed, Dean got antsy.

"When's dusk?" he asked out loud.

"Probably around five of the clock," said Elizabeth.

Even as she spoke, they heard the church bells toll the hour, and the sound of someone coming. But it was three guards who accompanied the jailer. Roger was not to be seen.

"The inquisitor wants you now." The jailer nodded at Dean, as he opened the door.

"What?" Dean demanded. "But he wasn't supposed to want me until tomorrow!"

"Who told you that?" snapped one of the guards.

"Um." Dean squirmed. "The guy that was here just this afternoon."

"He changed his mind," replied the guard.

The three men advanced. Dean hedged backward into the cell. Unsuspecting, they bore down on him. Backed up against the wall, Dean slowly sank to a squat. His hand slipped into the straw underneath him. He waited until the three men were almost on top of him.

"Now!" he yelled.

Straw flew as he whipped his sword out and charged. Robin sprang to her feet. She whirled around, pistol in hand, and fired at the jailer before he slammed the cell door shut. He fell backward grabbing his shoulder.

One of the guards swung around and cuffed Robin. She stumbled. The pistol fell and, still hot, skidded and sparked on the stone floor into the straw. Regaining her balance, Robin swung around and landed an elbow into the side of the guard's neck. He bent in agony.

Elizabeth tripped a second guard. She had the belt knife and went after him. He got a good grip on her hands and forced it from her. She sank her teeth into his wrist. Yelping, he let go. She punched him in the crotch. After struggling to her feet, she kicked him in the shin for good measure.

Dean still slashed at the third guard. The man barely had time to draw his own sword. He beat back the blows, backing up as Dean pressed harder. He made it through the cell door, then tripped over the downed jailer. Dean burst out and danced around the jailer's prone form.

"Fire!" yelled the guard.

Dean ignored him and bore down on the guard. The

guard picked up and ran off down the corridor. Only then did Dean turn. The straw in the cell crackled in a burst of bright flames.

"How the hell did that start?" Dean cried.

"The pistol," Robin yelped. "Get going!"

She grabbed Elizabeth by the hand and pulled her out of the cell.

"Dean, wait!" Robin stooped as Dean paused. From the floor, she grabbed two hats that had fallen off the guards. "Here, put this on. Maybe we won't look as much like prisoners this way."

"Good idea."

They ran after the fleeing guard. Three minutes later, five men appeared before them, carrying buckets of water.

"You there!" one of them called.

Robin grabbed Elizabeth's arm. "We're moving this prisoner before she gets away. She's one of those papists that started that fire."

"Pass then, and hurry back."

Once past the men, Dean let out a deep chuckle.

"We're not out of this yet, knucklehead," Robin growled. "We've still gotta get out of this joint. Do you remember how you got in?"

"I believe so," Elizabeth sighed. "But I do fear we missed the right corridor."

"How far back is it?" Robin glanced behind her.

Elizabeth grimaced as a group of guards came running through the crossing corridor.

"Too far," she said.

"Terrific," groaned Robin. "There's got to be another way out of here."

People ran about everywhere. No one took any notice of the threesome. Robin found a stairway and led the group down it after Elizabeth assured her they had come up a staircase when they were brought in.

"Maybe if I can find where I was," Robin muttered.

"There you are!" exclaimed a familiar voice.

They whirled around. Dean defensively stepped forward, his sword drawn and ready.

"It's me," said Roger. He stepped out of the shadows. "What are you doing out of your cell."

"The inquisitor changed his mind and decided he wanted to see Dean early," snapped Robin. "We decided we didn't want to stick around. Do you mind?"

"Not at all." Roger glanced back as another group of guards ran past. "I've been hoping you were behind this fire."

"Well, it was an accident," Robin conceded.

"A happy one." Roger nodded. "Let's take our leave. This way."

Robin was forced to follow. On the street, men ran with buckets of water, while hordes of others came to sightsee. Roger pushed Dean and Elizabeth one way.

"You two go with them," he directed, pointing into the crowd.

"Wait a minute," began Dean.

Robin saw some familiar faces, men from Master Chandler's congregation.

"Go ahead," she hissed.

Dean and Elizabeth hurried away. Suddenly Robin felt

lightheaded. She wavered. Roger had his arm around her in seconds.

"Make way!" he yelled. "This man is injured."

They stumbled along until they were in an alley away from the action. Robin leaned against the wall of a house.

"I'll be all right," she gasped. "Just let me get my head down for a moment."

She bent over. Roger checked her pulse at her wrist.

"Not good," he said. "You shouldn't be pushing it this hard."

Robin winced. "Would you rather I was resting back in the cell?"

"I wasn't discussing your options." Roger's voice was grim, but he couldn't help smiling. "I'm merely concerned. It's going to take most of the night to get to where we're going, what with hiding and all. It won't take that long to put out that fire, and they'll start looking for you as soon as it is."

"No kidding. Well, we'd better get hustling." Robin straightened quickly.

Too quickly. The world went spinning and Robin sank. Roger caught her.

"Damn," he muttered.

The rest house he planned on using was close by. He pulled Robin's inert form over his shoulder and hurried on.

Dean and Elizabeth spent the better part of their evening underneath the hay of a market cart. They arrived at an inn on the other side of the Thames several hours later. Master Chandler was there and delighted to see them.

"Praise be to the Lord you're safe!" he cried. "And where is Master Robin?"

"With that Roger clown," Dean grumbled.

"Who?" asked Master Chandler.

"Reverend James took Master Robin with him," said a man.

"Ah, yes." Master Chandler nodded. "That was the plan. To be truthful, we didn't expect any of you until dawn."

"We found a cart," said a young man. "Master Goodworth loaned it to us."

"That was very kind of him," Master Chandler said. "We must remember him in our prayers. As for you, Master Dean, Mistress Elizabeth, you must rest. We've beds for you. Come. You get some sleep and I'm sure Master Robin will be here quite soon."

Dean was a little reluctant but couldn't think of anything else to do. Elizabeth asked if there was a bit of bread she could have. It was provided, and she fell asleep soon after eating it.

At sunrise, someone woke Dean and Elizabeth.

"They're coming!" said the young boy.

Dean was out of bed instantly. Elizabeth joined him in the best room. The early morning chill touched everything. Roger carried in what looked like a shrouded body.

"Where's Robin?" Dean demanded.

"In here." Roger indicated the shroud.

"What?" Dean lurched forward.

"Robin is completely alive," Roger said. "He just passed out from the exertion. We couldn't wake him, so we put him in here. It made it a lot easier to get him past the Roundheads looking for you three. Why don't you help me get him upstairs and in bed?"

This was accomplished quickly. Robin stirred as they unwound the sheet. Roger shooed everyone out except Dean and Elizabeth. After getting rid of the sheet and Robin's boots, Roger pulled his little flask from the depths of his cloak.

"Oh my..." Robin muttered. Her eyes slowly opened. "What happened?"

"I told you, you pushed it too hard." Roger put the flask to her lips. "Drink this."

"What is it?" Robin sniffed at skeptically.

"Phenyl-trichloroacenol."

Her lip curled. "And what the hell is that?"

"A restorative. Now drink it."

Robin sipped suspiciously. Roger turned to Dean and Elizabeth.

"There," he said. "You can see she's all right. Now could you please leave and let her get some sleep?"

"You guys okay?" Robin asked.

"Fine," said Dean.

"Good."

Dean and Elizabeth departed. Roger turned back to Robin.

"I'm afraid I'll have to leave also," he said. "I've got a couple things to look into and you really need to be sleeping to get your strength back. I want you to sleep for at least another three hours, then take it easy. You should be mostly back to normal by noon. I'll be back by suppertime. After then we'll talk."

Robin looked away sadly.

"What's wrong?"

"I suppose I should be grateful to you," she said bitterly. "You did save our lives and I am thankful for that."

"But...?"

"For what?" Robin asked. "What are you going to do to us? After all, we only wrecked your experiment. At least that's what I'm assuming Elizabeth was."

Roger chuckled. "Well, yes, she is, and it wasn't wrecked. We'll discuss that later, and I am very much looking forward to the discussion. Fear not, Robin. You haven't escaped the frying pan for the fire. I'll see you tonight." He left.

Feeling oddly reassured, Robin settled back and went to sleep. When she awoke, Master Chandler was sitting by the bed.

"Oh, good," she sighed. "You're safe."

"I was similarly concerned about you." Master Chandler smiled.

She yawned. "How long have I been sleeping?"

"About four hours." Master Chandler looked out the window. "The church clock struck ten not long ago."

"Great." Robin eased herself up and pulled her legs over the side of the bed. "I can get up now."

"I thought you might be worried, so I went ahead and brought these up." Master Chandler pointed to the three sacks.

"You got them!" Robin pounced on them. "You didn't go back for them, did you?"

"I did."

Robin glared at him briefly. "They weren't that important. But I'm sure glad I've got them." Robin smiled. The bags meant she wouldn't have to depend on Roger anymore. Even if he didn't seem angry at them, she didn't quite trust him. "Well, this means we'll be taking off right away."

Master Chandler looked crestfallen. "Where to?"

Robin didn't notice as she looked through the bags. "I'm not sure. Maybe the colonies. Who knows? London hasn't worked out too well."

"I can't blame you." Master Chandler sighed. "Come, my son. Let me give you my blessing."

Robin bowed her head as he whispered the Latin words over her. He laid both hands on top of her head. He swallowed as he brought the hands to her cheeks and lifted her face to look at him.

"You have been so dear to me, my son," he said.

Robin suddenly blinked back tears. "I can't tell you what you've meant to me." She pulled away. "Listen, take care of yourself, will you? This martyrdom crap may be great for your soul, but it's damned hard on the rest of us. Okay?"

Master Chandler nodded sadly. "I suppose it would be. You be careful also."

"I will. Goodbye, Father."

"Goodbye, Robin."

Robin pulled on her boots and collected the sacks. With one long sigh, she looked at Master Chandler. She opened one of the sacks and pawed through it, making sure there was nothing in it but coins.

"You may as well take this," she said handing it to him. "We won't be able to use it where we're going."

"Are you sure?"

She strode out of the room, without answering and called Dean and Elizabeth.

"Come on," she told them. "We're leaving now."

"What about Roger?" Dean asked, scrambling after her.

"Tough potatoes."

"So where are we going?" Dean asked once they were on the street.

"Someplace where no one can see us, first," Robin replied.

"Does this mean we're going home?" Dean asked.

Robin turned on him. "Why do you have to keep on with that?"

"Perhaps it would be best," said Elizabeth.

"But..." Robin turned to her. "Dean is talking about our home."

"I know."

"The place with all the magic you don't like."

Elizabeth swallowed. "I know. But it seems like everywhere we go here, we get arrested. I know it's that Master Neddrick behind it."

"I was going to take you to another time," Robin said.

"Then why don't we just go to your time?" Elizabeth asked. "I believe I can learn to like it. I understand a little better now."

"I suppose," Robin grumbled.

"You don't want to go back, do you, Robin?" said Dean.

"Of course, I do," she replied. "Well, maybe not just yet. I don't know. I'm afraid if we go home, I won't get to come back. This machine seems to be run on batteries, and I don't know how much power we've got left. I'm pretty sure we've got enough to get home, but beyond that..."

Dean shrugged. "I guess I understand how you feel. But

I've had enough history to last me a lifetime. Please, Robin, can we? We're running out of places to go."

"Not by a long shot," Robin said. "But all right. Let's get out on the road a ways before we do. I don't think it would be nice to let anyone see us disappear into thin air."

Dusk fell as they came to the edge of the city. They spent the night at an inn, just for old time's sake. The next morning, they took their time leaving. Close to noon, Robin called a halt. They left the road. Dean grabbed Elizabeth's hand, then placed his other hand on Robin's shoulder. With a reluctant sigh, Robin focused on the coordinates for home.

Chapter Twenty

Roger growled and paced as the older woman next to him glared sourly at the screen in front of them.

"I told you that wasn't a switch on," she said. "Look at that arc there and how it sputters."

"I never said I disagreed with you, Cricklan," Roger replied testily.

Since there had been no way of knowing who had operated the timetron when it had apparently failed, Roger had insisted on going to London in the hope that he or some other time traveler would be the one abandoned. But Robin had insisted on leaving, he'd been told, and there was no question now that she'd used the machine last, presumably with Dean and Elizabeth in tow.

"I should have searched the candlemaker's more thoroughly," he grumbled.

"Roger, you know the folly of second-guessing yourself," Cricklan said, her eyes never leaving the screen.

He flopped down on a chair next to her. "You're right. Any chance of making out where and when they landed?"

Cricklan shook her head. "Possibly, but it all depends on how the coordinates were focused on. And that's assuming your Robin Parker was headed for her natal time. But there's not enough of a power pull here for them to have gotten far at all."

Cricklan circled a point on the tip of the arc and enlarged the image. She was a woman of predominantly African descent, with still smooth and relatively light-colored skin framed by coarse gray hair that had gone to dreadlocks, which balanced out the ball her body had become.

"She was headed for home," Roger continued. "She left all her money with Master Chandler. Even if she were headed for another time, she would have kept some of the gold angels, at least. Those could be melted down. She was headed someplace where she knew she had money already, and where else would that be but home?"

"And what about Elizabeth?" Cricklan asked.

Roger shrugged. "I don't know. We didn't get that far. I had to track down Donald before he turned in the whole Catholic community." Roger glanced at Cricklan. "I'm sorry about that."

Cricklan imposed a vertical grid on the image. "You needn't worry about my feelings. I've done my grieving where Donald is concerned."

Roger shook his head. Cricklan had never been one to dwell on past mistakes.

"I find it interesting, however, that after all the work you did on the bring forward experiment, you are more focused on this Ms. Parker than you are on Elizabeth," Cricklan observed.

Roger began pacing again, this time, he hoped, with a careless air. "Not really. I mean, I've only spent a couple hours total with the woman."

"You did a DNA analysis on her."

Roger shrugged. "I had to. We had to figure out who RP170 is. And it's not that I don't like Elizabeth, and I'm certainly committed to her if it comes to that." He sighed. "We've just got to find them, first."

Cricklan nodded. "I may have. Look here." She enlarged another image again. "It's right on the path of the earlier log line and the marker is right."

"And hardly any power pull at all. No wonder we missed it." Roger did a quick calculation. "And shit. This is the first stop on Donald's timetron's log line after he went to the U.S."

Cricklan nodded. "I had a feeling he had hooked into this station, and now I've got the proof."

"You'll have to bring this to the Board."

"It's about time I did, don't you think?" Cricklan put her hand on Roger's arm. "Why don't you stay focused on getting Ms. Parker back to where she belongs? I'll deal with Donald. I am his mother, and he does sometimes listen to me."

"Yes, well, it would appear I've got a little research to do."

Robin had forgotten about the crushing, sucked in feeling as the machine worked. She gasped as they landed. Catching her breath, she looked around. Something was very wrong.

"This isn't Irvine," Dean said nervously.

It wasn't. They were in a wooded area overlooking a highway very similar to the one they had left. Robin looked down. A small stream of black smoke dissipated into the breeze and a small black splotch on the side of the machine revealed the smoke's origin.

"Something is very wrong here," Robin said.

"Where are we?" asked Dean, getting a little frantic.

"I'd say pretty much where we were," Robin answered. "Probably a different time, though."

"The right one?" Dean looked hopeful.

"Not likely, judging from that highway."

As if to confirm it, they heard a soft rumbling. As it got closer, a soft jangling sound could be heard as well.

"There," said Elizabeth. She pointed.

A small black coach, drawn by two brown horses, approached from where London would be if Robin were right. The man driving it was wearing knee-high boots, close-fitting knee pants, a long black coat with a wide tan lapel that ran the length of the front and very wide tan cuffs.

"A tri-cornered hat!" Robin groaned.

"Isn't that from the American Revolution?" Dean asked.

"More or less." Robin sighed. "We're in the eighteenth century, at any rate."

"I don't quite understand," said Elizabeth.

"We've only gone ahead about a hundred years," Robin answered. "How far ahead, I don't know. We'd better do something about our clothes. If we rag them up, we should be okay, except for you, Elizabeth. Your dress is far too big and loose. Waists are supposed to be tiny now."

"Oh, no," Elizabeth sighed. She glanced at Dean.

Robin didn't notice. She looked around. The sky was a bright blue, with huge white clouds floating across. The patches of snow they had left back in the seventeenth century were replaced by wildflowers. A wet loamy smell filled her nostrils.

"Spring," she muttered. She removed her doublet and tore up her pants.

"What did you say?" Dean asked as he did the same to his clothes.

"It's spring," Robin repeated. "When we left it was winter."

"Say, that's right." Dean pondered it a moment, then considered a far weightier matter. "Robin, if this is the eighteenth century, and we were trying to go home, does this mean we're stuck?"

Robin caught her breath. "I don't know. I was thinking that Roger had tracked us down by tracing us through the machine, but it wasn't turned on in London, so when he found us there, I figured he has some other way to trace us. If that's the case, then…"

"Uh, Robin." Dean's face had a seriously pained look on it. "The machine was turned on in London. I turned it on the day after Twelfth Day."

"And Roger showed up two days later," said Robin. She turned on Dean. "What the hell were you doing?"

"I don't know!" Dean backed away, not sure what to say, but sure that he did not want to tell Robin about Elizabeth being pregnant at that moment in time. "I wanted to go home. I just did."

"Fat lot of good that's going to do us now," Robin sighed. She took a deep breath. "All right. Maybe there's something I can fix. Let's try to stay positive and in the meantime, let's get ourselves situated. Here, Elizabeth, take your apron and tie it as tight as you can above your bodice. That should make it look like it has more of a waist. Are we ready? Good. Let's head down that road. Maybe we'll find an inn that needs some help."

They spent most of the day walking alongside the highway instead of on it. The road was thick, oozing mud, with deep ruts and numerous rocks. Coaches were not infrequent either, and the first one they encountered nearly ran them over.

Close to two o'clock in the afternoon they approached the end of a section hemmed in by trees. On the other side of the thicket, they heard shouts. Robin led the way cautiously, stopping at the edge of the trees to see what was going on.

A coach that had passed them barely minutes before was stopped on the road by two men with scarves on their faces. One dismounted from his horse, while the other, still on his, held a pistol on the driver of the coach.

"Looks like a holdup," whispered Dean.

"No kidding," Robin whispered back.

"We'd better hide," Elizabeth hissed.

"Maybe not." Robin grinned. "I don't like the idea of bounty hunting, but we're broke, and I'll bet there's a reward for those two."

"Have you lost it?" Dean looked at her, aghast.

"Not really. Think about it, Dean. We're easily as big as they are, and they don't know we're here."

"But they've got guns!"

"They've got two shots. If we catch them from behind, they'll never know what hit them."

Dean looked at the men. A slightly rotund gentleman emerged from the coach and a younger man who looked like a clerk.

"I'll take the one on the horse," he said and took off running.

"That's not quite what I had in mind," Robin grumbled as she took off herself.

Dean vaulted onto the back of the horse. The animal staggered. Dean got his forearm around the robber's throat and reached for the pistol with his free hand. The man twisted, and the two fell to the ground and rolled.

Robin slammed into the other robber and tackled him. His pistol went flying. They rolled for a moment, then the man got on top. He raised his fist. Robin dodged and threw him off. They scrambled to their feet. The man whipped out his sword. Robin danced backward and drew hers. The man's blade was at least an inch wide. Robin's wasn't. She pressed the attack anyway. It startled her opponent. He dropped back and barely deflected her charge. Robin came in again, slashing fiercely. She overshot the man, as she'd intended, and brought her hilt crashing down onto the back of his neck. The man looked dazed for a second, then fell forward. Robin pounced on him and twisted his arm behind his back.

Dean and his opponent rolled in the mud. Both of Dean's hands locked on the wrist with the gun. Dean squeezed and tried to stay on top of the smaller man. One vicious turn and the pistol dropped. Dean scrambled after it. He grabbed it and turned to face his opponent's knife. The man froze. Dean cocked the flintlock.

He chuckled. "Go ahead. Make my day!"

"Dean!" Robin groaned. She strong-armed her man to his feet and looked around for something with which to bind him. "Couldn't you be a little more original?"

Dean slowly got to his feet. "Okay, nice and easy now, drop the knife."

The man did. Elizabeth emerged from the trees.

"We'll need some rope," she observed. She turned to the rotund gentleman. "Have you any, sir?"

"Piggot!" he called to the coachman.

"Yes, sir?"

"Fetch the young woman some rope."

"Yes, sir." Piggot reached behind him, then scrambled down from his post.

Robin and Elizabeth bound the two felons and sat them down next to the coach.

"Let's see what we have here," said Robin, as she searched them. "What's this? A bag of silver? And here's another. Are these yours, sir?"

"N-no." The gentleman shook his head. "I was just about to hand it over."

"Then I'll take custody of these." Smiling, Robin tied the sacks to her belt. "I'm not adverse to adding a little silver to my collection. Speaking of, I assume there's a price on these fellows' heads. Do you know how far it is to the nearest town where we can collect it?"

"Well, uh, yes, I — Anthony?" Still in shock, the gentleman looked at the clerk.

"I don't know, uncle." the young man replied. "I rarely travel this road."

"Robin, why don't we just tie them up in the trees?" Dean suggested. "We've got money now."

Robin nodded. "It'll be easier than a forced march. All right." She turned to the gentleman. "Well, good day to you, sir. Hope you don't get robbed again."

"But..." the man sputtered. "You're not going to rob us?"

"Rob you?" Robin looked at him, confused, then laughed. "Not us. We're honest folk. I know we look pretty grubby right now." An idea began to form. "Unfortunately, we met with similar fellows earlier today. We were lucky we escaped with our weapons and our skins."

"Indeed, yes." The gentleman mopped his brow with a huge lace-trimmed handkerchief. "Well, I owe you a great deal of thanks. To whom do I have the pleasure…?"

"Robin Parker, sir." Robin nodded her head. "And this is my brother, Dean."

"And the young woman?"

"I am Master Dean's wife," Elizabeth answered.

Robin started, as did Dean.

"Ah. Very good." The gentleman wiped his brow again. "I am Sir James Culpepper, and this is my nephew and clerk, Anthony Morgan. And, eh, what brings you people out here?"

"We're looking for a situation," Robin answered. "We used to be innkeepers in the city but fell on hard times."

"Hm." Sir James ran an appraising eye over Dean. "I shouldn't think you would, but by any chance do you have your letters?"

"Letters?" asked Dean.

Robin nudged his ankle. "Yes, sir. We can read quite well. Our pastor taught us."

"Indeed." Sir James smiled. "And can you write?"

"Sure," said Dean before Robin could nudge him again.

"Uncle, if I may be so bold," Morgan began. "My aunt, your wife, did request that you not…"

"You may not be so bold, Anthony. I will bring whomever

I please into my household. I brought you into my household. Come, you three. We'll talk and see what you can do."

Robin glanced at Dean, who shrugged. Elizabeth nodded.

"Well, thank you, sir." Robin smiled. "We'll do our best for you."

Dean sat with Piggot on the box, as there wasn't enough room inside the coach. There, Sir James looked Robin over more closely.

"An innkeeper, eh?" he said.

"At my father's inn, sir."

Sir James nodded. "Debtor's prison, I assume."

Robin nodded. "He made some poor speculations, I'm afraid. He died soon after."

"I dare say. Poor speculations. Must have been dealing in trade from the colonies. Bad mistake, with all the trouble there now. At least they've stopped dumping tea in the harbor. Not that I think firing on the King's Army is any better a thing to do mind you."

Robin coughed back a laugh. "I, uh, heard something about that. When did it happen?"

"Let's see. This is April. Was just about a year ago, then."

"1776," Robin muttered.

"No. Seventy-five it happened. This is seventy-six." Sir James punctuated the thought with a walking stick he'd left in the coach and picked up as soon as they were underway.

"Oh. Right."

"It's a damned nuisance, is what it is. That Mr. Pitt has been nothing but a bloody old fool, hasn't handled it at all well. The King's more a fool for listening to him. I'm simply glad I never got involved in that mess. The Orient. That's where I do my business. India. Most profitable. I've done very well for myself, as you can see. I've got a small estate in Devonshire, a house in Town, and…" He shifted. "A house in Bath. That's where I'm headed, at the moment. My wife and daughter are there, taking the waters. My wife has the gout. I've also got a son who's an officer in the army. It was no small thing to buy him that commission. As a matter of fact, he's stationed in the colonies, Philadelphia."

Robin tried not to grin. "How interesting."

"Oh, you know of Philadelphia."

"I've… heard of it."

Sir James lifted an eyebrow. "You seem very knowledgeable. Can you add at all?"

"Quite well. Except for his speculations, I kept all of my father's accounts."

"Indeed." Sir James raised both his eyebrows. "What about your brother?"

"He's good at adding, too." Robin nodded vigorously.

"Indeed."

They stopped in a small village just as darkness fell, and Sir James insisted on paying for a meal and a room for the three. After they had eaten and were about to settle in for the night, Elizabeth left to fetch some water. As soon as they were alone, Robin looked at Dean.

"Dean, do you know why Elizabeth suddenly wants to appear as your wife?"

Dean swallowed. "Well, I can guess."

"You two have been fooling around, haven't you?"

"Yeah. So?" Dean answered defensively.

"Why, Dean?" Robin groaned. "We came here to leave her. Is it really fair to start a relationship like that?"

"Well, we're not going to leave her anyway, so what's the big deal?"

Robin paused. She knew Dean had a point but was so angry about everything else that she needed a target.

"That's not the point," she snarled, finally. "Didn't you even think about Elizabeth's feelings?"

Dean rolled his eyes. "Yeah, I thought a lot about them. Face it, Robin, Elizabeth and I both knew we couldn't stay."

"But, Dean, she doesn't belong in the twenty-first century!"

"She sure as hell didn't belong where we were, any more than we did."

"Okay. But what if she gets pregnant?"

"That. Well, um..." Dean smiled weakly.

Robin closed her eyes and turned away. "She isn't."

"Well, Robin..."

She turned on him. "You idiot! Why didn't you think of that beforehand? Good lord, Dean, you know about birth control. Why didn't you protect yourself?"

"I did!" Dean's face was seriously pained. "We just forgot once. I swear it was only the one time."

"Well, that was one time too many, wasn't it? What are you going to do with a baby? How are you going to support it?"

"Isn't this Culpepper guy going to give us a job?"

"But what if we'd made it home?"

Dean shrugged. "I figured we'd get an abortion."

"It's so easy to say that, isn't it? But what about Elizabeth?

It's her baby, too. I swear, Dean, you are so irresponsible, you make me sick sometimes!"

"Irresponsible, huh?" Dean's voice dripped with anger. "Well, fuck you. I've had it, Robin. Little goody-two-shoes Robin taking care of baby brother. I'm not a baby. You want responsibility? Fine. We're gonna keep that baby, and I'm going to support it, and Elizabeth, even if we do get home. I don't know how, but I will."

They froze as Elizabeth entered the room.

"Oh, dear," she whispered.

Dean glared at Robin then turned. "Elizabeth, you and I are getting married just the minute we get home, do you understand?"

"Married?" she gasped, rejoicing, and terrified all at the same time.

"Yeah." Dean kissed her roughly, then strode out of the room.

Robin turned away and sighed.

"You know," said Elizabeth.

"How far along are you?" Robin asked softly.

"A month or so."

Robin swore. "I guess the first thing to do is to make sure you're taken care of."

"I'm not ill. Well, a little in the mornings."

"But you have to eat the right things, get the right kind of exercise. Damn. You can't trust the doctors here."

"A doctor?" Elizabeth had to smile. "I'm only pregnant."

Robin snorted. "Right."

"It's not entirely his fault, you know."

Robin nodded. "True. Are you happy with him?"

"Very. I don't understand why, but love seems to be important in these matters to you and Dean. I do love him, and he loves me. He's said so many times."

"That seems a surprise, though I don't know that it should be." Robin sighed. "That overgrown lunkhead. I don't know why he has all the luck. You'd better get some rest."

"So had you."

Robin nodded. "I hope he gets back soon."

"He will be."

Tired and miserable, Robin went to bed. The situation was unbearably grim. She hadn't let on to Dean and Elizabeth, but she doubted that they'd ever get home.

Chapter Twenty-One

Bath, the great English watering-hole of the eighteenth century, was a congenial place, Anthony told the three the next morning as they took off in the coach again.

"It doesn't matter who you are," Anthony said, explaining through a yawn that the inconspicuous, the near-great and the great mingled together in cordial peace. Gossip and minor intrigue flowed as freely as the water in the reeking baths for which the city was named.

"What rot," blustered Sir James.

A few hours later, he ordered the coach to stop on the outskirts of the city to get new clothes for Robin, Dean, and Elizabeth. He then took them to his house and presented Robin and Dean to Lady Culpepper as his two new clerks.

An imposing woman with an over-powdered face and almost clownish rouging, Lady Culpepper frowned at first.

"Clerks, my darling?" she said to Sir James skeptically. "You have my dear nephew, Anthony. Isn't he enough?"

Sir James hemmed and coughed for a moment. "Anthony is... eh, indispensable, my dearest. But my business is growing. Poor Anthony shouldn't be made to bear the work of three men, especially when I have these two fine strapping brothers to help. And look, here's Mr. Dean Parker's young wife. She'll be quite suitable as a companion for Deborah. You were saying just the other week how nice it would be to have one, a steadying influence on the girl."

"Yes." Lady Culpepper's eyes took Elizabeth in critically, then her eyes flicked over Dean and her expression grew much more approving. "I suppose she might, then. Well, perhaps Mr. Dean could help me with the household accounts. You know how trying I find numbers."

Sir James missed the nuance, but Robin held her breath and debated speaking up.

"That sounds quite satisfactory, indeed," Sir James said, his voice filled with relief.

The three were each assigned rooms and servants, a footman for each, plus a lady's maid for Elizabeth, a middle-aged widow named Mrs. Baskin. Fortunately, Mrs. Baskin immediately noticed a certain glow about Elizabeth and warned her not to let Lady Culpepper know.

"If you'll pardon me for being so forward, Ma'am, Her Ladyship will not look kindly on it," Mrs. Baskin said. "It would be indelicate, especially in front of her daughter."

Mrs. Baskin also showed Elizabeth how to tie her stays to conceal her delicate condition.

It didn't take long for the three to settle in. There was some minor trouble with the footmen until Mrs. Baskin kindly explained about vails – generous tips that were expected for the least service. Dean, for his part, found having his footman, a strapping youth named Timothy, to be quite useful. Robin's footman, Samuel, a thin man in his late twenties, proved to be rather sullen, although Robin wasn't sure if it was because she couldn't quite get used to having him around and so didn't make much use of him.

The work, itself, was basically accounting work, with some letter-writing thrown in. Both had a little trouble, at first, learning to read the script, and both were painfully slow at writing. That worried Robin, then she noticed that Anthony wasn't much faster. She also began to notice that Anthony wasn't always that sober.

Elizabeth, for her part, was a little at loose ends with hardly anything to do except read and chat with Deborah. Deborah turned out to be a pleasant young girl of seventeen. She was delighted with Elizabeth's accurate memory. Deborah constantly lost things, and it seemed Elizabeth was the only one who could track down the items.

Sir James was prone to blustering a great deal, but he was an otherwise harmless individual. He reminded Robin of a character she'd seen in a play from the period. As she saw more plays the longer they stayed, she decided that Sir James and others like him were the models for the stereotype of the bumbling, slightly pompous, father figure.

Dean was the only one who seemed to have a problem, though not with Sir James. Lady Culpepper grew to like him a lot, a little too much. Dean ignored her flirting with an easy grace that belied her determination. Seeing as though she supervised the household accounts, he couldn't entirely avoid her, but he did his best.

It seemed that the weeks quickly slipped into months. Robin spent what free time she had working on the time machine, or more accurately, staring at it. She figured out that a circuit had blown. The carbon scoring on the circuit card inside made that obvious. But what that circuit did she had no idea. The parts on the card were laid out in a way that made no sense in terms of the physics that Robin knew. She hoped she could figure it out from the way the card was laid out. Granted, that was assuming the various parts were what she thought they were, and that they were made of materials she knew.

She remained cheerful, though only for Dean's sake. He trusted that Robin would get the machine fixed. In the meantime, he was enjoying his work and watching Elizabeth's belly grow. Robin was glad he was adjusting so well, even if it was because he thought the situation was temporary.

Elizabeth was as content as could be. She and Dean were as good as married, she felt healthy, and Deborah was quite pleasant. She never did adapt to being so much at leisure but found various errands and did a lot of running and fetching, which made Robin happy because the walking was such good exercise. Robin also had Elizabeth stretch her legs in a squatting position and raise her arms to stretch out her back. Elizabeth thought it queer, but she was used to Robin's requests that way.

They followed the family as they moved from house to house. Because Dean had charge of the household accounts, he usually stayed wherever Lady Culpepper was. Deborah, who had her parents well managed, made a point of keeping with her mother so Dean and Elizabeth could be together. Robin stayed with Sir James, which often meant trips to London, while the others stayed in Devonshire or Bath.

By the middle of September, Her Ladyship's gout had flared up, which meant the family would remain entrenched in Bath for a while. In fact, Her Ladyship had ulterior motives for the stay.

"Lord John Merryville has elected to stay through Christmas," Elizabeth told Dean and Robin one bright morning. "And his friends will probably stay also."

"Fat lot of good it's going to do Her Ladyship," Robin answered. She faced the mirror in Dean and Elizabeth's room and pinned down curls on the side of her head. "Sir James absolutely detests those dissolute types, titled or not."

"I wonder how much that'll matter if Deborah finds her true love among them," chuckled Dean. He sat leaning back in a straight back chair with his feet propped up on a small table.

"Good question," Robin said. "Sir James will only be pushed so far."

"It'll be interesting to see how it falls out." Elizabeth giggled.

Robin picked up a small canister with holes in the lid and began shaking white flour over her hair. Within seconds, a white cloud surrounded her head. She sneezed several times.

"I'll sure be glad when this damned hair powdering goes out of style," she grumbled, sniffing.

She stepped out of the cloud and wiped her eyes. She had her own room, next to the one where Dean and Elizabeth were, on the top floor of the house, a privilege accorded them because of Robin's and Dean's status as clerks, which put them above the house servants. Anthony Morgan had his room on the same floor as the Culpeppers, but that was because he was family.

Robin spent most of her time with Dean and Elizabeth

partly for the companionship and partly because they had a nice large mirror that made fixing her hair a lot easier.

There was a knocking at the door. "Mr. Dean, Her Ladyship requests your presence," came Timothy's voice.

"I'm on my way." Dean swung his feet off the table and stood. "Oh, Robin, Her Ladyship saw Mr. Brumfield at the baths this morning. Sure as shooting that means a trip to the apothecary. You want Timothy to pick anything up for you?"

Robin thought. "No. I've got all the metals I can use right now."

"Okay." Dean turned to Elizabeth and kissed her. "I'll see you later, sweetheart." He put his hands on her tummy and waited. "Hey, Robin, feel this. It's moving again."

With amused indulgence, Robin walked over and placed her hand on Elizabeth's stomach. She waited patiently for the small lump to shift itself.

"Yeah, I felt it." She had many times before, and though she would never admit it to Dean, she was just as fascinated by the promise of new life as he was.

Elizabeth just laughed. Pregnancy was far too common an experience for her to find the same fascination in it that Dean and Robin had.

Dean hurried off. Elizabeth and Robin both departed minutes later, Elizabeth to eat breakfast with Deborah, and Robin to start yet another day of business with Sir James.

Dean knocked quickly at the door to Lady Culpepper's chambers.

"Who is it?" sang the aging soprano.

"Mr. Dean, M'lady."

"Do come in."

Dean took a deep breath and entered. Her Ladyship was on the prowl again.

"A trip to the apothecary's?" he asked shutting the door.

"Yes, later. For the moment, I've another service for you to perform." She was decked out in one of her India cotton gowns, with her mob cap on and the three small black patches on her painted face. The gown hid her stout figure. There was no hiding the wooden false teeth, however, or the thin wiry hair, white as her powdered wig, that poked out from underneath the cap.

"Yes, M'lady." Dean dreaded what would come next.

"The good doctor suggested that maybe if I were to have my feet rubbed, it might give me some relief. My maid has proven to be an utter imbecile at it. I was wondering if perhaps you might try."

Dean shrugged. "I suppose."

As he bent, he reflected there were worse things she could have asked. Dean was fairly proud of his talent for massage, although he preferred much younger females as "patients." Lady Culpepper's feet were soft from their daily soaking in the baths, and the fact that she did very little walking.

He told Robin about his adventure the next morning when she came in to fix her hair.

"Don't let Sir James catch you at it," she warned him. "That's one step shy of adultery."

"Hell, no," Dean replied. "At least, I hope he doesn't. But it's kind of hard for me to say no. She is the boss."

"True." Robin yawned.

"You stayed out very late last night," Elizabeth observed.

Robin yawned again and nodded. "Anthony insisted on

showing me a good time. The idiot. He got bombed out of his skull and lost damn near five guineas."

"I've heard you've been doing your fair share of gambling." Dean grinned.

"Why not?" Robin retorted with a snort. "It's the only vice left me. I can't stand smoking. I don't like being drunk and hate hangovers even more. And sex is out."

Dean sniggered. "You could always try making it with Tony the next time he gets smashed."

Robin glared at him. "Not only is that disgusting, it's utterly ridiculous."

"Well, if you're desperate."

"Dean, what happens to guys when they get that drunk? Besides, I'm not that kind of woman."

Dean rolled his eyes.

There was a knocking at the door.

"Mrs. Parker?" called the voice of George, Elizabeth's 13-year-old footman.

Elizabeth bounced up, tied her apron over her tummy and grabbed a fan off the table.

"Miss Deborah has just discovered her fan is missing," she sighed. She kissed Dean and ran out.

"I'd better get downstairs, too," Robin said.

She was hard at work, recopying accounts she had figured, when Sir James came into the study. Months of working at the eighteenth-century script had made it easier, but Robin found she still had to go slowly to prevent her twentieth-century handwriting from giving her away. Sir James looked over her shoulder.

"Ah, very good," he said. "I've a letter here from my broker with figures you'll want to add in."

"I've already taken the liberty of doing so, sir. Mr. Morgan opened it yesterday afternoon when it arrived."

"Very good." Sir James looked around. "But speaking of that young rascal, where is he? I've a letter I need to dictate."

"I really don't know, sir," Robin answered. "I'm afraid we were out rather late last night. He may still be asleep."

Disgusted, Sir James walked to the door.

"Richards!" he called out into the hallway. "Richards, go and rouse Mr. Morgan immediately." He paused for the reply. "If he's awake, then why isn't he down here? Oh, never mind. Just get him down here!" He turned back into the room, muttering angrily. "Damn relatives. If he weren't Sarah's nephew, I'd sack him. He's nothing but a nuisance."

Anthony Morgan proved to be more than a nuisance. He showed up half an hour later, stewed, and in no shape to take dictation. Sir James was furious. He sent his nephew upstairs with strict instructions to stay in his room until further notice.

"I should have left him in the country," Sir James fumed after Morgan had gone. "Town life is no good for simple minds like his. No willpower."

"Shall I ring for my brother so that he can take your letter?" Robin asked.

"Yes, yes, yes."

Robin went out into the hall and sent Samuel to find Dean.

"Parker!" Sir James barked as she returned.

"Yes, sir."

"You were out with Anthony last night?"

"Yes, sir."

"I assume he got drunk."

"Quite, sir."

"And you did nothing to stop him?"

Robin thought fast. "I did suggest he not drink so much. But my position is rather awkward, sir. I am only a clerk, and he is your relative."

"Indeed, yes." Sir James put his hands behind his back and began pacing. "But somebody's got to keep an eye on him. I shudder to think what my wife's family would do if he went astray while under my protection. Oh, they're a miserable lot when aroused. I should never hear the end of it. And you can imagine what Her Ladyship would be like. Her poor innocent nephew. Ha! The boy does nothing but make trouble for himself and everyone else. Parker, he is now your responsibility. I want you to keep him out of trouble. I can't be watching his every move."

"Begging your pardon, sir, I'm not at all sure I can either," Robin said, a little frantically. "Furthermore, he is bound to resent me taking a superior position to his. He'll most likely complain to Her Ladyship, and if she confronts me, I shall probably be forced to confess that you requested it."

Sir James growled. "Well, do your best, then. I'll deal with Her Ladyship." He did not relish the task.

Robin didn't blame him. Lady Culpepper could be quite a formidable creature when her wrath was aroused, and she was not inclined to be reasonable even under the best circumstances. In any case, Robin found her precious evenings devoted to chasing Tony Morgan about Bath, instead of working at the time machine.

Dean's evenings continued to be filled with whatever parties or balls caught Lady Culpepper's fancy. The goal, of course, was to get Deborah a rich, preferably titled husband, which meant Deborah was out most evenings, sometimes with her mother in tow. Sir James resolutely refused to go to any of the events and so Dean got the job of seeing the ladies to the door and accompanying their sedan chairs home.

Of late, however, with Lady Culpepper's gout acting up more and more often, Her Ladyship was forced to forego the festivities, which made her mood all the more predatory.

As for Deborah, she faced plenty of competition in the husband chase. Available young women outnumbered the available young men. Deborah had an advantage in that she was very pretty and a lively companion. She wasn't as hungry as the others, either. She wanted to fall in love and was prepared to wait as long as she needed to do so.

That Saturday night, Dean dropped the young girl at the Assembly Rooms for a ball, then went off to a nearby tavern for a brandy and to gamble a little. He quickly lost, so he returned to the ball to watch the dancing through the windows. He would have liked to have chatted with the footmen who carried Deborah's sedan chair, but the hierarchy among the servants was even more strictly upheld than among the upper classes. So, while Dean was an employee, he wasn't a servant, which put him well above their station in life.

The footmen were off gambling with the other footmen, but Dean decided to hang around the sedan chair anyway on the off chance one of the footmen would come back and actually talk with him.

As he leaned, bored, against the sedan chair, a young gentleman approached.

"Is that your mistress's chair?" the gentleman asked, timidly.

"It's the family's," Dean answered. "But, yeah, we've got the young mistress tonight."

"Indeed. Come with me."

Dean shrugged and followed. The young man led him to the ballroom doors.

"Please, point out your mistress," he asked Dean.

"Um…" Dean searched the crowd. "There she is, in the lavender dress, with the umbrellas in her hair."

"Ah, yes, that's her." He sighed.

This young gentleman had obviously seen a few too many plays and was playing the young lover role to the hilt. Dean turned to go.

"Wait! What is her name?" The young man grabbed Dean's arm.

"Deborah Culpepper."

"She is so beautiful. I'm desperately in love with her, and I don't dare speak a word to her."

Dean tried not to laugh. "Why not?"

"Good lord, she'd never hear me." The young man started pacing. "Who am I that she should?"

"I don't know. Who are you?"

"My name is Viscount Edward Acton, heir apparent to the Duchy of Cliveton." He offered a small nod of the head.

Dean shrugged. "Sounds pretty good to me."

"You think?" He smiled hopefully, then frowned. "Oh, no. Mine is only a small duchy, and there are so many others here with larger holdings. Besides, it's quite the fashion nowadays to eschew titles, at least among the young ladies. If only I were poor."

Dean chuckled. "If you want a hint, that won't make any difference with her. She wants to fall in love, it doesn't matter with who."

He bit his forefinger. "I couldn't. I just couldn't."

"Have you considered writing her a letter?" Dean asked.

"But... No, she'd never accept me."

Dean thought. "Listen. I've got an idea. It'll bowl her over. I promise."

"You do?" He looked hopeful again.

"Sure." Dean grinned. "Write her a letter telling her how you feel, but don't tell her who you are. Become her secret admirer. I guarantee you, she'll go nuts trying to figure out who you are. Keep it up for several letters, and by the time you reveal yourself, she'll be eating out of your hand."

The viscount all but jumped up and down. "Are you sure it will work?"

"As sure as I can be."

"A quill. I need a quill, and ink, and paper! Wait here. I'll be right back. And here!"

Dean caught the little sack with a quiet chuckle. He knew he should feel insulted. He wasn't a servant. Feeling the heft of the little sack, Dean looked inside, whistled softly, and swore.

"Sure beats gambling," he muttered.

Chapter Twenty-Two

The row of fine Georgian townhouses arced around Donald Long as he stood in the park at the center of the great circle. Leaning against a tree, he contemplated one house after another, not that it was easy to see where one house ended and the next began, they were so closely built together.

One of those houses was the one that the power pull had come from... Or would come from in another couple weeks or so.

He debated going around to the back and the servants' entrance. It seemed unlikely that the three would have achieved any kind of rank. Therefore, the servants' entrances would be the most logical place to keep an eye on.

A young footman suddenly appeared from the nearby street, walking quickly before a well-dressed youngish woman wearing a modest wig. At first, Donald assumed she was somebody's maiden aunt. But before he dismissed her, he realized that her face was familiar, indeed.

Surprised, he watched the footman, a young boy who was barely a teenager, ring the bell on a house, then hold the door for the woman. Donald frowned, then smiled. So that's where they were. The odd thing was that the girl didn't look pregnant yet. It didn't entirely make sense given the timing of the power pull, but who knew how long he'd have to get his hands on her and start the baby? Of course, it could have been Dean's, as they'd said. But Donald knew there was more than one way to get a woman pregnant, and if his plan worked, Dean and Elizabeth would be none the wiser. The problem would be getting his hands on the girl long enough to do it and wipe her memory. Sullenly mulling things over, he noted the number of the house and left.

Elizabeth, unaware that she had been observed, hurried upstairs to her mistress's salon.

"I've got the book you requested, miss." Elizabeth handed it over.

"Oh, joy." Deborah grabbed it.

"And it was the strangest thing, miss," Elizabeth continued mysteriously even though she knew full well what was behind it all. "But a young gentleman bumped into me, and I dropped the book. He helped me pick it up and asked me if I'd dropped this envelope. I said I didn't think so, but then I saw that it was addressed to you, so I said I must have. But honestly, I don't see how I could have."

Deborah tore open the envelope. "It's from him. Oh, Mrs. Parker, what did the young man look like?"

"I can't say. I didn't really look at him. I was too embarrassed. I'm sorry, miss. Besides, it's quite possible that the letter was in the book when I got it. It was being held with your name on it."

"Oh, wouldn't you know it," Deborah groaned. "This is the second letter I've had from this man. I told you about the one I got two nights ago, Saturday night. Pinned onto my cloak, it was. If only I knew who was sending them. He writes so nicely, and to be burning with secret passion. Oh, I'm completely enchanted, and I have no idea who he could be. Isn't it too wonderful to have a secret admirer?"

Elizabeth smiled, then turned her back lest she give away too much. Two days later, she pressed Robin into letter-carrying service.

"Deborah will begin to get suspicious if I keep bringing them," Elizabeth explained. "She's already wondering why I've never seen the man."

"All right." Robin took the letter and shrugged.

An hour later, she presented herself to Deborah.

"Excuse me, Miss Deborah, but I found this last night. It wouldn't happen to be yours, would it?"

Deborah snatched the letter and tore it open.

"Yes, thank you," she replied suddenly dignified. "Where did you find it?"

"On Mr. Morgan, Mistress. It was falling out of his pocket."

"Oh, no, not Anthony." Deborah looked ashen.

Robin smiled. "I doubt it was his. That's not his hand, for one thing. I got the impression the letter had been put in his pocket by someone else."

"Then I'll have to question him."

"I wouldn't bother. I seriously doubt he'll remember anything about it. He was somewhat inebriated last night."

"Somewhat?" Deborah laughed. "Well, you're very kind in your assessment, Mr. Parker. But you do have a point. Thank you much for rescuing this, and good day."

"Good day."

Robin left, chuckling to herself. Later that evening she chased after Morgan as he left the house.

"Wait!" she called, running to catch up.

"Parker!" Morgan groaned. "Why are you following me about all the time?"

Robin gasped as she came up. "I thought we were friends."

"I suppose."

"You also owe me a brandy for that wager you lost last night."

Morgan looked surprised. "What wager?"

"You don't remember?" Robin asked.

Morgan swallowed. "Uh, of course, I do. I remember it perfectly. Are you sure you won?"

"Positive." Robin clapped him on the back. "And there were plenty of witnesses, so you can't back out of it."

Morgan sighed. Robin sighed and walked with him. He was already half-crocked. A textbook alcoholic, Robin thought. There hadn't been any wager the night before, or any other time. Robin took advantage of Morgan's shaky memory frequently. She paid him off just often enough to keep him from getting suspicious in his rare lucid moments.

It was impossible to keep him off the bottle. The best Robin could do was make sure he got home in one piece every night, and that he was sober enough to work the next day. Sir James was somewhat sympathetic once Robin had him search Morgan's room, and he found all the hidden bottles there. For a drunk, Morgan could be slippery and quick. More than once he'd ditched Robin's vigilance and sent her searching around the city for him.

He gave her the slip again that night but didn't go far.

Robin found him in the next tavern on the road, drinking and playing dice with some other clerks near his age.

Sighing, she bought a tankard of ale and joined the group on the fringe of the game. Morgan sat across from her. Behind him, at a table away from the group, two gentlemen discussed something intently. One laughed and uncommonly white teeth flashed. His mustache was a dark reddish-brown, and his hair, though powdered, showed a few auburn strands here and there.

Robin thought he looked familiar. Trying not to stare, she tried to place him. He smiled with a nasty gleam.

Robin swallowed as her heart bounded into her throat. It was impossible, then again, it was all too likely. The man was Master Neddrick, which meant he wasn't from the seventeenth century at all, but another time traveler like Roger.

Robin kept her cool. He hadn't noticed her, or if he had, he hadn't recognized her. Robin wondered why he was chasing them. They had messed up Roger's experiment. Robin had a strong feeling Neddrick had nothing to do with that. But he obviously had some connection to Elizabeth. And if he had tracked them down, why hadn't Roger?

It crossed Robin's mind that if Neddrick was there, that meant he had a working time machine. It was some small hope, but not much. It would be too dangerous to reveal themselves, or to even find where he was staying, let alone steal the thing.

Neddrick abruptly got up and left. Robin debated going after him. Then Morgan got to his feet. She hesitated one moment too long. Neddrick was gone. She shrugged and got a good grip on Morgan's swaying form. With a grim sigh, she decided Neddrick would find them before she found him.

She didn't tell Dean or Elizabeth about her evening's encounter. There didn't seem any point in exciting them, and there was always the chance that Dean would do something rash before she could stop him. She remained preoccupied with it, however. The next night she kept her eyes open as she followed Morgan about.

Noting her distraction, Morgan slipped away earlier than usual and disappeared more completely than ever. Robin was furious with herself for losing him as she had. Close to one in the morning she made some discreet inquiries.

A couple of footmen finally answered Robin's request in the affirmative. They directed her to a bright house on a dark alley not far from the Assembly Rooms. Shaking her head, Robin knocked.

A scantily clad woman ushered her in. Several more lounged about in the salon she was shown into. Robin gulped as she realized in just what kind of place she was.

"Take your pick," suggested an older, made-up woman in velvety tones. "It's a shilling a turn."

"Um, actually I came to inquire after one of your clients."

A lovely young thing with a towering wig and white, white skin slid close up to Robin and stroked her cheek.

"Are you sure you wouldn't like a turn with me?" she asked in a beguiling voice.

"N-n-no." Robin stepped away. "I-I'm really not on the market. Honest. Um. I just came to get my friend. He's a little loaded right now, and if I don't get him home fast, my boss will skin me alive. His name's Morgan, Anthony Morgan."

The older woman nodded. "Tony. First floor, second door on your right."

"Yeah." Robin swallowed again. She certainly didn't want to go barging in on someone… "Right. Um. Thanks. I'll be right back."

There was blessed silence behind the indicated door. Robin opened it and peeked inside. The light from the hall fell upon Morgan sprawled face down on the bed with nothing on. Robin went in. She tried to wake him and failed. Robin gathered his clothes together and got his breeches and shirt on him. At least his purse was still full. Grunting, Robin heaved him up and home.

The next day was Friday and another ball night for Deborah. That evening, draped from her wig was a special lace veil with tiny seed pearls worked into the pattern. A bouncing country jig sent it floating to the ground. Deborah, as usual, never noticed. But a timid young gentleman did. Unobserved, Lord Edward Acton picked it up and slid it next to his bosom.

The next day, the Culpepper house was in an uproar. Deborah was desolate over the loss of her veil. Sir James was not happy about it, either. It had come from Venice and had cost a pretty penny. All the servants stayed out of the way as much as possible to avoid Sir James' ranting and Deborah's sorrow.

Late that afternoon, one of the kitchen maids came back from the marketplace with a letter for Deborah. Deborah was ecstatic and rang for Elizabeth.

"He's got it!" Deborah exclaimed as Elizabeth entered the room.

"I beg pardon, miss?"

"My secret lover. He has my veil. He's keeping it next to

his heart. Isn't that beautiful?" Deborah whirled around in joy.

"Yes, miss. But what are you going to tell your father?"

"My father?" Deborah stopped whirling. "Oh. What can I tell him?"

Elizabeth thought. "That a friend has it, and you've let her borrow it?"

"Oh, Mrs. Parker, you're a genius. He won't like that much, but he'll have to admit it's safe. With any luck at all, he'll have forgotten about it by tomorrow."

"Yes, miss."

Sir James had forgotten about the veil by that evening. He was more preoccupied with a letter he had just received. He had Robin write the reply, giving his permission to let Mr. Farquhar visit Miss Deborah Culpepper on the morrow, Sunday. Robin dispatched it with Samuel, who didn't seem all that happy to be sent.

Robin had only a passing interest in Mr. Farquhar. She hadn't met the man but knew that Sir James had dined with him at least twice the previous week. Sunday afternoons she had off with Dean and Elizabeth. They had planned to spend that afternoon at the Summer Gardens, but rain changed their plans. Dean and Elizabeth went straight up to their room. Robin paused in one of the salons while Samuel fetched a snack for her.

On her way upstairs, Robin passed the sitting room where Deborah was having her interview with Mr. Farquhar. Just out of curiosity, Robin put her ear to the door and listened.

"Then you didn't send the letters," Deborah was saying.

"No. The only letter I sent was to your father, yesterday."

The voice sounded familiar. Robin opened the door a crack and peeked in.

Deborah looked away from her guest sadly. "Oh, how silly of me. I merely thought… After you were so kind to me at the ball the other evening. I beg your pardon for making such an assumption."

"You may have it." It was Neddrick. Robin shut the door. "What was that?"

"Oh, just one of the servants, I'm sure," Deborah answered. "Ours are harmless, but you know how nosy they can be."

"Yes, indeed."

Robin hurried upstairs to Dean and Elizabeth's room. They were asleep. Robin left a note instructing them to not go downstairs until the next day.

Not that the next day was any better. Neddrick/Farquhar dropped by again to conduct business with Sir James. Robin heard about the visit beforehand and manipulated an errand that kept her out of the house for the day. Dean and Elizabeth had been carted off earlier that day with Lady Culpepper and Deborah to visit with a friend in Cheltenham.

Robin spent the next three days dodging Farquhar. Dean spent his days dodging passes from Her Ladyship. Thursday, she caught him, more or less.

"Parker, you've done so well with my feet," she told him after summoning him to her room. She was wearing her India cotton overgown, but it hung open revealing her stays and panniers underneath.

"Thank you, M'lady."

She smiled archly. "My back has been very sore lately."

Dean hesitated. "It has?"

"That wretched coach trip, you understand." Lady Culpepper arranged her thin gown around her ample bosom. "Why they can't make those blasted things more comfortable, I've no idea."

"They do bounce a lot, M'lady."

"Do you think you could apply those marvelous hands of yours to my back?"

Dean grimaced. "Couldn't that get us into trouble?"

"How do you mean, Parker?" Her smile was almost menacing.

"Well, your husband might get the wrong idea," Dean answered and almost immediately regretted it.

She chuckled. "That's if he finds out. But he's in Bath. We're here."

"Yes, M'lady."

"You wouldn't like it if I complained to him about your insubordination, now would you?"

"No, M'lady."

"Then have at it."

"Yes, M'lady."

Dean had at it reluctantly. Somewhere in the back of his mind, he remembered there were laws against sexual harassment on the job. But that was in the twenty-first century. He couldn't wait to get back home.

The little group got back to Bath the next day to find Mr. Farquhar had serious intentions for Deborah, and Sir James liked him. Lady Culpepper was aghast because the man wasn't titled, and wasn't that rich, either. Deborah was upset because she didn't like him. She'd been relieved to find he wasn't her secret admirer and liked him even less after that. Dean and Elizabeth were scared, at first, when Robin told them who Mr. Farquhar was.

"I suppose he's chasing us," Elizabeth said. "But poor Deborah. I shouldn't want her to be married to such an evil creature as Master Neddrick, I mean, Mr. Farquhar."

"Assuming he stays married to her," grumbled Dean. "He'll probably knock her up then head off to some other ti—Wait." The thought slowly manifested itself in his brain. "If he's here, then he had to have a way to get here. Robin, you think maybe this guy's got one of those time machine thingies?"

"I think that's a safe bet," Robin said. "The trick will be getting it."

"Well, hell." Dean started pacing. "Find out where he's staying, and we'll go get it. Hell, I'm happy to do a little breaking and entering."

"No." Robin turned on him. "Are you out of your mind, Dean? Think about it. We messed up Roger's experiment. I know he didn't seem mad at us about it, but Farquhar sure seems to be. Maybe there's a reason, and do you really want to give the time travel people more ammo against us by stealing another machine?"

"Hello? He's not going to loan it to us. How else are we going to get home?"

Robin gulped. "Well. I don't know. Give me some time to think about it. In the meantime, we've got to make sure this Viscount Edward gets his bid in for Deborah's hand. Dean, I want you to promise me you won't go after Farquhar's time machine."

"Come on, Robin."

"Dean, promise."

Dean glared at her. "All right. I promise. I won't go after his machine."

"Good." Robin sighed. "Why don't you take charge of giving Lord Edward the royal shove in the right direction"

Dean snorted. "Oh, right. Just give me the easy job. This guy is a total weenie."

"Good," said Robin. "Then getting him to do what we want him to do should be no problem."

"I can think of a few things to say to him," Elizabeth said quietly.

"Even better," said Robin. "I've got to go think. And it's Friday. I get to go chase Tony all over town."

That evening, Deborah stayed home and sulked. Lady Culpepper convinced Sir James that they desperately needed to be seen at the theatre, and he, grumbling, went along with her. With Robin chasing Anthony, and Elizabeth nearby to provide help with Deborah, Dean decided to fetch Lord Edward.

He found the young swain sighing in the vestibule of the Assembly Rooms.

"My good Mr. Parker!" he exclaimed. "You're here. But where is your mistress? She's not ill, I hope."

Dean clapped the young man on the back. "She's perfectly well, but pretty unhappy. She's got another suitor, you know."

Lord Edward sighed even more deeply. "I've heard. I suppose she's accepted him."

"She hates him."

"Are you sure?" Lord Edward brightened.

"Cross my heart."

"Oh, this is wonderful news." Lord Edward sighed with joy this time.

Dean shook his head. "It's not all that great. Sir James really likes the guy. You've got to do something and fast."

"What?" Lord Edward looked panicked.

"Reveal yourself. Talk to her."

"Me?" The viscount practically squeaked.

"Come on. She's at home right now and her parents are gone. We'll sneak you in."

"But I..."

Dean got a good grip on the frightened young man's arms and started him down the street.

"Look, I promise you, she's head over heels in love with you and she doesn't even know who you are," Dean said.

"But if she finds out." Lord Edward trembled visibly.

Dean squeezed his arm reassuringly. "She'll love you. Trust me. Just talk like you write to her. She eats that stuff up."

"But..."

"Shut up. You sound like a motorboat."

"A what?"

Dean grinned sheepishly. "Never mind."

At the house, Dean took Lord Edward in through the servants' entrance. Lord Edward was too nervous to notice. Dean sent his footman upstairs to have Elizabeth get Deborah into the back salon. Dean waited there with Lord Edward until Deborah appeared, pushed in by Elizabeth.

"But at least my wig!" Deborah pleaded as Elizabeth shut

the door. Dean slid around the room as she turned and started.

"Oh! My Lord!" She dropped a curtsy. "I must beg pardon for my appearance."

He swallowed. "You are more beautiful now than I have ever seen you."

Outside, in the hall, Dean and Elizabeth muffled their laughter and continued listening.

"You are most generous, My Lord."

"Oh, please. I am your humble servant, Edward. You don't know how I have loved you."

"But your letters..."

"They couldn't come near to expressing my true feelings for you. They are but a shadow of what my heart holds for you. I have worshipped you. See, your veil which I found, it is my most sacred relic. I've kept it here next to my heart since I found it. It has saved my very life many times over when I thought I would die from not having you."

Deborah sighed. "Yes, you are the one. You can't imagine how I've longed to see your face. I knew from the moment I read your first letter that we would be true lovers."

Dean and Elizabeth could bear it no longer. They went upstairs and had a good long laugh.

"Oh, dear," said Elizabeth, wiping her eyes. "I feel so unkind laughing like this. I'm afraid we must sound like them sometimes."

"I'm not that bad." Still chuckling, Dean wrapped her up in his arms. "I love you, Elizabeth, and I don't mind saying so, but I'll say it without the glop."

"I'm glad you do." She reached up and kissed him. "And I love you, too."

Chapter Twenty-Three

Donald paced casually in the Culpepper drawing room. A time traveler developed patience naturally. At least, that's what the Board said was true. Donald had his doubts about that. Still, the girl was within his grasp. That satisfied him, even if the ensuing formalities would take a little time to get through.

The only thing that bothered him was that he had not had a glimpse of her since that first day he had arrived. Or the others. He knew they were part of the household. His research on that score had been thorough enough. But since the few dinners he'd had with Sir James had failed to turn up the three, Donald was forced to woo that fool girl in an effort to insinuate himself into the household.

Robin, DeanDean, and the girl had to be around someplace. He'd seen the girl, and that power pull had come from the Culpepper house. The girl hadn't generated it. As far as Donald knew, she and the other two had no way of knowing he was there, so he doubted they were hiding. But where were they, especially Robin, who was the most dangerous of the three?

Donald shuddered. That Robin seemed to be staying one

step ahead of him didn't make sense. Donald idly wondered whether he wanted to get the girl or get Robin.

Sir James walked in.

"Ah, Mr. Farquhar, good day." The old man seemed in a pleasant enough mood.

Donald nodded. "Good day, Sir James."

"You do not wish to visit my daughter today?"

"Perhaps later." Donald put on his most ingratiating smile. "I would like to discuss an urgent matter with you first."

"Regarding?" Sir James signaled a young footman. "Some tea? The girl just brought it up."

"Yes, I saw. Thank you." Still smiling, Donald cursed inwardly. "The matter does concern your daughter."

"Indeed." Sir James rubbed his hands together expectantly.

Donald nodded at the footman as he accepted the cup of tea. "I've become quite fond of her."

"Indeed." Sir James' eyebrow lifted as he watched the footman stand expectantly looking at Donald.

"I realize this is rather sudden." Donald moved away from the footman. "But I've been given to understand that you are looking for a husband for her."

"I am," said Sir James, as he watched the footman elegantly sidle up next to Donald. "I am indeed."

Donald turned an exasperated glare at the footman and moved away. "I would imagine she has quite a full list of suitors, but I should hate to lose my chance with her simply for lack of speaking my intentions, eh, sir."

"Indeed."

There was an awkward pause as the footman again placed himself expectantly next to Donald. Donald was about to move again when he suddenly remembered the blasted vail. It took no small effort to hide his disdain as he dropped the piece of silver into the young man's hand. The footman, for his part, made no effort to hide his disdain as he withdrew.

"Insolent beasts," Sir James grumbled cheerfully. "Now to your business. You'd like to be considered as a suitor, eh? Well, young man, what are you prepared to offer my daughter?"

"Fifty pounds a year allowance, plus any clothes she needs, and upon my death, should she survive me, her dowry and all my possessions, providing they go to our children upon her death."

Sir James nodded. "Very generous."

"I'll also raise her allowance as my means prove capable."

"Indeed." Sir James smiled approvingly. "I must admit you make a very impressive offer. You've got very good references, too." He paced about, musing. "Still, she is my only daughter. I would like to ensure her happiness, as well."

Donald clicked his heels. "I will make her happiness my foremost priority."

"Indeed." Sir James stopped pacing. "Well, Mr. Farquhar, I think I can see my way to letting you press your suit. Let's not say anything to Deborah or Her Ladyship just yet. Take some time and win my daughter's heart first. We can draw up a preliminary contract Tuesday afternoon, if you will."

"Very good, sir. Thank you."

"Would you like to see Deborah now?"

"I would, thank you."

Outside in the hall, Robin ran up the stairs. She knocked

first on Dean and Elizabeth's door, then burst in when admitted.

"Damn and blast!" She slammed the door shut.

"What's the matter?" asked Dean. He had his breeches on and lounged on the bed. Elizabeth rested at the table.

"Neddrick, alias Farquhar." Robin leaned on the door. "He just asked Sir James for Deborah's hand, and Sir James all but handed it over."

"Oh, no!" gasped Elizabeth.

"'Oh, no' is right," grumbled Robin. "The only thing I can figure is that he's marrying Deborah to get at you, Elizabeth. But why?"

Elizabeth thought. "Perhaps he hopes to get to us by joining the household. He strikes me as too proud to come in as a servant."

"But how could he know we're here?" asked Dean.

"I have no idea," said Robin. "But he must. Why else would we be taking such a drastic measure to insinuate himself into the family?"

"We'll have to quit," grumbled Dean.

Robin glared at him. "And where are we going to find jobs? People don't just change employers willy-nilly here, you know."

"Well, how much longer before you get the machine fixed?" Dean complained.

Robin sighed. "Dean, there's a good chance I'll never get that machine fixed. Half the materials it's made from haven't been discovered yet."

"So boost Neddrick's," said Dean.

"It looks like I'll have to," Robin said.

Elizabeth shook her head. "I know you don't like stealing, Robin, but it is the only way."

"That's for sure." Robin began to pace. "You're certainly in no shape to run for it. Not to mention it's getting harder to cover up your condition."

"I know." Elizabeth pulled her India gown over her ample belly. "But if I must run, I must. Until then we must do what we can to save Deborah."

"We do have to do that much," Robin grumbled. "What are the odds of Lord Edward getting in there before the contract is drawn up?"

"So long even Anthony wouldn't bet on them," Dean snorted.

Robin winced. "We've really got to light a fire under that clown now if we're going to keep Elizabeth out of Neddrick's hands and keep our jobs."

"Well." Dean got up. "That's my job. I'll leave the felonies to you, Robby."

"You're so generous, Dean." Robin's lip curled. "The hard part is going to be finding out where Neddrick's sacked out. I'm tied up here all day with Sir James, and all night with chasing Tony around. Elizabeth, why don't we make that your assignment."

Elizabeth frowned. "I'll do my best. Perhaps if Deborah wrote him some sort of letter. I could have George deliver it instead of Andrew."

"Andrew?" Robin asked.

"Deborah's footman," Dean explained.

"Yes," said Elizabeth. "If George delivers it, then I could

find out where. I might be able to get Andrew to tell me, but George is far more likely to."

"That's all very well and good," said Robin. "But why on earth would Deborah want to write a letter to Mr. Farquhar? She doesn't like him."

Dean grinned suddenly. "I bet I could do it. I could write the letter for Deborah. I can forge her handwriting easy. I'll write him a hate letter. I mean, who's gonna know?"

"Uh, Deborah?" Robin replied. "And that's just for starters. Dean, it's insane."

"Not really," Elizabeth said. "Although I think it would be better if Deborah did the writing. I expect she'll be calling for me any minute now, wanting to know how to discourage Mr. Farquhar. All I have to do then is suggest writing him a note saying that she'd prefer it if he focused his attentions elsewhere. There's nothing improper in that, and all I have to do is see to it that George makes the delivery."

It seemed simple enough. But Elizabeth couldn't get Deborah to cooperate. Apparently, Sir James had let his daughter know that he highly approved of Mr. Farquhar and that she was not to discourage him. Dean was a little more successful with Lord Edward. While the nervous suitor refused to speak with Sir James, he did agree to ask Lady Culpepper's advice on the matter. What occurred during the interview that Monday, Dean never found out. He avoided Her Ladyship as much as he could without losing his job.

Lady Culpepper sent for him constantly, to the point that Sir James began to notice her unusual interest in his clerk. Tuesday morning found Sir James fuming about it to Robin.

"Don't think I'm accusing you, Parker," he grumbled. "But

I wonder if your brother is aware of how indiscreet such things are."

"He's very aware of it, sir," Robin replied. "He's trying to avoid the situation, but, well, this is very awkward, sir."

"I'll be damned if it isn't. I know what you're trying to say."

"I don't mean to offend or accuse, sir," said Robin, nervously. "It's just the way things appear. I'm sure Her Ladyship's intentions are perfectly innocent, as are my brother's. He just doesn't know how to handle it properly."

Sir James sighed. "Your lies are very kind, Parker. I've heard the servants talking, and I'm not the blind old fool they think. Her Ladyship is behaving exactly as it appears. Well, I'll be damned if I'm going to be a cuckold, even if I have to remove a perfectly good clerk from my household."

Robin gulped. "Yes, sir."

"I can see you don't like the idea. I'm afraid you'll just have to live with it. I refuse to be made a fool of by a member of my own household, even if it's innocently."

"Yes, sir."

"The greatest difficulty is that he has made himself quite indispensable." Sir James began pacing. "I'll have to find someone else to take his position before I let him go." He stopped and looked at Robin. "Pray don't say anything to your brother just yet. It will take some time to find a replacement and I shouldn't like him to be uncomfortable."

"Thank you, sir," Robin replied as she pondered how she could sabotage Sir James' employee search.

There was a knock on the door.

"Yes?" Sir James asked.

The door opened.

"Mr. Farquhar is here," said the butler.

"Thank you, Barnes. Send him up."

Robin waited until the door had shut. "I'd better get those other accounts done, sir. They're in my room."

"No. I'll need you to take dictation." Sir James popped open his snuff-box and took a pinch.

"Why don't I get Morgan?" Robin fought to keep her voice steady. "He's much faster at it than I am."

Sir James snuffled, then dabbed at his nose with a lacy handkerchief. "This is too important to take a chance on Anthony messing it up. And I don't want to have to remember all the details when you come back to get the corrections when you re-do his work."

"Yes, sir." Robin swallowed and resolved to remain cool. She didn't think Neddrick would take a chance on telling Sir James she was from another time, if only because she could make the same accusation.

When Farquhar came in and saw her, a brief smile flickered across his face.

"Good day, Mr. Farquhar," said Sir James cheerfully.

Farquhar smiled again. "Good day, Sir James."

"I'm glad to see you're on time." Sir James dabbed at his nose again. "This is my clerk, Parker. He'll be taking down the contract as we dictate it."

"He will?" Farquhar stressed the "he" with an insinuating glance at Robin.

"Parker is an excellent clerk," protested Sir James. "His work is extremely accurate. I have every confidence in his abilities."

Farquhar simpered smugly. "I beg your pardon, Sir James.

I wasn't questioning his abilities. Merely... Well, he does seem rather young. No beard to speak of."

Robin glared back at Farquhar. "Sir James is aware of my unfortunate accident."

"Ahem. Indeed," said Sir James, growing a little red in the face. "Not something one wishes to discuss."

Robin turned back to Sir James. "Excuse me, sir, what is the contract we are to draw up?"

"We are going to start a marriage contract between Mr. Farquhar and Deborah," said Sir James proudly.

"Mr. Farquhar?" Robin feigned surprise. "I understood it was the other young man that Deborah favored."

"That letter writer? Bah!" Sir James grandly whipped out his handkerchief. "If he hasn't the nerve to show himself, then he shan't have my daughter."

Robin shot an icy glance at Farquhar. "Perhaps he's waiting to be sure he's won the mistress's heart, rather than going ahead and marrying a woman who doesn't like him very much."

"What rot. I did and I've managed—" Sir James stopped suddenly. "I'll take that into consideration, Parker. Eh. This isn't the final contract, in any case. Fetch your quills and paper. We've work to do."

"Yes, sir."

That evening, Robin fumed in Dean and Elizabeth's room.

"He promised the damned moon!" she groaned. "And I had to take it all down, knowing damned well he has no intention of keeping it. What's worse, he'll get off scot-free. He'll take off for another time, and never get caught."

Elizabeth nodded. It was pointless to remind Robin of the increasing pressure. Robin was all too aware of it.

Two nights later, a Thursday, Robin lost Morgan again. He left quite a trail. Robin made all the usual inquiries, including ones at the brothel, and a couple others, and found that Morgan had stopped in at most of the places and left before she arrived.

She was closing in on him, when, as she left a tavern, two largish men met her at the door, and escorted her to a deserted road.

"We understand your name is Robin Parker," said one, a pasty looking fellow with a large brown mole on his chin.

"Yes," Robin answered.

"Last Monday night, you played a few rounds with our master, Mr. Beverton, and lost quite a bit of money."

Robin frowned. "I don't believe so. I don't know any Mr. Beverton, and I spent Monday night attending my master in his home."

"Mr. Parker, you signed your name to several notes, and promised Mr. Beverton should have the money Tuesday." The man's grip tightened on Robin's arm. "It's Thursday, and Mr. Beverton has received no money."

"I don't sign notes." Glaring, Robin pulled herself up.

"You did Monday."

"I was... Oh, damn! That Morgan!" Robin added a few other epithets. "I know what happened. A colleague of mine has signed my name to his notes. Take me to your Mr. Beverton. He'll tell you I wasn't the one who gambled with him Monday night."

The man with the mole on his chin thought it over, then

nodded at his companion. They escorted Robin to a coffee house frequented by gentlemen. Mr. Beverton sat at a table playing cards with Morgan. He looked up as he noticed his servants entering.

"Ah, Daniels, Simpson," Beverton said as they came up. "I needn't have sent you out after Mr. Parker. Here he is. Who is this young man?"

"The real Robin Parker," Robin growled. She yanked Morgan up out of his chair. "Tony Morgan, you are dead meat. I oughta turn you in to your uncle!"

"No! Robin, please don't!" Swaying only a little, Tony seemed much more sober than he probably was.

Robin rolled her eyes. "Are you paid up?"

"To me, he is." Mr. Beverton smiled. "In fact, he's even won a little."

"Aren't you one lucky SOB." Robin scooped up the coins. "Well, if you can lose in my name, you can win for me also. Thanks for the money. Mr. Beverton, my pleasure."

Robin shoved Morgan out of the coffee house. "All right, you brainless alky. How many other notes have you signed my name to?"

Morgan shrugged. "I don't know. Not many. A few."

"I'll bet."

"How much?" Morgan burped and giggled.

In response, "Get out of here!" Robin tightened her grasp so Morgan cried out. Furious, she propelled him home.

The next day, she had another piece of dubious luck. Sir James wanted a message sent to Mr. Farquhar's lodgings. Though Robin knew that message delivery was Samuel's job, she decided to use her footman's sour disposition as an excuse and delivered the note, herself.

Farquhar was out when she arrived. Robin debated for a moment, then decided it would be worth it to look around, at least. Given that Farquhar was expected back at any minute, she doubted she'd be able to steal the machine, but she'd be able to get the lay of the land, as it were, for a future visit.

"Which is Mr. Farquhar's room?" she asked the footman at the door. "My master was most adamant that he get this letter. If I were to slide it under his door, that should be adequate assurance."

The footman hesitated. Robin pulled out a couple silver shillings from her pouch and held them up. The footman sighed. Heavily. Robin dug in her pouch for a crown piece, plus the two shillings, all of which ended up with the footman. But Robin did get the information she wanted.

After sliding the envelope under the door indicated, she paused. Downstairs, she could hear the door opening and the footman greeting a resident. Farquhar's voice answered, with a certain snideness, as if he was only being polite because it was expected of him.

While there probably was a servant's stair, Robin decided it would not be politic to use it. That left only the main stair, and Robin did not want an encounter with Farquhar. SoSo, she slid up the main stair only so far as she could avoid being seen.

Fortunately, Farquhar went straight to the door the footman had said was his. His hand on the doorknob, he suddenly paused and listened. Robin pulled back into the stairwell and held her breath. Slowly, she edged around and saw him looking behind him as if he had reason to believe he was being followed. Somehow, he missed checking the stairwell and entered his room.

Robin let her breath out and as quietly as she could, slid past his room and out of the building.

She didn't go back that night. Friday was Morgan's big night out, and Robin felt it would be wise to make sure she and the others still had jobs in case something went wrong.

Sunday the sky was a brilliant blue with huge white clouds scudding across. Dean and Elizabeth insisted that Robin join them for a walk in the nearby park.

"SoSo, what's the big joke you wanted to tell us about yesterday?" Dean asked Robin as they strolled among the trees.

"Oh, that." Robin snickered. "Sir James got a letter from his son in the Colonies."

"What about it?" Dean shrugged, unimpressed.

Robin couldn't contain her grin. "Think, Dean. What year is this?"

"1776."

"What happened in 1776?" Gleefully, Robin poked him in the ribs.

"The American Revolution." Dean twisted to avoid another poke. "That's old news. Besides, like you said, if we look at it from everyone here's point of view, it is ridiculous that they could win the war."

"I know. But listen to the latest. Captain Culpepper made a copy of a certain document that went on display over in Philadelphia, where he's stationed. It starts 'When in the course of human events it becomes necessary for one people to dissolve the political bands which have connected them with another...'" Robin waited expectantly.

"That sounds familiar," said Dean. Elizabeth shrugged.

"It damn well better." Robin chortled. "Come on, Dean, you know what it is. A Declaration by the Representatives of the United States of America."

The light switch went on in Dean's head. "That's not the Declaration of Independence, is it?"

"Of course, it is, you lunkhead!"

Dean frowned. "But doesn't that start 'We the people...'?"

Robin groaned. "That's the Constitution."

"Oh, right. I remember now."

"But why is this declaration so amusing?" asked Elizabeth.

"Because the hot-headed rebels who drew it up are going to do the impossible and win the war," Robin replied. "What the Declaration goes on to say is that the Colonies are no longer part of England. Of course, everyone here doesn't know that yet."

"It sounds like treason to me." Elizabeth shook her head.

Robin shrugged. "For the moment, it is. But in another fifty years or so, Britain will be friends with the United States."

"Hm." The whole idea sounded incredible to Elizabeth.

"Hey, Elizabeth, that's our home we're talking about," said Dean. "Where Robin and I come from, and where we're all going to be living. This is just the beginning."

"I know." Elizabeth sighed. "You've told me."

Robin smiled. The news would be hitting everywhere soon. As she listened to a couple older gentlemen converse, she realized it had reached some people already. The men were aghast at such a preposterous move. They deserved it, Robin thought with a surge of patriotism for her homeland.

That evening, however, any glee was quickly squelched. As usual, on Sunday evenings, Sir James gathered his household for dinner, and as always, that Sunday, he insisted that his clerks be there, along with the young Mrs. Parker.

The group gathered in the salon before the meal, dressed in their best. Sir James was less than pleased about what was going on in the colonies but was confident that his son and the rest of the King's army would put down the rebels in no time. But his bluster seemed somewhat distracteddistracted, and Robin soon realized why. Lady Culpepper was eyeing Dean with obvious hunger. Dean stayed as close to Elizabeth as possible without taking up the same space.

When dinner was announced, Lady Culpepper attempted to slide up next to Dean that he might escort her in to dinner, but Robin slipped in first and gently took her arm.

"My Lady," Robin whispered softly, as they walked into the dining room. "I know you're fond of my brother, but I don't think you want your husband to find you out. If he does, then my brother will be gone."

"Impertinent beast!" Her Ladyship hissed back, then stopped and laughed as she noticed the others staring. "A silly joke. But Mr. Parker, I do think you should be more discreet around a lady."

"I will endeavor to do so," Robin replied.

Dinner went more smoothly than usual, but Sir James' eye wandered over to Dean far too often for either he or Robin to feel comfortable.

Chapter Twenty-Four

Masked and gloved, Robin gently turned the knob on the door to Farquhar's room. It was locked. What would otherwise be considered odd didn't surprise Robin in the least. But it did make things more difficult.

Fumbling in the dark of the hallway, she found the broken key she'd brought along and slowly inserted it in the lock. She had practiced on all the doors at the Culpepper house. The key had worked there. Robin's nerves were on edge, which made the extra twists necessary. The gloves weren't necessary at all, except that Robin couldn't remember when fingerprinting was discovered, and she wasn't about to take any chances.

The door opened with a loud squeak. Robin's heart stopped. She looked up and down the hallway. No one stirred. She slipped in and shut the door.

About fifty years before, it had been made mandatory that all houses in Bath be responsible for lighting the streets. The lamp kept by the inn shone its light through the open window.

As Robin searched, she wondered how much longer Deborah would keep Farquhar occupied. It was a little strange that he had come visiting on a Monday night, but Robin wasn't complaining.

She hurried through the chest at the foot of the bed. It was empty but for a couple shirts and a pair of breeches. The wardrobe cabinet was empty, too. Robin softly tapped on the walls, and everywhere else she could think of, hoping for a secret panel. She didn't find one.

Under the bed was a cloth sack. Robin grabbed it. There was something lightweight in the bottom, not the time machine. It was in pieces, whatever it was.

That's when Robin heard the step in the hallway. She scrambled out of the window onto the ledge outside.

She made it out just in time. Farquhar burst the door open. She heard him angrily stomping about the room, searching.

Robin crept along the narrow ledge. She almost lost her grip when a dangling rope bumped her. Catching her breath and her composure, she recognized what it was. It was connected to a beam at the top and center of the house. Weighted at the bottom, and on pulleys, it was used to bring invalids and furniture too big for the narrow doorways into the house.

Robin tugged at it. It had plenty of tension on it. She took a deep breath. Three stories was a long drop to the hard cobbles below. But then she heard Farquhar rousing the house. She gripped the rope and floated down.

She hit the pavement just as the front door opened. Running hard, she dodged into the first alley she could find. Farquhar and his landlord pursued. As she turned the first corner she came across, she removed the mask and gloves.

She stuffed them in the sack she still had and stuffed all that under her waistcoat. Two more quick turns, and she figured she might be safe enough for a quick rest and readjustment.

There was a garbage heap next to her. She dumped the gloves and mask there, under some rotting cabbage. The sack folded around its pieces into a small flat bundle about the size of her palm. This she stuffed down the front of her pants.

She heard Farquhar's shout come from the street she'd just left. She ran again, around one corner, then another, straight into someone. He flailed about, further entangling Robin.

It took some effort, but as Robin began to disentangle herself, she realized she'd run into Morgan. He reeked of stale brandy and bad perfume.

"Who are you?" He squinted at Robin and veered.

"It's me, Parker," Robin hissed. An idea hit her. Morgan was too drunk to know the difference. She could say anything now and he'd swear it was true. "I'm taking you home again. I picked you up a while ago, remember?"

"Oh, yeah." Morgan belched.

"Come on." Robin steered him out of the alley onto the main street.

They'd only gone a short distance when Farquhar dashed out from a side street. His landlord appeared a moment later.

"There you are!" Farquhar exclaimed, stopping Robin and Morgan. "You broke into my room!"

"Me?" Robin looked taken aback. "Why on earth would I do that?"

"You know why," Farquhar snapped. "You were there, not five minutes ago."

Robin smiled. "I beg your pardon, sir. Five minutes ago, I

was wrestling Mr. Morgan, here, out of a bordello in the immediate neighborhood."

"You're lying!" Farquhar screamed.

"Sir," the landlord pointed out. "The man we were chasing had on a mask and gloves."

"You'll find them back there somewhere." Farquhar snapped.

"Even if you do," Robin said. "It still doesn't prove I was wearing them."

"Search him!" Farquhar ordered the landlord. "He's got my sack."

The landlord nervously patted Robin's waistcoat pockets.

"He's not carrying anything, sir," the landlord said.

Farquhar glared at her. "Very well, then. I'll deal with you tomorrow."

"Good evening, then." Robin nodded, then pushed Morgan on home.

At the house, she dumped Morgan in his room, then went to her own and lit a candle. She removed the sack from her pants and opened it. The pieces were small circuit chips, just like the ones inside her machine. Her heart leaped with joy. If she couldn't have the machine, these were the next best thing. She spent the rest of the night poring over the chips, trying to decide which ones she needed.

She was still very sleepy the next afternoon when Sir James called her into his salon.

"Mr. Parker," he said severely. "Mr. Farquhar was just herehere, and he made some very nasty accusations against you."

Robin nodded. "I'm not surprised, sir. He made the same accusations last night."

"And..And...?"

"I didn't do it." Robin shrugged. "I was bringing Mr. Morgan home."

"He obviously can't prove otherwise, but I've reason to believe he may have something in his accusation, though I didn't say anything of the sort to him. I overheard one of the servants mention she'd seen you trying to unlock the front salon door with a broken key."

"Oh." Robin briefly debated denying it but realized that if one had talked, the others would soon enough.

"Have you nothing else to say for yourself, Mr. Parker?"

"I'm sorry, sir. I must confess, I did break into Mr. Farquhar's room. But I beg of you, please hear me out. I had a very good reason, sir." Robin took a deep breath, trying to remember all the strands of the excuse she'd made up the night before. "Deborah lost some letters she had written. They were innocent jokes, but in the wrong hands, they could have been extremely damaging. Unfortunately, Mr. Farquhar acquired them. He was holding them over Deborah's head, and head and threatening to make them public. Deborah begged me to retrieve them. She also insisted that you not know about them. She had me swear I wouldn't tell you. She was afraid you'd be hurt, so I must ask you not to say anything to her. It would upset her terribly if she was aware that you knew. Anyway, that's what I went to Mr. Farquhar's room for. I've since burnt them. I felt it was my duty to this family to protect it."

"I see." Sir James nodded. "Well, I can't find any fault with that, although I disagree with your conclusions about Mr. Farquhar's intentions. You have to watch out for Deborah. She tends to exaggerate a great deal. But you did what you should have under the circumstances. Don't worry. I won't mention the matter to her, as long as you're certain the letters have been destroyed."

"I even stirred up the ashes, sir." Robin sighed with relief. Sir James was even easier to spin than she'd thought.

"Very good then. We'll let Mr. Farquhar think someone else burgled him. Now about those accounts from yesterday."

"Yes, sir. They're right here." Robin fetched them quickly.

The following Thursday was not a good day for anyone in the Culpepper house. It began an hour before dawn. Robin got up early to work on the time machine. She heated the iron poker from her fireplace and melted the sheet of tin she'd acquired. Holding her breath to prevent breathing in the deadly substance, she mixed in lead powder, a common cosmetic of the day.

As she put the top on the powder can, she heard movement from Morgan's room. Something was afoot. Morgan never stirred before nine in the morning, and only rarely that early. Robin heard his door open and close.

She was torn. She needed the machine fixed as soon as possible. But if Morgan got into any more trouble before she could, it might endanger her position.

She grabbed a cloak and scarf. Hurrying out the front door, she spotted Morgan leaving the circle. She ran as swiftly as she could without clattering too loudly on the cobblestones. Morgan glared at her as she caught up.

"What are you doing here, Parker?" he sulked.

"I was going to ask you the same thing," Robin said.

Morgan sniffed and held up his head. "I'm walking. Can't a man have any peace?"

"Tony, you and I both know you don't go walking around at five-thirty in the morning." Robin roughly grabbed his shoulder. "Where the hell are you going?"

"Down the river a bit."

"Why?"

Morgan groaned and looked away. "I got challenged to a duel."

It was Robin's turn to groan. "And you're going to fight it?"

"What else can I do?" Morgan whined.

Robin shook him. "Plenty. Good lord, Tony, dueling's illegal and stupid besides."

"I don't have any choice," Morgan said resolutely.

"Don't give me that. You forget everything else. Why do you have to remember this?"

"I will not be thought a coward." Morgan twisted in her grip.

"Tony, with your memory, nobody will think that."

"I'm sorry, Robin, I must."

"Terrific." Robin rolled her eyes, then decked him.

Morgan came to as Robin pulled him up from the ground.

"Hullo!" called a young gentleman of around twenty.

Robin turned to him and his three companions.

"Who are you?" she demanded.

"Mr. William Southby," said the gentleman. "I've a duel to fight with that young man you've bagged."

"I'm sorry, Mr. Southby," Robin replied. "Mr. Morgan is not in any shape to duel."

Neither was Southby. He was steady on his feet, but with a tendency to list to his right. Morgan lurched up.

"I'll fight you now!" he bellowed and drew his pistol.

"Tony, you idiot!" Robin grabbed for it.

Morgan caught her wrong and she fell in front of him. There were two gunshots, and Morgan fell on top of her.

"The constables!" someone cried.

Morgan groaned. Robin eased herself out from underneath him. Morgan groaned again as she rolled him onto his back and bent over him. Blood oozed out of a hole in his right upper arm.

"Damn! Now you've gone and done it!" Robin yanked his handkerchief out of his coat pocket.

"What's going on here?" an imposing constable asked.

"We were attacked," Robin answered. "My friend here was shot. Could you help me get him home?"

It wasn't very hard to bring Morgan along. The constable left them at the servants' entrance to the house. The cook, Mrs. Ferris, was just up and helped Robin bring Morgan in and lay him out on a work tableworktable.

"The master isn't going to like this," Mrs. Ferris commented as Robin eased Morgan out of his coat, waistcoat, and shirt.

"No kidding. Here, bring that candle closer." Robin probed the wound. "I'll be damned. I can see the ball. Get me a bowl of clean water and that small pair of tongs. Good, you've got a kettle already boiling. Dip the tongs in there first."

"But why?"

"Just do it. Thanks. Now hold that candle close again, and hold this arm down." Swallowing back the bile, Robin inserted the small tongs.

Morgan flinched and moaned. Robin dug the ball out.

"Well, that's that," she sighed straightening. "Do you have any clean cloths for bandages?"

"Yes, here."

Robin tied them on, then took Morgan upstairs to his room. After making sure no one was about, she went to her room and got the rubbing alcohol. She dosed the wound, then returned to her own room and collapsed on the bed.

Later that morning, Dean answered his summons to Lady Culpepper's room with the usual dread.

"Oh, Mr. Dean," she complained. "It's my back again. You must rub it. No one else can help."

Dean took a deep breath but didn't move. "M'lady, with all due respect, this is really making me nervous. What if your husband comes in?"

She sniffed. "He won't. He's too busy with his accounts. Now, hurry up and rub my back before I complain to him."

"Yes, M'lady." Defeated, Dean went to work.

Dean was rubbing the back of her neck when Sir James knocked and walked in.

"Well, Sarah, I'm here at your request— Parker— Parker! What are you doing?"

Dean yelped and bounced away.

"He insisted, James!" wailed Lady Culpepper. "It's all his doing."

"My doing?" Dean sputtered.

"Parker, to your quarters until further notice," Sir James snapped. "And you may as well start packing."

Furious, Dean stomped out. Robin had just powdered her hair when Dean burst into the room. He explained angrily what had happened. Robin swore.

"I think she set me up, too," Dean grumbled. "Sir James was talking like she'd asked him in there."

Robin groaned. "Shit! How could I have missed it? Of course, she set you up, Dean. Good lord, last Sunday. Don't you remember before dinner when she was flirting so outrageously with you?"

"That was hell," Dean said.

"No. That was trying to get Sir James jealous."

Dean grimaced. "Like, duh. Why the hell didn't I see that coming?"

"At least now I know how to spin it," Robin said. "I'm not blaming you, Dean. It's not your fault." A bell rang. "That's Sir James. Listen. Whatever you do, stay put. You can't afford to take off with Elizabeth in her current shape. And I might have the machine fixed, so we really have to be sure we stay together now. Okay?"

"Sure."

Robin ran downstairs to the salon. There she found two constables in the salon with Sir James.

"Mr. Parker, what is the meaning of this?" Sir James demanded.

Robin smiled as ingratiatingly as she could. "Of what, sir?"

"These two gentlemen say you were involved in a duel this morning, and that you've been passing bad notes."

"I was trying to prevent the duel, sir." Robin took a deep

breath. "As for the bad notes... Well, begging your pardon, sir, I'm afraid Mr. Morgan has been using my name as cover for his misdeeds, which, no doubt, he will not remember. I do have a witness I can bring forward who will confirm that this has happened."

Sir James snorted. "What about this duel?"

"Mr. Morgan again, I'm afraid." Robin shrugged. "I caught him leaving this morning. I was bringing him back when his opponent showed up, and they both drew guns. Before I could stop them, they fired. Mr. Morgan received a flesh wound in his upper right arm. I removed the ball already. I checked him about half an hour ago. He's a little feverish, but he should heal well, providing he doesn't take sick from it. I don't think he will. The wound looks clean enough."

"Are you satisfied, gentlemen?" Sir James turned to the constables.

"We've only his word for it," replied one.

"What would it profit me to place the blame on my master's nephew?" Robin said. "If I were to accuse him wrongly, it might save me from you, but would have dire consequences from my master. Besides losing my position, he'd probably hand me right back to you. I would be in just as bad a shape."

They couldn't argue with that, and so left. Sir James glared at Robin.

"You were supposed to prevent trouble," he said, finally.

"I did my best, sir. I truly regret that it wasn't good enough. However, it could have been much worse if I hadn't followed him."

Sir James growled in defeat. He left the room to go sulk in his chambers. Robin went about her work.

Around three in the afternoon, Elizabeth left with Deborah for a walk. An hour later, Elizabeth returned with a letter for Sir James. She and Robin watched as Sir James' face turned bright red with fury as he read the letter.

"Sir?" Robin asked. "What's wrong?"

"What do you know about this?" He turned on her.

Robin looked back, puzzled. "About what?"

"She ran off and got married!" Sir James sputtered.

"She what?" Elizabeth gasped.

"Got married! To that little mouse with the title." Sir James paced the room furiously.

"May I see the letter, sir?" Robin neatly detached it from his hand as he prowled past.

"How could she?" the older man fumed, then turned on Robin and Elizabeth as they read the letter. "And how could you let her?"

"Begging your pardon, sir, we didn't let her do anything," said Elizabeth. "She merely told me that she'd forgotten a shawl here at the house and asked me to fetch it back and at the same time deliver the letter to you personally. Otherwise, she would have sent the footman."

"And you?"

Robin gulped. She doubted explaining that she'd been too busy trying to keep Morgan out of trouble would sooth the angry man.

"I had no way of knowing, sir," she said. "I don't see much of your daughter at all."

Sir James sputtered again. "You knew nothing of this? Either of you?"

"No, sir," said Robin.

"And who does she marry? Viscount Edward Acton." Sir James snorted. "One of those young titledyoung, titled hellions. Damn and blast! And after I worked so hard to find a responsible young man for her."

"Sir, if I may be so bold," Robin said carefully. "I've come across this Lord Edward, and I understand he's not like his peers that way. I also understand that the Duke of Cliveton, his father is a very virtuous man, and very powerful, in spite of his rather small duchy."

"Small comfort that is in light of a willful daughter! Damn and blast! It's all her mother's fault. She spoiled the girl with all these notions of a rich and titled husband. Marrying well. Bah!" Sir James suddenly stopped in his tracks. "Oh, my god, how am I going to tell Sarah?" His eye fell on Elizabeth and Robin could see the painful memory of that morning flashing before him.

Robin decided to pretend that she knew nothing about it. "Sir, as you just said, Her Ladyship has been very much in favor of your daughter getting just such a husband. Perhaps if you emphasized that."

"Enough of your effrontery, Mr. Parker. Do you think I'm as easily managed as the rest of my family?" Sir James' again grew alarmingly red. "You and your brother have brought nothing but trouble to this house. And after I showed you nothing but the greatest of kindnesses!"

"We are indebted, Sir James," Robin said through her teeth.

"And this is how you repay me?"

Robin lost it. "How I...? I've only busted my hump for you! And you had trouble brewing long before we got here. Who was keeping an eye on Mr. Morgan before I came along? Huh? I heard about those fines you had to pay for him back in London. And if you really wanted your daughter to be sensible, why the heck didn't you teach her to do your books? Instead, you let her lay around all day with nothing but romantic poems and novels and then you wonder why she's trying to live a fairy tale. And as for your wife, maybe if you'd spent some time paying attention to her, she wouldn't have had to come on to my brother to get you jealous enough to notice her!"

"Wha— -what? Jealous?" Sir James was beyond speech, but Robin noticed that he was sort of listening.

"Yes. She wanted you to pay attention to her. She doesn't care about Dean. She cares about you. Didn't she send for you this morning? You can't believe she forgot she had when she told Dean to rub her back, can you?"

"But she said…"

Robin rolled her eyes. "Do you honestly believe that after the way she chased Dean all over the salon Sunday past? Come on. He was glued to Elizabeth and doing everything he could to keep away from her. Why on earth would she be that obvious if she didn't want you to notice her?"

Sir James kept opening his mouth and making little sounds, but no words formed.

"Bah!" he finally snorted and drew himself up. "Leave me! We'll come to terms tomorrow."

Robin swallowed. She didn't like the sound of that.

Elizabeth went to comfort Dean. Robin finished her work for the day, then retired to her room. She spent the night sleeping off and on, working on the machine. She had to make it work. There was no doubt in her mind that she, Dean and Elizabeth would be thrown out onto the streets the next day.

And while Elizabeth was little more than six months along, she hadn't once seen a doctor. There were all sorts of things that could go wrong, and there weren't any hospitals where they were. They had to get home for the baby's safety as well as Elizabeth's.

As the night wore on, Robin became more and more driven by her fears. The troubled dreams she had when she dozed didn't help. Robin could only guess that she was doing the right thing. Not knowing was almost worse than her fear of failure.

As dawn touched the sky, she sat back and surveyed her work. There was the generator she had built in the early days out of a coffee grinder and speaker wires from Dean's iPhone, just to be doing something. The player, itself, had been torn apart for other possible parts. These were scattered about, mixed in with the parts she'd taken from Farquhar's room. On a china plate sat the lump of improvised solder, with the long iron poker cooling next to it. In the middle of the mess was the time machine, with the cover removed. Robin had just finished soldering what she hoped was the right chip to the circuit card.

Taking a deep breath, she pressed the switch on the side. The top glowed. Robin smiled. Then a thin stream of smoke appeared. Bright sparks flew, and white smoke billowed over the whole circuit card. Robin bounced back.

When the smoke cleared, she poked at the card. Every last circuit had burnt out.

Robin gazed at it, numb. Slowly, the depth of the disaster sank in. Drained of hope, she rested her arms on the table, buried her face in them, and cried.

Chapter Twenty-Five

The window of time in which the power pull was to occur was ridiculously short, unless, of course, you were spending the night on a park bench waiting for it to happen.

Roger shifted once more, hoping that the tree across from the Culpepper home would continue to provide sufficient cover, especially now that dawn lightened the sky over the square. Fortunately, the constables had only come by once and had been noisy enough on their approach to warn even the deafest of malefactors.

Shifting again, Roger kept his gaze steady on the one lit window among the townhouses on the row. He put his spyglass to his eye once more and saw Robin bending over something, then sit back.

In his week in Bath, he'd had little trouble finding out all that Robin, Dean, and Elizabeth had been up to. All he'd had to do is pose as the greengrocer's assistant, and the Culpepper's cook told him everything in exquisite detail. It hadn't taken him long, either, to pin Donald down. Fortunately, Donald had developed the habit of not noticing his inferiors, making it even easier for Roger to remain unseen. Donald's landlord had told Roger, again in the guise of the greengrocer's assistant, all about the burglary in Donald's room and the missing sack. And it had been perfectly easy to slip into the house, and Robin's room, where Roger had found the parts and Robin's work.

The problem had been deciding whether or not he should intervene. After all, it was possible that it would be him and not Robin who would generate that power pull. Roger had decided to wait, but as the night continued to fade, he debated intervening again. He furtively checked a small dial he had under his sleeve. Nothing had registered yet.

Except that the dial began to glow just as Roger caught a flash of light from Robin's window. That was it. He put the spyglass to his eye again and saw a look of horror on Robin's face. Roger hurried over to the house. Given all that cook had had to say yesterday afternoon, Roger could understand Robin's horror. Whatever had happened, she had every reason to believe all was lost. The poor thing had no way of knowing she'd just saved herself and the other two.

Silently, Roger slipped through the sleeping house. He stopped at the upstairs doorway, listening. Robin's soft sobs were on the other side. He eased the door open, slid through and quietly shut the door.

The charred mess on the work tableworktable told the story. Roger chuckled softly. Still engulfed in tears, Robin didn't seem to hear. Roger cleared his throat.

"Dean?" she sniffed as she turned around. She jumped. "Oh!" Wiping her eyes, she composed herself. "Oh. Roger."

He smiled. "Hello."

"How did you find us?"

Roger pointed. "Your experiment on the table there."

"This?" Robin almost burst into tears again. "It just blew up on me."

Roger looked at it more closely. "Well, all the chips are in the right place. Which one originally blew?"

"That one." Robin pointed.

"That makes sense, then what..?what...? Ah, here's the answer. Tin solder, isn't this?"

"Yeah. It's not very pure, either. I had to use the lead powder the ladies use on their faces to mix with it."

Roger shook his head. "It wasn't the lead. Tin can't conduct ion frequencies. It overloads, as you just saw."

"Oh." Robin sniffed. "I did my best."

"A pretty impressive best, I assure you." Roger gently put his hand on her back.

Robin snorted. "Not really. I ripped off the parts from Mr. Neddrick, I mean Farquhar."

"Donald Long." Roger's voice didn't quite sneer, but Robin could tell that Donald was not one of Roger's favorite people. "That's his real name."

"I don't know why he's after us," she said.

"When you say 'why,' are you asking what's his external objective, or the psychological issues driving his behavior?" Roger settled himself on the end of Robin's bed.

Sniffing, Robin chuckled. "He seems to want Elizabeth."

"That would be the external objective. Although I'm sure now he'd like to take care of you and Dean, as well."

"Ah. The ever-popular revenge theme." Robin sighed. "But why was he so hot on Elizabeth?"

Roger shook his head. "It's not so much Elizabeth as it is taking over the experiment she was involved in. I must confess it was originally his idea. And I not only gave him the credit for it, he got to make the presentation to our board. The Board simply decided that Donald might be less than humane in the execution, so they gave it to me instead."

"Experiment?"

Roger smiled guiltily. "I know it sounds awful, but I promise you, the whole project was thoroughly vetted so that it would be completely respectful of Elizabeth's identity and privacy and freedom of choice." He paused. "As far as she could make a choice. When we chose her to remove and bring forward, I could only promise a certain adventure and myself as her husband. She wasn't capable of understanding the rest."

"Oh." Robin thought. "Uh-oh. You're not still planning on marrying her, are you?"

"That." Roger sighed. "I've been told that she's Dean's wife, so I strongly suspect that Dean has made a stronger claim."

"You have no idea how strong." Robin looked at her time machine and sighed.

"Robin, you didn't fail just now," Roger said. "Given your lack of knowledge and the lack of materials, you've given yourself a fighting chance. One of my colleagues was convinced that you three were forever lost. And when we saw that power pull, she was certain that Donald or I had generated it. She refused to believe that you could have been the one."

"I guess." Sadly, Robin picked at a chip. "SoSo, you're going to take us home now?"

"Yes." He smiled as her face fell even further. "Don't

worry. You'll still be traveling. We just have to get through the debate."

Robin grimaced. "How hard will it be?"

"It's one of the strictest rules of time travel," Roger said. "You just don't bring people beyond their natal time. You wouldn't believe the debate that went on to get the Board to agree to bringing Elizabeth forward."

"Hm." Robin thought. "I hope they don't get upset because I was already there."

Roger looked at her, puzzled. "The base unit?"

Robin smiled weakly. "Well, when we found Elizabeth... Actually, Dean found her first, then went and got me. Anyway, I started checking out the consoles you had in the room, and I sent myself to your time. That's how I figured out it was a time machine. I came right back, to within three minutes of when I left."

For the first time, Roger looked angry. "You didn't. Damn you. Oh, hell. You wouldn't know better. Robin, don't ever try that again. The timetron is only accurate to within plus-minus three days. That's why you never go to any time within a week of your previous visit or departure. You don't want to run into yourself."

Robin snorted. "I almost did. The only thing I can't figure is why I was able to land back in the castle at the exact time and day I set and haven't been able to since."

Roger thought. "The power source. That's one of the reasons I chose that castle to hide Elizabeth. There's a power source there for the time machines. As it turned out, I was able to get the machine to set me down at the exact time I set it for, as well." He sighed. "As you can see, Robin, there's still a lot we don't know about time travel, which makes it all the more dangerous for you to be traveling on your own. You know even less."

Robin sighed. "I suppose."

"Well." Roger thought something over, then decided it was better not to say anything just then. "Let's get your stuff packed." He paused. "I'm curious. Which do you like more? The time machine or the history?"

Robin stopped clearing her work tableworktable long enough to think. "You would have to ask that. I mean the technology is so amazingly cool, even though I don't understand it entirely. But I also love the history, really seeing the world as it was. That's why we've been here so long. Well, in the seventeenth century. We were trying to go back home when the machine blew. I should have figured out that Elizabeth wasn't going fit in after the second village we went to tried to hang us."

"What happened in the first?" Roger asked.

"Oh, we ran afoul of a very narrow-minded clergyman and got ourselves accused of witchcraft."

"I see. And the second village?"

"That was the crooked steward. We ran a better inn than he did." Robin smiled. "In a way, I wish we could have stayed. We'd made a lot of friends in the village. I really got a kick out of talking to the pastor. He went to Oxford. As a matter of fact, I think he knew an ancestor of mine. He said I was just like this Lady of Hawkesland."

"Hawkesland?" Roger looked at her with amused amazement.

Robin, busy stuffing her sack, didn't notice. "Something

like that. He seemed really thrown because I was a man, or he thought I was. The lady's husband was Lord James Haverfield, Earl of Hawkesland. Lady Eleanor was her name. That's funny. I just thought. Eleanor is my middle name. What a bizarre coincidence."

Roger swallowed. "More bizarre than you think. Maybe I'd better go wake Dean and Elizabeth."

"Wait." Robin put her hand on his arm. "Why are you letting go of Elizabeth so easily?"

"Because I never thought the experiment would work in the first place," Roger said, although there was clearly more to be said.

"Is there some other reason why this experiment is important, Roger? I mean why would this Board thoroughly vet things and want to make sure you'd be humane about it for something this, uh, Donald wanted to do on a whim. Especially since you didn't think it would work."

Roger sighed. "I can't really tell you. Except…" He looked at her thoughtfully. "Well, I expect you're going to know sooner or later. Our world is facing the extinction of humankind. For a lot of complicated reasons that we really haven't got time to go into now, fertility rates are so low, it's entirely possible that humans will die out in another three or four generations. If something isn't done very, very soon, the gene pool will get too small to regenerate."

"But what about fertility treatment? Even in my time, there's a lot that can be done."

Roger winced. "Most of those advances are now outlawed, and for very good reason." He stopped as he heard movement below. "Another very long story. And it sounds like we'd better get a move on."

Robin decided to wake Dean and Elizabeth, herself. The two were packed within minutes, largely because they didn't want to bring much with them, and what they did want had been packed the night before in anticipation of being kicked out.

Robin decided that the least she could do is leave a note for Sir James, but when she went to deliver it, she found Sir James emerging from his wife's rooms, wearing his dressing gown and nothing else. Sir James went beet red, but with embarrassment.

"I'm so sorry, sir," Robin stammered. "I didn't think you would be up so early."

"Well, I…" He coughed politely, then smiled. "I've been thinking about what you said yesterday afternoon."

"Oh, I apologize for that, sir."

He waved her off. "Perhaps it was said in haste, but there was the bitterness of truth in those words. I like to think of myself as a rational man, which means I should be able to bear the truth, even when unpleasant. I owe you an apology, Mr. Parker. You and your brother and sister-in-law have always shown tremendous loyalty to me and to my family. I should never have doubted you. I am a changed man, Mr. Parker. What on earth is that?"

Banging sounds and the cries of the kitchen staff echoed up through the hall.

"Sir!" yelped the cook's son from below stairs. "It's Mr. Farquhar. He's brought a gang of men. They're wrecking the kitchen!"

"He's angry about that contract," Sir James said to Robin. Then he called downstairs. "Send Mr. Farquhar to me in the back salon."

"But he's after the Parkers!" the cook's son bellowed back.

"He'll find them there." Sir James turned to Robin. "Get your brother and his wife out of here. I don't know how long I can hold him."

"Thank you, sir."

Robin ran upstairs. Roger, who had heard the commotion, was just emerging from her room.

"It's Farquhar," she gasped. "I mean whatever you said his name was. He's apparently after us and brought the cavalry with him to make sure he gets us."

"Nothing like an enlightenment to ruin a favorite tactic," said Roger.

"What?"

"Charges of witchcraft."

Robin shook her head. "Never mind that. Sir James said he'd try to hold him in the back salon.

"Excellent." Roger went to the door. "I'll see what I can do to calm him down."

He left as Robin gathered her two sacks together and took a last look at the room. Then she hurried to Dean and Elizabeth's room, knowing that they'd heard the commotion.

Only the cause of the commotion was already in Dean and Elizabeth's room, assisted by two thugs, each of whom was bigger than Dean. Donald had one hand wrapped tightly around Elizabeth's upper arm and the muzzle of a pistol pressed against her temple.

"Perfect," Donald said. "I have everything I need." He nodded at the thugs. "Marshall, Timkins, you will take care of the Messers Parker, just as I told you. As much as I'd like to be around for that part, I'm afraid I've more important business with this young lady."

"Except that your experiment has already failed," Robin said coldly. "You might be able to put Elizabeth on the suspend an, but what about her baby?"

"What?" Donald looked at Elizabeth more closely. "Your daughter. How? And how do you know about the suspend an?"

"Roger's here," Robin said. "In this house."

"Damn, it's a trap." Donald waved at the thugs. "Go find this Roger. He's the one I told you to keep a lookout for. Find him now!"

The thugs were barely out of the door when Dean pounced on Donald. The two rolled on the floor with Dean's hands locked on the wrist of the hand that still held the pistol. Robin pulled Elizabeth and the sacks from the room.

"Is this everything?" Robin whispered to Elizabeth.

"Yes. Dean said we won't need much where we're going."

Robin glanced down the hallway. The thugs had hurried down the servants' stairs, leaving the door to the stairwell wide open. Dean burst into the hallway, slamming the door shut just as the crack of pistol fire went off.

Robin and Elizabeth scurried after him down the front stairs. At the next to last landing, Robin paused.

"I've got to get Roger," she said. "You two get to the cathedral as fast as you can. We'll meet you at the communion table."

"But—" said Dean.

"It'll be harder for them to catch us if we split up," said Robin.

She waited just long enough to make sure Dean and Elizabeth were down the stairs, then Robin headed toward the back salon.

As she came up on the room, she could hear the scuffling going on within. Flattening herself against the hallway wall next to the door, Robin eased around the open doorway and peered into the salon.

Roger was locked in a wrestling match with either Marshall (or Timkins), with Sir James, now dressed, but looking somewhat disheveled, backed into the sideboard across from Robin, a pistol limply grasped in one hand. Timkins (or Marshall) lay in a corner unconscious. Donald was on the other side of the doorway from Robin, but far enough into the room that he couldn't see her.

Donald still had his pistol, but instead of aiming at Roger, he raised it toward Sir James. Robin rolled the rest of the way into the room, grabbed an inkwell off a nearby table and hurled it at Donald. The inkwell caught him in the upper arm, and though Donald recoiled, he didn't drop the pistol. He whirled around and finally saw Robin.

"That's it, Farquhar," Robin hissed. "Leave Sir James out of this. I'm the one you wantwant, and we all know it."

"Yes, you are," Donald said, smiling and raising the pistol.

Robin's eyes were glued to the muzzlemuzzle, and it seemed like an eternity before the gun went off. The odd thing was that the shot went wild, shattering a China sconce behind her to the left. Slowly, she realized that Donald was on the ground, a gasping Sir James above him and looking quite pleased with himself.

"I've sent Samuel for the constable," Sir James said over the crashing sound of a desk splintering under the weight of two grappling men.

Roger was on top, but Marshall (or Timkins) scrambled out from underneath and took off running. Donald slowly pulled himself to his kneesknees, but Sir James applied his foot to Donald's backside and gently knocked him back down. Roger got up, panting.

"Well, Sir James," Robin said. "You saved my life. I guess we're even."

"Yes, well a good clerk is worth a great deal," Sir James said.

"I'm just afraid we can't stay," said Robin. "My friend, Roger, here, has brought me good news of my family's fortunes and Dean and I must go and oversee it alleverything. Thank you for everything, sir."

"Wait!" Sir James mopped off his face. "You said that Mr. Farquhar here really wanted you?"

"Yeah," said Robin. "That's part of the news. He was, uh, my father's business partner who had heard about the reversal of our bad fortune and wanted Dean and me out of the way. I had never liked him. In any case, that was why he wanted to marry Miss Deborah. To get at us. I didn't say anything because I couldn't prove it and he didn't because, well, it's obvious he couldn't."

"Hm," said Sir James. "That explains why you didn't support the match. All's well that ends well, I say. Are you sure you must leave?"

"Yes, and quickly, sir. Um, my mother is all alone and needs protection."

"I see. Well, Godspeed."

"You, too, sir."

Roger nodded. "It was good to meet you, sir. Perhaps we shall meet again under more pleasant circumstances."

"Indeed."

Donald lifted his head. "Robin Parker. Do you know who the father of Elizabeth's baby is?"

Robin glared at him. "Of course I do."

"Don't be too sure," Donald growled with a snigger.

"Oh, hush, you vile creature." Sir James kicked Donald in the side for emphasis.

Robin nodded at Sir James then she and Roger hurried out.

"We'd better not count on Sir James being able to hang onto Donald that long," Roger said as they got onto the street. He paused long enough to grin at her. "That was some pretty fast thinking."

Robin shrugged. "I told Dean we'd meet them at the cathedral."

"All right. Follow me." Roger started down the next alley.

Robin stopped him. "Do you know where you're going?"

"Yes. I've been here several times."

"When, and how long ago?" Robin glared.

"About twenty years past, and twelve years back on my natal time continuum." Roger grinned. "And I've been here for a week already."

"Great. I've been living here for the past six months. We'll go through the marketplace." Robin headed down the street.

"You are stubborn, young lady," said Roger, scrambling after her.

Robin didn't bother to glare at him. "Don't you 'young lady' me. You're just a kid, yourself."

"I'm a lot older than I look."

"They all say that." Robin looked behind her. "Damn. He's coming, and he's got reinforcements. Let's go."

Donald shouted as he and three more thugs came after them. Robin and Roger dashed into the market, already busy with the common man's business. They dashed around stalls, hoping to lose Donald and company. The four men spread out and covered a lot of ground fast.

Robin and Roger wound up backed into a corner next to stacks of cages containing chickens.

"Don't say it," Robin grumbled as they ducked behind the cages.

"Say what?" asked Roger.

"I told you so."

Roger shrugged. "We can still get out of this. But we should split up. You take my timetron."

Robin pushed it back at him. "How will you get back?"

"We have ways." Roger shoved the time machine into her hands. "It's too complicated to go into now. That's another reason you shouldn't be time traveling. Promise me you won't until I get to you."

"All right. Only to get home. I promise. But how will you find us?"

Roger looked back into the marketplace. "You'll want to hide. Find someplace you can stay for a couple weeks. And use money, if at all possible. Your debit and credit cards can be traced, although I don't think Donald has been able to break into those records. Then, when you're settled, turn the machine on for a couple minutes and turn it right off. Donald can't trace this machine, but I can. Now, go!"

Roger reached up and pushed over the cages. Squawking hens went everywhere. Roger took off right away. Donald and the others chased after him. Robin waited a moment, then ran off in the other direction.

A minute later, she arrived at the cathedral, panting heavily. Dean and Elizabeth appeared from a side apse as she came clattering up the aisle.

"Come on," Robin gasped. "Roger's led them off after him, but they'll be after us as soon as they discover I'm not with him."

Robin led them outside and around the building's side to a courtyard lined with shops. The Summer Gardens were across the square and down some stairs. On the other side of the gardens was the Avon River. Robin hurried Dean and Elizabeth there.

The gardens were deserted at that early hour. Pleasure boats for rowing on the river lay piled on the bank in anticipation of the winter. Dean and Robin turned one over and set it in the water. Carefully, they got Elizabeth on board and shoved off.

Just over an hour later, Robin decided that they had gone far enough downstream. She and Dean maneuvered the boat aground.

"Okay," said Robin when they were all safely on the shore. "Let's all get touching."

"Uh, Robin," Dean said. "Shouldn't we be trying to get more modern?"

Robin smiled softly as she entered coordinates. "Actually, I think we'll be safer if we stay period. We're going back to L.A. People will probably think we're on some sort of movie shoot, but if anyone asks, we can tell them we're part of a living history group. Everyone touching?"

Certain that everyone was, Robin took a deep breath and focused on home.

Chapter Twenty-Six

It was hard to tell which was worse, the bone-crushing sensation of the machine or the roar of noise that greeted Robin, Dean, and Elizabeth as they landed.

"Where are we?" Dean hollered over the sound of a jet engine taking off.

"Los Angeles International," Robin yelled back. They were in the parking lot. "Lots of places we could go from here, just in case Donald finds a way to follow us. There's the shuttle to the airport. Let's get on. I've got to get to an ATM."

The driver stared at the three as they boarded the bus.

"It's a joke," Robin said, nervously. "We belong to this living history club, and we've got this friend that's coming in, and, well, he's supposed to freak when he sees us, figuring he got the wrong era, and… It'll be funny. Really."

The driver chuckled. "Sounds like a good one."

Elizabeth kept her head down during the short ride. At the terminal, Robin found an ATM readily enough, got the money she wanted, then got change.

"Why?" asked Dean.

"We'll need it for the trains so we can get back to Pasadena," Robin told him. "Elizabeth, you okay?"

"I am all right," she sighed. "It's noisy and things move so strangely. But I'll get used to it."

"Trains?" asked Dean. "What trains?"

"Wake up, Dean," Robin snarled. "Los Angeles has public transportation now. We'll take the bus to the Green Line to the Blue Line to the Red Line to the Gold Line. There's a stop about half a mile from my house."

They got more stares from people as they waited on the various platforms for the electric trains. Robin got a fix almost immediately on the date and time – late morning, one day before the date she'd programmed. It was almost mid-afternoon when they finally got to the porch of Robin's house. Robin unlocked the door quickly and jammed everyone inside.

"We're not safe yet," she told them. "How are you doing, Elizabeth?"

She smiled softly. "You keep asking me. I said I am fine."

"Okay. Good." Robin looked at Elizabeth again. "Geez, Elizabeth, your stays are really straining."

"I know. My dress feels very tight."

"I should have something upstairs that you can throw on until I can get you those clothes we bought before we took you back to your time." Robin looked around. "I'm going to shower first, then head over to my office. That's where I sent our luggage. Dean, you'd better start combing that flour out of your hair. If you try washing it out, it'll turn into big sticky globs."

Robin found an old t-shirt and athletic shorts for Elizabeth and then set to work combing out flour and getting showered. The worst part was that she knew she shouldn't linger. But she couldn't resist the glory of hot water running down her back after so many months without any running water at all. She also paused while toweling off, enjoying the scent of a clean towel. After getting dressed in jeans and another shirt, she stuffed her hair under her hat, then headed out.

"Robin!" proclaimed the receptionist, a young man named Alex. "I thought you weren't going to be back for another couple weeks, at least."

"I'm not and I'm not here," Robin said, genially. "Would you get on the P.A. and let everyone else know I'm not here? I am merely a figment of everyone's imagination."

"Hey, Robin," said Steve Wasserman, her partner. "How was England?"

"Great, and I'm not here."

"Can we pretend you are and will you look at this little glitch that—"

"No! I am not here." She looked over at Alex. "Make that announcement. Now."

"Seriously, Robin," Steve continued as Alex started the announcement.

"No way, Steve." Robin moved quickly toward her office. "I'm just here to pick up some stuff that I had sent here from my triptrip, and I am out of here."

"But when are you coming back?" Steve remained hot on her heels.

Robin paused. It was a better question than she'd anticipated. "Uh, in a couple weeks or so, according to plan. I got back early from Europe to deal with... To deal with some family stuff. I'm just going to pick up my boxes and get out. Okay?"

In the end, Robin needed Steve to help with the boxes, so she looked at the glitch, had a much longer conversation than she wanted over how to fix it, and then left, feeling slightly unnerved by the whole experience.

Back at the house, Robin gave Elizabeth her clothes. When Elizabeth had changed, Robin could have sworn that Elizabeth's tummy had grown even since she had left an hour before.

"SoSo, what do we do now?" asked Dean, after he had changed into his modern clothes.

"We hide," said Robin. "I've just called Dad and he said we could use his cabin for a while."

"Yeah, but won't what's-his-name be able to find us through Dad's name?" Dean said.

"Not really. Dad bought it under some corporation deal with that company that owns the patents on his inventions. It'll be pretty hard to trace it to him. We can use it for free, which means we won't have to use credit cards, which are traceable. And it's pretty secluded, which means we'll be able to help Elizabeth adjust more slowly."

"We can't stay here?" Elizabeth asked, grimacing slightly.

Robin shook her head. "Too easy for Donald to trace. But the car trip shouldn't take that long."

"I will be all right," Elizabeth said, resolutely, although her face betrayed her fear.

They left shortly afterward. Robin was less than thrilled that their first meal back in their own time had to be fast food, but Dean wasn't complaining.

"Aw, come on, Robin, these are the best burgers on the planet," he proclaimed as they ate in the car.

Robin didn't answer. She knew she should concentrate on driving, but all she could think about was what to do after they got to the cabin. And how they would explain Elizabeth to their mother. And whether time travel would be forever denied her. And when would Roger come?

The drive was not the most pleasant or easy. Rush hour traffic was in full force and while Elizabeth was amazed by the huge number of cars also on the freeway with them, at least, she wasn't frightened by high speeds simply because Robin couldn't get going any faster than twenty-five miles per hour. By the time the traffic had eased, Elizabeth was a little more accustomed to moving quickly, even twenty-five miles an hour being exceedingly fast for her experience. She even managed to watch out the window as the suburbs of Southern California flew past.

It was closing in on dark when they finally arrived at the cabin in Big Bear. Dean got Elizabeth inside and warned her about the lights, as Robin brought in the luggage. The cabin was more of a large house decorated in rustic mountain style, with a huge vaultedhuge, vaulted ceiling in the living room and a second story with three bedrooms.

"Woh, this place is pretty cool," said Dean, looking around.

"Haven't you been here before?" Robin asked.

Elizabeth suddenly grabbed the back of a sofa and groaned.

"What's the matter?" Dean yelped.

"Nothing," she gasped. "I've got to go to bed though. It's

too soon, but I've gotten so big suddenly. Maybe the baby will be big enough."

"You're in labor." Robin looked at her in shock.

"Yes." Elizabeth nodded, as the contraction subsided.

Robin swallowed. "How long?"

"Since before we left your home."

"In labor?" Dean squeaked. "Why didn't you say anything?'

"Because I knew I had time and we couldn't stay there, anyway," said Elizabeth.

"Great," Robin grumbled. "How fast are the pains coming?"

"Fast. Oh, no. Here it comes again." Elizabeth doubled over.

Robin checked her watch. "Hell, that's less than two minutes. We've got to get you to a hospital!"

"I'm not going anywhere!" Elizabeth snapped. "Except to bed."

"We can't deliver a baby here," groaned Dean.

"It looks like we're going to have to." Robin looked around. "Oh, hell, how do you do this?"

"You don't do anything," laughed Elizabeth. She grimaced as another pain took over. "Except catch it. I've got all the work to do. We'll need something to wrap the baby in, some water to clean it with, and a good sharp knife."

"A knife? For what?" Dean's panic grew.

"To cut the cord."

"No. We won't do that," said Robin. "But you're right about the other things. Let's get you upstairs. The master bedroom has a bathroom there. We'll have all the water we need. Dean, give me a hand."

Dean helped Elizabeth into the room while Robin turned down the bed and laid out some towels to protect the sheets.

"Dean, you'd best fetch that water," Elizabeth said through clenched teeth as she sat down on the bed.

"We've got water in there." Robin pointed. "And he's staying right here. I can't do this alone."

"But he's a man!" Elizabeth protested.

"So do I stay or go?" Dean asked frantically.

"Do you want to see your kid born?" Robin demanded.

"Well, yeah, but I figured I'd get to go to class first."

"Class?" Elizabeth looked at them bewildered. "You have to learn how to have a baby?"

"I know it sounds ridiculous," Robin said. "But you learn how to relax with the contractions, breathing and all that. And he learns how to coach you. I've heard it works really well. Anyway, fathers are always in the delivery room with the mothers. Let's get you undressed."

Elizabeth gulped. "In front of Dean?"

"Oh, for crying out loud, Elizabeth, that's how he got you this way!"

"Um, Robin, it wasn't," Dean said.

"Huh? Oh, never mind. Dean, go get some more towels. They should be in the bathroom closet."

He left.

"All I need to remove are my drawers," Elizabeth said.

She groaned, then pulled the underpants off. Dean reappeared, then grimaced with her as the next contraction took hold.

The pains came fast and hard. Elizabeth cried out again and again. Beads of sweat broke out on her forehead.

"When the head comes," she gasped when she could. "Check that the cord isn't around the neck. Oh, no!"

"Keep talking, Elizabeth." Robin coaxed, although she already knew what to do from her first aid classes. Anything to keep Elizabeth's mind off the pain. "Tell me everything I have to do."

"Turn the head. Turn it to... to... the shoulders are right." Elizabeth broke down in sobs.

Dean squeezed her hand. "Hey, it's alright, honey. You're gonna be okay. You're gonna be okay."

It was almost as hard on him as it was on Elizabeth. The pain was terrible, and he was helpless to relieve it. Yet, even so, as the labor progressed, he got calmer and focused on reassuring Elizabeth.

Elizabeth grunted, straining all of a sudden.

"Don't push yet," Robin ordered.

"But—"

"Don't push until you absolutely must. Whatever you do, try not to."

"That's right," said Dean. "We've got to make sure you're completely ready to have this kid."

Elizabeth nodded and cried out as the contraction hit yet again. Dean mopped her brow with a damp washcloth, then gave her another to suck on. Robin went and washed her hands to the elbows.

Ten minutes later, Elizabeth strained again.

"Don't push," Robin ordered.

"I have to!" Elizabeth shrieked.

Robin helped her bend her legs, then swung a bright reading lamp around. She aimed it right where the baby would be coming. The contractions slowed down a little but remained just as hard.

"Okay," Robin said. "Push with the next contraction and push for all you're worth. Dean, you'd better start cheering her on. She's bushed."

"Help me sit," Elizabeth ordered.

Dean pushed her up from behind as she strained even harder.

"Enough," she gasped as the contraction died.

"That's a good idea," Robin said. "Try and rest where you can, Elizabeth."

"I've no choice," she murmured. Her breath caught. "Help up!"

Dean shoved her into place. "Come on, Elizabeth, push that baby out."

Robin helped spread her legs. "Hot damn, Dean! I can see the head!"

"Yeah?" Holding Elizabeth up with one arm, Dean reached and looked. "I can see it, too. Won't be much longer now."

Elizabeth nodded and sank backward. As tears slipped from her eyes, Dean gently let her down. Seconds later, he helped her up again.

"It's coming." Robin encouraged. "Just a few more pushes, Elizabeth. Just a few more."

Elizabeth sank back again. "Water."

Dean handed her the washcloth. She sucked greedily, then yelped. Dean heaved her back up.

The head came fast. Robin watched, transfixed in wonder as it emerged. Dean peered anxiously over Elizabeth's shoulder. Poor Elizabeth was almost too tired to know what was going on.

As the chin cleared, Robin checked to make sure the cord was not around the neck. It wasn't.

"Okay, we've got a chin and there's no cord," she announced.

Elizabeth sobbed and nodded. Robin gently held the head, then jostled out the top shoulder, then the bottom. Elizabeth gave one more push, and the rest slipped out.

The tiny purple body was covered with blood and a light white mucus-like substance. Robin pinched the bottom, and the baby sprang to life with a loud, coughing wail.

"It's a girl," Robin muttered, then louder, "It's a girl. We did it!" Her tears flowed. "You guys have a girl and she's all right."

Elizabeth sank back onto the pillows, half laughing and half sobbing.

"And I'm alive," she whispered.

"Of course, you are." Dean sniffed and wiped his eyes.

Robin wrapped the still crying infant in a towel and handed her to Dean.

"Dean, no." Elizabeth gasped.

"It's okay," Dean said, grinning. "I know how to hold a baby. See?"

Elizabeth smiled and nodded. "She's hungry."

"Are you sure you're up to feeding her?" Robin asked as she held Elizabeth's legs and waited for the placenta.

"I don't think she'll go that far," said Dean. "She's still hooked up."

"Get the knife and cut the cord," Elizabeth said.

"Nope," said Robin. "There's a better way to handle it. Here comes the placenta." She caught it in a towel. "Yuck. What a mess. We'll wrap it up with the baby, then take you to the hospital and get the cord cut there."

"But why?" Elizabeth asked.

"Because of germs, Elizabeth. We don't want to take a chance on infecting the baby, or you, for that matter." Robin laid the placenta on top of the baby and wrapped them both together in another towel.

"She's so small." Dean gazed at her in wonder.

"Let me nurse." Elizabeth pulled herself up on the pillows and reached for the baby.

Dean handed her over. Robin watched for a minute, then began clean upcleanup operations. Dean laid his hand on the baby's back and lovingly kissed Elizabeth.

"She's beautiful," he whispered.

Robin turned away. Something in her ached with loneliness. She tried telling herself that she wouldn't have to deal with diapers and two o'clock feedings and other such nonsense. Even that proved to be small consolation. She quickly collected all the soiled linens and hurried out to the garage where the washer and dryer were.

While Robin was gone, Elizabeth prevailed upon Dean to get a knife.

"She does have a point about those germs, you know," Dean said, bringing the knife in.

"But it's not good to keep the cord on."

"True." Dean went into the bathroom and came back with a bottle of rubbing alcohol. "This'll take care of Robin's problem."

He poured the alcohol over the knife, then handed it to Elizabeth. She made short professional work of the cord, then handed the bundle with the placenta to Dean.

"It should be burnt."

"Hm." Dean looked around. "Good thing there's a fireplace in here, especially one with gas logs."

Elizabeth looked at him, puzzled, then jumped as he turned on the gas and touched a match to it. The little bundle crackled merrily but sent a rather nasty scent into the room.

"What smells?" asked Robin, coming in. She saw the towel in the flames. "Terrific. I did know what I was doing, you know."

"So does Elizabeth," said Dean. "And she was worried. I thought it would be better if she could relax."

Robin couldn't argue. Exhausted, she pulled out a dresser drawer and lined it with the last two towels.

"This'll do for a crib until we can get something better," she said. "We're going to have a hell of a time taking showers tomorrow, though. We've used every last towel in the place."

She took the drawer over to the bed.

"Thank you," said Elizabeth. "For everything."

"No sweat," said Robin. "You take it easy and rest up. I figure there's no rush to get to the hospital now. We'll go in the morning."

"Okay," said Dean. "Goodnight."

"Goodnight."

Robin left the room elated and down, both at the same time.

Chapter Twenty-Seven

Through half-closed lids, Robin watched the room she was in slowly grow lighter as the daylight outside slipped in through the cracks in the drapes. She would have rather been sleeping, but her mind was far too full, in spite of her exhaustion.

She was home. Sort of. At least, she was back in her own time, although she wasn't sure she felt like she belonged there. Elizabeth had given birth to Dean's little girl. Robin's niece. She was an aunt. She wasn't sure that made any more sense than time travel. About the only thing Robin knew was that she wanted to do more traveling.

She rolled onto her back and opened her eyes. Robin looked at the little specks of light on the floor and guessed that it was later than early morning, but not midmorning yet. It was odd how she'd come to check the position of the sun rather a clock. Looking around the room again, she saw that there was a clock on the bedside table that appeared to be running. Eight a.m., or more precisely eight twelve a.m.

Fuzzy with sleep, she stumbled out of bed and went to the bathroom. That felt normal, at least. Still wearing her night t-shirt, she went downstairs and headed for the kitchen.

Yes, there was coffee. That felt reassuringly normal, too,

even though she had lived over a year without a coffeemaker. But there was comfort in the former routine, and so she made coffee. Coffee in the eighteenth century was strong enough, but not always consistent. And for all she had made fun of pre-ground coffee from cans, the familiar consistent product smelled awfully good.

Mug in hand, she went into the living room. The timetron had somehow landed on the couch in all the rush and turmoil. Robin picked it up and turned it on and then off again a few seconds later. Within minutes, there was a knock on the door.

Robin was not terribly surprised to see Roger on the other side.

"Morning," she mumbled. "Come on in."

"Thanks," said Roger as he followed her into the living room. There was an awkward pause as if Roger wanted to say more.

"Didn't you say that machine is only accurate, like, days or something?" Robin flopped onto the couch and motioned for Roger to do the same.

He sat across from her on the nearest easy chair. "Plus, minus three days. I've actually been here for two. I saw you guys come in last night. I didn't think Elizabeth was that far along."

"She wasn't." Robin yawned. "Sorry. I just got up. I didn't think you'd show up so fast when I turned on the machine."

"It's easy when you've got the time pinned. But she *wasn't* that far along?"

Robin chuckled. "Yeah. We had a baby last night. A girl. She's a little moose, actually. Full-term, as far as I can tell.

But Elizabeth swears she counted only six months. We'll take them to the hospital later. Elizabeth insisted on cutting the cord last night, so I figure there's no rush."

"You may not have to go at all," said Roger. "I've got enough training to do an initial scan to make sure she and the baby are all right."

Robin thought that one over. "Cool. I was trying to figure out how I'd help her get acclimated to this century before the baby came as it was. After last night, I think she could use a little breathing room before forcing an emergency room on her."

"Good call."

"I've just got to figure out how to get a birth certificate for the baby. I could call the county, I guess." Robin sighed.

"That reminds me." Roger shifted and pulled a packet out of his biker jacket. "Elizabeth's papers. There's a passport, copy of her birth certificate, a California ID card and a Social Security card."

Robin opened up the envelope. "These look really good. How did you get them?"

"It's very simple, actually. We do it all the time to establish a personna in a given time. And they are legitimate, so if Elizabeth loses her ID, or needs to change it, she can get new paperwork."

"Wow." Robin yawned and stared moodily at her mug. "Oh. Can I get you some coffee?"

"Sure. I'm guessing you haven't had breakfast yet."

"I'm not even sure there's any food in the place. It doesn't get used that often, so there's not usually perishables in the fridge." Robin lifted herself off the couch and stumbled into the kitchen. "How do you want your coffee?"

"Like I always do."

Robin, turned, puzzled. "And how am I going to know that?"

He chuckled, guiltily. "That's right. I'm sorry. I'll drink it any way I can get it."

"Oh?"

He shrugged. "Side effect of spending too much time when you can't get it at all."

Robin handed him a mug. "Well, you've got it black. If you want sugar and creamer, they're right here." She pointed to the jars of powdered creamer and sugar next to the coffee maker.

She glared out into the living room, watching him take his first sip through the corner of her eye. He seemed pleasant enough. Light blond hair, hazel eyes that were slightly narrowed. He looked mostly Caucasian, but not entirely. His body was trim enough, not perfect, but no particularly bad rolls, either.

Then there was that calm. On the surface, he didn't seem to give a damn about anything, but after a while, Robin realized he just didn't worry. He reminded her of somebody who had lived a very, very long time. An old soul, she thought.

The stairs creaked. Robin looked across the half wall separating the kitchen from the open dining room to the stairway. Dean was slowly stumbling downstairs.

"Is Elizabeth awake?" Robin asked.

Dean looked at her through half-open eyes. "Yeah. Have we got any tea?"

"For you or for her?"

"Both," Dean grumbled. "Oh. Hi, Roger." He stopped at the entrance to the kitchen and yawned. "I thought I heard voices."

"Is the baby awake?" Robin asked.

Dean nodded. "Elizabeth is feeding her. What about that tea?"

Robin began rummaging through the cupboards. There was tea. But Robin's assumption that there wasn't much else in the cabin to eat was correct. She volunteered to run get breakfast, and Roger volunteered to join her. The ride out to the nearby town's small grocery was filled with meaningless chitchat that was, nonetheless, oddly comfortable, Robin thought. And as they waited at the checkstand to buy the Danish and other basic groceries, Roger's hand slipped into Robin's. Blushing, she pulled it back.

"Oh," Roger said, suddenly nervous. "I'm sorry. I didn't realize I'd done that."

As soon as they got back, Roger asked to see Elizabeth and the baby, and Elizabeth agreed to let him up. Robin was astonished to see that even overnight, the baby had grown and matured.

"My lord, she looks like she's a month old already," Robin gasped.

"I know," said Elizabeth, from the bed, where she was propped up by pillows. "Dean assured me, she was smaller last night."

"I'm sure she was," said Roger, who was holding up the baby's hand and pressing it against a small hand-held screen. "Well, preliminary tests indicate she's healthy. I'll be able to get a better reading on any genetic pre-dispositions when I run the saliva test. The other good news is that her cells seem to have settled down, so she'll grow more normally now."

"Huh?" asked Dean.

"It's a side effect of being in the drop," Roger explained. "It excites cell growth. Elizabeth is the first person to go through while pregnant, but it doesn't seem to have had any negative effects on your baby. It just made her grow faster, is all. Which probably explains why she came so early and yet was a full-term baby." Roger looked over at Robin. "I wish I'd known about the baby before we got separated."

"That. Well..." Robin sighed. "Roger, I don't know if you'll believe me, but I was going to tell you. Only we got a little side-tracked if you'll remember."

"Too true," Roger said. "And Donald made sure I knew that at least one part of the experiment had worked. That Elizabeth was pregnant."

"Are we going to be running from this Donald for the rest of our lives?" Elizabeth asked.

Roger shook his head. "No. I can't say more, but, no, not the rest of your lives. And you'll be safe in Pasadena." He smiled as he handed the baby back to Elizabeth. "So, what is your baby's name?"

Elizabeth smiled as she looked up at Dean. "Her name is Robin Mary. Robin for her aunt and Mary for my mother."

Robin felt her face grow hot. "Oh." Tears filled her eyes. "Wow. That's... That's...."

She never finished.

Dean laughed. "Aw, come on, Robin. How could we not?"

Smiling, Roger picked up Elizabeth's free hand and pressed it to his small screen.

"Looks like you're doing well, also, Elizabeth," he said, looking over the read-out. "Goodness. You didn't even get any vaginal tearing pushing that little moose out. Uterus is receding nicely."

Dean looked at the read-out. "Geez, how can you tell all that from just putting her hand there?"

"It's neuro-radiopathy," Roger explained. "It uses modulated x-rays to tap into the nerve impulses and spectrometry to read blood density and things like that to spot problems. It's reading completely normal on tissue soundness and pain, which it wouldn't have if there had been any tearing. And the position it notes for the uterus is right in line with where it should be this many hours after childbirth. How are you feeling, Elizabeth?"

"Tired," she said.

"How about emotionally?" Roger sat down next to her.

"I am fine," she answered, a little stiffly.

"Really?" Roger asked. "Not feeling overwhelmed or frightened by all the strange things in this world?"

"In this time," Elizabeth corrected, then fell silent.

Dean gently pushed Roger up from the bed and took his place. "Honey, it's okay to talk about how you feel. It'd be weird if you weren't all scared and messed up by things here."

Elizabeth sighed. "I am here now. I want to accept it and learn to like it." She sniffed. "It's not so bad. Being in magic carriages and strange lights and everything. It's not bad at all now."

"I'm sure you're doing very well," Roger said, reassuringly.

"But at the same time, having a baby and having to adjust to this very different time, that's a lot to handle, Elizabeth."

Robin smiled. "Roger's right, Elizabeth. This world is pretty strange compared to what you've been used to. If you get scared or something, no one is going to think you don't want to be here."

Elizabeth smiled weakly. "I do want to be here. It's only that if I keep thinking about how much all these strange things frighten me, all I'll be is frightened all the time. You accept them as normal, so I'm trying to look at them the same way."

Roger nodded. "That's very brave, Elizabeth, and not a bad way to look at things. But if it gets to be too much, you do need to talk about it."

Robin Mary squawked suddenly.

"I'm tired, now," said Elizabeth, "and my baby needs to be fed."

"Well, then we'd better leave," Roger said.

He followed Robin out of the room.

"Isn't that great," he said, sliding his hand onto Robin's seat.

"Roger!" Robin slipped away and glared.

"Damn." Roger's sigh was genuine and a little tortured.

"What's wrong?" Robin asked.

"I can't stay." Roger hurried down the stairs. "I thought I was going to be able to, but it's clear I can't. Where's your timetron?"

Robin walked over to the sofa. "I suppose hiding it from you wouldn't work."

Roger paused. "No. And you don't really want to do that." He held his hand out.

"A lot you know about it." Sourly, Robin put the machine in his hand.

"You don't understand, Robin." He reached his hand out to her then self-consciously pulled it back. He used his finger to trace something on the top of the machine. "Things were… Will be going badly. In my natal time. I can't tell you right now. You just need to trust me." He stopped and looked at her, his eyes penetrating, yet warm. "I need you to promise me two things. One is that before you do anything else, you'll see to it that Dean and Elizabeth are well settled in."

"What the hell else am I going to do?" Robin grumbled. She glared at him. "I'm not going anywhere or anywhen."

"Yes, you are."

"What?" Robin gaped, too afraid to believe that it could be true.

"Robin, this is serious. Things are very bad when I'm sending you. I wouldn't do it, except that it was the best plan I could think of. I can't tell you more." Roger handed her the timetron. "But when Dean and Elizabeth are settled, I need you to go to the coordinates I entered."

"You mean I get to time travel again?"

"Of course." Roger smiled. "Robin, I wasn't going to stop you. I just needed to get you trained. You're good, but there are things you didn't know and you needed to learn them. I mean, need."

"Roger. That's…"

His face became serious again. "I just don't want you rushing off from here. It doesn't matter when you leave, you'll be right where you need to be, whenever you leave here. So make sure Dean and Elizabeth are okay, first."

"They're not in any danger, are they?"

"They'll be fine. I promise."

"How can you be so sure?"

Roger grimaced. "I can't tell you. Just trust me."

Robin folded her arms. "And what makes you so sure you can trust me?"

"I can't tell you." Roger smiled again and started to reach out to her. "Yeah, I've got to go. This a lot harder than I thought it was going to be."

Robin's heart lurched. "Am I going to see you again?"

"I can't…" He stopped and moved close to her. "What the hell. You'll see me when you land. In fact, you'll see me for a really long time. Many times."

He put his hand on her cheek and kissed her long and deep and passionately. Robin almost felt her legs giving way.

"Now," he sighed as he pulled away. "I've got to get the hell out of here before I cause any more trouble."

He pulled out his own timetron, closed his eyes and vanished.

Robin stared at the empty space for several minutes.

"Robin?" called Dean from the landing. "We saw the lights go. Did Roger leave or something?"

"Yeah. He left." Robin pulled herself together. "Everything okay up there?"

"Everything's fine."

"Good." Robin took a deep breath. "Great. I've got some laundry to finish and if Elizabeth's up to it, we'll make some plans."

"Great. We've already talked some things over."

Robin nodded. She looked at the time machine in her hands, then slowly laid it back down on the couch. She would be time traveling again, very soon. But first, she had Dean and Elizabeth to take care of. There would be time enough for that.

Coming Soon - Book Two of the Trilogy

Time Enough

Robin has plenty of work to do to acclimate Elizabeth to life in the Twenty-First Century. Elizabeth is feeling overwhelmed. Dean is determined to step up and do what he needs to do to support his new little family. Robin is feeling lost and longing to time travel again.

When Dean insists on making good on his promise to marry Elizabeth by taking her to Las Vegas, Robin is worried. But the lights of The Strip are not half the problem. Donald Long shows up and he's making the worst kind of trouble. Robin flees with the timetron, only to discover that things are just as bad as Roger had told her. Maybe even worse. And there is one more trip into the past that will hopefully set Donald right.

Other books by Anne Louise Bannon

I'm so glad you liked this book! Check out my other novels, available in print or ebook at your favorite retailer:

Freddie and Kathy Series:

Fascinating Rhythm

Bring Into Bondage

The Last Witnesses

Blood Red

Operation Quickline Series

That Old Cloak and Dagger Routine

Stopleak

Deceptive Appearances

Fugue in a Minor Key

Sad Lisa

These Hallowed Halls

Old Los Angeles

Death of the Zanjero

Death of the City Marshal

Death of the Chinese Field Hands

Daria Barnes

Rage Issues

Mrs. Sperling

A Nose for a Niedeman

Brenda Finnegan

Tyger, Tyger

Romantic Fiction

White House Rhapsody, Book One and Two

Fantasy and Science Fiction

A Ring for a Second Chance
But World Enough and Time

And I would be honored if you left a review for this and any of my books on GoodReads or any other retail site. It really helps.

Connect with Anne Louise Bannon

Thank you for sticking it out this long! Please join my newsletter. It's the best way to stay up-to-date on my upcoming projects, blog posts and even games and giveaways.

Sign up here: http://eepurl.com/zH0Ab

Or connect with me on your favorite social media platforms:

Visit my website: http://annelouisebannon.com
Friend me on Facebook: http://facebook.com/RobinGoodfellowEnt
Follow me on Twitter: http://twitter.com/ALBannon
Connect on LinkedIn: http://www.linkedin.com/in/annelouisebannon

About Anne Louise Bannon

Anne Louise Bannon is an author and journalist who wrote her first novel at age 15. Her journalistic work has appeared in Ladies' Home Journal, the Los Angeles Times, Wines and Vines, and in newspapers across the country. She was a TV critic for over 10 years, founded the Your-FamilyViewer blog, and created the OddBallGrape.com wine education blog with her husband, Michael Holland. She is the co-author of Howdunit: Book of Poisons, with Serita Stevens, as well as author of the Freddie and Kathy mystery series, set in the 1920s, the Old Los Angeles series, set in 1870, and the Operation Quickline series, plus several stand alones. She and her husband live in Southern California with an assortment of critters.